SCIONS OF CHANGE

THE CURSE AND THE CROWN
BOOK 4

LINDSAY BUROKER

Ker'ruk Lands
Havartaft Estate
Preserve
Strait of Torn Towers
Port Jirador
Frost Harbor
Stillguard River
King's Highway
Evardor Mountains
North Dakmoor Sea
Justori Pass
Kingdom of Zaldor
Old Beyrok
Potato Patch
Potaraki River
Sand and Sage
Sandsteaders
South Evardor Mountains
Tirak River
L-ro Vamorka Islands
Tirak Valley

1

Each time into the wilderness, a new experience, a new adventure.

~ Ranger Founder Saruk

"When you said, 'let's go into the preserve to get more honey,' you didn't mention stopping at creepy druid ruins where *extremely* mobile vines would hiss and flick at me."

From the top of a thick stone slab covered by moss, Kaylina Korbian waved a dismissive hand at her brother—her *half* brother, if her recent research could be trusted. Since that research had involved receiving visions from a sapient plant, it was possibly suspect. But her sister's memories about the green-haired man who'd visited their mother before Kaylina's birth did corroborate the story...

"You're not a ranger or enemy of the preserve, so they shouldn't hurt you or do anything alarming," she replied, pushing aside moss in search of Daygarii runes for her brother to translate.

"Hissing and flicking counts as alarming. Did you know—"

Frayvar shrieked, sounding more like a little girl than the seventeen-year-old accountant, chef, and rational-minded half of their meadery-and-eating-house business that he was. "That vine slithered over my boot like a snake. That's *tremendously* alarming."

"But it didn't hurt you. An actual snake would be more concerning."

"You're far too blasé about this. We just looted a hundred pounds of honey from that valley across the lake." Frayvar pointed at the packs strapped to Levitke, the blue-furred taybarri who'd been kind enough to come along and help carry the honey, then thrust his arm toward the blue water shimmering in the midsummer sun.

"It's not looting if a brand on the back of your hand matches the mark on the side of the beehive."

"You're sure about that? You consulted with the bees you were thieving from?" Frayvar jumped back, putting more distance between his foot and the vines.

"When I put my hand on the hive, it tingled pleasantly."

"Oh, there was *tingling*? Why didn't you say so? I'm vastly reassured." Frayvar frowned toward her perch. "You should have your sword in case you need to cut a vine that tries to strangle you." He looked toward Levitke again—or maybe the beautiful, bejeweled sword in its scabbard strapped to her back.

The blade had once belonged to Vlerion's brother, but he'd given it to Kaylina a few weeks earlier, and she'd dutifully put it to work more than once. The memory of Spymaster Sabor's death wafted through her mind.

"I've attempted to cut those vines with swords before," Kaylina said, pushing the thought aside. "It didn't go well."

"Yeah, but you're stronger now. From all that ranger training, right?"

"I'm positive it wouldn't make a difference."

Levitke padded into the water lapping at the shoreline,

appearing warm or maybe bored. Though taybarri and other animals were drawn to Kaylina and liked helping her—a boon she'd never believed she deserved—she vowed that they would head back to the city soon. It took hours to trek to Port Jirador, and the taybarri would want her dinner.

The afternoon was pleasant, however, with birds chirping in the trees around the ruins, fowl paddling among lilies in the lake, and insects buzzing in the air. The mountains looming beyond the preserve still held snow, but southern-born Kaylina could walk outside without four layers of clothing now, and this beautiful area spoke to her blood, inviting her to stay and relax.

Not finding anything to translate on the slab, Kaylina slid to the ground and wandered deeper into the ruins to seek out more promising structures. She passed a plaque surrounded by magical flowers that buzzed with power, but she'd taken a rubbing from it on a previous visit and knew what it said.

These lands are protected by the magic of the Daygarii... Step with care. Enemies... will be slain. One species may not subsume another. When imbalances occur, and one species dominates, fear not, for all will return to equilibrium eventually. The universe... appoints protectors to ensure that in balance the world thrives.

It gave some insight into the ancient druids, but what Kaylina longed to find was information on how to lift Vlerion's curse. He was still exiled on his family estate, waiting to be questioned about Sabor's death. Kaylina had killed the spymaster, drawn into a fight with him to defend the then-unconscious Vlerion, but he'd taken the blame and was awaiting judgment.

Finding a way to lift the curse that compelled him to turn into a beast when his emotions were roused might not do anything to solve *that* problem, but Kaylina had promised him—and his mother—that she would use her newfound druidic power to do so.

As a commoner and a newcomer to the north, she had no idea

how to help him with the crown or the law, unless she stepped forward and took the blame on herself. But he'd done that to protect her. As he'd pointed out, his station as a ranger and an aristocrat from a respected family—one that had ruled over Zaldor until his ancestor had abdicated—ought to shield him somewhat. He believed he would receive a more lenient sentence than she would.

"I hope you're right, Vlerion," Kaylina whispered, missing him, though it had only been a few days since she'd visited and they'd shared a picnic on the lakeside dock on his estate. He wasn't in chains or a dungeon. He was fine. "For now," she murmured, well aware that the situation could change once the new spymaster, a man named Milnor, who'd apparently been Sabor's second, completed his investigation.

Kaylina climbed atop a pile of toppled slabs and rubble for a better view of the ruins. She tried not to think of how Vlerion, having changed into the beast to battle enemies in this very area, had chased her into a gap in the rocks because he'd longed to mate with her. As much as she cared for *Vlerion*, and wanted to be with him, she was terrified at the idea of the beast taking her, something that had almost happened more than once.

"Another reason to get that curse lifted," she murmured, thinking of the scars on the neck of Vlerion's mother, of her warning that women didn't always survive mating with the cursed men of the Havartaft line. Since Lady Isla had been married to one of them, she knew better than any.

The elevated position improved Kaylina's view, but she couldn't tell if any of the piles of ruins would be more useful than others. If there had once been a library in the ancient settlement, she couldn't tell now. Any books or scrolls the druids might have kept were long gone.

She eyed the leaf-shaped brand on the back of her hand. It *had* tingled when she'd touched the hives to remove a portion of the honey from within, hives that had been placed by the druids centuries earlier. Further, the brand always drew her toward the ruins when she was near. She hadn't intended to stop to poke around in here, but a hunch had told her it might prove fruitful. An hour later, she feared it had been her imagination.

"Is there anything here that can help with the curse?" she whispered to her hand, keeping her voice soft, lest her brother hear and tease her. "With Vlerion?"

The brand didn't tingle, warm, or do anything to suggest it was anything except a mark on her hand. She was on the verge of climbing down when another thought came to her.

"Is there anything here that could give me information about my father? Or help me find him?"

The plant in Stillguard Castle—the *sentinel*—had given her a vision of him, a green-haired man with skin the color of a red cedar tree. It hadn't, however, shared whether he lived or remained in this world.

A hint of warmth came from the brand, and her arm lifted of its own accord. It pointed toward a circular half-wall on a hill overlooking the garden where magical flowers had once shrieked a warning about Kar'ruk warriors approaching. Fortunately, they'd been silent today.

Kaylina scrambled down from the rubble, waded through waist-high flowers, some of which were still blooming, and climbed the hill to the circular area. When she stepped onto the stone wall, she could see the lake. Frayvar stood on the beach near where Levitke waded, his fists on his hips. He looked toward the ruins, noticed Kaylina gazing his way, then clutched his chest and crumpled to the ground.

She squinted at him and called, "Did your heart give out or are you melodramatically letting me know you want to leave?"

He flopped onto his back, hand still over his chest. "The great magical druid danger wafting from those ruins threatens to wither my organs and disintegrate my bones. My collapse will soon be complete, and carnivorous vines will consume my body."

"So... melodrama."

"My death will be your fault."

"I'll feel extremely guilty about it."

"As you should. You'll also be bereft of your chef. Do you think people will come for your mead if there aren't fine meals to serve alongside the goblets?"

"I could buy some tins of crackers to dole out."

Horror twisted his face. "I really *am* dying after hearing that."

Levitke padded out of the water, sniffed him, then licked his cheek.

"Let me know if you have any final words, and I'll include them in a letter to Grandma and Grandpa." Kaylina turned away, trusting the taybarri would let her know if her brother withered, disintegrated, or was consumed.

She studied the circular area, looking for clues. Tall grasses and plants she couldn't name filled the hilltop, some growing out of gaps in the stones that comprised the wall. In the center, a spherical object almost hidden by leaves, grass, and vines rested on a pedestal the same green as the vegetation.

"Hello, what are you?" she murmured and pushed her way to it.

Vines, branches, and the grime of the ages covered the sphere, and she struggled to brush it clear. She pulled out her knife, thinking it would be easier to study if she sliced away the vegetation, but she hesitated. Though she didn't sense magic emanating from the plant matter, the nearby alarm flowers might object to damage to any growth within the ruins. She didn't want them to start keening again. That noise had nearly incapacitated her.

She returned the knife to her sheath and rested her palm on the grimy sphere. It was cool, no hint of magic about it, but she willed her power to prompt the vegetation to shift away from it.

She'd convinced vines to move before, though she didn't know *how* she'd done it, other than wishing they would.

In case it helped, she focused on the brand. The sentinel had said it didn't have power itself but somehow helped her access her own.

As Kaylina stood there with her hand on the sphere, she realized the lake and trees around the ruins had grown quiet. When had that happened?

She bit her lip. The last time all the wildlife had fallen silent here, Kar'ruk warriors had been in the area. After the invaders had been defeated in Port Jirador, the rangers had swept through the countryside, including the preserve, and made sure none remained, but what if some of the Kar'ruk had returned to foment trouble? As far as she knew, the Virts—the rebels who called themselves the righteous and virtuous—were still trying to find ways to overthrow the king and better their working conditions.

Kaylina was about to give up and return to the city with Levitke and Frayvar when her hand warmed. The vegetation slithered aside, and some of the hardened grime flaked away. Under her fingers, the sphere flared with green light, green light and *energy*. A strong buzz vibrated against her palm and ran up her arm.

Startled, Kaylina sprang back. Her heels tangled in the vegetation, and she fell to her butt. She winced at the pain and also with the certainty that the shrieking flowers would wake up.

But they stayed dormant. And the preserve all around remained quiet.

The warmth in Kaylina's hand intensified, and an urge to return to the sphere filled her.

"If Vlerion were here, he would tell me this isn't wise," she whispered as she pushed herself to her feet. She flexed her tingling hand, then stepped back up to the sphere. "As I've told him often, wisdom isn't my forte."

A pulse came from the back of her hand. Did it seem reassuring, or was that her imagination?

Thus far, the brand had helped her, and the sentinel had also helped her, even if it did so by murdering people who wished her harm. The druid magic was, as her brother said, dangerous. But...

"So far, it's been on my side." Shoulders tense, Kaylina rested her hand on the sphere again, the green light shining up between her fingers.

Power flared, and an image of her father formed in her mind. No, not in her mind. It appeared in the air above the sphere, hovering there.

More power flowed from the sphere and into her until her entire body buzzed. Then the energy reversed, seeming to be drawn from within her so it could pour into the sphere.

Weakness made her legs leaden, and she would have pulled away, but the image of her father continued to float in front of her. It was lifelike, almost as if he was there with her, looking the same as in the vision the sentinel had given her.

"Can you hear me? Can you *help* me?" Kaylina whispered as more energy was sapped from her. "Ideally, before I collapse. Even more dramatically than my brother did."

A final drawing of energy left her slumped against the pedestal. The image of her father dispersed, the wisps billowing outward in all directions.

What did *that* mean?

That was her last thought before she crumpled to the ground and the world went dark.

2

A man will mind his own affairs only until what he cherishes is threatened.

~ Tenegarus Grittorik, lieutenant of the Righteous and Virtuous

The sky was a deep green. That couldn't be right.

From her back, Kaylina gazed up at it, picking out stars here and there between the shadowy branches that partially blocked the view. Where was she? Still in the preserve? Her memories were fuzzy, but she recalled touching something, then collapsing.

A dark figure came into view, head cocking to the side as it gazed down at her. As he *gazed down at her. Vlerion. He wore his leather armor and ranger blacks, with his sword belt at his waist.*

"You've done something unwise," he remarked calmly.

"As we've discussed, I'm prone to that."

"Indeed. It's probably your youth."

"You're only a few years older than I am."

"True, but I was forced to grow up young."

When his brother had died—been killed by rangers because he'd turned into the beast. Vlerion didn't say that, but she knew he was thinking about it. They'd come to know each other well these past months.

"It's fortunate that you and your wisdom are here to guide me," Kaylina said.

"And my sword is here to protect you." He tapped the hilt, then knelt beside her, touching her shoulder. "It would have done so more effectively if you'd told me you were coming out here and had invited me along." Though his touch was gentle, his tone was stern.

"You're in exile and supposed to stay on your estate."

"Yet I would have come if I'd known you needed protection."

"I know, and that's the problem." Kaylina clasped his hand. "This is a strange dream."

"Because I'm admonishing you?"

"No, that's perfectly normal, but you're not usually wearing so many clothes when you feature in my dreams."

She'd lost count of how many times she'd awoken from a sexual dream about him, disappointed to find herself alone, disappointed every time she remembered that they couldn't be together in the real world. The dreams, alas, were never long enough, never satisfying *enough.*

"Ah, yes. I understand." His blue eyes gleamed, the sternness replaced by humor. "You're not clothed at all *in my dreams."*

"Not at all? Even at this chilly northern latitude?"

"Never. Once you were partially wrapped in a bear hide for warmth."

"The epitome of fashion." Kaylina imagined her southern, island-living family having sarcastic words about such a clothing choice.

"Fear not. I soon removed it." He touched her cheek.

She longed for more and reached up to him, but he patted her on the shoulder and leaned back.

"This time, I'm here to protect you until you wake," Vlerion said. "And until he comes."

"He?"

"You called someone."

Her memory remained fuzzy. "Called?"

"Yes, loudly. Like a Kar'ruk raider blowing a war horn."

Now, she remembered the magic flowing out of that sphere. But who *had she called?*

Something jostled her, and Kaylina woke. Her eyes were gritty with exhaustion, and she groaned at the effort that opening them took. The back of her hand throbbed. Had it been doing that the whole time she'd been out?

Around Kaylina, the world had grown dark, with stars out in the night sky. At least it was a *normal* night sky, not a green-tinted one.

An owl hooted nearby, and crickets chirped. As in the dream, she lay on her back, but, this time, she noticed the discomfort of pebbles underneath her, and pain asserted itself all over her body. Her head ached, and she could feel a lump even before she touched it. She must have cracked her head on something when she'd fallen.

She looked around for the pedestal and ruins, but she was by the lake now, lying on the pebbly beach. Two men sat in the dark at her side, and two taybarri lay on their bellies nearby. Levitke and... was that Crenoch?

"Vlerion?" she asked the larger figure, night's shadows hiding both of their faces.

"She's awake," Frayvar blurted with relief.

"Yes." Vlerion rested a hand on Kaylina's shoulder, not unlike he had in the dream.

Or... had that been a vision?

"And asking about *you*." Frayvar harrumphed like an old man. "Kay, *I'm* the one who risked my life to drag you out of those loathsome vine-sprouting ruins."

"I thought you said Levitke got her out." Vlerion pointed at the taybarri.

"She did after I attempted and failed to do so because vines were hissing at me like cobras. But I still risked my life."

"Did they hiss at Levitke too?" Vlerion asked.

"Yeah, but she's fast and could dodge them and get to Kay. Dragging her out was dicier."

"Dragging?" Kaylina mumbled.

Maybe *that* was why her entire body hurt. She envisioned the taybarri tugging her by the scuff of her neck over ruins.

"Yes, we were afraid to leave you there," Frayvar said. "Looking back, I think the vines were protecting you, but I didn't know what *happened*. You didn't answer, and you were out for hours. After Levitke got you, she ran back for help. Taybarri are *very* good companions."

Levitke lifted her head, swished her tail, and whuffed. Crenoch yawned and rolled onto his back with all four legs in the air.

How late *was* it? It had been afternoon when she'd touched the sphere. And Vlerion...

"You're supposed to be in exile," she whispered, afraid he would get in trouble for coming out here.

"As you might imagine," Vlerion said, "when your taybarri showed up at the estate without you, I was concerned."

"I actually asked Levitke to get Doc Penderbrock," Frayvar said. "Taybarri may be good companions, but they have minds of their own."

The crickets stopped chirping. Vlerion noticed right away, and his hand dropped to the hilt of his sword as he gazed around.

Levitke rose and padded over to gaze solemnly down at Kaylina.

"Maybe she thought I needed a protector rather than a doctor." Kaylina rolled to her side, wincing at the pain from so many parts of her body. Had someone been there offering her healing draughts, she wouldn't have rejected them.

Vlerion helped her sit up. "Something's out there."

Crenoch also rose, stance rigid as he looked toward the trees behind the ruins.

Kaylina remembered the part of the dream about how she'd apparently *called* someone. When she'd touched the sphere, she'd hoped she could somehow reach out to her father, but, if he lived at all, he was probably halfway around the world. After all, he'd met her mother on the sun-drenched Vamorka Islands, where monkeys chattered in the trees and lizards scuttled over warm rocks above sandy beaches.

"I'll get my sword." Kaylina pushed herself to her feet, Vlerion's hand under her elbow supporting her.

He always supported her, the moon gods bless him. When he protected her, it touched her, but when he helped her achieve the things she desired... that made her love him. A word she needed to speak aloud to him one day.

The grass and leaves between the trees rustled.

One day when they weren't in trouble.

Was that the wind? Or an animal? Or something more *dangerous* than an animal?

Thanks to her druid heritage, Kaylina didn't usually have to fear forest creatures, but if the Kar'ruk had returned to the preserve, they wouldn't be mollified by her blood. If anything, they would want to use her—*it*—because they believed it could convey some power.

A wolf howled in the distance.

"There are people out there." Vlerion gazed toward the trees where the rustling had originated, but he also glanced toward the opposite shoreline, keeping an eye on everything.

"Human people?" Kaylina asked as the two taybarri shifted,

also facing the trees. Their large floppy ears twitched, no doubt hearing more than she could.

"What other kind of people would there be?" Frayvar whispered. He'd crept closer to Vlerion.

Kaylina had her sword out, too, but she couldn't blame her brother for believing an experienced ranger would be better able to defend them. "Don't tell me you've forgotten the Kar'ruk."

"Oh. No, but I thought they were gone." Frayvar glanced toward the ruins and the trees, shifting his weight nervously. "I don't have my cast-iron pan."

Vlerion looked at Frayvar.

"His weapon of choice," Kaylina explained. "He smacked one of my kidnappers with it."

"Yes, I recall you mentioning his heroism." Vlerion's attention returned to the trees.

"It's possible he was defending his cherry-mint glaze rather than me," Kaylina said, "but it *was* a heroic action."

"Both were in danger," Frayvar said.

"Ranger lord," came a call from the trees, the female speaker hidden by shadow. "Few of your kind have entered the preserve since the Daygarii determined you enemies of this place."

"I'm aware," Vlerion said.

"Do you defend she who has returned to the land of our ancestors? Or do you imprison her?"

The voice sounded human—the speaker didn't even have an accent, except for a faint drawl that wasn't common in the capital. But who was *she who has returned to the land of our ancestors*? Kaylina? She was the only female on the beach, but…

"I protect Kaylina Korbian and enforce the law." Vlerion sounded a touch pompous. Was he implying that he believed the speaker was a criminal? "Who are you?"

"Loyal kingdom subjects who mind the mountains and the preserve." The female speaker and three men stepped out from the trees. The darkness made it hard to see faces or determine if they were armed, but they had shaggy forms. Did they wear furs? "We heard the call," she added, taking a few steps closer, but the group stopped twenty yards away.

"Uh," Kaylina said. "I wasn't trying to call *them*."

She had no idea who *they* were but was surprised normal humans would have sensed whatever magic that sphere had sent out.

Her brand warmed, and she frowned down at it.

"Mountain men and women." Vlerion lowered his sword but didn't sheathe it. "They're usually hunters and trappers. They have villages in the Evardor Mountains, but I didn't know they entered the preserve. I trust they don't hunt here."

"We would not be so foolish," the woman responded, though Vlerion had spoken softly. "Some of us have an interest in these lands and visit them, but even we do not dare go against the wishes of the Daygarii. We have not forgotten what they desire—or that they punish those caught by the sentinels remaining in the area."

The sentinels? Like the plant in the castle?

With her hand still warm, Kaylina scrutinized the shadowy people, wishing for better light. Maybe it was her imagination, but now that they were closer, she sensed something about them. Something unusual. The people of Jirador didn't rouse her brand.

"Even you, you said?" Vlerion asked. "Are you special?"

"*We* like to think so," the woman said. "We are not noble, of course, in the way of the kingdom, but our ancestors were in these lands before gold was discovered and outsiders flocked to the area and built the great capital."

With those words, Kaylina realized what was different about them. What was *special*, as Vlerion had asked. She didn't know how she knew, but with certainty, she whispered, "They're descended from the druids as well as humans."

Vlerion eyed her. "Like you?"

"I... maybe?"

"Are you drawn to them, Crenoch?" Vlerion asked.

The taybarri yawned, then ambled over to nudge Kaylina's pocket.

She had treats in there for Levitke, to thank her for carrying all the honey, but doled out a couple for Crenoch. After all, he'd brought Vlerion all this way to help her.

"Not as much as to you, apparently," Vlerion said, answering his own question.

"My pockets may be more interesting than hers," she said.

"Are you *certain* you are her protector, ranger lord?" one of the men asked.

Was he looking at Vlerion's sword?

"Your kind have no reason to love those with the blood of Daygarii flowing in their veins," the man added, pointing at Kaylina.

She shifted, uncomfortable that strangers knew that about her. But if she could sense that something was unusual about them, maybe they could tell the same about her.

"I believe he is different," the woman said before Vlerion could answer.

"He is *cursed*," another man said.

"He is Lord Vlerion," the woman said. "A respected ranger and a descendant of the Havartafts, they who once ruled the kingdom. His squad came through our village last winter and helped Keenor and Draks hunt down the rabid malikar that leaped over our wall and slew one of our children."

"That does not mean he's suitable for or interested in protecting her," the man said. "She has called for the help of her kind. We cannot leave her in anything but trustworthy hands."

Kaylina opened her mouth to vouch for Vlerion, but the snap of a branch came from the forest behind the ruins.

Rustling followed, along with heavy footfalls that caused more snaps.

"The zenlevars will determine if the ranger truly protects her and if he is worthy of doing so." The man pointed in the direction of the snaps.

"Uhm." Kaylina lifted her finger. "That's not necessary. Vlerion and I are friends. He protects me and does it well, thanks."

The group looked in her direction but didn't respond to her statement.

A chilling roar came from the trees. The woman shifted, drawing aside her fur, and produced a lantern. She un-shuttered it and turned up the flame, then set it on the ground and backed away. The men followed her lead, also moving away from the light.

"The zenlevars will decide," she agreed.

More snaps came from the woods. Whatever zenlevars were, they didn't pad silently among the trees like cats or wolves. Kaylina dug through her memory for a picture to go with the name, certain they were described in the ranger handbook.

"These people must be *anrokks*," Vlerion said quietly, "and have the ability to command animals."

"Well, I have that ability too." Kaylina willed whatever was in the woods to go away.

It was the taybarri who responded to her comment—and her will. Levitke and Crenoch growled, wide tails swishing on the pebbly beach in agitation, and moved to stand with her.

Vlerion noticed they chose her instead of him and gave Crenoch a sad look, but he didn't say anything. Kaylina hadn't forgotten his admission early on that he'd grown up adoring the taybarri and that it disturbed him that they, fearing the beast, did not adore *him*.

"Help *Vlerion*," she whispered to them as shaggy dark creatures padded out of the woods. "Please."

The taybarri growled toward the new animals and opened

their jaws to reveal their fangs, to show that their amiable demeanors and floppy ears didn't keep them from being powerful predators.

As more and more zenlevars came into view, the lantern light doing little to provide help for human eyes, Kaylina worried her side was outmatched. With wide-set eyes, stub ears, and broad faces and jaws, the four-legged creatures were as large as horses and as muscled as oxen. They didn't move as lithely as felines, but they emanated power.

If Vlerion turned into the beast, he might be able to handle them, but Kaylina didn't want that. Already, too many people knew about his secret. She'd worked hard to keep it from her brother and those she'd interacted with. If Vlerion turned in front of these people, they might tell every villager in the mountains.

3

Often we are defined by what others misunderstand about us.
~ Lady Professora Nila of Yarrowvast, Port Jirador University

Again, Kaylina tried to draw upon her power and assert her will on the zenlevars. A few of them glanced at her, but they gave steadier looks to the mountain men—to those who also had druid blood. She sensed a bond between them, that the big predators had worked with these people before. When they growled at Vlerion, she also guessed they knew he was different and believed that the beast magic that cursed him made him a threat.

As the animals strode closer—Kaylina counted eight of them—Vlerion considered the mountain men. Thinking that if he attacked *them*, he might capture one and force the others to call off the animals? That could work. But if it was on his mind, he didn't contemplate the thought long, instead crouching to face the animals. Maybe attacking humans, even humans with strange druid blood, wasn't honorable for an aristocrat sworn to protect kingdom subjects.

Kaylina leaned her sword against her leg and drew her sling. *She* wasn't an aristocrat and didn't care about honor, not when it was being used to disadvantage Vlerion.

Before she could aim her sling, the animals charged. As one, all eight rushed toward Vlerion.

Levitke leaped out to meet their charge. Vlerion swung up onto Crenoch's back, and they sprang into the fray together. The taybarri's jaws snapped, keeping the predators at bay, as Vlerion swung down from above. He angled his sword toward eyes and throats and other vulnerable targets.

But the shaggy animals were as fast as the taybarri. His sword delivered glancing blows, but the zenlevars darted away, evading the brunt of the attacks, then leaped back in. They either snapped at Vlerion's legs or lunged for the taybarri, trying to take Crenoch down to reach his rider. Levitke flanked them, attacking from behind, but there were so many.

Kaylina scurried back, afraid she would be in the way. The animals paid her no attention. Of course not. She was an *anrokk*. They might not obey her, but they wouldn't attack her.

Since they wanted to *kill* Vlerion, she couldn't take any solace in that. She snatched up her sword as Crenoch flashed to avoid four zenlevars charging him and Vlerion.

"Kay," her brother blurted from behind her. "Stay back."

She didn't. Oh, she didn't rush into the fray—thus far, few of Sergeant Zhani's sword-fighting lessons had addressed what to do against fanged foes—but she ran closer to the water. She skirted the battle to angle toward the fur-clad mountain people. They'd started this, and they—she hoped—could stop it.

A yelp of pain sounded as Vlerion lopped off the ear of a zenlevar that had been caught off guard by Crenoch disappearing and reappearing behind it. Though briefly discombobulated by the taybarri magic, the animals recovered and ran across the beach, focusing on Vlerion and Crenoch instead of

Levitke. She surged after them, biting at their heels and hindquarters.

Crenoch spun as two zenlevars tried to circle behind him. He used his tail like a club as Vlerion leaned out, slashing into the back of an attacker's neck. Another yelp pierced the night as his blade sank deep. One zenlevar that Crenoch clubbed stumbled away, thudding into a tree.

Had the numbers been even, Vlerion and the taybarri would be winning, but more of the predators rushed out of the woods to replace those that were injured.

Kaylina crept closer to the group of people. Either the darkness hid her better than she expected, or they were so mesmerized by the battle that they didn't notice her. As the snarls, snaps, and thuds coming from the frenzied skirmish grew more intense, she raised her sword and ran toward the onlookers.

At the last second, the woman spotted her and tried to leap back. But Kaylina was faster. She caught the woman by the arm and swung the sword toward her throat. The blade bumped against the woman's shoulder, making Kaylina wince. How had all the people who'd grabbed her and put a blade to her throat these past weeks done it so effortlessly?

"Practice," she muttered.

The alarmed woman tried to pull away, but Kaylina had the strength to hold her in place.

"Stop the attack!" Kaylina didn't add, *or I'll cut the woman*. She couldn't threaten humans, especially not when they seemed to be, however misguidedly, trying to assist her. "It's against the law to attack the king's rangers, and I'm a ranger in training. I'll do what I must to stop this."

The men who'd been so mesmerized by the fight finally turned.

"Dola!" one blurted.

Was that the woman's name? Kaylina felt guilty about grabbing her, since she was the one who'd spoken decently of Vlerion, but her odds were better at effectively restraining another woman.

One man drew a knife but looked at Kaylina instead of attacking. "You'd hurt one of your own?"

"I am a ranger trainee," Kaylina said as one of the taybarri yelped in pain.

Damn it. Irritation surged through her, and she again tried to will the zenlevars to leave them alone. When that didn't work, she imagined a wildfire sweeping through the woods and burning everything—animals included. She tried to thrust the alarming imagery into the zenlevars' minds, though she had no idea if she had the power to share visions—or threats.

"Stop the attack, or I'll arrest you all," Kaylina yelled, though it was ridiculous. Unless Vlerion helped her, she would be hard-pressed to arrest anybody.

Surprisingly, the snarls and snapping of jaws halted, as if her threat had worked. No, she realized as the zenlevars glanced wildly about. It was the imagery that must have worked, overriding the feelings of loyalty the animals felt toward these people. They couldn't have seen flames, but they ran toward the lake and leaped into the water. Without looking back, they swam for the far side.

"What happened?" one of the men blurted, glancing from Dola to the retreating zenlevars.

"She overrode us." Another man pointed at Kaylina. "Her blood is stronger than ours. As we knew when we heard the call."

"She doesn't need protection!" Dola whispered harshly, as if she dared not speak loudly with Kaylina's sword against her neck.

"Oh, she does," one man said. "Maybe not from us or from him, but the future is chaotic, and she is in danger. She would not have called otherwise."

Kaylina grimaced as she looked toward Vlerion. She had, however inadvertently, brought this battle to him.

Fortunately, he remained fully human, giving no hint that the beast threatened to rise. She hadn't even caught him humming, as he often did to help keep his equanimity. Vlerion breathed heavily, but, as she'd observed before, he was far more likely to lose his calm—to have his emotions riled and cause the beast to emerge—when those he cared about were in danger. His own fate seemed to matter less to him.

Now, he stood on the ground between Levitke and Crenoch, the taybarri panting as they licked wounds. Had Vlerion been hurt? Kaylina couldn't tell. He was always so stoic about hiding his pain.

When he walked toward her, sword out with zenlevar blood dripping off and darkening the pebbles, he didn't limp. He emanated power, danger of his own, like the predator he was. His gaze was charged as it raked Kaylina. Did he worry that *she* was injured? No, he'd been the one in peril, but he'd come through unscathed, and she couldn't help but admire him as he approached.

Admire him and long for him, as drawn as ever by the beast—by *him*.

She made herself look away, reminded that others were here. Even if they hadn't been, she couldn't have joined with Vlerion. Not until she figured out how to lift his curse.

He stopped, standing at Kaylina's side. Realizing she'd forgotten about her brother while she'd been admiring Vlerion, she looked down the beach to check on Frayvar.

He'd followed his own advice and found a clump of mossy rocks to take cover behind. His head poked above them as he watched the goings-on, but he seemed content to remain back there until he was certain the danger was past.

"You were going to arrest them?" Vlerion asked mildly. "Did you bring shackles? Enough for four people?"

"No." Kaylina lifted her chin, deciding he couldn't be too badly wounded if he was teasing her. "But there are vines all over the place. As you well know, they have impressive tensile strength."

"I am aware of that, yes. I suppose for one who can command them, they would do."

"Please let me go," Dola whispered. "We didn't mean... We thought we were helping. We thought you *wanted* help." She flicked her hand toward the man with the knife.

He lowered it and stepped back.

"I'm sorry about that. I meant to call... someone else." Kaylina moved the sword away from the woman's neck and released her.

Kaylina shifted close to Vlerion, wanting to emphasize that they were together, not enemies. His sword remained in hand, and she suspected he was dubious about the group and didn't know if they would prove a further threat. He lifted his free hand to her shoulder though, gripping her gently.

"You did well," he said softly, no hint of the earlier teasing in his tone.

Kaylina felt she should have been able to divert the zenlevars earlier, but she reminded herself that she'd had no training in magic. She had no idea what her power could do or how to effectively draw upon it. Glad for his praise, she leaned into him.

"Why did you sound a call if you didn't need help?" one of the men asked her.

"I was..."

Vlerion looked at her with his eyebrows raised. A reminder that he'd arrived later and had no idea what she'd done in the ruins. She'd *been* there and didn't entirely know what she'd done.

"I'm looking for someone," she said as much to him as the onlookers. "A druid."

"They have passed on from this world," Dola said.

"Not all of them. There was at least one around as recently as, oh, a little over twenty years ago." Kaylina pointed at herself.

Dola studied her. "I see. You are a half-blood."

"I think so. From what I've been told."

Told by a plant...

"I've not seen one before," Dola said.

"Would you know if any full-blooded druids had come through the mountains? Or this preserve?" Kaylina wondered if her father could have visited the area without them knowing about it.

"If they came near us, we would sense it, but not if they remained many miles away. The preserve is quite large." The poor lighting made it hard to tell, but this speaker sounded like he was older than the others. "In my lifetime, you are the first with the ability to activate the ancient artifacts."

He pointed toward the ruins.

"I touched a grimy sphere, and something happened," she whispered to Vlerion, feeling his curious gaze upon her.

"And that activated an artifact?" he murmured.

"Apparently."

"I knew you were special." Vlerion squeezed her shoulder.

"I told you *that* when we met. At least, I let you know I'm not normal." Kaylina didn't know if *not normal* was an official synonym for special, but it seemed plausible. Maybe she would consult her wordsmith brother later.

"Did you? I mostly recall you flinging a sling round at my head."

"Yes, that was how I let you know. That was clearly the action of someone different from the norm."

"That is true. *Most* people regard rangers with polite respect and don't hurl weapons at them." Vlerion shifted his gaze from her to the group. His voice remained mild, and, despite the dangerous battle, he didn't seem that offended that they'd *hurled* deadly animals at him.

The group had started to back away, the men avoiding Vlerion's gaze, but Dola remained up front, and she lifted her chin as she met his eyes.

"You are a mighty fighter, Lord Vlerion, despite your curse."

Vlerion's lips thinned. All his life, he'd done his best to keep the family curse a secret. He couldn't be pleased by how many people knew about it these days.

Kaylina worried, as he did, that the Virts or his other enemies would use that knowledge against him. When the Virts had run their rebel newspaper, they'd been trying to prove a link between the beast and the rangers and claim Vlerion was a threat to everyone and needed to be killed.

"I am a ranger," he replied to Dola. "I've trained many years at swordsmanship."

"You are a worthy protector for she who called." Dola waved toward the dead zenlevars.

Crenoch whuffed, and Levitke swished her tail, batting a pebble down the beach.

"I am fortunate enough to have *many* worthy protectors." Kaylina waved toward the taybarri, not wanting them to feel slighted. They had leaped into battle as readily as Vlerion.

"I suspect... you will need them." Dola backed up to join the men. "I am not certain whether to wish you luck in receiving the answer you seek from your call or not. The Daygarii... did not like humans." She looked at her comrades and then at Vlerion. "Should they return to this world, it may not be for the good of mankind."

Dola and her comrades exchanged worried murmurs as they turned and soon disappeared into the dark preserve.

Kaylina bit her lip, hoping she hadn't condemned anyone by activating that artifact. All she wanted was to meet her father and learn from him if she could. The man her sister had described hadn't sounded cruel—he'd made the children toys, after all—but what if he wasn't the one who came? As she'd already learned, others had heard her call.

A nudge at her hip distracted her from the dark thoughts. Levitke prodding her pocket.

"Ah." Kaylina reached for the package of honey drops she'd brought along. "Worthy protectors should be rewarded, of course."

The two taybarri nearly shoved Vlerion aside as they scooted closer, their big heads and twitching nostrils converging on Kaylina's hand. Large tongues lapped the homemade sweets off her palm.

"Should I be envious that your other worthy protectors are the ones being rewarded?" Vlerion asked.

"Probably." Kaylina wiped her palm, using a furry taybarri shoulder as a towel, and used her other hand to pull another honey drop out of her pocket. "Did you want one?"

She stepped closer to Vlerion, smirking as she offered it, holding it between the thumb and forefinger that hadn't been slobbered on. She had to lift her hand high and turn toward him to keep the taybarri snouts from swooping in to take it first.

"It *was* a taxing battle."

She held it out to him, expecting him to use his hand to take it, but he lowered his mouth to her fingers. His gaze held hers as his lips made contact, tongue sliding over her skin as he tasted the treat. It was a far different sensation from the animals licking her, and a surge of heat swept through her body, bringing instant arousal. She caught herself stepping closer and watching his lips, watching his tongue slide over the treat, tasting it before taking it. He was watching her in turn—noticing the effect his touch had on her—and the memory of his prowess in the battle returned to her.

Heat pooled in her core, and she wanted—

"Is it safe to camp here?" Frayvar wobbled as he walked up the pebbly beach toward them.

Vlerion stopped teasing Kaylina, took the treat, and stepped back.

She blushed and also stepped back. It was good, she told herself, that her brother was here, not disappointing.

"Taybarri eyes are keen, even in the dark," Vlerion said. "We can travel through the night and make it back to the city by dawn."

Frayvar groaned. "Aren't you tired after all that fighting? We were out here all day, and it's past midnight, isn't it?"

Vlerion opened his mouth, as if to say *of course* rangers didn't get tired, but Frayvar yawned, which prompted Kaylina to yawn as well.

She *was* tired, especially considering she'd been unconscious for however many hours. She remembered how her hand had been throbbing when she'd woken and wondered if the brand had been doing something on her behalf while she'd been knocked out. Continuing the call? She grimaced at the thought, now worried about the possible repercussions for what she'd done.

"We can rest for a few hours," Vlerion said, eyeing her.

She closed her mouth, wishing that yawn hadn't slipped out. He probably wanted to get back to Havartaft Estate before anyone noticed he'd departed. Men exiled to their manors were not supposed to take jaunts into the preserve.

"We can snooze on the taybarri backs," Kaylina said, waving to Frayvar and hoping he wouldn't argue.

He either didn't see her wave or ignored it, instead groaning dramatically. *Melodramatically*.

Vlerion lifted a hand. "We'll camp. There may be more dangers in the preserve than usual in the aftermath of..." He looked toward the ruins, but all he finished with was, "these events."

Kaylina winced. The call *she'd* made.

"It will be safer to wait until daylight to travel," Vlerion added.

"Oh." Frayvar brightened. "Good."

It was only as Vlerion said he would make a fire and left to gather wood, giving her a long look over his shoulder as he went up the beach, that she wondered if he was worried about making camp out here with her. They'd never spent a night in close proximity to each other. Did he worry that he would be inordinately drawn to her and do something that could rouse the beast? Or vice versa?

She shifted her weight, wondering if she should argue more strongly for leaving, but her brother had already flopped down on the beach.

"This is a good spot," he mumbled, using a pack of honey for a pillow. "Not cushy but free of weird vines."

"As all beds should be," Kaylina murmured.

"*Yes.*"

4

Under the stars, confidences may be shared that hide from the sun's brilliance.

~ Ganizbar, the poet

Wrapped in her cloak and lying down, Kaylina scooted closer to the fire that Vlerion had made. The cold seeping down from the mountains defied the calendar's promise that summer had come. Up the beach, the taybarri slept with their faces under their furry tails.

Back home, nighttime temperatures were rarely chilly, the semitropical ocean breezes whispering across the beach never bringing jackets to mind. But here, even when the days were sunny and warm, the nights cooled considerably, making one glance toward the glaciers in the nearby mountains, glaciers that never melted.

Before settling, they had pushed the bodies of the dead zenl-evars into the lake in the hope that scavengers wouldn't be drawn to their camp, but Kaylina doubted the corpses had floated far. They'd mused on burning them but had decided they would leave in a few hours and could let nature handle the clean-up.

Kaylina put another branch on the flames.

"You're cold?" Vlerion asked from a log he'd pulled near the fire to sit on.

He had to be tired, but he hadn't yet lain down, instead murmuring something about keeping watch. With Frayvar already snoring, the fact that he'd curled into a tight ball the only indication that he was also cold, he wouldn't be a candidate for standing guard. Kaylina had offered, but Vlerion had waved for her to get some rest.

"I'm fine." She smiled at him and deliberately didn't pull her cloak tighter to give away the lie. She *was* cold, especially since the pebbles underneath her seeped warmth out of her body. "We weren't planning to spend the night or we would have brought blankets."

"You weren't planning to traipse through druid ruins, activating artifacts with the power to knock you unconscious?" Vlerion's tone was light, and he returned her smile, not looking like he blamed her for doing that or that he wanted to call her unwise.

Again, Kaylina found herself appreciating his support. How long had it been since he'd pointed out her perennial failing of not calling him and other aristocrats *my lord* when she addressed them? Before his exile, he'd talked up her mead and their new eating house to other nobles, ensuring many people had come to their opening night. He'd even been responsible for a prominent wine critic coming by, the woman later publishing a flattering article about the mead. They'd received numerous bulk orders since then, and the seats had been full each night for dinner. Vlerion was... amazing.

"If you keep looking at me like that," he said, "I'll be tempted to come over there and personally keep you warm." His tone remained light, but his eyes had grown intent—*hungry*—and she knew exactly how he wanted to keep her warm.

She tried not to think about how desperately she longed for that, but her heart thumped in her chest, belying her. It took a lot of willpower to look into the fire instead of at Vlerion. She didn't want to make things hard for him, to inadvertently invite him to join her. He'd pointedly sat across the fire from her, laying out his own cloak behind the log to later use as a blanket.

"Kaylina," he said softly in the tone of a man with a secret to share.

She looked back to him.

He opened his mouth but glanced at Frayvar before speaking. She doubted her snoring brother would hear anything they said, but Vlerion came around the fire to sit behind her.

Anticipation swept through her, along with the memory of his lips on her fingers. She resisted the urge to scoot toward him, to wrap her arms around him. She did roll over to look at him, wondering what had brought him over.

Vlerion settled on his side, propped on his elbow and facing her, not touching her, but only a small space was between them now. A small space that would be easy to make disappear.

"I had a discussion recently with Sergeant Zhaniyan," he murmured.

Kaylina blinked. That wasn't what she'd expected him to bring up.

Sergeant Zhani had accompanied Kaylina out to Havartaft Estate when she'd gone to visit Vlerion in exile—Captain Targon had apparently insisted on Zhani acting as a chaperone, lest Kaylina and Vlerion be tempted to *hare off together* before matters were settled in regard to Spymaster Sabor's death. Because of that, it didn't surprise Kaylina that Zhani and Vlerion had spoken at some point, but what could they have discussed that he would bring up in the middle of the night?

"About my training?" she asked.

"Not exactly." Vlerion gazed at her, as if she might guess his thoughts, but she had no idea what he had in mind. "You know she was trained as an herbalist by her people before coming here, right?"

"Yes. She once gave me..." Kaylina stopped herself before explaining the drug Zhani had given her to prevent pregnancy if she found herself involuntarily—or *voluntarily*—with a man. That had been after one of the sage assassins had cut her shirt open and called her *appealing*. "Something," she said vaguely when Vlerion raised his eyebrows, waiting for her to finish.

His brows drew together in concern. "Medicine? Are you all right?"

"I'm fine." Kaylina waved dismissively, regretting that she'd brought it up, but Vlerion continued to look concerned. "After the incident with the sage assassins, she gave me..." She lowered her voice even further, though her brother continued to snore. "A contraceptive. Just in case."

"Ah," Vlerion said, though his brow remained furrowed.

Was he worried she'd underplayed how her encounter with the assassin had gone? The guy was dead, so he'd been suitably punished for whatever thoughts he'd had about her, but she didn't want Vlerion to think she'd experienced something worse than she had.

"Zhani knows how I feel about you too," Kaylina added. "I think she was trying to be helpful in case... Well, she doesn't know that we can't. You know."

"Yes." His gaze drifted from her face to follow the outline of her side, highlighted by the fire behind her. Her hip, the curve of her breast. "I well know," he added, a husky note in his voice.

The awareness of his desire for her always ignited her equally demanding desire for him, and she lifted a hand to his jaw before catching herself. The fire highlighted his face as well, casting shadows, drawing attention to the hard line of his jaw, his cheekbones, and the parallel scars that he'd received from his father long ago, when the man had been the beast. Maybe they should have made him unappealing, but they didn't. She wanted to touch them, to touch him.

Vlerion drew a steadying breath and caught her hand, pressing it to the ground between them.

"We need to be careful." He glanced toward Frayvar with significance.

He wasn't, she realized, afraid that her brother would overhear, not now, but worried the beast would erupt and hurt them. Kaylina doubted her brother would be in danger, since Vlerion's alter being would think of exactly what *he* was thinking about now. It would desire what he desired, so *she* would be the one in danger. That was... also something to be avoided.

Kaylina nodded and swallowed, her mouth dry, to let him know she understood.

"I only wanted to tell you that she mentioned a certain herb that I might use so that I could..." He cleared his throat and looked away, though he didn't release her hand. "I'd mentioned that I enjoyed training with you but that we couldn't because, ah..."

"I know." Kaylina well remembered one of their earlier practice sessions, one in which they'd been drawn by each other's sweat-dampened skin and heaving chests and had ended up embracing—and almost rousing the beast. They'd been in the middle of ranger headquarters, a courtyard with witnesses nearby. Witnesses who could have become victims to the beast if Vlerion had lost control. Worse, the rangers might have killed the beast. "Sergeant Zhani was a good choice. She's a good teacher."

"Yes."

It occurred to Kaylina that Zhani, with her knowledge of plants, might be someone to ask about the vial that Spymaster Sabor had used on Vlerion, throwing it to the ground, the contents somehow forcing the beast to change back into a man. Kaylina had almost asked Doc Penderbrock about it, but since he didn't know about Vlerion's curse, she hadn't wanted to risk revealing anything. Instead, she'd given the broken vial, with its vague smudge of dried blue liquid in the bottom, to her brother to research.

As smart and educated as Frayvar was, he didn't have any expertise with plants and medicines. Zhani, on the other hand, might have an idea what the substance had been. If it was something safe that could be used to make the beast change back if he was endangering others... it would be worth it to figure out where to find more of it. *Very* worth it.

Since Vlerion was gazing at her—wondering at her thoughts?—Kaylina pushed those musings away to focus on him.

"I liked training with you too," she said. "You're patient and hardly ever try to convince me that types of trees and plants are useful memory devices in recalling certain combinations of moves. The Sweeping Frond hasn't helped me defeat Zhani in battle yet."

He snorted softly. "I believe plants are good memory devices for *her*."

"Because she's an herbalist." Kaylina looked curiously at him, still wondering what he had in mind. What herb had Zhani recommended to him and why?

"Among other things, yes."

Kaylina waited to see if he would expand on that—more than one person had implied Sergeant Zhani was more than a ranger—but he switched topics.

"She spoke of a plant called altered chasteberry. It doesn't grow in this area, but some apothecaries reputedly carry the unaltered and occasionally the altered versions. She said she would look into it for me."

"Uhm, okay. Because it does what?"

"Reduces libido. She mentioned it might make it easier for us to train." His voice turned dry. "Me specifically."

"Oh, if we took it, we'd be less, er, horny?" Kaylina rubbed her face, her cheeks warm. This wasn't what she'd imagined him coming over to chat privately about.

"Yes." Vlerion touched his chest, as if to indicate only *he* would need to take it.

As if she wasn't as drawn to him as he was to her. Admittedly, she could probably keep herself from pouncing on him like a panther if he showed no interest in her. But...

"Are there side effects?" she asked.

"None that sounded that onerous."

"So... yes." Kaylina frowned at the thought of him taking some unpleasant medicine—or was it more like a *poison* since it had a negative effect on the body?—indefinitely until she could find a way to lift his curse. Was that what he was considering?

"It was my understanding that it wouldn't be necessary to take it continuously but only in... situations in which arousal would be... inconvenient. Difficult not to act on."

The pauses made her believe Vlerion found the discussion as awkward as she. At least they were able to talk about it. She couldn't imagine doing so with any other man. But he was the person she could lean on. Who appreciated her.

"Are you that eager to train me?" Kaylina squeezed his hand.

"It's not that. Sergeant Zhani is sufficient for that. But... you saved my mother even when her machinations were to blame for her—and *your*—peril. And you've stood at my side in battles, helping the city and the rangers. Even when these things had nothing to do with your dreams and goals." He paused to give her a significant look. "Did you investigate the ruins here because you sought to *call* someone or because you were looking for a way to lift my curse?"

"I did promise you and your mother that I would do that. I *want* to do that." Badly.

"That you care means a lot to me." His eyelids drooped. "You know I wish to reward you."

"Oh," she whispered as his thumb brushed the back of her hand. He'd alluded before to the kind of *reward* he had in mind for her, and the thought titillated her, but… "Wouldn't that be less, ah, interesting for you if you weren't… excited about it?"

"Less interest would make it easier to focus on your pleasure."

"Oh," she repeated, enticed but also a little embarrassed as she imagined being naked and writhing in his arms while he was calm and detached. That embarrassment didn't keep her from wondering what he would do when he had her in such a position. "I'd prefer if you didn't have to take anything. I would want you to enjoy… us." She waved between them with her free hand.

"You've given me hope that we'll both find enjoyment one day. If anyone has the power to lift my curse…" He released her hand but only so he could brush his fingers along her jaw. "I believe you do. But until then…"

His gentle words and tender gesture shouldn't have aroused her, but his every touch did that. Sometimes, all he had to do was *look* at her, and her entire body flushed with desire. Maybe they both needed to take that berry to counteract the magic—the obsession—in their blood, the pull between them.

"You should not wake yearning and alone because of *my* problem," he murmured.

"I would rather wake with you…" An image of them together in bed, *both* naked and enjoying each other's company came to mind.

"I know."

She always wanted to call him a cocky and haughty aristocrat when he said such things, but he was right. And he did know it.

"You don't need to reward me, okay?" Kaylina said. "Not in a way that would make things more difficult for you. Besides, you've already done a lot for me. I know you were behind many of those people, especially the aristocrats, showing up at our opening night."

"That wasn't difficult. I merely mentioned your business here and there."

"It wasn't difficult to get people to come to a cursed castle and try the drinks of an unknown commoner who's been in nothing but trouble since she arrived in the city?"

"Word was already getting out about your mead."

"But you helped it get out. Thank you. Some of those people run businesses of their own and put in bulk orders. We've been making enough to hire help and keep everything rolling along." The swift success was why they were here in the preserve, gathering more honey for future batches of mead. "It's wonderful, Vlerion. It's my dream."

"Not your *only* dream though." His fingers trailed from her jaw to her throat then brushed along her side.

Clothing didn't make the gesture less enticing, less erotic, and she tilted toward him, always wanting more.

"Vlerion," she whispered, not the protest she meant it to be. Instead, it came out with a hitch, a desire for him to keep touching her.

He leaned over her, bringing his lips to hers. It was supposed to be a gentle kiss without passion, probably one of parting before he returned to his side of the fire, but he'd already primed her libido, and she groaned and arched up into him, returning the kiss hard and hungry.

For a moment, he responded in kind, his hand cupping her through her shirt, his tongue drinking her in, but he made himself let go and pull back.

"Later," he whispered, though his gaze remained on her lips.

Later... after he had that plant?

She shouldn't have wanted him to give her satisfaction without knowing any of his own, but she couldn't keep from whispering, "Okay," and longing for it.

He nodded curtly, rose, and walked stiffly not to the other side of the fire but into the woods.

"I'll stand guard," he called back as he disappeared, and she imagined him satisfying himself with his hand, alone in the shadows. Or could he find even that relief? She didn't know if giving in to that amount of lust might bring out the beast.

Shaking her head, she stared up at the stars. She wished she'd found more in the ruins than a sphere capable of knocking her out. How could she lift Vlerion's curse so they could finally be together?

5

Centuries of uneventful stability may pass until a year comes when the world is irrevocably changed.

~ Prophet Tenolarc

Kaylina woke at first light, feeling more aroused than refreshed, since she'd dreamed of Vlerion. This time, he hadn't been calling her unwise. He'd been bringing her to great heights of passion while wearing his clothes and an utterly calm expression. Was that what would happen once he consumed the altered berry? Her dreaming mind must have thought so. His detachment certainly hadn't kept her from passionate dreams.

Hoping she hadn't been making any noise, she turned toward the ashes of the fire, a few orange embers still providing warmth and light. On the far side, Vlerion sat on his log, watching her, his eyes intense.

She rubbed her face, worried she *had* been making noise. Fortunately, her brother hadn't woken yet.

"Did you sleep at all?" Kaylina asked Vlerion but doubted he had. Not if he'd considered himself on watch.

"Plenty these past nights at home, with no work to occupy me."

"Well, that was a solid no."

He managed a smile that drew some of the intensity from his eyes and looked toward the lake. "It's fine. I—"

He rose, hand going to his sword, his gaze whipping toward the path that had brought them into the area. The taybarri had been snoozing near that section of the beach, but they were also rising. They must have heard something.

Levitke bounded over to stand next to Kaylina. Crenoch whuffed and swished his tail.

"Does that mean trouble is or isn't coming?" Kaylina pushed herself to her feet.

Levitke looked at her pocket, then bared her teeth in the direction of the trail. No growls accompanied the gestured, so Kaylina doubted a serious threat approached. The glances toward the pocket might mean Levitke felt the need to defend whatever honey drops remained.

"More taybarri," Vlerion said, "and presumably rangers."

The grimness in his voice surprised Kaylina until she remembered that he wasn't supposed to be in the preserve. He wasn't supposed to be anywhere except on his family estate.

"You should hide," she whispered, rushing to stand at his side.

She almost stood *in front* of him as voices sounded in the trees, a distinct, "Almost there," among them. But it wasn't as if people would miss seeing the taller and broader Vlerion behind her. And he did nothing to indicate he would grab Crenoch and hide in the woods. He lifted his chin as he faced the trail, doubtless too *honorable* to consider doing anything but accepting whatever punishment came as a result of his choice.

"It's a pain in the ass following all the tenets in that book, isn't it?" Kaylina muttered.

Vlerion arched his eyebrows and glanced at her, but the first rider appeared before he could reply.

"Yes, they're up here, Captain," Sergeant Jankarr said, his own eyebrows rising as he rode onto the beach with his taybarri. "Together, like you said."

"Of *course* they're together," came Targon's exasperated voice.

He and two more rangers on taybarri followed Jankarr onto the beach, Targon aiming his scowl at Vlerion and Kaylina like a javelin. "You're supposed to be on your estate, Lord Vlerion."

"Levitke found me and informed me that Trainee Korbian was in danger," Vlerion said.

"She informed you, did she?" Targon turned his scowl on Levitke, who swished her tail and bared her teeth again, guarding the honey pocket from the newcomers. More than one taybarri had its snout turned upward, nostrils sampling the cool dawn air—and probably noting not the honey drops in her pocket but the heavy pouches of pure honey in the packs. "I didn't realize any of our young taybarri had developed speech."

Kaylina almost pointed out that Levitke *had* spoken telepathically to her before, but that probably had more to do with her druid blood than the ranger mounts developing the ability to project words to humans. As far as she knew, only the silver-furred elders could do that.

"When she showed up at the estate without Kaylina, I knew she was in trouble," Vlerion said.

Targon looked Kaylina up and down, his dark mood not disturbing him so greatly that he couldn't let his gaze linger on her chest.

Not unlike Levitke, Kaylina bared her teeth, though the gesture was for Targon rather than his honey-seeking mount.

"She looks fine to me." Targon didn't leer for long before focusing on Vlerion again.

"She has recovered since I arrived," Vlerion said.

"Woke her with a kiss, did you?"

"Something like that. Does an inquisitor or the new spymaster seek me?"

"Not yet. Not as far as I know. After last night's events, your inquiry is probably on hold."

"Events?" Vlerion asked.

Behind Kaylina, Frayvar stirred, wiping crud from his eyes and blinking blearily at the rangers.

Targon gestured at Jankarr. "I sent the sergeant to inform you as soon as I heard. You'd know by now if you had been where you were supposed to be."

Chin up, Vlerion waited for his captain to get to the point.

Jankarr was the one to speak first. "The king is dead, Vlerion."

Surprised, Kaylina didn't react for a long moment.

Vlerion's only response was to grow grim. Very grim. "An assassin?"

His eyes darkened with... was that self-recrimination? He couldn't blame himself, could he? Because he hadn't been there to defend the elder King Gavatorin?

"No," Targon said. "At least not from what I was told. The newly appointed Spymaster Milnor—" an eyebrow twitch was his only acknowledgment as to *why* a new appointment had needed to be made, "—sent word that Gavatorin died of natural causes. Old age. Of course, there are drugs that can kill while simulating that, and I believe his personal physician is examining the body, but Gavatorin is—*was*—old." Targon shrugged. "Either way, I received orders to round up all the rangers in the field." He delivered another eyebrow twitch toward Vlerion. "Also those waywardly disobeying their exile. With the Virts always poised for an uprising, and Prince Enrikon gone whoring and gambling down in whatever manor the royal family owns along the southern coast, there could be trouble in town this week."

"Will the senior lords accept the prince as the next ruler?" Vlerion asked.

"They'll have to. He's Gavatorin's only acknowledged heir."

"Maybe you should volunteer for the gig, Vlerion." Jankarr smiled, and it sounded like a joke, but his eyes were wistful.

"I've no right to rule," Vlerion said, meeting Targon's eyes.

Kaylina didn't know if that was true—just because his ancestor had abdicated didn't mean he couldn't be considered if there wasn't another good option, did it?—but she understood why he wouldn't push for it. The same reason his ancestor had walked away from the throne. A king couldn't be a danger to his own people whenever he lost his temper. Or—she glanced at Vlerion—felt lustful toward a woman.

"You *do*," Targon said, "but you're even younger than Enrikon. People would object."

"*I* wouldn't," one of the thus far quiet rangers said from behind Targon and Jankarr. He nodded politely toward Vlerion. "He's proven himself in battle and never whores or gambles or has any vices at all that we've seen."

"Except breaking his exile," Targon grumbled.

"I don't understand why he *is* exiled, my lord," the ranger said.

"Find Sabor's corpse and ask it." Targon pointed at the taybarri. "Mount up. I don't know *what's* been going on out here—" when he'd ridden up, he must have noticed the torn-up ground and thrashed vegetation where the battle had occurred, because he looked pointedly in that direction, "—but you'll all come back to the city with me." He scowled at Frayvar and Kaylina. "Don't you two have an eating house to run?"

"My brother started all the meals before we left, and we have staff who handled the service." Kaylina hoped that was true—when she'd originally left with Frayvar for this mission, she'd assumed they would make it back by the time dinner began. "We came out to gather honey to make more mead."

"That's the dire reason you had to break your exile, Vlerion?" Targon asked. "Sating your sweet tooth?"

"Trainee Korbian was knocked unconscious in the druid ruins," Vlerion said. "For many hours. It was concerning."

"More concerning is why anyone would lack complete common sense and go *in* those ruins," Targon said with disgust, turning his mount toward the trail.

Vlerion's significant nod toward Kaylina promised he appreciated what she'd been trying to do in there. She wished she'd found something to help him. Instead, she'd apparently called out over who knew how many miles to everyone with druid blood.

"Come on," Targon grumbled, waving for them to follow.

Kaylina and Frayvar climbed onto Levitke's back. She gave no indication that she minded the load. With their sturdy builds, the taybarri could carry—and pull—more than horses could, but since Kaylina had learned how intelligent they were, she hated using them for toting burdens. She slipped a couple of honey drops to Levitke before they joined the others.

"Vlerion," Targon added as they headed down the trail, "you'd better hope nobody who dislikes you noticed your absence."

Jankarr gave Vlerion a sad look over his shoulder.

"The king's death and what will happen next to the kingdom should be people's primary concern now," Vlerion said.

"It *should* be." Targon's tone suggested it wouldn't be, not for everyone.

Kaylina shook her head, wondering how it was that some people adored Vlerion and wished he were king while so many others wanted him dead.

6

A pharmacist always has a potion.

~ Sage Frally

The sun was high in the sky by the time Kaylina and the rangers rode out of the preserve and onto the highway that followed the Stillguard River toward Port Jirador. Grassy green fields rolled away from either side, eventually reaching the cultivated lands of noble families with estates close to town, rows of crops growing high as summer reached its peak.

Usually, people were out working in those fields while sheep and cows grazed on the grass, but Kaylina barely saw anyone today. Word must have gotten out about the king's death. Were people in mourning? She hadn't gotten the impression that King Gavatorin was that beloved, except perhaps by those who had used his growing senility as an excuse to draw power to themselves and influence decisions. Spymaster Sabor came to mind. Kaylina doubted he'd been the only one scheming behind Gavatorin's vacant eyes.

"Riders coming." Sergeant Jankarr pointed at the highway ahead.

Two people in ranger blacks were leaving the city fast, their taybarri loping at top speed.

"I see them," Captain Targon said.

"That's Sergeant Zhaniyan," Kaylina blurted, spotting her raven-haired ponytail flopping on her shoulder as they rode.

"And Corporal Ged." Jankarr lifted a hand.

It didn't sound like the riders were expected. Targon grimaced. Expecting trouble?

Zhani and the corporal slowed to meet their group.

"Captain," Zhani said with relief in her voice. "And Lord Vlerion."

"We're here too," Jankarr said dryly, waving at his chest and toward the two other rangers in the group. After a pause, he smiled and pointed at Kaylina too.

Jankarr hadn't joked with her, not the way he first had, since she'd saved his life in the preserve. Because she'd done it *weirdly*, she knew, by spouting a word that had come to her out of nowhere and commanding the semi-sentient vines to release him. At least he was still willing to acknowledge that she existed.

Zhani nodded toward them but focused on Targon and Vlerion. "We came out to warn you. The new spymaster—Milnor—stomped into ranger headquarters this morning. He implied he's researching whether the king *really* died of natural causes, and he was on his way out to Havartaft Estate to question Lord Vlerion about... I'm not sure." Her green eyes grew troubled. "He said the inquiry was long past due. That was it, right, Ged?"

The corporal nodded.

"We were worried he would be irked when he rode out to the country and Lord Vlerion wasn't there." Zhani nodded to him.

Targon sent a dark look over his shoulder at Vlerion. "It's too late. You won't beat him there, even if you dangle Korbian's honey drops in front of Crenoch's nose to convince him to sprint across the countryside."

"I know," Vlerion said. "The road is the fastest way there."

He didn't look like he cared that much about getting back in time to please the new spymaster—or even ensure the man didn't have more reasons to be suspicious of him.

Kaylina wished Vlerion *would* care. She lamented that her choice to go into the preserve had resulted in him breaking his exile—and that he would now get in trouble for it.

"What kind of *unnatural* causes that Lord Vlerion could have been responsible for from a distance might have killed a man?" Frayvar asked.

Zhani spread her arms. "There are many ways to poison someone, but I cannot imagine a ranger employing any of them. I did get the impression that Milnor already knew he wouldn't find Lord Vlerion at home and was deliberately going out, with a couple of witnesses along, to prove that he's not there."

"To imply Vlerion could have been out last night poisoning the king?" Targon asked sourly.

"I don't know, Captain, but if he wanted to throw suspicion in Vlerion's direction..."

Targon sighed.

Zhani's words about knowing of poisons reminded Kaylina that she wanted to ask the sergeant about the substance in the vial.

Targon looked at Vlerion again. "You'd better come back with me to headquarters. Whenever Milnor ambles back through, maybe someone with flexible integrity will say you were there last night." His tone suggested *he* wouldn't.

Crenoch whuffed.

"*You're* not a sufficient witness," Targon told the taybarri. "We all know your integrity can be bought for honey and a pat from an *anrokk*."

Crenoch must have understood the comment, because his big

head swung around to regard Kaylina. Levitke also whuffed, maybe agreeing that it was a good time for honey.

"I'll have to resupply my pockets when we get back," she murmured to them.

"I'll deal with Milnor and whatever he believes," Vlerion said coolly, "without asking for anyone to lie on my behalf." His aloof gaze promised he would never do such a thing and was insulted that his captain would suggest it.

Targon only grunted and waved for Zhani and the corporal to turn around and ride with them.

"Captain?" Kaylina asked. "Since we were gone much longer than planned, my brother and I need to check on Stillguard Castle and make sure nothing went wrong last night. If it's all right, we'll veer off when we get to town."

She groped for a way to request that Zhani come along. At the least, Kaylina wanted a few minutes to talk to the sergeant about the vial. Maybe identifying the substance wasn't a priority right now, but, since Sabor had used it to knock out the beast, its existence was a threat to Vlerion. What if the new spymaster knew all about it and had a stash in a pocket for when he faced Vlerion?

"This is a time when ranger duties supersede *mead making*. You'll come to headquarters with the rest of us, Korbian." Targon flicked a dismissive hand toward Frayvar, as if to say he could handle their business since *he* wasn't a ranger.

Kaylina clenched her jaw, tempted to remind Targon that she hadn't volunteered to become one of them. He'd bribed her, if not *strong-armed* her, into agreeing to it. "The small amount of training I've received isn't going to help anyone if there's a coup."

Kaylina didn't know if that was what he expected to happen, but, as they rode closer to the city wall, Targon kept eyeing Port Jirador like it housed vipers.

"It could be helpful if you recruit a pack of stray cats." Targon glanced at her.

Kaylina froze. Was that comment meant to inform her that he knew she'd killed Spymaster Sabor? That it hadn't been Vlerion? And that Targon even knew *how* she'd done it? He hadn't been in the alley to see that battle, but Kaylina believed her mead-making rival, Jana Bloomlong, had witnessed it through a window. What if she'd blabbed the story all over town by now?

"Do you want me to continue with Korbian's training today, Captain?" Zhani asked.

"Yes. Until you're ordered otherwise." Targon pointed at Kaylina. "Your skills may be needed if trouble arises in the city." His voice lowered to a grumble. "*All* of our skills may be needed today."

"The sentinel—the plant in our tower—could help if there's trouble," Kaylina pointed out, trying a different tactic.

She supposed she didn't *need* to return to Stillguard Castle, and if she trained with Zhani today, Kaylina could ask about the vial, but her instincts told her it would be a good idea to check in. Or maybe she was just being stubborn and didn't want to give in to Targon's wishes.

Vlerion gazed at her without comment, though he probably wondered what she was up to.

Targon scowled at her. "The plant could help if you're allowed to go up to its tower to caress its leaves?"

"My honey-water fertilizer entices it more than leaf caressing," Kaylina said.

"That right? And here I thought druids were into rubbing leaves. Fine." Targon pointed at Zhani. "Take Korbian and her brother to the cursed castle and have your training practice there."

"Yes, Captain."

"But I want you and her to return to ranger headquarters tonight," Targon added. "I'm expecting trouble."

"Yes, Captain," Zhani repeated.

Kaylina almost pointed out that the sentinel had helped her

defend Stillguard Castle—and herself—numerous times, and it would be safer for her to stay there, but Targon might be worried about having enough people to keep peace in the streets, not about their personal safety.

Fortunately, the group rode through the city gates unchallenged. The streets, like the fields, were eerily quiet, with scant people out. Those who were stood close, speaking in hushed tones, and fell silent as the rangers passed.

"I have an idea about something," Kaylina said to Vlerion as they rode down the street that led toward Stillguard Castle.

He arched his eyebrows. "This may not be the time for schemes."

"Or it may be the *perfect* time for schemes." She smiled reassuringly at him, tempted to mention the vial, but she didn't want to with so many other ears nearby. Besides, he might not be as interested as she in a substance that could force the beast to change back into a man. In Sabor's hands, it had made him vulnerable. *Defenseless*, since he'd not only changed back but lost consciousness at the spymaster's feet. "I'll tell you more later," was all she said. "Be careful with Milnor, please. Getting in trouble is *my* job, not yours."

He snorted. "That's a career neither of us should pursue."

"And yet, I seem destined for it."

She said it jokingly, but his eyes grew grave, and he said, "Be careful today," before leaving Kaylina, Zhani, and Frayvar at the front gate to Stillguard Castle. For some reason, Jankarr gave them a long look over his shoulder before the group rounded a corner and disappeared from view.

"He's been acting oddly lately." Zhani must have caught the look.

"Jankarr? He thinks I'm weird." Kaylina let Frayvar get off first, then swung down from Levitke's back.

"You are weird." Frayvar sneezed three times, then glared

around, as if the quiet street were to blame. "Our whole family is weird," he added.

"That's a truth." Kaylina patted Levitke. "You can go back to ranger headquarters with the others if you want. Or I can bring out some breakfast for you. But you might not want to come into the courtyard. The plant is allowing Vlerion inside the castle these days, but it may still be suspicious of rangers and their mounts in general."

"I *did* wonder when you suggested this place for training." Zhani peered through the wrought-iron gate toward the tower, but the sunlight made it hard to see the plant's glow. "I am rather notably a ranger." She waved at her leather armor, black uniform, and sword.

"We can train by the waterfront out back." Kaylina lowered her voice. "I had another reason for wanting to speak alone with you."

"You mean you *didn't* want to spend hours blocking and parrying this morning? Imagine my surprise."

"I don't avoid our exercise that often, do I?"

"No, but you complain vociferously during it."

Kaylina hadn't realized she was being that obnoxious, but she *had* mentioned to Zhani frequently that she'd never wanted to become a ranger. "Sorry. I'll try to do that less. Frayvar, will you get that vial out of the kitchen and bring it out here, please?"

He'd opened the gate to go inside but paused. "Which vial?"

"How many are in the kitchen?"

"Well, I've been collecting oils, extracts, macerated herbs, vinegars, oh, and did you see the nutmeg alternative I prepared with clove? I'm excited to try it." Frayvar smiled, far too perky for someone who'd slept on the ground. Of course, he'd been snoring most of the night, not staying up, pining for Vlerion.

"The broken one I gave you and asked you to research."

"Oh, the apothecary I took it to scraped most of the residue out of that, but I'll see what's left."

"Did the apothecary learn anything about it?" Kaylina looked at Zhani, who was waiting patiently, her eyebrows lifted.

"He used some chemicals and tools on it to see if there were any reactions that might offer clues to what it was. He also wondered why there was dried fur on the vial. But he ultimately wasn't able to identify it. Some compound was all he said."

"Well, bring out what's left. Sergeant Zhani is a ranger, so I'll bet she likes dried fur."

A statement that prompted Zhani's eyebrows to lift further.

Kaylina waved away the silly comment. She was tired and punchy.

Levitke whuffed.

"Bring out some of the salted lamb and dried fish too, please," Kaylina added, reminded that she'd mentioned breakfast to Levitke.

"Oh, good idea," Frayvar said. "I'm starving. I have some capers that go great with the fish. Oh, and the new infused herb oil that I made will be delicious drizzled over it. Maybe some cheese too."

"It doesn't need to be that fancy for Levitke." Kaylina patted the taybarri's blue-furred shoulder.

"I wouldn't mind those things," Zhani said. "They sound delicious."

"I take it back, Frayvar. Fancy it up."

Levitke whuffed agreeably. Maybe taybarri also liked herb oils.

"I remembered that you know a lot about plants," Kaylina said when she and Zhani were alone, "and was hoping you could look at a vial and might have an idea about what the substance that was inside did. No, I *know* what it did. What I'm wondering is what it was and if more might be available in the city." She waved vaguely, not knowing where an apothecary shop was, and started unstrapping the honey packs from Levitke. "There's a little bit of a dried residue inside the vial. It was liquid, uhm, last week, I guess."

"You believe I can look at a week-old residue and know what it is?"

"Maybe?"

"The apothecary who presumably has a microscope and other tools for examining substances would be a better bet. I doubt it'll even smell like much after that long."

"Well, it doesn't sound like he or she figured it out. And you're... knowledgeable about more than ranger things."

Zhani's *hmm* was skeptical, but she held out her hand when Frayvar returned with the broken vial. There were scrape marks through the blue residue in the bottom, presumably from the apothecary taking samples.

"Here you go, Fray." Kaylina handed him one of the packs of honey she'd removed.

He grunted as he accepted it. "It's so lovely when people turn the creative genius of a chef responsible for more than half the business's income into an unpaid assistant."

"You're welcome to pay yourself. We're making money now, aren't we?"

"Not enough to fix my back if I throw it out toting your honey," he grumbled, shambling back into the courtyard.

"He's only seventeen, if you can believe it," Kaylina told Zhani. "He grouses more than Grandpa. I guess I'll have to find time to buy or make him a gift to show my appreciation though. He *has* contributed a lot to our success thus far. More than I've had time to contribute. I did agree that his name for the place could become the official name. You know, to honor him. Everyone is still calling it Stillguard Castle though."

Zhani, busy holding the vial up to the sunlight and sniffing the contents, didn't respond. Frayvar returned with a trencher of fish and meat for Levitke and two plates for Kaylina and Zhani.

"You're a wonderful brother," Kaylina told him.

"Yes, I most absolutely am." Frayvar waved toward the tables in the courtyard. "There's a guy out back drinking mead by the kitchen. He wants to see you. He's been here before."

"Okay." Kaylina smiled, touched that they already had regulars who came repeatedly.

"You said you know what it does?" Zhani asked, not seeming to notice the plates or that Frayvar had come out at all. Levitke noshed happily at the trencher he'd delivered. "That would help me a lot more than looking at this residue. I'm aware of many plants and how they affect the human body. I assume this was used on a person?"

"Ah, sort of."

"Sort of?" Zhani eyed the broken top of the vial. "It wasn't thrown at a taybarri, was it? Or some other animal?"

"No… I did see one used on Crenoch that seemed like an acid. It made his eyes and nostrils water, and he backed out of a fight, so it must have hurt a lot." Kaylina frowned at the vial. She should have realized Zhani might need to know the context of how it had been used. She hadn't told Frayvar that, so the apothecary couldn't have known, but that might be why she hadn't yet gotten the answer she needed.

She slumped against the courtyard wall. So many people had unearthed Vlerion's secret, but *she* hadn't told anyone, and she couldn't. She'd promised him that she wouldn't.

"That sounds like a dreadful substance," Zhani said. "One rangers wouldn't want their enemies to discover."

"Yeah." Kaylina waved at Levitke, who was daintily enjoying her food. When more than one taybarri was around, they ate like ravenous bears, but she savored hers when no other snouts were present to veer in and steal morsels.

"This wasn't an acid." Zhani held up the broken vial, sounding certain.

Kaylina spread her arms, not knowing. She remembered how Vlerion's wound-covered naked body had looked that night—he'd been burned, stabbed, and attacked with acid—but she didn't know how much he'd endured at the hands of the pirates and assassins and what Sabor had done before she'd shown up. The spymaster had been standing over unconscious Vlerion with a dagger, not vials dripping substances, but there *had* been shattered glass in the alley.

"What did it do?" Zhani prompted again. "Without knowing that, I'm at a loss."

Kaylina sighed. "It caused someone to lose consciousness, but that may have only been due to blood loss after a battle." Due to the beast magic wearing off, she thought but didn't say. "That's happened to him before. What I'm sure this did was temporarily remove the magic of a curse." She bit her lip, afraid saying even that was too much.

Zhani leaned over to look through the gate and up to the tower. "Something on the plant? Oh, or is this about those sage assassins that were after Lord Vlerion? There's an altered plant back home that they consume that enhances their natural attributes—strength and agility and the like."

"I..." Kaylina started to say no, but what if Sabor had been carrying the vial around because it could nullify the sage assassins' superhuman abilities? He'd been dealing with them, after all. He might have worried they would turn on him. Now that she considered things, it would have been surprising if he'd had a substance along to nullify the beast. Until that week, Sabor had never *seen* the beast. Oh, he would have researched the curse, but, as Vlerion had said, his own ancestors had studied it assiduously over the generations. If an antidote to the beast change, which this essentially was, had been discovered and written about, the Havartafts would have known about it. "Yes."

"That was a long pause."

"I'm a big thinker."

"Uh-huh."

"Are you aware of substances that can nullify the assassins' magical advantages?" Kaylina asked.

"I am. The one that comes to mind is usually sneaked into a drink to be consumed though." Zhani tapped the broken lip of the vial. "You said this was thrown?"

"Yes."

"I have a book in my quarters on altered plants from the high desert. Mind if I take this with me? I can read up and see if I find anything."

"Of course. Thank you for looking. Here." Kaylina handed one of the plates to Zhani, wanting to thank her and hoping she enjoyed the food. "You can take this with you."

"You want me to go now?" Zhani's tone turned dry. "Targon told us to train."

"Maybe if you give him a piece of herb-oil-drizzled fish, he'll forget about that."

"I don't usually bring him food." Zhani cradled the plate protectively to her chest, as if to say she wouldn't have shared this even if she brought the captain's every meal. It *did* smell good, and Kaylina looked forward to breakfast herself.

"I'll come to headquarters for training once I make sure everything is okay here. Will that work?"

"For me, yes."

"Targon's probably going to be too busy with other problems to worry about how my swordsmanship is progressing today." Kaylina waved toward the royal castle perched on its plateau overlooking the harbor and the city.

"True."

"Hello?" came a man's voice from the courtyard. A familiar sandy-haired fellow held up an empty goblet as he walked toward the gate. "Ms. Korbian, would you sell me a refill, please?" He offered an affable smile.

Kaylina recognized him. It was the Virt who'd come by before the grand opening to tell her Jana Bloomlong was plotting against her—again—and to say he hoped Kaylina would consider helping the rebellion.

Zhani peeked through the gate, and the man—Grittor was the fake name he'd given Kaylina—flinched when their eyes met. Since Zhani wore her uniform, there was no doubt about her occupation, and the Virts had to have learned by now not to be caught by the rangers. When Kaylina had described Grittor to Vlerion, he hadn't recognized him as one of the known leaders, but that didn't mean Zhani hadn't seen the man before.

"Who's this?" Zhani didn't sound suspicious—more like she was wondering if she needed to help Kaylina with a threat.

"He's..." Kaylina could have said he was a Virt, and maybe Zhani would have searched him or questioned him, but she hesitated. The message Grittor had delivered last time—that Bloomlong was trying to hire poor people to make a scene at Kaylina's opening night—hadn't come to fruition. He'd said he'd been discouraging his people from accepting the job. She had only his word as to whether that had been true, but after he'd paid for her mead and said nice things about it, she was disinclined to rat him out. Besides, she'd already told Vlerion about him. "A customer," she finished after a long pause.

Zhani regarded her. "More big thinking?"

"*Tremendous* thinking." Kaylina smiled at her. "If you could research that substance, I'd be infinitely pleased with you."

"So pleased you would stop grousing during our training sessions?"

Kaylina had already vowed to herself to do that so she didn't have to feign an enthusiastic, "*Yes.*" She added, "I'll even be delighted when you compare jab-punch-kick combinations to trees and bushes."

"Really?" Zhani's tone turned dry. "You would be the first."

"I'm stunned that the young men you recruit aren't delighted when you tell them about the oak-hickory-maple."

"Yes, me too."

Zhani eyed Grittor for a moment but glanced at Levitke and must have decided Kaylina had a suitable protector. She saluted before walking away, taking the plate of food and vial with her.

Grittor nodded gravely at Kaylina, maybe realizing she could have sicced Sergeant Zhani on him. "Sorry to interrupt, but I don't have a lot of time. I've been waiting here since dawn for a refill."

"We don't open at dawn." Kaylina stepped through the gate and into the courtyard. The sentinel wasn't trailing vines out its windows and down to attack, so it probably didn't believe Grittor a threat.

"I'd hoped my charm might get me invited in before hours, but you weren't home."

"No. I was collecting more honey for my mead."

"Ah. Of course. I'll be happy to pay for a drink." Grittor dug out a crinkled five-liviti bill. "But I admit I came to ask you about things of more import." He looked significantly in the direction of the royal castle.

Kaylina's stomach sank as she realized this might be about the king's death, something that, she had a feeling, was going to affect her and Vlerion, whether they wished it or not.

7

Pull one weed in the garden, and ten more sprout forth.
~ Grandma Korbian

Kaylina took Grittor's money, retrieved his requested strawberry mead, and joined him at a table in the courtyard behind the kitchen. The afternoon sun warmed the spot pleasantly. Clanks floated out a nearby window, Frayvar unpacking the honey and organizing the pantry, but Kaylina and Grittor were ostensibly alone. Though the sentinel hadn't grown any vines to menace Levitke, she remained outside the courtyard walls, heading toward the river for a drink, the last Kaylina had seen.

"How else can I help you?" Kaylina waved to indicate the freshly poured goblet, but she immediately regretted opening herself up for requests. Last time, Grittor had tried to recruit her to help all the Virts, and she didn't want to get involved with them.

"I was wondering if you could satisfy my curiosity."

"That'll cost you more than five liviti," she said, certain this would come around to him wanting her to use her druidic power on the behalf of the Virts.

"Ten?" Grittor smiled, pulled out another bill, and waved it in the air.

Kaylina snorted and pointed for him to put it away. "I don't know if I can answer whatever questions you have, but go ahead and ask."

"Okay." He looked toward the back gate—there wasn't anyone in sight—and also toward the open kitchen window. Then, in a low voice, he said, "Spymaster Sabor is dead."

"I've heard that." Kaylina raised her eyebrows to suggest it was old news—old news she didn't want to talk about. She'd expected him to bring up the *king's* death.

"There are some rumors that, when he was killed, he had sword wounds but also claw marks on his body."

"Huh." Kaylina laced her fingers together on the table, trying not to give anything away.

She was tempted to ask if he'd spoken to Jana Bloomlong, but if he had, and she had shared everything she'd seen from her window overlooking the alley, Grittor would know exactly how Sabor had ended up with claw and sword wounds.

"A lot of people have died with claw marks on them this summer," he continued. "People in the city, where such things are rare."

"It's been an eventful summer."

A soft clink floated out the window, followed by, "Oh, I forgot we had fresh oregano." Frayvar was close enough to listen to the conversation but possibly too distracted to do so.

"Yeah. We know." Grittor waved at his chest and also vaguely toward the city. To indicate the Virts in general? "We know there's a beast in the area that attacks humans, but we also know the Kar'ruk were behind some of those earlier deaths, making it *look* like a beast had done it." He curled his fingers in the air to mimic claws raking at someone. "Maybe they were behind *all* the deaths, at least during that time period."

"That's right."

Kaylina didn't mention the role she'd played in unearthing the Kar'ruk scheme. The last time Grittor had come, he'd implied he'd known she had found the press being used for the rogue newspaper the Virts had been publishing—and that she'd led the rangers to it. Targon had ordered it shoved off a cliff in the mountains so it couldn't be used again.

Grittor opened his mouth for his next question, but the back gate rattled. Levitke's snout appeared, bumping the bars. The taybarri looked at Kaylina, then toward the front of the castle, then back.

"Trouble?" Kaylina guessed.

Levitke swished her tail in agitation.

"More trouble than that Frayvar didn't bring you seconds?" Kaylina willed her magic to let her understand the taybarri. It had worked a few times before.

The brand on the back of her hand warmed slightly.

Levitke's voice sounded in her mind: *Human law. Rulers.*

Kaylina looked toward the front of the castle again. Was that the clatter of horse hooves on cobblestones? The city was so quiet today that she had no trouble hearing noise through the courtyard walls.

Grittor was watching her. She didn't think she'd done anything that would indicate she was drawing on her druidic power, but he glanced at her hand, as if he somehow knew. The brand wasn't glowing, as it had done before, but maybe she scrunched up her face oddly when using magic.

"She *is* troubled that she only received one meal," Kaylina said lightly.

"She's a big animal. I imagine she needs lots of food."

Despite her agitation about whoever was coming, Levitke whuffed in blatant agreement.

"Someone representing law enforcement is coming," Kaylina said, the hoofbeats drawing closer and halting. It sounded like the horses were outside the front gate. "You might want to go."

"I haven't finished my mead." Grittor held up the goblet.

She wagered what he really meant was that he hadn't finished asking her questions. She wouldn't mind if he never did that but waved to the kitchen door. "Wait inside, then." A clang sounded, someone throwing open the front gate. "And tell my brother to have his heavy frying pan ready."

That prompted Grittor to wrinkle his brow, but he did go into the kitchen.

Kaylina was tempted to hide inside as well. Instead, she walked through the courtyard and rounded a front tower as a man lifted a fist to knock on the door.

Two armed guards in gray uniforms with blue trim stood there, handcuffs dangling from their belts along with swords and pistols. Had they come to arrest her?

Behind them, a middle-aged man stood dressed in rich blues and blacks, including a beaver-fur hat. Two pistols hung from holsters on his belt, along with a dagger long enough to excavate an elephant's trunk. He had a neatly trimmed salt-and-pepper mustache and beard.

Two more guards waited behind him, and stallions stamped and pawed at the cobblestones out front. A few of them looked nervously at the castle—or maybe the tower.

Kaylina stopped underneath its window in case the sentinel had the urge to toss vines out to protect her. She didn't know who her visitor was but trusted Levitke's assessment that he represented trouble. He didn't look like a mead aficionado.

"Ms. Kaylina Korbian," the man said in a deadpan voice as he looked coolly at her.

Vlerion had a similarly emotionless voice when he was working on keeping his calm. She doubted this was a relative who was cursed to turn into a beast and had to do the same.

"That's right," she said. "Do you want to see a tasting menu?"

"My lord," he stated.

Ah, another one of those.

"Oh, are you? Sorry. You're not wearing your I'm-an-aristocrat name tag. Do you want to see a tasting menu, my lord? For you and your friends?" Kaylina waved at the guards. "I give half off to the stalwart men and women who work to protect the city and the crown."

A new policy she'd made up on the spot, but one she would be happy to implement if it kept her from being arrested.

The guards at the door looked wistfully at each other.

"I'd heard from Captain Targon that you are an irreverent commoner," the man in the hat said.

"Yup, the word gets around. Who might you be?" She pointed at his chest.

"I am Lord Darlintor Milnor, the new spymaster for the crown. I've recently replaced the heinously murdered Spymaster Sabor and am seeking details about the events revolving around his dreadful demise."

Kaylina badly wanted to object to the notion that Sabor had been murdered, heinously or otherwise. At the worst, they'd been trying to kill each other in a fair fight. But since Vlerion had taken the blame, she couldn't say any of that.

"That sounds like an important job that can stir up a thirst. I'd be happy to extend the half-off discount to you as well. Can I get you a dry mead? You look like the type to eschew sweetness of any kind in your drink."

And your life, she added silently.

"I have a few questions for you, Ms. Korbian. As part of my inquiry." Milnor's gaze lifted to the tower.

With the sun out, the glow remained unnoticeable, but she had no doubt he knew the sentinel resided up there and had heard about its powers.

Kaylina resisted the urge to play dumb. This guy probably was as well informed on everything as Sabor had been. "Okay," she said and shrugged, as if answering a few questions wouldn't be a big deal.

Never mind that her heart thumped noticeably in her ears. Why was it so quiet today? Ah, yes. The king's death.

"I'm attempting to learn precisely how my predecessor died," Milnor said. "Tell me what happened the last time you saw him."

"Do you want to know how he died or the events of that whole night, such as how the assassins he hired to kill Lord Vlerion were after me and his mother? They kidnapped us and locked us in a pirate ship to use as bait in a trap." Kaylina watched his face, trying to guess how much he knew about what Sabor had done. Had he been in the dark as to Sabor's plans to raise a beast army to help him rule the kingdom? Or had Milnor been in on it?

His face gave away nothing as he gazed steadily at her. "Tell me how he died."

"He was trying to kill me because I didn't call him *my lord* often enough, and Vlerion killed him."

All right, that wasn't the *exact* version of the story she and Vlerion had agreed to give if they were questioned, but it was close.

"His corpse was maligned by both claw and sword marks."

It seemed *everyone* knew about that.

"Yup," Kaylina said. "That's what you get when you pick a fight with Vlerion."

The guards behind the spymaster frowned, looking at each other in confusion. The other two were peering through one of the front windows, either because someone had wandered up to the vestibule or they were daydreaming about half-price mead.

Milnor squinted at her, but, unlike the guards, he didn't appear confused. "There was also what I believe to be cat fur on the legs of his trousers." His eyes narrowed further. With suspicion? Or was that *certainty* that she had been involved? Or... responsible?

Kaylina groped for a response. She hadn't expected anyone to figure out that a stray cat had assisted her. Bloomlong must have had her nose pressed to the window to spot every detail of that battle.

"That's weird," she said. "I wouldn't think Sabor was the type to attract cats."

"I believe the feline was under the influence of someone with the power to command animals," Milnor said.

"Really? Sounds kind of farfetched. What would a cat do in a sword fight?"

Milnor held up a finger toward the guards, then walked toward Kaylina. She tensed, wondering if she should have run inside to grab her sword, but what would she do with it? Get in a fight with *another* spymaster? *Kill* him?

As Milnor approached, Kaylina retreated several steps, putting her back to the stone wall of the tower. She didn't look up at the window, but she was tempted to silently call to the sentinel for help. But that might condemn her, prove that she had the power to command plants and animals. Right now, Milnor might not know for certain what she could do—what she *had* done. If he did, why would he have bothered coming to ask her questions?

He didn't step close enough to touch her, but he stood close, his back to his men. Surprisingly, they were the same height. He might have been more intimidating if he'd loomed a foot over her, but Sabor hadn't been that big of a man either, and he'd been a capable fighter. If not for his injuries and that cat's help, Kaylina never would have bested him.

"Will you be more open with me if there aren't others to overhear? Or do you wish me to take you inside for questioning under the influence of kafdari root?" Milnor delved into a pocket and pulled out a foil-wrapped ball, holding it up between two fingers.

Kaylina stifled a groan. She hated that stuff. Even if she hadn't objected to speaking the truth to him, she wouldn't have wanted to bare her emotions. She would doubtless end up babbling about her feelings for Vlerion, how unfair the curse was, and how hot she was for him. Her face flushed at the prospect of such mortification.

"What do you want to know that you don't already know?" Kaylina shrugged to feign casualness she didn't feel. "He was the beast during their fight. I'm sure you know all about his curse. It was probably *his* hair that you found on Sabor's clothes."

"The beast was protecting you?"

"The beast always protects me."

"With claws. He doesn't wield a sword in that form."

Was that a question? Milnor didn't sound certain, so she assumed he hadn't seen the beast in action.

"I'm not sure. His paws are hand-like."

"You were there, and you're not sure?"

"I'm not sure of the beast's exact capabilities."

Milnor fingered the foil-wrapped ball of kafdari root. "The killing blow was made by a sword. I believe you did it, either to help the beast or simply because you wanted Sabor dead."

I did it to help *Vlerion*, she wanted to cry. "A lot of people probably wanted him dead, but I'm no murderer. I've barely started learning to fight with a sword and only because Captain Targon forcibly recruited me to become a ranger. I'm a mead-maker, not a warrior."

He looked her up and down, not checking her out as a woman, Kaylina sensed, but assessing her *warriorness*. "I believe the kafdari root will be necessary. You continue to lie to me." His eyes narrowed. "Just as Lord Vlerion did."

Uh-oh. Had he spoken to Vlerion at headquarters already?

Kaylina shifted uneasily. What had Milnor learned? What if Vlerion was now in a dungeon?

"Did you question him with the kafdari root?" She doubted the spymaster had. Otherwise, there would be little point in him questioning her.

Milnor pressed his lips together. "As Captain Targon was quick to remind me, those of noble blood may not be questioned using torture or under the influence of drugs. They can be arrested for crimes but not put to death unless it occurs as a result of a mutually agreed upon duel."

"Vlerion would be happy to duel with you." Kaylina smiled.

Milnor did not. "I believe *you* would be happy to duel with me as well."

"Nope, not interested. Thanks. How about you take a couple of bottles of mead and go? I'll give you one entirely for free." The offer galled her, and she hoped he didn't take her up on it.

"We will stay until my questions are answered." Milnor started to reach for her, but a couple more horses trotted up to the gate, and he paused.

A high-ranking Castle guard peered inside. "Lord Milnor? The queen wishes you to attend her."

Irritation sparked in Milnor's eyes.

"She said it's about the prince—the succession," the guard added.

"Tell her I'll see her shortly." Milnor jerked his head toward the keep. "Come, let's sit you down and feed you some truth root."

Kaylina was on the verge of calling up to the sentinel for help when the ground in the courtyard trembled.

Surprised, she planted her hand against the wall for support. The guards also looked around in surprise, spreading their arms to steady themselves. Milnor squinted at her as the horses outside snorted and stamped in concern.

One took off, hooves thundering down the road, and a guard

shouted after it. Distant cries of alarm promised other people in the city were experiencing the same troubles.

The ground continued to tremble, and glass shattered somewhere in the castle. Remembering the chandeliers that had broken when she and Frayvar first moved in—the sentinel letting them know it wasn't pleased—Kaylina looked up at the tower. Nothing had changed up there, as far as she could tell, and her brand wasn't warm or tingling.

Levitke roared from behind the castle.

"I need to check on her," Kaylina blurted and bolted around the corner before Milnor could stop her.

The ground kept trembling as she ran through the back gate and found the taybarri under a tree, her brown eyes huge as she looked around. She snapped at the air, as if an invisible enemy might be responsible for the trouble.

"It's okay," Kaylina called, patting the air with her hands. "It's only a... an earthquake."

Was that right? Such events didn't occur in the Vamorka Islands, an area known for hurricanes rather than shaking earth, so she'd never experienced one.

The ground soon stilled, so maybe she'd guessed right. Maybe the earthquake had been natural, and the plant hadn't been responsible.

That didn't keep her from projecting her thoughts toward the tower: *You* weren't *responsible, right?*

The sentinel didn't answer, but that wasn't surprising. It rarely spoke telepathically to her, instead favoring visions and sometimes a sharing of emotions. Such as indignation. She didn't get anything now. Since the sentinel had never caused an earthquake before, at least not in the time she'd lived in Stillguard Castle, she doubted it had done anything to spark it.

Kaylina stepped up to Levitke's side and patted her on the shoulder. "It's all right."

The taybarri issued a concerned cluck, then sniffed Kaylina's pocket.

"You need a honey drop to help you recover from the ordeal?"

Levitke whuffed again and gazed deeply into her eyes.

Obviously, Kaylina translated.

Milnor and two guards rode around the outside of the castle, stopping their horses when they spotted her.

"I may need a honey drop too," Kaylina muttered, fearing nothing had changed, that they would question her.

The spymaster seemed surprised to find her outside the back gate. What, had he thought she would run off into the wilds at the first opportunity? She sighed wistfully. No, she'd endured being a fugitive before and didn't want to go through that again.

"I need to see what the queen wants." Milnor waved at the guard who'd shown up before the earthquake. "I'll return later to finish your inquiry." His look of significance promised he would shove the kafdari root down her throat at the beginning of their next chat.

"Can't wait," Kaylina muttered.

Milnor squinted at her.

She added a, "My lord," that might have come out more sarcastic than sincere.

As he rode off, looking coolly back over his shoulder at her, she knew she wouldn't escape a second encounter with him unscathed.

8

A FAVOR DONE TODAY MAY BE RETURNED TENFOLD IN THE FUTURE.
~ Winter Moon Priest Dazibaru

"I wonder if Sergeant Zhani knows of any plants or concoctions to dodge the effects of kafdari root," Kaylina said when Spymaster Milnor and the guards were gone.

Levitke, her only audience, nosed her pocket again.

"I'm out of honey drops, but I'll go inside and get some. Afterward, will you take me to ranger headquarters? I'm worried about Vlerion and need to check on him."

Levitke whuffed, apparently over her trauma from the earthquake.

Kaylina patted the taybarri and headed for the gate.

Grittor stood in the courtyard, a few steps from the open kitchen door. Kaylina paused. She'd forgotten he was in the castle and wondered if he'd listened in on the conversation.

A few clunks, clanks, and a grunt wafted out from the kitchen. Either the earthquake had wreaked havoc on the pantry organization project, or Frayvar had been so into it that he hadn't *noticed* the earthquake. Either was possible.

"The new spymaster sounds like a lovely fellow," Grittor said.

"Oh, yeah. I adored him instantly."

"After listening to you two chat—sorry, but I couldn't help but overhear..."

"Uh-huh." As a practiced eavesdropper herself, Kaylina didn't know if she could blame him for listening. Not without being hypocritical.

"Well, it was what *wasn't* said, wasn't it?" Grittor asked.

Kaylina folded her arms over her chest. What did he want?

"We'd already figured some of that out. That's partially why I came." Grittor lowered his voice. "We knew Spymaster Sabor was behind a lot of our troubles. We've been fighting, like I told you, to get better working conditions, and we've done a little sabotage here and there to try to make our points, but until this spring, we hadn't tried... Well, nobody was talking about assassinations or killing people as a solution to our problems. We always worried about what the ramifications would be to our loved ones. And the hangings—those weren't the first hangings. But a while back, Sabor started talking with Cougar and a couple of the other leaders. I'm not important enough to know all that was going on, but... I do wonder. I think Sabor was as much to blame as some of our people. Like he might have been egging our leaders on, you know? Trying to get the Virts to escalate the situation so he could take advantage of the chaos or use it as an excuse to assert his authority."

Kaylina shrugged. She sympathized with the Virts, especially if Sabor had been messing with them too, but she wanted to check on Vlerion, not speculate on what the spymaster's motivations had been.

"Some say he even was behind the murdering of the nobles," Grittor continued. "The tax collectors and finance lords who were killed this spring. *We* got blamed for that. But I never thought those murders made any sense, even for Cougar."

"Sabor proved himself manipulative and ruthless," Kaylina said.

"Yes. I think... Well, what I came to ask is if we owe you a favor." Grittor gazed frankly at her. "For getting rid of him."

"You don't owe me anything. Except liviti bills when you come for mead." She smiled, hoping he would accept the answer and drop it. All these people wanting to know if she'd been behind Sabor's death were making her nervous.

Grittor hesitated. "Do we owe *Lord Vlerion* a favor?"

Was that his way of asking if Vlerion had killed Sabor? And implying he knew all about the beast? The *real* story about the beast, not the stuff the Virts had been printing?

Kaylina remembered the journal she'd found by the press, the article that had been about to be published. It had detailed specifics about Vlerion being the beast. By finding and destroying the press, she and the rangers had kept it from being printed, but they'd never learned which of the Virts had been penning the original articles.

Since Vlerion might already be in a position where he needed assistance, she hesitated to dismiss the idea of the Virts owing him a favor. They might not have the power to do anything to help, but they were a big organization with a lot of ears. Who knew how much influence they truly had?

"I wasn't going to bring up Jana Bloomlong again," Grittor said when she didn't answer. "I already told you she was trying to get some of our people to sabotage your grand opening, and I dissuaded them from accepting the dubious work."

Kaylina nodded.

"It seemed like the right thing to do, and I wasn't looking for a reward for it. But now..." Grittor cocked his head as he considered her. "Now I wonder if the moon gods have let us know that was the correct choice because of the choice *you* made. You and him? If you and Lord Vlerion were responsible for Sabor's death, we *do* owe you."

"Look, I'm not unsympathetic to your cause, and I don't think Vlerion ever has been either, but we didn't..."

Should Kaylina lie? When Grittor already seemed to know?

His eyebrows rose.

"I'll just say..." She chose her words carefully. "Vlerion has no regrets about Sabor's death."

That was the truth, at least.

Grittor grunted softly. "Is that your way of saying he's on our side?"

"I wouldn't go so far as to claim that, but, given the choice, he wouldn't *oppose* you and what you're trying to achieve. As long as laws weren't being broken, laws he's sworn to uphold as a ranger, he probably wouldn't object to you protesting the working conditions." Kaylina shrugged, not wanting to commit Vlerion to anything. Besides, the Virts, whether influenced by Sabor or not, had been breaking laws left and right. For all she knew, they were behind the king dying of *natural causes*.

"I think I see what you're saying." Grittor nodded.

Kaylina hoped he hadn't taken more from her words than she'd intended.

"Did you or your people have anything to do with the king's death?" Kaylina realized Targon might appreciate it if she could get that information. She especially wanted it if Milnor was setting Vlerion up to appear responsible.

"Not that I'm aware of." Grittor's words and shrug seemed genuine. "The king was old. It might have been his time."

"Yeah."

"If the prince dies of natural causes too, then it might be suspicious."

"I would assume so, yes." Kaylina pointed to the kitchen. "I need to help my brother clean up." That wasn't exactly what she meant to do, but she hoped Grittor would take the hint and leave.

"I understand." He nodded toward her. "Thanks for the drink and... perhaps more. If we *can* help you with anything, let me know."

She lifted a hand, though she didn't intend to ask the Virts for assistance.

After Grittor walked away, Kaylina jogged inside, intending to grab her sword and some honey drops, then head to ranger headquarters.

But a pulse of energy flowed over her. Originating from the sentinel, she had no doubt.

Frayvar stuck his head out of the pantry. "Did you feel something?"

"I think the plant wants to have a chat," she said before wondering if he'd been asking about the earthquake. He often didn't sense magic the way she did.

He grimaced. "Just with you, right?"

"Probably. You know your job is to haul me away from the magic if it knocks me out."

"You think that's going to happen *again*?"

"I hope not."

It *had* become a distressingly regular occurrence.

"Levitke is outside if you need to send her for the doctor and his smelling salts," Kaylina added.

"I asked her to do that before, and she got Vlerion instead."

"Vlerion doesn't have smelling salts. He would have to wake me with a kiss."

"Ew." Frayvar's comment came out as one of their staff, Sevarli, walked into the kitchen.

"Hi." She waved brightly at Kaylina and Frayvar. At sixteen, she seemed delighted with the job, the tips, and everything about life in general. "Did you feel the earthquake? It was *epic*."

"Earthquake?" Frayvar scratched his head, then picked up a box that had fallen to the flagstone floor. "I thought I bumped the shelves."

Maybe Kaylina had been right not to assume that he'd noticed it.

"Oh, Frayvar. A messenger from the royal castle came last night. He delivered a letter for you. For both of you, I think." Sevarli hurried to a drawer in the kitchen and pulled out a fancy envelope with three wax stamps sealing it closed.

"The royal castle?" Kaylina couldn't help but pause.

"A letter for *me*?" Frayvar pounced on it. "Maybe the royal chef heard about my exquisite lamb dish—Professora Vesimoor promised she would write it up even though she came to critique the mead. Oh, maybe the chef wants my recipe." Even more excitement infused his voice, and he hopped a couple of times as he added, "Or to invite me to the castle to prepare it."

"I'm sure that's it," Kaylina said. "Their own culinary staff is surely incapable of serving an adequate meal for the king's funeral."

Frayvar nodded eagerly, missing her sarcasm.

With their luck, the letter was more likely to contain a threat from a chef who resented that he'd made a similar dish and now had it out for Frayvar. Jana Bloomlong's face floated through Kaylina's mind.

"The message came before the king's passing, I believe." Sevarli tapped her forehead as she ducked her chin in a gesture to pay respect to the dead—and request they not haunt the living.

Frayvar tore open the letter so vigorously that the wax seals flew off, bouncing off the stone of the hearth. One almost hit Kaylina.

"You have more strength than people give you credit for," she murmured.

"He's very determined and passionate about his craft." Sevarli smiled at Frayvar.

He was too busy reading to notice. That seemed typical for most of their interactions. If Kaylina found time, she would attempt to play matchmaker, since Sevarli clearly adored him. Too bad Frayvar's *ew* at talk of kissing suggested he might not yet be mature enough to have a girlfriend. Create award-winning dishes that took days to prepare, yes. Talk to women, no.

"Oh, huh." Frayvar's shoulders slumped as he deflated.

"Not a request for you to serve the royals lamb?" Kaylina guessed.

"No. It's good news for the business though." He forced a smile and nodded to her. "It's the mead they're interested in. The head of the kitchen staff in the royal castle heard all about it and has invited us to the castle. Well, me, specifically. Maybe you're not mentioned because of that poisoning kerfuffle—"

"The poisoning kerfuffle I had nothing to do with," Kaylina said.

Ignoring that, Frayvar held up the paper and continued. "I'm invited to bring our five most exquisite meads to the castle as soon as I can prepare them for a tasting. If they live up to expectations, and the wine steward deems them a good match for the menus there, he may be interested in putting in an ongoing order. Oh, that's good news. What a victory for the business, Kay."

"That would be amazing." Kaylina bit her lip to keep from saying it would be a victory over the awful Jana Bloomlong too. As she well remembered, Bloomlong was the current mead supplier to the royal castle. Current or *former*? "If the queen allows it."

She frowned. It was possible the wine steward was in charge of ordering beverages and was making this decision on his own. If the queen found out, would she quash the notion of Kaylina or her business selling mead to the castle? Was it too much to hope that the prince would, after he took the reins of the kingdom, send his mother off to some distant part of Zaldor where she couldn't meddle?

"Our mead is so good that she'll *have* to allow it." Though usually oblivious to other people's feelings, Frayvar might have noticed Kaylina's chagrined expression. "Her tastebuds won't permit otherwise."

"You have to admire his optimism," Sevarli said.

"I'm the pessimistic one in the family," Kaylina said.

"She is that. Considering I'm the rational, thoughtful, and pragmatic one—and she's the schemer—you might find that surprising, but her funks mess with her mental facilities." Frayvar looked at Sevarli while tapping his temple and shaking his head at the woeful state of Kaylina's mind.

"I do appreciate you discussing my mental health with the staff," Kaylina said.

"They need to be warned about it in case they come in one day and find you curled up with a book and a blanket and moaning to yourself."

Sevarli giggled.

The girl even appreciated his wit? Frayvar definitely needed to notice he had an admirer and give her a kiss. Or at least agree to collaborate on a secret sauce with her.

A second pulse of energy flowed into the kitchen, an edge of insistence to it, and Kaylina winced. She shouldn't have allowed herself to be distracted.

Sevarli lost her smile, gripped the counter, and peered around in confusion. Frayvar also glanced around before looking to Kaylina. They were sensing something too.

"I'll check on it." Kaylina pointed in the direction of the tower.

They might not sense as much as she when it came to magic, but those pulses were strong enough that they'd felt something. She jogged up the stairs, hurrying to the tower. She still wanted to get to ranger headquarters to check on Vlerion, but it would be good to ask the sentinel if it knew anything about the sphere she'd touched in the druid ruins. And hear whatever information it had to share.

The chair she used to climb through the hole in the floor to its perch remained where she'd left it, a crate on top of the cushion. She supposed she could rebuild the stairs one day, but it wasn't as if she had much time between ranger training, making mead, and dodging interrogations from spymasters.

Before she poked her head through the floor, a vine flopped down, twitching toward her.

"Just when I think you're getting less creepy," Kaylina said to the great pot that held the magical tangle of vines and branches that called itself the sentinel. "Though I wouldn't have minded if you'd dropped that out the window to strangle the new spymaster."

No, that wasn't true, and she shouldn't encourage the plant. As she'd been thinking earlier, she would be in even *more* trouble if her actions resulted in the death of a second spymaster.

"Do you think it would be pointless to hope that Prince Enrikon, or whoever ends up in charge, will be a good and strong leader who doesn't let his spymasters run amok?"

The plant pulsed energy, an impatient vibe attached this time, and lifted the vine toward her forehead. She grimaced, knowing it wanted to communicate with visions that it would share once it touched her, but there was a chance she hadn't been joking with her brother and that the experience would leave her unconscious.

"Okay, but I need to go soon, so don't knock me out, please."

Kaylina swung up through the hole and knelt on the floorboards, noticing the lack of dead leaves on them. A week earlier, when she'd been up delivering the honey-water fertilizer that the sentinel enjoyed, she'd swept and dusted the room. No new leaves had fallen, and the plant continued to glow purple instead of the ominous red that it had before she'd started feeding it. As she'd feared more than once, she might be making it more powerful by trying to keep it healthy and happy, but it pleased her to know something she was fertilizing was doing better.

The cool tendril that had been poised shifted in, a few leaves rustling, and touched her temple. She braced herself for the visions.

Her own memories were what the touch dredged up. The previous day's exploration in the ruins and finding and touching the sphere. The sentinel slowed the replay of her memories at that point and seemed to study the pedestal that held that item—the *artifact*, as the mountain men had called it.

Ah. The word floated faintly through her mind.

Let me guess, she thought, trusting it would understand her silent words. *You felt the call that I accidentally made.*

Yes.

Not expanding, the sentinel continued to root through her memories, including her being knocked out—always something delightful to linger on—and waking up with Vlerion at her side.

He's still faithfully protecting me, Kaylina said, though the plant hadn't asked.

She wanted to make sure it didn't misunderstand anything and revoke its invitation to Vlerion. Well, not exactly an invitation, but the sentinel had said he could visit her in the castle, in his human form, and it wouldn't attack him. They hadn't tested that yet, but she hoped they could soon.

You've the ability to command him with your power.

That's not why he's protecting me, she protested.

He is drawn to you. The plant showed her another memory, one it had shared before of spying on her and Vlerion kissing and embracing in the courtyard.

Her cheeks flamed. He'd helped save her from kidnappers right before then, so it had been natural to kiss him. Ardently.

Yeah, yeah, she said. *His beast is drawn to my* anrokk *and vice versa. We know all about it.*

In his human form, he is not a danger to you.

She reined in further snark since the plant was agreeing with her. *Do you know what that sphere thing is? Is that what you called me up to ask about?*

Not that it had asked anything. It was presumptuously sifting through her mind *without* asking.

I sought clarification.

And you're all clarified now? Like a fine butter?

Other sentinels have been roused, the plant said, ignoring her snark.

What does that mean?

You are coming into your powers. The world has been waiting.

Uhm, what?

Change comes.

Look, I just want to meet my father and talk to him. And find a way to lift Vlerion's curse. That's what I was seeking in the ruins, not to change anything. Or rouse *anything.*

Craters of the moon, did the world need *more* plant sentinels? She had her hands full dealing with one, one that had killed countless humans in the centuries since it'd been left to watch over the castle. No, it had been left to watch over the whole city. She remembered it showing her the vine that it could grow up through the tower roof to spy on Port Jirador and the countryside. Keeping an eye on the pesky humans who'd once dared hunt in the protected druid preserve.

Maybe you can tell the other sentinels that they can go back to sleep, she added when the plant didn't respond.

Change comes, it repeated, drawing its vine back from Kaylina's temple. It had gotten what it wanted.

"Great," she muttered.

9

Many doors may be opened by a kind word and a bottle of alcohol.

~ Sandsteader proverb

Fortunately, the plant didn't knock Kaylina unconscious after their conversation, so she was awake when a woman called her name from the stairs. At first, she thought it was Sevarli, but that sounded more like...

"Sergeant Zhani?"

"Yes, where are you? There's a—" Zhani swore as something clanged on stone. Her sword against the wall?

Kaylina also swore and swung down from the plant's room, almost knocking over the chair as she landed. Why had Zhani come into the castle?

"Are you okay?" Kaylina called as she ran down the narrow hall and swung into the wider one that led to the first floor.

"Yes, just questioning my life choices," came a call from the stairs. It sounded like Zhani was backing down them. Quickly. "Especially the one made thirty seconds ago."

"Go outside." Kaylina spotted a vine waving menacingly from the stair railing. She hadn't known the sentinel could grow them out of wood as well as the stone walls. "I'll come out to see you."

She was about to attempt to use her power to shoo the vine back into the ether and tell the plant Zhani was a friend, ranger uniform or not, but the sergeant spoke again.

"Vlerion's in trouble."

"Milnor?" Kaylina guessed, worry clenching her gut.

Damn it, she'd been afraid of that. If not for the sentinel's pushy pulse of magic, she would have gone straight to ranger headquarters.

"Yes," Zhani called.

She'd backed into the courtyard and waited with her sword in hand. Her taybarri, Bludashar, stood shoulder to shoulder with Levitke at the gate. They'd been wise enough to stay outside. When Kaylina didn't see Frayvar or Sevarli in the kitchen, she understood why Zhani had come up. There hadn't been anyone to send to get her.

"What happened?" Kaylina grabbed her sword from the kitchen and joined Zhani in the courtyard. "Is Vlerion okay?"

"Spymaster Milnor came to ranger headquarters and demanded that Lord Vlerion be locked up in the castle dungeon until his investigation has been completed. Milnor said his preliminary evidence indicates Vlerion was responsible for Sabor's death."

"Well, of course. Vlerion stepped forward and took the blame for that."

Zhani nodded without surprise. She'd heard the story. "Milnor also said he might be responsible for the king's death."

"No way. Vlerion is loyal to the crown—even though the royals don't deserve him. Besides, he was with me last night."

"I guess that's part of the problem, that he wasn't on his estate when people went looking for him."

Kaylina bent forward and gripped her knees, almost dropping the sword.

"I don't know what's going to happen," Zhani continued, "but I heard Targon say something about... He thinks Milnor might make Vlerion disappear. The law would protect an aristocrat from a lot of crimes, and in some cases, they're considered above suspicion, but royal spies have ways of skirting the law and not getting in trouble."

"I'll bet."

"Targon looked like he might attack Milnor, but Vlerion waved him down and went along with the spymaster. Targon fumed a bit, then stalked out of headquarters, saying he was going to talk to the queen. I don't know what good that will do. Petalira married the king and bore him his son, but her heritage doesn't give her a right to rule on her own. She's not in charge after his passing. And the prince hasn't arrived yet."

Kaylina knew about Targon's relationship with Queen Petalira but had no idea if it involved favors beyond him entertaining her in bed. Even if it did, Kaylina wouldn't count on Targon being able to talk the queen into helping. Kaylina hadn't gotten the impression that the woman liked Vlerion. And, given his lineage, Petalira might consider him a threat to her son's right to rule.

"I have to go to him," Kaylina said. "Vlerion is so damn *noble* that he might let them—*his superiors*, I'm sure he would call those toads—lock him up. Or worse."

Would Vlerion let the spymaster or queen execute him? He wasn't *that* loyal, was he? He would fight. The beast would come out. Right there in the middle of the castle. And they would get what they deserved.

Kaylina clenched her jaw and shook her head, afraid Vlerion

wouldn't *let* the beast come out. He would do anything to protect her, but would he disobey orders to save himself?

"I don't know," she muttered.

Of course, if *she* were there and threatened by the new spymaster...

"What?" Zhani asked.

"I don't know how I can help him, but I have to." Kaylina straightened and pointed in the direction of the royal castle on its plateau. "I need to join him up there and ensure he... makes the right choice."

"If only you knew someone with an invitation to the royal castle," came Frayvar's voice through the kitchen window as he returned from whatever errand he'd been on to eavesdrop.

Kaylina scratched her jaw. She'd forgotten about the letter. "You think they want you to show up this very day with mead samples?"

"Of *course,*" Frayvar said.

"When the king is likely being prepared for people to pay their last respects before the funeral?"

"What better time for a delicious but appropriately somber and respectful mead?" Frayvar asked. "The blackberry would be perfect. Or the *lavender*-blackberry mead. No, no. That's sweeter. They'll want a rich and dark melomel, ideal for grieving."

"Just what I was thinking when I made it."

"You... have a plan to get in?" Zhani asked Kaylina.

"I think so."

"What will you do once you're in the castle?"

"Get everyone drunk on mead so I can walk Vlerion out without people noticing," Kaylina said.

"I am skeptical that plan will work."

"Well, we can at least get everyone in the kitchen smashed. And from there... we'll see."

Zhani gripped the hilt of her sheathed sword and gazed

thoughtfully toward the distant castle and then toward the two taybarri watching them. "Do you want me to come with you?"

She wore the expression of someone who knew she would get in trouble for helping but was offering to do so anyway.

"Targon didn't ask you to assist me, did he?" Kaylina couldn't imagine that Targon had even thought about her since returning to the city.

"No. He didn't tell me to come here at all. I'm supposed to be in the armory with my squad, helping Sergeant Nandari clean weapons and making sure the cannons mounted on the walls of ranger headquarters are supplied and ready in case the city erupts in chaos."

"You'd better return to do that then. Thanks for offering to help though. You're a good trainer. *Much* better than the men at ranger headquarters that I've worked with." Except Vlerion, she thought, smiling sadly—and with worry for him. He'd done a wonderful job training her. He'd been calm and respectful. He was a good man. Why were those idiots in the royal castle all gunning for him?

"Because of my superior ability to demonstrate and explain concepts?" Zhani asked. "Or because I never ogled your chest?"

"*Both* of those things." Kaylina ran inside, grabbed a bottle of the lavender-blackberry—since they wouldn't need that for the royal tasting—and brought it outside. "Here. In case you need to drink to our memories."

Zhani started to reach for it, but she paused as the words registered. "You're not planning to get yourself *killed,* are you? What are you going to do?"

"Get Vlerion out of there. Whatever it takes."

"I shouldn't allow this." Zhani accepted the bottle of mead but looked like she was considering clubbing Kaylina over the head with it to knock her unconscious.

"But you will because you're a kind and supportive mentor.

Besides, those vines over there will strangle you if you attack me." Kaylina waved toward one of the walls where a couple of green tendrils that had sprouted from the mortar pointed toward them. *Watching* them.

"Blighted orchards," Zhani blurted when she noticed them. "I thought I was safe when I came outside."

"The sentinel has orchestrated many attacks on enemies in the courtyard." Kaylina rested a hand on Zhani's back to show the vine minions that she was a friend—and also to guide her mentor to the gate. "Will you take Levitke back to headquarters with Blu? Frayvar and I had better rent a horse or mule, something innocuous."

Kaylina had a feeling the royal kitchen staff had sent out the invitation independent of the Castle Guard or anyone higher up, and she didn't want to draw attention by arriving on a ranger mount. With luck, whoever was at the gate wouldn't remember her, especially if Frayvar did the talking.

Levitke's head came up with an indignant snort. *Mule!*

The word rang in Kaylina's mind even though she hadn't been attempting to use her power to understand the taybarri.

"You're too noble, fearsome, and linked to the rangers." Kaylina patted Levitke. "Will you please return to headquarters with Sergeant Zhaniyan?"

Levitke gave her a grave you're-making-a-mistake look.

"If Vlerion and I aren't out of the castle by tomorrow, you can bring the entire taybarri herd up there, rip open the portcullis—again—and batter down the doors to charge inside and retrieve us."

One of Levitke's floppy ears twitched with interest.

"You can even leave droppings on the marble floors that some future spymaster can complain about it." Kaylina smiled slightly, remembering Sabor's snark on the subject.

"If they try to kill Lord Vlerion, *I* might come leave droppings too," Zhani said, her face sour.

"That's a strange battle tactic for a human, isn't it?"

"I suppose. This whole situation is frustrating though. We can't attack our own people." Zhani swung onto her taybarri's back. "Oh, I almost forgot." She delved into a pocket and pulled out a leather-wrapped packet. "These are for you."

"What are they?" When Kaylina accepted the packet, glass clinked inside.

"Four vials of an elixir made from altered zeatora berry."

"This isn't another contraceptive, is it? I haven't had any time for situations that would have led me to need the other ones."

Not that she wouldn't have loved to join Vlerion in the woods the night before...

"No. I found the apothecary who made Spymaster Sabor's elixirs. He's the official apothecary to the royal castle, so it wasn't hard. He said altered zeatora berry elixir is the calming agent that was in the vial you gave me. He remembered selling it to Sabor recently. These elixirs are the right blue color, so I believed him, but he did give me a blank look when I asked about the liquid's effects on magic. I suspect Sabor was the one to learn about that."

"Oh, that's great to know what it is, but I don't need..." Kaylina trailed off, gazing down at the packet.

Wasn't it possible that she *would* need the elixir? The next time the beast reared up at an inconvenient moment, one of the vials might work to halt the change.

"They could be helpful." Zhani lifted a hand, refusing to take them back.

"Yeah, I might be able to use them. Thank you."

"You're welcome, but there's one more thing you need to know. The calming agent, even if magic doesn't come into play in any way, has side effects. Swallowing it would be deadly. It's usually turned into a vapor."

Kaylina nodded. She'd assumed that from the broken vial Sabor had thrown to the ground.

"Also, if the dose isn't measured correctly, if the recipient gets too much… it could stop the heart."

"Uh." Kaylina held the packet out at arm's length. She couldn't risk using something like that on Vlerion. No matter what.

"It's unlikely that would happen," Zhani hurried to say, "since it's quite pungent, and your target will pull back instead of breathing it in deeply, but I didn't want you to be surprised. Just in case."

"I don't think…" Kaylina tried to give back the packet.

But Zhani leaned away and shook her head.

"Keep it," she repeated, "Just in case."

Kaylina eyed the packet bleakly, tempted to throw it in the river, but Vlerion wasn't the only person out there who possessed magic. If her guess was right, Sabor had been carrying the elixir around to deal with the sage assassins and their powers.

"All right." Kaylina forced a smile. "I hope I won't need it, but thanks for finding it for me."

"You're welcome. Be careful at the royal castle. It's as dangerous as this one." Zhani eyed the vines before nudging her mount to get him pointed toward the river trail. "Let's go, Blu. We have weapons to clean."

Levitke and Blu huffed out breaths that sounded more like sighs than their usual whuffs.

Kaylina closed the gate, hoping she hadn't made a mistake in sending Zhani away. She also hoped there wouldn't be a need for Levitke to charge up to the castle with the whole herd. That might start the city chaos that she'd been worrying about earlier, even if it had nothing to do with the king's passing.

"All right, Fray," Kaylina said, joining her brother in the kitchen. "I'll pick a few meads and find a mule. Hopefully, I'll be back in time for the evening meal."

"You don't want me to come along? My name is on the invitation."

"Don't you need to start preparing for the dinner service soon? Especially since you haven't hired an assistant chef yet."

"Sevarli helped me cut onions, carrots, and celery yesterday."

"So you're ready to leave her in charge of creating your signature dishes?"

"No."

"I'll be fine by myself." Kaylina hoped that was true and tried not to second-guess her choice to go alone.

"You rarely are. You *need* people."

"I know. Once I hook up with Vlerion, I'll have him." She caught herself before patting her brother on the shoulder, lest he complain about unnecessary touching. "Keep the eating house running, Fray. We're off to a good start. We can't let a little regime change upset the apple cart."

10

A FELINE CAN BE A FINICKY COMRADE BUT A REWARDING ONE.
~ *Queen Henova*

Kaylina found an aged donkey to rent to pull a tiny cart loaded with mead samples. She carried some of the most precious bottles in a padded bag hung over her shoulder, wanting them jostled as little as possible on the walk through the city. It would have been preferable if the wine steward had come to Stillguard Castle for a tasting, so the mead would have been properly rested and chilled in the root cellar, but that wouldn't have gotten her in to see Vlerion.

More people were out in the streets than earlier in the day. Kaylina didn't spot any sign of the fighting the rangers were worried about—not yet—but the kingdom subjects spoke in hushed tones, aside from protestors on several corners, who held up signs sharing political opinions. Very few were in support of the prince.

Replace the monarchy, one read.

Fairness and equality for all.

Time for a change, one read, making Kaylina think of the sentinel's words. *Change comes.*

A little girl carried a sign that asked for Queen Petalira to become the next ruler.

Kaylina couldn't get behind that one.

One reading, *Vlerion Havartaft, the true heir,* made her stumble and look twice.

If the spymaster, queen, and whoever else had been running things during Gavatorin's reign had seen that sign, or others like it, that might explain why Vlerion had been dragged to the dungeon. It might have little to do with Milnor's investigation and more to do with them worrying he would be a threat to their plans.

"Vlerion doesn't even *want* that job," Kaylina muttered, the bottles clinking softly as she led the donkey up the road ascending the plateau and toward the castle gate.

She had to find him before something dire happened. Unfortunately, Vlerion wouldn't be in the kitchen with the wine steward. Earlier, she'd been joking when she'd said she would get the staff drunk so she could sneak off, but that might have to be her plan, unless chance gave her an opportunity to slip away and snoop.

Two guards stationed outside the gate watched her approach without expression. With the portcullis down, there was no chance she could amble inside unchecked, not that she'd expected that. The guards held blunderbusses in their arms in addition to having swords and daggers belted at their waists. They looked like they expected trouble.

Kaylina withdrew the invitation and waved it in the air before approaching the men. One of them sneered dismissively at the donkey and cart, as if certain she was a panhandler coming up to peddle wares. Well, dismissal was better than wariness or a call to arms, which was what she might have gotten if she'd ridden up on a taybarri.

"Nobody's allowed into the castle today," one guard told her, waving away her letter without looking at it.

"I'm delivering mead for the kitchen staff." Kaylina held the invitation up, ignoring the wave. "It's a tasting. They requested it."

"Not today. The king passed. We're in mourning." The speaker squinted at her, as if her face was familiar and he was trying to place it.

"Hence the need for mead," Kaylina hurried to say, hoping he wouldn't identify her. "They want something appropriate for the funeral. Preparations have already begun, I assume."

"What kind of mead maker wears a sword?" The other guard had been eyeing her.

"There are protestors and rebels and who knows what else in the streets, and I'm traveling alone. I'd be foolish *not* to wear a sword."

Another guard wandered up to the gate from inside. He wore more rank on his collar and was older and scowling. He studied her through the bars.

Kaylina smiled sturdily, not prepared to give up, but what would she do if these guys wouldn't let her in? She didn't sense any meandering outdoor cats or dogs nearby that she might call upon, not that furry animals weaving between the guards' legs would help in this situation.

She thought she sensed a cat inside—maybe in the kitchen?—but she didn't know how far to trust her intuition. Still, she attempted to will the animal to tell the staff that an important visitor was outside. She promised it some of Frayvar's smoked fish if it showed up at Stillguard Castle later. Whether it was let outside here, she didn't know, but she didn't have anything else to offer it.

"I know her," the senior guard said.

"Is she trouble, sir? She looks like trouble."

Kaylina touched her chest in innocence. She'd barely said anything. How could they have already labeled her as that?

"She's the one who was accused of poisoning the queen and was a fugitive."

"Yes, but I was cleared of that accusation. I'm a mere mead maker, and your own people have requested my presence." Kaylina willed a greeting—and an image of a delicious goblet of chilled mead—in the direction of the kitchen, hoping one of the staff would come out to override the guards and let her in. Unfortunately, she hadn't had much luck using her fledgling druid powers to influence human beings. "Technically, they don't need me there for the tasting. I could write a few notes and wait outside, I suppose, but if they want to serve something excellent that conveys the right mood for the funeral, they'll want to consult me." She waved at the cart and hefted her own bottle-filled bag. "That'll be a big event, won't it? Important people from all around."

"The taybarri queen vouched for her." The senior guard's tone was so gruff that Kaylina couldn't tell if he meant the statement to exonerate her or as an accusation.

"Oh, yeaaaah," one of the other guards said, the word drawn out with awe or maybe wonder. "It was so amazing when they came to the castle. They were *beautiful.* And I heard them speak into my mind, just like the legends say. Were you there for that, Drokon?"

"Yeah, the silver taybarri are gods-blessed, no doubt."

"Come back tomorrow," the senior guard told Kaylina. "Nobody's allowed in today."

Kaylina groped for something else to try. Maybe she should have brought Levitke with her after all. Though she might have had to paint the taybarri's fur silver to be invited inside.

A door in the courtyard thudded open, and meows floated out. Cranky meows. Was that the cat she'd sensed?

Kaylina peered between the bars, trying to see what was happening, but the door was out of sight. The senior guard looked back as the meowing continued.

"Here, you little beast," a woman said. "Quit complaining."

A black cat with white socks trotted into the middle of the courtyard and sat down, looking at the gate. No, looking at Kaylina.

That prompted all three guards to frown at her. Maybe this hadn't been the wisest use of her powers. But a gray-haired woman in a white apron walked into view and also peered through the gate.

"I have the mead for the tasting," Kaylina called, though she'd never seen the woman before and had no idea if she had any knowledge of the invitation. "From Stillguard Castle."

"Oh, *that* mead?" one of the guards outside said. "I got a taste of that the other night. Maxol stole some from Laverton, who had way more than he needed, and he let me have a sip. It was really good." The guard, who'd previously sneered at the donkey and cart, looked at them with interest.

"Ah, the invitation," the woman said. "I'd forgotten. The king..." She glanced toward the balcony that the king and queen had once walked out on to address the taybarri elders. "It's a day of mourning, but... I wonder if any of those meads would be good at the funeral. We have instructions to make plans."

"Most certainly," Kaylina said. "I brought a couple of varieties with that in mind."

"Oh, well, let her in, men. Please. The funeral meal is an event of paramount importance. Only the coronation of Prince Enrikon will require more thought and planning."

The two outside guards made a face at the prince's name as one relieved Kaylina of her sword. She twitched, not wanting to let it go, but she could understand why they wouldn't allow her in armed.

"*King* Enrikon," the senior guard corrected and glared at his men as well as the woman.

She didn't acknowledge the correction, only putting a fist on her hip and pointing at the portcullis.

"Isn't that up for debate?" one guard whispered to the other as the senior man stepped back, ceding to the woman's wishes. "The queen... I heard she had plans."

"The queen *always* has plans. Nothing's going to come of that."

"The prince is her son. He'll have to do what she says."

"No, he won't. He'll pack her off to peel carrots in Potato Patch if she butts in."

"I doubt he even knows where that is. There aren't any race-tracks or dice tables there, just crops."

After the senior guard raised the portcullis, Kaylina led the donkey slowly into the courtyard, wanting to hear the men's gossip. A few months ago, she wouldn't have cared one way or another who ruled the kingdom, but seeing Vlerion's name on that sign, and hearing people mention him as a possibility, made it much more personal. If Vlerion ended up killed because *other* people thought the Havartafts should return to the throne...

"This way, dear," the woman said, almost tripping over the cat as she turned to lead Kaylina toward the door. "I'm Chef Anja, and I'll take you to the wine steward."

"Thank you."

The cat had stopped meowing but rose, evading the chef's feet to amble over and walk beside Kaylina. She would have to remember to put fish out for it later, to go with the milk she'd been leaving out for the first cat who'd helped her—and the twenty or thirty strays that were coming by regularly to avail themselves of the offerings.

"You're a strange beast," the chef told it, then waved at a stable boy, who was sneering dismissively at the donkey, much as the guard had done. Maybe only taybarri and pedigreed horses were allowed in the courtyard of the royal castle.

"Cats are independent sorts," Kaylina offered, hoping the woman wouldn't think to associate *magic* with its antics.

"That's a certainty."

The stable boy unhitched the cart and unloaded the two crates of mead it carried. A pair of servants came to take them, as well as the bag Kaylina carried, and they followed Kaylina and the chef inside.

As they walked, Kaylina looked all around, hoping to catch a glimpse of Vlerion, but she didn't expect it. He could already be in the dungeon deep in the plateau under the castle. Even if he wasn't, she wouldn't likely run into him down this narrow hallway, visited more by the staff than residents and guests.

The chef led her past supply closets, storage rooms, and a huge pantry with so many exotic spices that Frayvar would have either fainted from being overwhelmed or leaped inside, eager to organize them.

When they entered the kitchen, heat rolling off stoves and a hearth browning flat bread, the chef waved grandly to a corner with a table where Kaylina could set up. Several staff made pleased exclamations when the mead bottles were unloaded from the crates. Maybe this had been discussed before the wine steward had extended the invitation.

"At least getting them drunk shouldn't be that hard," Kaylina murmured as someone brought over crystal goblets.

"The prince is here!" came a cry from the hallway. A young maid stuck her head into the kitchen. "The queen's ordered him to attend her. Right away. They're going to the lilac parlor!"

Kaylina assumed the information was given so the kitchen workers could prepare drinks and snacks, and several of the staff *did* spring to pantries and cupboards, but several others ran toward the maid. She held a finger to her lips and gestured for them to follow.

"I'll be right back," Kaylina said to the young man setting out goblets and lining up her bottles of mead.

He blinked at her.

She held up a finger in the same gesture the maid had used, then hurried after the other staff. They'd already disappeared into the hall, but she was in time to see the last person dart behind a tall cabinet of dishes that opened outward to reveal a secret door. It started to swing shut on hinges, but Kaylina made it and joined the whispering people heading down a narrow passageway between stone walls. Light seeped in from cracks near the ceiling and in spots with other hidden doors.

Kaylina tried not to make any noise, but when someone glanced back and saw her, she didn't say anything. The woman only grinned and held a finger to her lips, as the maid in the lead had. Kaylina had either been accepted into the pack of castle staff, or it was too dark for them to realize she wasn't one of them.

The group slowed as several people in the front whispered *ssh* and crept forward in silence. Someone in the lead eased a sliding bookcase aside a couple of inches, the spot reminding Kaylina of the secret door in Captain Targon's office. This city was overflowing with secret passageways.

"Mother," came a stern male voice from a spacious room that did indeed have lilac-painted walls. That was all Kaylina could see through the gap. "I don't know why you're presuming to tell me what to do. I'll certainly take your *suggestions* under advisement, but I am a grown man."

"You haven't been acting like one for the last ten years," Queen Petalira said. "How many women did you bring back with you in that ridiculous carriage with the *mattress* in it? And how much of the kingdom's money did you lose gambling on the racetracks and arenas this past month?"

"Neither is any concern of yours, nor will my hobbies affect how I rule *my* kingdom."

"Your father's will hasn't been read yet. You're making assumptions."

"I'm the only heir, Mother. Unless he was a randier old man than I assumed. I *know* his first marriage didn't result in children."

In the dark passageway, the staff scarcely breathed as they listened in. The way they hunched forward, hands on their knees and ears cocked toward the door, all having made room for the others, as if they'd practiced this, made Kaylina suspect she wasn't the only regular eavesdropper in the group. To think, Vlerion and Targon had implied she was *odd* for listening in on conversations.

Admittedly, she didn't care that much about hearing these two insult each other. She only wanted to know if Vlerion's name came up and hoped to learn where in the castle he was being held.

"He was randier than you'd think," the queen said tartly. "He may very well have other heirs stashed away. Don't make assumptions."

"*I'm* his designated heir, Mother. He told me back before he went daft from old age. You're welcome to stay around and enjoy the life you've been privileged to have here—"

"As if *I'm* the only one who's enjoyed privilege. Don't think I don't know you constantly had Financier Falgor send you money from the king's coffers."

"I am the heir, and I had a right to that money. I have a right to *all* of it. This is *my* kingdom, Mother, and you'll not nag me. Not if you want to stay here and enjoy your life of ease."

"Being your mother isn't as much *ease* as you'd think."

The prince scoffed. Kaylina had never met the guy—or even seen him yet—but she already didn't like him. Maybe he was the reason Spymaster Sabor and however many others had been scheming for control. Maybe they'd even plotted the prince's demise.

"Don't be melodramatic, Mother. Your role here isn't *that* significant."

"How lovely of you to assume so when you've barely been in the capital these past ten years."

"It's dreadful and *cold* here. Why our ancestors—no, why the Havartafts—thought all those years ago it was a good idea to move the seat of power to this frigid mountain land, I don't know."

"The gold, dear," Petalira said.

"Gold can be exported, Mother."

They fell silent, and a couple of the women in the shadows glanced at each other. Afraid the queen and prince had realized the bookcase had been moved and they had eavesdroppers?

Petalira sighed loudly enough that they heard it in the hall. "Why don't you get some food and rest, and we'll talk more later? You'll want to pay your respects to your father, I'm sure."

"Yes, the entire trip here, I couldn't wait to look at a corpse. Really, Mother. He hadn't spoken to me in ten years. I—"

Someone knocked at the parlor door. Kaylina almost jumped. She imagined guards storming in to tell the queen and prince about the eavesdroppers in the secret passageway.

"My pardon for the intrusion," a familiar male voice said. Was that Milnor?

A couple of Kaylina's fellow eavesdroppers stiffened, and two backed up, almost bumping into her. Did they want to leave? Yes, several patted her and the wall as they retreated.

They didn't move so quickly that Kaylina thought they believed they were about to be caught. Maybe they simply knew better than to spy on a spymaster?

Kaylina flattened herself to the wall, having no intention of missing Milnor's report. She would cheerfully eavesdrop on anyone.

"Who are you?" Enrikon asked in a flat tone.

"That's Milnor," Petalira said. "Spymaster Sabor's successor."

"What happened to Sabor?"

"We'll update you later," Petalira said.

Kaylina wished the queen would share the update now, one that would reveal what they believed had happened that night.

The prince grunted but was probably tired after his travels, because he didn't object to leaving. By the time Petalira was alone in the parlor with Milnor, Kaylina's co-eavesdroppers had disappeared.

She wavered, knowing she should hurry out as well. In the dark, the staff might not have realized she wasn't one of them, but she was sure to be missed when everyone returned to the kitchen, and they couldn't find the mead lady…

But Milnor started speaking, and Kaylina inched closer to the bookcase opening. If he brought up Vlerion, and revealed where in the castle he was, Kaylina would abandon her mead to find him. Once she rescued him, they could find a way out together, fighting back-to-back through the courtyard if they needed.

"I've got Vlerion, Your Majesty," Milnor said politely, not snubbing her because her husband was gone.

"What are you going to do with him?"

"What do you *want* me to do with him?"

Petalira sighed. "I don't know right now. He's never shown any interest in taking back the throne—my understanding is that none of the Havartaft men have—but it's hard not to see him as a threat right now. I always thought it would be best if he didn't exist, if that entire line ended. But my husband was afraid of him—afraid to cross him."

Milnor hesitated. "Do you know the reason why, Your Majesty?"

"I know about the curse, yes. Yet another reason he's a threat."

"Yes, Your Majesty. I'm certain I can… end that threat, but you should let me know soon if that's what you wish. I feel obligated to point out that once Enrikon is coronated, I'll be bound by duty and honor to obey *his* wishes."

"I doubt he cares one way or another what happens to Vlerion Havartaft. If they've spoken more than five times, I don't know about it." Petalira's tone turned dry. Or maybe bitter. "I am wounded to hear that you won't be bound to obey my commands anymore after that."

"My apologies, Your Majesty, but you are not..."

"Yes, yes, I'm just the woman who endured Gavatorin in her bed for thirty years and bore him an heir. I'm a nobody."

"Not that, surely, but... you are not in charge."

"Of anything anymore. Your reminder is a blade to the heart."

"My apologies," Milnor repeated.

"Sabor and I worked together for a long time. *He* would not have cast me aside. He acknowledged I could have a role in his plans."

"I don't have plans, Your Majesty. Other than to do the duty I was trained for, that which I took an oath to do."

Kaylina could have respected him for that—if he hadn't been threatening to make Vlerion disappear.

Milnor lowered his voice and added, "I do plan to avenge my predecessor's death."

Kaylina grimaced. That was another reason she couldn't respect this guy. Sabor had been an ass who'd deserved what he got and didn't warrant *avenging*. All she regretted was that there would be consequences. She had to make sure those consequences didn't fall onto Vlerion's head.

She leaned closer to the opening, wishing they would say where Vlerion was. The dungeon under the castle? Her skin crawled at the idea of going down there again, but she would if—

A cool steel blade pressed against her throat an instant before a strong hand gripped her arm.

Shit.

11

*W*HETHER ONE IS CAUGHT OR NOT, EAVESDROPPING ALWAYS HAS *consequences.*

~ Spymaster Yeroknor the Senior

"Who are you?" the owner of the dagger asked softly.

Kaylina's jaw drooped in surprise. It was a woman's voice.

One of the maids? Their supervisor who rounded up wayward staff who used the castle's passageways for eavesdropping? No, this person knew just how to grab Kaylina and where to hold her dagger—even in the dark. Weapons expertise would be an odd skill for a maid.

"I'm from the kitchen," Kaylina breathed.

Not exactly a lie...

A thump came from the parlor. The door closing? Kaylina couldn't hear voices anymore and suspected Petalira and Milnor had left. She'd hung out longer than she should have, and she hadn't learned anything extra. And now...

"You are not on the staff," the woman said.

"No, I run a meadery and was invited up to give a tasting to the wine steward."

"Ah, you're the druid girl."

"No, I'm the *mead* girl." Maybe Kaylina shouldn't have argued. That blade remained against her throat, cold and deadly.

"With druid blood. Korbian."

"Yeah, nice to meet you. Who are you, by the way? Would you like to try the mead?"

"Do you find it difficult to execute tastings from secret passageways far from the kitchen?"

"It adds an element of challenge, but I like that. Who are you?"

The grip on her arm tightened, surprisingly strong for a woman. Her voice was above Kaylina's ear, meaning she had to be near six feet tall.

"What are you doing back here?" her captor asked. "Who sent you to spy?"

"I was in the kitchen when the staff said the prince had arrived. They were the ones to open a hidden door to this passageway. I was curious so I followed them."

All true...

The woman snorted, warm breath stirring Kaylina's hair. "The staff *is* full of eavesdroppers who do their best to outdo each other when it comes to gossip."

"I wondered what will happen next to the kingdom," Kaylina said, though maybe she shouldn't have offered up anything other than what was asked. "Uhm, have you seen Lord Vlerion, perchance? He was supposed to help me with the tasting, but I can't find him."

"Oh, yes. I'm certain a ranger aristocrat pours drinks for you."

"Well, no, but he's supporting me in my business endeavor. His mother was even thinking of investing at one point."

After a pause, the woman said, "I have heard that he's been talking nobles into visiting that cursed castle."

"For the delicious mead served there. Why don't you put away that dagger, and I'll take you to the kitchen, and you can try some yourself."

The grip on her elbow shifted to her shoulder, and the woman forced Kaylina to turn around, the dagger still at her throat. "Walk."

"Okay." Kaylina tried to lead the way toward the kitchen, which she thought she could find again—the maid gaggle hadn't taken many turns—but she doubted that was their destination.

"Turn right," the woman stated.

Kaylina did so, her hunch proven correct. Soon, the passageway led up stairs that she bumped and groped over in the dim lighting. The woman removed the dagger from her throat, but Kaylina sensed it remained close and that her captor could sweep it back in at any time.

On the second floor, they took several more turns, finally entering a passageway so narrow that her elbows bumped the walls. She brushed against hard stone that protruded, making the way even tighter. The back of a hearth?

"Did Lord Vlerion kill Spymaster Sabor?" the woman asked, startling Kaylina.

She sought an answer that would neither condemn Vlerion nor belie what they'd both already said. She longed to protect him but knew he didn't want her to get herself in trouble.

"He was there when Sabor died," Kaylina said.

"As were you." Her captor tightened her grip, stopping Kaylina.

"Yes, that alley was a busy place."

"Milnor is skeptical that you had anything to do with it. Only the cat fur makes him wonder."

"Huh."

Tense, Kaylina waited for the woman to press her further—and return that dagger to her throat. But she used it to scrape at the stones. To prod a hidden switch between them?

Yes, a soft click sounded, and a door swung open, revealing an office with floor-to-ceiling bookcases, a sofa, a desk, leather chairs, and someone sitting in one of them. Someone familiar.

"Vlerion," Kaylina blurted as his gaze swung toward the hidden door.

His eyebrows rose, and his lips parted as she walked out. Judging by his surprise, he hadn't heard that she was nearby.

"Kaylina, what are you doing here?"

"Enacting a plan to rescue you." She managed a smile, but she felt silly voicing the words. She didn't know whose office this was, but it was far from the dungeon she'd imagined him in. He wasn't even bound or shackled, nor was there a guard at the door, though she supposed a whole legion could be standing outside.

At first, he didn't stir, but when the woman walked out behind Kaylina, he rose, muscles tensing. He glanced toward the hand gripping Kaylina's shoulder and also noticed the drawn dagger.

"Will that rescue be hard to accomplish with an armed spy at your back?" Vlerion asked, his tone more mild than Kaylina expected.

He squinted at the woman, but he didn't threaten her, nor did that dangerous spark light in his eyes, the one that suggested the beast might appear to protect Kaylina. She interpreted his body language as he was concerned but not yet worried.

"A spy? She wouldn't give me her name after she ambled up and thrust a dagger to my throat." Kaylina glanced over her shoulder, aware of the woman standing uncomfortably close. There were enough lights in the office to reveal that she had pronounced cheekbones in a lean face, her angles a little too hard to be considered beautiful, though Kaylina would call her handsome, especially if her shoulder-length dark-blonde hair were down instead of pulled back in a tight braid. "It was rude," she added.

"Spies aren't known to be the epitome of politeness," Vlerion said.

"Really, my lord," the woman said. "Haven't I always been civil with you?"

"Reasonably so. More so than Sabor and Milnor, at least."

"That wouldn't take much," Kaylina muttered.

Vlerion looked toward the closed wooden door at the front of the office, presumably the official exit. "There are a number of guards out there," he said quietly.

"Yes," the woman said, probably knowing all about them.

Kaylina spread her arms, not sure what to say or do. She didn't know if she'd joined Vlerion as a prisoner here or if this woman might be an ally. Or at least not an adversary?

"Are you in as much trouble as I thought you were, Vlerion?" Kaylina asked.

"Milnor and I were having a chat when the prince returned."

"That... answered my question less than you might think."

"I don't actually know the answer. What do you think, Lady Shylea?"

The woman snorted softly. "I'm no more a lady than Targon is a lord."

"Targon *thinks* he's a lord," Vlerion said.

"He thinks he's a lot of things. The arrogance is impressive given how many times we were beaten and told we were excrement as kids."

Kaylina stepped away from the woman—Shylea—and looked back and forth between them. "I'm a little lost."

"And yet you found the secret passageways in the castle," the woman said dryly.

"I told you I followed the staff into those. And that's not what I meant."

Vlerion extended a hand toward the woman. "Kaylina, this is one of the spies who works for—*worked* for—Sabor. She's also Targon's twin sister."

Kaylina rocked back. As soon as he said it, she could see the resemblance, but... "Targon has a sister? He never said anything about it—her."

"He discussed his family with you at some point?" Vlerion asked.

"Well, no, but he's so... It's hard to imagine women in his life who aren't—" Whores, Kaylina thought but kept herself from saying, realizing Shylea might find that insulting. Maybe she respected her brother. Though... the words she'd voiced didn't quite suggest that.

"Yes," Vlerion said dryly, as if he knew exactly what Kaylina was thinking.

"Spies don't wish to be talked about," Shylea said. "I serve the crown, the same as he does, and our father paid for us to have an education and the training we desired. Of course, I had to sneak off for my combat training, since sword fighting wasn't deemed appropriate for women of noble—or half-noble—birth back then. I wanted to become a ranger, the same as he, but that wasn't allowed then either." Bitterness flashed in her eyes as she eyed Kaylina.

Great, someone else disliked her for reasons Kaylina didn't want anything to do with.

"I had training and talent enough that then-Spymaster Jalkoran noticed and gave me work," Shylea said. "He was loyal to King Gavatorin Senior, and I believed in what I was doing. The work was right, protecting the populace and the crown."

"And now?" Vlerion asked.

Shylea hesitated and glanced toward the door, though it remained closed, no sounds suggesting the guards had their ears pressed against it.

"Things have been murkier of late," she said quietly.

"Yes." Vlerion nodded sadly at her.

Distant calls came through the door from the hallway, which had been quiet until then. It didn't sound like the guards or anyone immediately outside, but a few thunks and clangs echoed from somewhere on the floor. Maybe the prince was stirring things up? Ordering people about? Or maybe the staff had come upstairs to help unpack and prepare whatever rooms he claimed.

Vlerion, apparently not that worried about the goings-on in the castle, walked around the desk to hug Kaylina. Though she hadn't expected it, she leaned against his chest, always welcoming his touch.

He patted her gently while looking over her shoulder at Shylea. "Kaylina is not a threat to the crown. She's been swept up in events because Targon has recruited her to be a ranger, and the cursed castle has recruited her to... I'm not entirely sure what it wants from her. But nothing to do with human politics, I think. It serves the druids—or their memory."

"I'm aware of the plant," Shylea said, her tone neutral.

Kaylina wished the woman would go away so she could talk to Vlerion alone. Since Milnor had finished his discussion with the queen, he might be on his way back to the office.

"I was trying to learn what happened to Spymaster Sabor," Shylea said, "since, from what I've heard, you haven't been forthright with Milnor or even Targon. The spymaster was wounded by both claw marks and a sword; that implies two different attackers."

"Do you care that much what happened?" Vlerion stroked Kaylina's hair as the conversation continued without her.

She felt awkward being talked around and wanted to suggest that she and Vlerion slip into that passageway before Milnor returned. But would Shylea allow that? It was doubtful she would be a match for Vlerion if he decided he wanted to leave, but Vlerion also might not be willing to attack Targon's sister.

"He was my boss," Shylea said after a long pause.

"I've long had the impression you weren't that pleased to be in his employ."

"He was overly ambitious and working at odds with his oath. That put me at odds with *my* oath."

"It's best for the kingdom that he's gone," Vlerion said. "He was trying to put his plans in action. If it's discovered that the king died of some poison, he might very well be to blame, a plan he enacted before his end, though I'm not certain of that. Sabor probably needed more time before he was ready for the kingdom's figurehead to disappear."

"Time to ensure his army was birthed," Kaylina muttered.

Shylea might not have caught that. She frowned over, a question in her eyes, but Kaylina didn't repeat the words.

"He sought to betray the king and rule the kingdom himself," Vlerion said, drawing Shylea's gaze back to him. "I don't think you would be doing anything wrong by not wholeheartedly pursuing the one who slew him."

"Tell Milnor that."

"Oh, I did. Swaying him will be difficult."

"Well, he's *my* boss now." Her mouth twisted, the bitterness less hidden this time. "I've served in this capacity longer than he. He was a *doctor* for twenty years. I don't deny that his experience in that field makes him valuable, but I..." She frowned toward the secret door and didn't continue.

"Sabor didn't respect women," Vlerion said. "He wouldn't have named one as his successor. You *do* have more experience than Milnor, at least in this role."

"It doesn't matter," Shylea said, though Kaylina sensed that it did. "*I'm* not ambitious. I've only ever wanted to serve the kingdom and..."

"Have interesting adventures?"

"Yes. Since I couldn't become a ranger and have a taybarri, I had to find them somehow."

Amazing how many people became rangers so they could ride taybarri. Kaylina thought of loyal and delightful Levitke and admitted it had swayed her—a lot more than Targon's bribery.

"I can't decide on my own to drop the investigation," Shylea said, bringing the conversation back to the topic Kaylina wished she would forget.

"I'm only suggesting that we move on, that the details of that night don't need to be recorded." Vlerion gazed steadily at her. It wasn't exactly an order, but his face was stern, one of a commander addressing a subordinate.

But Shylea wasn't that, was she? No more than Targon.

Still, she was the one to lower her head and study the floor. "If I left that exit undefended, would you walk out it, Vlerion?" She waved to the secret passageway, the wood-paneled door still ajar.

"*Yes*," Kaylina said emphatically.

Vlerion sighed and didn't move to leave. "If I disappear during the middle of his inquiry, Milnor will have justification to mobilize the guards—even the rangers—to have me hunted down."

"He's not going to let you leave, Vlerion," Shylea said softly.

"I think she's right." Kaylina leaned back to look at Vlerion's face as she gripped his arms. "I heard him talking to the queen."

"You were eavesdropping?" he asked mildly, not appearing concerned about the rest. "Again?"

"To learn all I could to *rescue* you. You should be grateful for my tendencies, which, by the way, don't seem rare at all. Half the kitchen staff was spying on the queen's conversation with the prince. How do you think I found them?"

Vlerion looked at Shylea.

"It's like I told her." Shylea waved toward Kaylina. "The staff are busybodies and gossips. Besides, they want to know what their future holds. Understandably so. The prince hasn't been around much lately, but everyone who's worked here a long time remembers what a spoiled brat he was and how he dragged the female staff off against their wishes."

"So you're eager to serve him," Vlerion said.

Shylea made a sour face. "As eager as you are, I'm sure." She shifted her hand toward the hidden passageway. "Go ahead, Vlerion. This may be your only chance to leave without..." She glanced at Kaylina. "I know what you can become. What you *will* become if threatened. It would be better for us all if a repeat of the dungeon massacre didn't happen here among the guards and staff."

Vlerion sighed again, this time looking at Kaylina. He might have staved off turning into the beast when he'd been alone, but now that she was here and could be threatened...

"You can come stay at Stillguard Castle instead of ranger headquarters until we see what happens with the succession," she offered. "Who's going to get you there? The plant is protecting it."

"The plant protects *you*," Vlerion said. "It would happily hang me from the rafters with one of its vines."

"It *would*, but it won't. We've got a deal." Kaylina rested a hand on her chest. "Besides, it said you're welcome now, remember?"

"I'm positive *welcome* isn't the word it used. Does it even use words?"

"Sometimes. Usually, when a tendril is touching my head. That aside, it didn't strangle you with vines after you groped me in the courtyard under the tower. How much more of an invitation do you need?"

Belatedly, Kaylina decided one shouldn't discuss physical relations in front of strangers.

Maybe Vlerion didn't agree, because he snorted and said, "You groped me as much as I groped you."

Well, Shylea wasn't a stranger to him.

"That plant sounds more intelligent than I was led to believe," she said, observing their discussion with bemusement.

"It said you could come visit me," Kaylina added to Vlerion. "In human form, anyway, which is the form I prefer."

"The form we *all* prefer," Shylea murmured.

More clanks and distant calls sounded on the floor. Was there more going on than the staff moving the prince and his entourage in?

"You could disappear in Stillguard Castle while we figure things out," Kaylina urged. "Or until Sabor's death is forgotten. Maybe the prince will be so busy fending off enemies that he'll have to keep Milnor busy ferreting out plots, and Milnor won't have *time* to have you hunted down."

"I shouldn't feel wistful at that notion, I suppose," Vlerion said.

"It's not an impossible one," Shylea said. "He does have enemies who oppose him."

Glad the woman was supporting her, sort of, Kaylina added, "If we took the catacombs to reach Stillguard, people wouldn't have any idea where you'd gone. Is there still a tunnel leading from the dungeon to there?"

"That was walled up immediately," Shylea said, "and the tunnel filled in."

"Too bad. But we can find another way." Kaylina tapped her lip. "If it hasn't been too long to be suspicious, I could return to the kitchen, do the mead tasting, and then get the donkey I rented. If you scrunch up, we could fit you in that cart under some hay. There would be hay in the stable, right? I didn't bring enough mead to cover you with bottles. Besides, those might be empty by now." She looked to Shylea again, realizing they would need help for this new plan. How much of an ally might Targon's sister be?

"Nobles don't *scrunch*, Kaylina," Vlerion said. "Or *hide*."

"Commoners do. I'll show you how. It's easy."

Shylea laughed softly. "I'd heard she was irreverent but not how much of a schemer she is."

Kaylina lifted her chin. "I just want to help Vlerion."

She wanted to make sure the damn spymaster didn't have him *executed*.

Shylea eyed them—or their closeness, Vlerion's arms still around Kaylina and her gripping him. "I see that."

She smiled without condemnation. At least *she* didn't seem to think Kaylina was trying to land herself a noble for his wealth—as that awful Lady Ghara had suggested.

"Targon's reports may not have been adequate," Vlerion said. "Strange that he accuses *me* of being overly brief."

"Believe it or not, he doesn't report to me. Nothing that he doesn't write up in the official papers, anyway. Sabor was always irked about that and certain Targon was hiding things about the ranger organization."

"Is that why he suborned Jankarr?" Vlerion asked.

Kaylina gaped at him.

Oh, she'd noted that things that happened around Jankarr seemed to get reported quickly, but she liked him—even if he'd stopped being as friendly and affable with her. She hadn't wanted to believe he would do anything to harm Vlerion or the other rangers.

"I believe it was more of a strong-arming. That was his style. And Jankarr isn't the only one. Watch your words." Shylea stepped away from the passageway while leaving her arm extended toward it. Making it clear Vlerion should leave.

"I always do," he murmured, considering the doorway but not yet moving.

Another shout sounded in the hallway. This one closer.

Someone knocked on the door and opened it. Kaylina jumped, shifting away from Vlerion to stand in front of the secret opening, though she wasn't tall enough to hide its existence.

The knocker didn't stick his head in, only saying, "Spymaster's coming back, Lord Vlerion."

"Thank you," Vlerion said.

The door closed again.

"You have more people looking out for you than I expected," Kaylina said.

"Sabor's death freed that up somewhat." Vlerion nodded to Shylea, took Kaylina's hand, and—thank the moon gods—headed for the passageway. "He was ruthless and made sure nobody dared take action that wouldn't please him. Everyone knew he was someone you didn't dare cross."

"*You* dared," Kaylina murmured.

"Not as much as *you* did." Vlerion smiled at her, his eyes proud, even if he'd probably been exasperated with her at the time.

"As we've discussed, I'm not that wise." Kaylina stepped into the passageway, eager to shut the door, though it wasn't as if Milnor didn't know about it. Even if that had originally been Sabor's office, the spies had to know about every hidden passage and bolt-hole in the castle, if not in the entire city.

Vlerion paused before stepping fully in. He looked back at Shylea, raising his eyebrows.

"I'll stay and try to buy you a few minutes. I was supposed to report to him at the start of my shift tonight anyway."

"Very well. Be careful." Vlerion nodded gravely to her. "Milnor might not be as ruthless as Sabor, but I have no doubt he expects compliance."

"Oh, yes."

12

There are thoughts privately held that may not be publicly shared, not until the majority turns.

~ Abayar, founder Sandsteader Press

Vlerion pulled the hidden door to the spymaster's office shut, plunging the tight passageway into darkness. Still clasping Kaylina's hand, he led her a couple of steps toward the stairs, but she slipped out of his grip and stopped.

"Don't you want to hear what he says?" she whispered.

In the gloom, she sensed more than saw Vlerion turn. "He *knows* about this passage, and he'll know the guards didn't let me out the main door."

"Yeah, but—"

"And I don't know this castle well. We'll have to hide somewhere and escape later or get out before he raises—"

A door in the office thumped. "Where's Vlerion?"

Milnor.

Vlerion found Kaylina's hand and gripped it again, but she resisted being pulled away.

"Just for a minute," she breathed, well aware that Vlerion had the strength to hoist her over his shoulder and carry her.

"He wasn't here when I came in, spymaster," Shylea said.

"His *taybarri* didn't break him out."

"Uh, no, spymaster. I wouldn't think so. I came to report for tonight's duty. Does the prince's arrival change anything as far as my—"

"The taybarri *wanted* to break him out," Milnor said, raising his voice over hers. "I have no doubt. That male is his mount, and I think the female belongs to the Korbian girl. *She's* in the castle too."

"Ah, yes, spymaster. But the prince. Do we need to—"

"I want those two, and I want them executed," Milnor said. "The girl had a role in Sabor's death; I know it for a fact now. Spy Yevarro just got back from questioning Bloomlong. Korbian delivered the killing blow. The beast hurt Sabor, but *she* killed him. A commoner from some backward island down south. The *gall*."

Vlerion did as Kaylina had feared, stepping forward and hoisting her more easily than she'd picked up her bag of mead. She found herself draped over his shoulder with his arm around her legs and her face pressed into his back. Vlerion broke into a jog, somehow finding his way in the gloom without tripping or bumping her against the wall.

Only after he descended the stairs did she risk lifting her head and speaking. "How did the taybarri get in? They can't flash through gates, right?"

"Correct."

She imagined the portcullis ripped from its mounting hardware. A group of taybarri had done that before, after all. "Do you think we can ride out without being killed?"

"We'll see."

"Do you think we can stop in the kitchen for the mead I brought? If there's not going to be a tasting..."

"*No*."

"There were a lot of bottles of mead. I hadn't even opened them yet."

"No."

Vlerion set her down and pushed against a wooden portion of the wall, sliding something rectangular a couple of inches outward. Another bookcase? Or maybe a grandfather clock? Either way, it wasn't the entrance the staff had used.

Kaylina knew collecting her mead wasn't a priority—more than ever, she had to make sure Vlerion escaped the castle—but she couldn't help but wish she could retrieve it.

"Will you follow me the rest of the way out?" Vlerion asked quietly as someone ran past the clock, not noticing the way it was shifted slightly out from the wall. "Or do I need to carry you to the courtyard?"

"Is that where we are?"

They weren't near the kitchen where Kaylina had first entered the maze of hidden passageways. She had no idea where in the castle they *were*, but Vlerion had to know these routes better than he'd implied.

"We're not far from it," he whispered as someone else clattered past—a guard in chainmail with weapons jangling on his belt.

A roar sounded. That was Levitke.

"They're not being subtle, are they?" Kaylina whispered.

"Taybarri aren't known for that. You didn't answer my question." Vlerion put a hand on her waist.

"I can run."

"But *will* you?"

"There's nobody to eavesdrop on here."

Or so she thought. An irritated male voice came from the end of the hall, the direction opposite the roars. "Someone get those cursed beasts out of my courtyard. How did they get inside?"

"They won't let themselves be captured, Your Highness!" someone called.

"Then *shoot* them."

Vlerion growled. He didn't have his sword, but that didn't mean he wasn't a threat.

"They're taybarri, Your Highness," came the shocked response.

"Just get *rid* of them."

"Yes, Your Highness."

Another growl emanated from Vlerion's throat.

"Do you need to hum?" Kaylina whispered, resting a hand on his back.

"I might."

They waited for whatever guard had been responding to the prince to race down the hallway toward the roars. But nobody passed by the clock again. Maybe this hallway didn't connect to the courtyard after all?

Another ferocious roar sounded.

We're making our way out to you, Kaylina thought, imagining Levitke's face and willing the words to reach her. *Don't let yourselves be captured or shot, please. Otherwise, we'll need to escape on a geriatric donkey.*

The next roar sounded indignant as well as ferocious.

Vlerion risked pushing the clock farther from the wall and leaning out for a better look.

"The hall is empty," he said after a moment.

"That's... odd, isn't it?"

"Yes." But he slipped out, waving for her to follow.

Kaylina did but looked in the direction the prince had been shouting from. Though some more noises came from the end of the long hallway, he wasn't in view. Neither were any guards.

A whisper of cool night air, salty from the harbor, came from the same direction as the taybarri roars. Kaylina didn't have to be urged again to run after Vlerion as he headed toward an open door leading to the courtyard.

As she'd suspected, they were in a different part of the castle from the kitchen. Alas, there was no opportunity to pop in and retrieve her bottles.

"If they don't send my mead back," she whispered as she ran after Vlerion, "I'm going to have Frayvar send them an invoice."

"*That's* your biggest concern right now?" Vlerion glanced back, amused despite their predicament.

"Not my biggest, no, but it's *a* concern. The blackberry mead is really high quality."

"Aren't they all high quality?"

Kaylina lifted her chin. "Yes, they are."

Vlerion stopped at the door to the courtyard to look out.

"There are guards… but they're not trying to grab our taybarri. That stable boy holding his arm might have. Foolish."

"You don't try to grab a taybarri unless you have honey drops in your hand. Everyone should know that."

Vlerion leaned out farther. "The taybarri saw me and are heading this way. The gate is closed, but they've gotten through it before."

Crenoch and Levitke appeared, running toward them.

"Watch for weapons fire," Vlerion warned. "Get on and stay low."

"Got it," Kaylina said.

The taybarri stopped in front of the door, turning to bare their fangs at anyone who dared approach while offering their backs for their riders. Kaylina, afraid of guards on the ramparts who might have blunderbusses aimed at them, mounted as quickly as Vlerion. Night had fallen while she'd been inside, but there were lights aplenty in the courtyard for guards to take aim.

On Crenoch's back, Vlerion took the lead, the taybarri loping toward the gate, snarling menacingly as they went. Staying low, Kaylina glanced toward the castle walls as Levitke ran after them. There *were* guards up there, and they did have blunderbusses, as well as bows and swords, but she didn't see anyone with a weapon lifted.

When she and Vlerion approached the gate, the grumpy senior guard who'd reluctantly let Kaylina in before lifted an arm. But not to stop them. He pointed at someone, and the portcullis rolled up.

"Oops, it's malfunctioning, sir," the guard operating it called cheerfully. "*Again.*"

"We'll have the engineer check it in the morning," the senior guard said, standing aside so the taybarri could ride through.

One guard even stepped out to hand Kaylina's sword to her.

Vlerion lifted a hand toward them. Kaylina gaped at the guards. As the taybarri carried her and Vlerion toward the road that descended down the side of the plateau, her shoulders were tense. She expected at least *one* of the men to do as the prince had ordered and shoot them. True, the prince had ordered the taybarri shot, but Kaylina trusted he would like her and Vlerion dead too. Milnor, at the least, wanted that.

Despite her concerns, no weapons fire trailed them down from the plateau.

"What just happened?" Kaylina asked as they neared the bottom.

"King Gavatorin is dead," Vlerion said, as if that explained everything.

But he gazed thoughtfully back up at the castle as they rode into the city streets, and Kaylina didn't think he'd expected this outcome either.

13

Rejection perceived as spurn ensures future infernos doth burn.

~ *"The Mating Season" by the bard Nogorathi*

Despite Kaylina promising that the sentinel would *welcome* Vlerion, or at least allow him on the premises without launching vines toward his throat, he insisted on returning to ranger headquarters. No guards, assassins, mercenaries, or anyone else armed and angry chased them through the streets. A single horse-drawn carriage had come down the plateau after them, but it hadn't been in a hurry and might not have had anything to do with their departure. It was as if Kaylina and Vlerion had been released from the royal castle with heartfelt claps on the back and an invitation to return anytime, instead of riding out against the wishes of the queen, the prince, and the spymaster.

Admittedly, the queen hadn't seemed to care much about Vlerion's presence in the castle, and the prince's main objection had been roaring taybarri making too much noise in the courtyard. But Spymaster Milnor… he wanted Vlerion dead. No doubt there.

Again, Kaylina debated how to sway Vlerion to return to Stillguard Castle with her. The sentinel might not be willing to protect him, but it had proven it would protect her and the premises, and, as long as she stood next to Vlerion, that should include him. Further, fewer enemies might think to look for him there, at least at first.

"You needn't come with me," Vlerion said as they approached the gate to headquarters, a yawning ranger watching them approach. "I'm certain your brother wants your help, and I doubt Sergeant Zhani is waiting inside with practice blades to resume your training."

An eyebrow twitch was the only indication he gave that he knew there hadn't been any training whatsoever that day. It wasn't Kaylina's fault she'd been busy. Part of the time that she'd been busy, she'd been trying to rescue him.

"Frayvar *would* like my help—you know he's bereft without my presence—but he'd like *your* help too. Why don't you come back with me? I'll show you how to wash dishes. As a nobleman, you've probably never learned that important life skill."

"I've washed my mess kit numerous times while patrolling the mountain borders, and new rangers often help in the kitchen during their early years of training. If you haven't spent time at the sink here yet, I'll make sure the staffing sergeant knows you yearn to experience all aspects of rangerdom."

"Goodness, Vlerion. I invite you home so my cursed castle can protect you, and you fantasize about arranging extra duties for me. That's rude."

"As you've accused aristocrats of being before."

"Not without merit."

"Indeed." Vlerion smiled but didn't slow his mount as they rode up to the gate, the guard pushing it open for them.

If the young ranger knew Vlerion had been detained in the royal castle, he didn't comment on it. Kaylina hoped there wouldn't be further trouble that night but suspected the only reason it hadn't followed them down from the plateau was that Milnor hadn't yet learned Vlerion was gone.

In the courtyard, Vlerion pulled Crenoch to an abrupt stop. Levitke almost ran into his rump. She *did* step on his tail, which resulted in him turning his head and snapping his teeth at her. She bared her own teeth, then phhhted her tongue against them.

"You were right to expect trouble," Vlerion told Kaylina, ignoring the interplay between the taybarri and looking at a black carriage in the center of the courtyard. Four beautiful stallions were harnessed to it.

"Is that it?"

Vlerion grunted. "Probably."

There was nothing remarkable about the carriage except that six Castle Guards were stationed around it. Across the courtyard, the door to the office building opened, and Captain Targon jogged out. He noticed Vlerion and Kaylina—glancing twice and seeming surprised at their presence—but headed toward the carriage without hesitation.

Its door opened, and a cloaked person with a fur-trimmed hood covering his face stepped out. Or was that *her* face? The cloak made it hard to tell until the woman held up a hand toward Targon while looking at Vlerion.

From that angle, enough lamps burned around the courtyard to reveal her face. Queen Petalira.

"Uh-oh," Kaylina muttered, worried the woman had found out that she'd eavesdropped and wasn't pleased about it.

But how could she have beaten them here? She must have left the castle right after they had and taken another route, the driver hurrying to beat them here. Maybe she'd even been in the stable, getting ready to depart while Vlerion and Kaylina had ridden out.

Was this the carriage they'd seen coming down from the plateau behind them?

Petalira's gaze remained on Vlerion. She didn't look at Kaylina, didn't acknowledge her in any way.

Vlerion lifted his chin with his usual haughty aristocratic pride. Since *he* hadn't been eavesdropping, he wouldn't have a guilty conscience about it.

"Can we help you... my lady?" Targon asked, not drawing attention to her rank—her identity—since she'd come incognito.

"I have a proposition for Lord Vlerion," Petalira said.

"For Lord... Vlerion?" Did Targon sound offended? Since *he'd* been the recipient of the queen's... propositions before?

Kaylina doubted Petalira had sex in mind tonight. Even if she thought Vlerion, who was thirty years her junior, would be open to that, she'd admitted she knew about the beast curse. She wouldn't be foolish enough to try to entice him into her bed.

At least Kaylina thought. And hoped. She couldn't keep from frowning at Petalira.

"Yes. It has nothing to do with you, Captain. I will speak with Lord Vlerion in private." For the first time, Petalira looked at Kaylina but only to frown at her.

Targon also looked at Kaylina, but all he said was, "You can use my office, my lady."

"Lord Vlerion?" Petalira extended her hand in the direction of the two-story building.

Stiff and with palpable reluctance, Vlerion slid off Crenoch's back.

Kaylina also dismounted and stepped toward Vlerion, as if to take Crenoch and Levitke to the stable together. The taybarri were smart enough to do that themselves, but it gave her a reason to get close to Vlerion.

"I should have gone home with you," he murmured.

"*Obviously.*"

He gave her a wry look.

"It's not too late to run. The gate is still open." Kaylina kept herself from saying the sentinel would be delighted to threaten Petalira if she and her men pursued them. It probably wasn't appropriate to fantasize about such things, even if the queen had once had her thrown into the dungeon.

"I'll see what she's here to *propose*."

"Not what she proposes to Targon, I hope," Kaylina said.

Vlerion snorted. "I shall also hope that."

Petalira folded her arms over her chest, doubtless not used to being kept waiting. She looked like she might command Targon or maybe her guards to assist Vlerion in walking more swiftly to the office. But he touched Kaylina's arm, then headed in that direction before the queen could start issuing orders.

Cloak sweeping over the stone ground of the courtyard, Petalira moved to walk at Vlerion's side. She rested her arm on his as they strode toward the office building.

Kaylina stared, surprised by the familiarity. From her eavesdropping, she hadn't gotten the impression that the queen liked Vlerion.

Targon stepped back to make room for them to pass. If the touching surprised him, he didn't show it, but he *did* watch it, his gaze trailing them as they entered the office building and headed up the stairs by the door.

Kaylina absently patted Crenoch and Levitke while debating if she might eavesdrop on another conversation tonight. Since she'd twice listened from the back entrance to Targon's office, she knew how to get to it, but... with the captain standing in front of the door, it wasn't as if she could amble in.

She willed him to go away, but, not surprisingly, nothing happened. Sadly, there weren't any trees nearby. If one had been planted by the office building, she might have convinced it to whack him with a branch, but there were only two in the courtyard, and they were on the far side. Alas, fantasizing about one's superiors being mangled by branches was probably also not appropriate.

"I'm going to try to listen in on that conversation," Kaylina whispered to the taybarri. "Can you guys feed and groom yourselves?"

This time, they both made phhht noises with their tongues, but they sashayed in the direction of the stable. Levitke paused to use a rear foot to scratch her belly. By luck, or more likely design, she positioned herself to block the six guards' view of the office building.

Kaylina walked in that direction, taking the assistance as a sign that Levitke approved of her plan to eavesdrop. Crenoch also paused, whuffing a few times at the stallions hitched to the carriage. They were amiable whuffs, but the horses looked at him with wide eyes. Taybarri were, after all, predators. The exchange drew the attention of the guards.

Unfortunately, Targon remained outside the office building, and his gaze swung from the door to the taybarri and finally to Kaylina as she approached. His eyes narrowed, and she had a feeling he knew right away that Crenoch and Levitke were helping her.

"I need to use the lavatory," she told him.

"As you know, there are several nearby and appropriate for the use of trainee rangers." Targon pointed toward a door by the stable.

"Yes, but I prefer the one in the visiting officer quarters." Kaylina pointed through the door toward the end of the hall where that suite accessed the secret passageway that led to his office. There wasn't much point in coming up with a more convoluted excuse—he would see through anything she said.

"I'll bet. You're a pain in the ass, Korbian."

"As you've mentioned numerous times before."

"I keep waiting for Vlerion to flog some reverence into you, an amount appropriate to your *menial* station in life."

He'd mentioned that numerous times before too.

"Earlier, he suggested extra duties such as dish washing to me."

"Good."

"I need to find out what's going on," Kaylina said. "I overheard Spymaster Milnor talking to the queen in the castle."

Targon grunted without surprise at her admission of eaves-dropping.

"Look, it's important. Milnor wants Vlerion dead, and Petalira wants… I don't know what exactly, but she doesn't like Vlerion."

"Oh, I'm aware of what she likes and doesn't like."

Right, they slept together regularly.

"She may be planning to get rid of him right now, when they're alone." Kaylina stepped closer to Targon, wishing she dared lunge past him to the door, but he was a strong and fit ranger. He would have no trouble stopping her. "Sabor had potions that he could fling around. Maybe she's got something similar. He's noble and wouldn't raise a hand against her, even if he was in danger."

Kaylina didn't believe Petalira could kill Vlerion, but she would throw out anything and everything she could think of that might sway Targon. Even if the captain didn't adore her, he liked Vlerion and tried to protect him.

Targon sighed, glanced toward the taybarri still blocking the view of the guards, then gripped her elbow. "Come on."

Though startled by the touch, Kaylina followed him into the building. Targon kept the grip as he walked down the hall with her. She was tempted to object to his unwelcome touch, but they were going in the direction she wanted. She must have bristled and glared noticeably, however, because he released her.

"I suppose if I'm too handsy with you, you'll convince one of the trees around headquarters to fall on me," he said.

"I *was* lamenting that there are only two in the courtyard."

"I don't doubt it." Targon didn't sound worried. "Good thing I got rid of the potted plants in here that my predecessor liked. He thought rangers should embrace nature. I prefer to embrace it outdoors."

He led her into the suite she'd mentioned, heading for the secret door at the back. He opened it and stepped inside.

Kaylina hesitated. She hadn't imagined Targon eavesdropping *with* her. When she'd been alone in the dark passageway with Vlerion, she hadn't worried, but Targon ogled her chest far too often for her to want to be alone in the dark with him.

He paused and looked back, maybe guessing the reason for her hesitation. A gentleman would have promised not to touch her or do anything untoward. *He* leered at her chest, his eyes glinting with humor.

"How badly do you want to listen?" he asked.

"You're an ass. My lord."

Targon's eyes slitted at the insult. "And you're *so* in need of flogging. If I didn't think—*know*—Vlerion would be furious—and dangerous—I'd handle your discipline myself."

"Does your sister know how often you fantasize about beating women?"

"It's trainee rangers and upstart commoners that need a firm hand, not women specifically. And I'd ask when you met Shylea, but they're already talking, I'm sure." He pointed toward the passageway ahead, then headed up it, leaving her to decide how badly she wanted to listen in.

"Badly," Kaylina muttered, then braced herself and followed Targon into the dark.

14

A CLEAR HEAD AND A CALM DEMEANOR MUST BE ADOPTED TO DEAL WITH those who manipulate.

~ "Royalty and Politics" Scribe Menalow

Kaylina crept through the dark passageway, her fingers on the dusty wall for guidance. She remembered how to get to Targon's office but couldn't see a thing and worried about bumping into obstacles. At night, with few others in the building, sounds would carry.

She found the stairs and climbed, not encountering Targon. He hadn't waited for her.

When she stepped onto the landing at the top, the sound of voices reaching her ear, she swept out with her arm, not wanting to run into him. The air was empty, the landing so quiet that she wondered if he'd turned somewhere along the way, heading to another spot from which to eavesdrop.

"You don't think Targon will mind, do you?" Petalira's voice came distinctly through the bookcase that marked the hidden entrance to the captain's office.

"He will, but he won't say anything to you about it, Your Majesty." Vlerion's tone was distant and aloof, his voice coming from the far side of the office. It sounded like he was lingering by the door while the queen wandered around, doing who knew what.

"I wouldn't have expected to be able to experience such delight in the office of someone as rough and uncouth as he."

Kaylina glanced into the darkness, as if she could see Targon and gauge his response to being called uncouth, but not a sound came from the landing, and she again questioned if he was there with her.

"Do you enjoy such experiences, Lord Vlerion?" Petalira patted something. The desk? A chair?

Kaylina frowned. The queen wasn't suggesting they have sex in the office, was she?

No. It was silly to keep thinking the queen was here for that reason. Just because she slept with Targon didn't mean she wanted the same from Vlerion. Even if she *did*, Kaylina didn't need to worry about Vlerion giving in to her. He was… they were… Well, if anyone was going to get to have sex with Vlerion, she was, damn it.

"I do not," he stated.

"Never? Do you worry about losing your… equanimity?"

There was a long pause. Was that the queen's way of telling him she knew his secret?

"I do prefer to keep my mind sharp and my emotions in check," Vlerion said coolly.

"Even in bed?"

If Vlerion answered, it was with his face instead of words. Kaylina clenched her jaw, wishing she could spring out there and stand in front of Vlerion to protect him from whatever feminine wiles Petalira was attempting to employ.

But Vlerion, she told herself firmly, didn't need protecting. Only if something happened that threatened to bring out the beast might she have justification to intervene.

Something clinked softly in the office. A bottle against a glass?

The faintest of exhales—more a slight grunt of understanding than a sigh—came from the corner of the landing. Targon *was* up there.

"Are you sure you don't want some?" Petalira asked, and Kaylina realized she'd poured a drink. *That* was what she'd been talking about.

"I'm sure."

"It may make my proposal sound more appealing."

"Then I'm *certain* I don't want any alcohol."

Petalira laughed, the sound rich but not entirely genuine. Maybe she didn't want to be here, proposing… whatever she intended to propose. Was it possible she was *nervous*?

"So mistrustful, Lord Vlerion." A pause followed as Petalira sipped from her drink. Or maybe gulped down a deep and bracing amount. "You're aware, I trust, that my son has returned home."

"I heard."

"Enrikon has made it clear he doesn't believe I should continue to have a role in running the kingdom, even though I've spent the last ten years having a great deal to do with the daily decision-making and long-term planning. Gavatorin had been losing his sharpness for years, though we kept it from the public, to honor him."

"And so the public would believe the decisions being made were his," Vlerion stated.

"As the king, *his* decisions were never questioned."

Not exactly a *yes* but it amounted to the same.

"Enrikon," Petalira continued, "believes he'll simply unwind everything we've been working toward and be the sole decision-maker going forward. Never mind that he spent his youth evading his tutors and has had *no* involvement with running the kingdom these past years. His father wanted him to show more interest, to start to take on duties in the government, but he wasn't inclined." She took an audible drink. "Until now."

Vlerion said nothing. He had to be wondering why she was telling him all this. *Kaylina* wondered why.

"One isn't supposed to speak ill of one's children," Petalira continued, "but it is what it is. He's thirty and acts like a boy. He would run the kingdom into ruin. I don't intend to let that happen."

"Your Majesty," Vlerion said, "if your proposal tonight is to hire me to assassinate him, that is not an assignment I would accept. I am certain Spymaster Sabor left a book of contacts with an extensive list of people who could take on the duty, should someone who was in your employ not be willing to do it."

"I'm not looking to have my son *killed,* Lord Vlerion." She truly sounded horrified.

Too bad. The prince had been snotty. Kaylina doubted anyone would miss him.

"Then what?"

"For the senior lords and ladies to come together, as is their right in our government doctrines, to reject Enrikon's claim to the throne and instead stand behind another. Enrikon could return to his life of avarice and ease, and I would even continue the exceedingly generous allowance that his father approved for him, however galling it is for the kingdom's money to go to that."

"You would," Vlerion said, his tone flat.

"Yes, me. I know what you're thinking, that *my* blood, though aristocratic, is not *royal*, that my only claim to power has been through my husband. That is all true." Her voice grew bitter when she added, "As I'm well aware. As those I've sought support from have already told me. The aristocrats would not back me as the situation stands. Even though it is right for the kingdom. They know that. *You* must also know it. You've met Enrikon."

"Numerous times," Vlerion said.

"You can't tell me you want to serve him."

Vlerion didn't answer. Kaylina wished she dared slide the bookcase open a couple of inches so she could see their faces, but it was so quiet in the building... She couldn't risk even a whisper of noise.

"But you'd have to. If Enrikon is coronated, your oath as a ranger that you swore to King Gavatorin and the kingdom would extend to him."

"I'm aware."

A long silence fell, and Kaylina imagined the queen staring intently across the office at Vlerion.

"You've a blood tie to the throne. A *direct* blood tie. If Enrikon had not come into existence, the nobles would have asked if your family wanted to return to rule before reaching out to those with weaker ties. And since you are the only male left alive in your line..."

"What is it that you want from me, Your Majesty?" Vlerion asked.

"I wish to propose to you, Lord Vlerion." Vlerion must have given her a blank look because Petalira clarified. "I wish to *wed* you, Lord Vlerion."

Kaylina's jaw descended, possibly all the way to the floor.

"You what?" Vlerion sounded almost as stunned.

"The nobles will back you if I tell them to," Petalira said, "and if we were to marry, nothing would change for me. I'd have the same power, the same right to make decisions, even if they still had to be in my husband's name." That bitterness lingered in her voice.

Kaylina realized this was a move of desperation for her. How not? Petalira didn't like Vlerion. She couldn't want to marry him and let him take the credit for whatever she did, the same as Gavatorin must have.

"I have no desire to marry you, Your Majesty." Vlerion was back to cool and calm.

"I have no doubt, but we do what we must for the good of the kingdom."

"You assume your influence has been good for the kingdom? When there have been riots, invasions, and assassination attempts? In this year alone?"

"The existence of the scheming, power-hungry *Virts* doesn't mean I've not been a good queen. Besides, it's not as if I've made decisions alone. You know Sabor had a hand in things, and Lord Grifhan has blackmailed his way into a position of power. And Gavatorin's hand-selected Lord of Foreign Affairs butts in on a daily basis." Sounding exasperated, Petalira took a deep breath—and possibly another drink—before continuing. "If you joined me, we could push them out. You must have ideas. I... wouldn't insist that you be a figurehead." Despite the words, her tone made it sound like a figurehead was exactly what she wanted. "I would be open to ruling jointly, as long as I continued to have a place and influence in areas that I consider important. What do you say, Lord Vlerion?"

Another long silence fell.

Kaylina stared into the darkness, again wishing she could see their faces. She didn't think Vlerion would consider this, but she couldn't help but hold her breath, waiting for his answer.

"I have no desire to rule, Your Majesty, nor do I wish to wed you."

"I already told you," Petalira snapped, frustration bubbling over, "it's not about what you want. It's for the good of the kingdom. As a ranger, it's your duty to work toward that end."

"But it is not my duty to marry you."

"If you're worried about your buxom little female, I don't care about her. Rut with her every night if you wish. Just come to the royal bedchamber often enough that the staff doesn't gossip, so others believe we have a legitimate marriage. I'm not *that* old and dreadful. Just ask your captain."

"We do not discuss sex."

Petalira snorted. "*All* men discuss sex. Often and crudely. Listen, I slept with Gavatorin, by the grace of the most patient gods, even though he was a wizened raisin who could barely find his cock with his own hand."

Kaylina swallowed, getting more details than she'd bargained for—than she'd wanted—during this eavesdropping session.

"You'd be severely less tortured being with me," Petalira added. "You might even find my experience makes up for my lack of youth, though, if I've gotten the gist from the snatches of conversations I've heard, we might not want you to find the experience too stimulating."

"Queen Petalira," Vlerion said, a hint of exasperation creeping into his earlier detached calm, "I will not marry you. If I wanted the throne, I wouldn't need to wed you to make a claim on it."

Yes. Kaylina clenched a fist. That was a good point. If she grasped the political history well enough, he had as much of a claim as Prince Enrikon.

"You would find the route to obtaining it easier with my assistance," Petalira said stiffly. "Do not think that just because a few guards looked the other way when you fled the castle to escape my spymaster that you would have everyone's support. I'm experienced. I could guide you. You've proven yourself a heroic ranger fighting in the city and on the borders, but you're a young man who's rarely at court. You'd need guidance, advisors. People you could trust."

Only the need to stay silent kept Kaylina from scoffing. As if Vlerion could trust Petalira.

"That young mead-making frill can't advise you on anything," the queen added.

The need to stay silent also kept Kaylina from throwing aside the bookcase, springing into the office, and strangling the queen.

"Your Majesty," Vlerion said. "Kaylina is far from a frill, and you would have been better served making a friend of her. Regardless, I will not consider your offer. Let us finish this meeting."

"Yes, let us. But one last word for you to think over. Spymaster Milnor, as it presently stands, believes you were responsible for his predecessor's death, and he wants you dead. He has the means to make that happen."

"Sabor also thought he had the means to make that happen," Vlerion said coolly, "and Sabor is dead."

"Not by your hand. I've talked to Jana Bloomlong. I know what happened in that alley. He threw some potion and knocked you out. You would be *dead* if not for the girl stepping in."

"The girl with the power of the ancient druids."

"So I understand. Strange to think that such a ditzy young thing has power of any sort. At least she's loyal to you, eh, Vlerion? I hope you're tonguing her to climax multiple times every night, because she deserves a good time for standing at the side of someone so practiced at making enemies."

Kaylina almost rocked back, cheeks flaming at the turn in the discussion, at such bluntness about sex coming from a royal. How could Vlerion—all the rangers, for that matter—have ever sworn loyalty to these people? None of them deserved the rangers *or* the taybarri.

A faint click sounded. A door opening?

"You will leave now, Your Majesty." Vlerion gave the order in the same tone that he used when he commanded his rangers.

"Do not also make an enemy of me, Lord Vlerion," Petalira said, ice in her tone. "Even if the king is dead, it's not acceptable for you to give me orders."

"Then it will be even more unacceptable if I carry you over my shoulder and toss you into your carriage."

"It's a mystery as to why people want you dead."

"It is," he said agreeably.

The door thumped shut.

Trusting the queen had left, Kaylina slumped backward, thinking she would find the wall to lean against for support. Instead, she encountered Targon and jerked away. He must have moved closer to hear better. She *hoped* that was the only reason he'd moved closer.

"Careful," he said, sounding far more amused by the situation than she, "all that talk of tongues and climaxes got me excited. I won't be able to contain myself if you rub up against me."

"That's *not* what I was doing."

The bookcase slid aside, lantern light brightening the landing and revealing Vlerion's silhouette. Kaylina sprang into his arms, possibly an overly dramatic gesture. She told herself she was disturbed by the queen's threats, not because she'd accidentally bumped into Targon. Hugging Vlerion was a natural reaction to the situation he found himself in.

He wrapped an arm around her while glaring at Targon, who remained on the landing, arms folded across his chest as he casually leaned against the wall. "Relax, Vlerion. And don't give me your beast eyes. I didn't touch her."

Kaylina leaned back to look into Vlerion's face, afraid his eyes *would* have the glint that signaled the beast might soon rouse. She hadn't meant to alarm him.

But he merely looked irked. Probably with the queen and the day's events more than with his captain.

"I was a perfect gentleman," Targon added, strolling into the office.

He frowned at a bottle of expensive whiskey sitting open on the desk next to a half-full tumbler. Was *that* what the queen had been drinking? Straight? She *had* needed bracing for that conversation.

"Be careful if you marry her," Targon said. "She likes her drink and gets demanding in bed once she's fortified herself with it."

"I expected to find Kaylina eavesdropping back there," Vlerion said, squeezing her to let her know he hadn't minded. "I didn't think *you'd* listen in."

"I like to know what shenanigans are being discussed in my own office. Korbian also told me that Milnor wants you dead. She thought the *queen* might want you dead too. I imagine this was a surprise." Targon smirked at Kaylina.

Was he truly amused by all this?

"To all of us." Vlerion released Kaylina and looked at her. "You were right. I should have gone with you to your castle. Maybe I still should. Then your plant could wave its vines at anyone who comes by, wanting to embroil me in plans to further their ambitions."

"You think more people might proposition you?" Targon sat in his seat, tossing his legs up on the desk. "Or should I say *propose* to you? Lord Grifhan and Sabor used to hang out. Maybe Grifhan wouldn't mind a husband."

"I prefer your dour moods to your jubilant ones, Captain," Vlerion said.

"I'm positive nobody has ever said that before, certainly nobody I command."

"And yet, it's a truth."

Kaylina patted Vlerion on the chest. "You're very welcome to come stay at Stillguard Castle, but I can't promise the sentinel will attack conniving aristocrats unless they threaten me. I talked it into letting people come in since I didn't want potential customers being scared away. Or killed."

"She admits she talks to plants, and you still want her in your arms," Targon said. "It's been fascinating watching this relationship develop."

"The plants talk back," Vlerion said.

"Oh, I believe it."

"I'll chat with it and see about adding conniving aristocrats to the list of forbidden people," Kaylina said, hoping Vlerion *would* come back with her. "If nothing else, the castle's reputation might make them think twice about approaching you there."

"Yes." Vlerion looked wistful.

"You'll enjoy staying there. There aren't skeletons in any of the rooms anymore, and it's been weeks since the castle moaned or a chandelier fell." Kaylina glanced at a clock. "Even better, we're about halfway through the hours of the dinner service, so those dishes I mentioned will be piling up in the sink." She patted his chest again. "Frayvar and I would love your strong ranger arms to assist with them."

Targon blinked. "You're going to wash dishes for her?"

"To escape proposals? I might."

Targon looked shocked—or maybe scandalized. Did the queen not ask him to perform domestic duties after sleeping over?

"I've washed dishes for you, Captain," Vlerion pointed out.

"*All* trainees wash dishes for the kitchen. Except, now that I think about it, I don't think *she* has. How have you escaped that duty, Korbian?"

"I suspect my training has been atypical."

Targon grunted. "*You're* atypical."

"Yes, she is." Vlerion smiled and rested a hand on Kaylina's shoulder.

Though she was aware of Targon watching them, she couldn't keep from leaning into Vlerion, loving that he didn't mind that she wasn't normal. And she loved that he wasn't normal either.

"I can't imagine what you've done to earn it," Targon said, "but she looks at you a lot more adoringly than Petalira does."

"She's a much more appealing soul than the queen is." Vlerion wrapped an arm around Kaylina again.

"I can't deny that. Even if she's mouthy and only says *my lord* when she wants something from me. Like access to my secret passage." Targon smirked as if that was supposed to be a sexual innuendo. Knowing him, it probably was. "You'll stay at ranger headquarters though, Vlerion. As much as the idea of you wearing an apron and washing dishes tickles me, nothing has changed. You can feel the tension when you walk through the city, and now that the prince is back... it's going to get tenser. The rangers will likely be needed at some point to deal with protestors and plotters."

"Stillguard Castle isn't far." Kaylina gripped Vlerion's arm, wanting him close.

She didn't believe he needed her—or her castle—to protect him, especially when her earlier *rescue* had been unnecessary. But now that he was of interest to people, for far more than his abilities as a ranger, she couldn't help but want to be close to him, to watch out for him. And it was possible the sentinel *could* help if enemies desiring to do more than wed him showed up.

"It's far enough," Targon said, "and the rest of our rangers still can't go in there, right?"

"I wouldn't advise it," Kaylina said.

"*You* can stay in headquarters here, if you two want to be close, but since Vlerion is always on the edge of losing control around you, I can't imagine you two are doing as much with tongues as the queen thinks."

A low growl in Vlerion's throat promised he didn't want his captain discussing their sex life—or lack thereof. Kaylina agreed wholeheartedly, even if she didn't growl.

A soft knock sounded at the door.

"What?" Targon looked at the clock, exasperation crossing his face.

Past his bedtime, was it?

The corporal who'd been guarding the gate earlier poked his head inside. "There's someone to see Lord Vlerion, Captain?"

"Someone *else*?" Targon asked.

"Yes, my lord. The woman we weren't supposed to know is the queen has left with her guards, but another woman showed up. She's wearing a cloak and was being furtive and wouldn't give us her name, but she has a newspaper and said Lord Vlerion would want to see it. It, uhm, has his name in it."

The corporal looked at Vlerion but quickly shifted his gaze toward the floor. Embarrassed? No... He almost looked scared.

Something told Kaylina he'd seen more than Vlerion's name in the newspaper.

15

The obvious maelstrom on the horizon gives us less trouble than the surprise gust that knocks into us from behind.
~ Elder Taybarri Ravarn

Kaylina stuck to Vlerion's side as they descended the stairs to leave the office building. She had a hunch about the identity of the furtive woman but didn't know how Jana Bloomlong would have gotten a newspaper that nobody else had seen yet. Kaylina *assumed* nobody had seen it. If a story about Vlerion had gone out that morning, a story with something in it capable of alarming that corporal, all the rangers would have been talking about it.

Boots clomped wearily on the stairs behind as Targon trailed them.

"If this new woman proposes to Vlerion," he said, "I'm going to start to get envious that I don't get that kind of attention from the opposite sex. I'm twice as handsome as he is."

"You're also twice as old as I am." It didn't sound like Vlerion's heart was in the banter. His eyes were grave as they walked into the courtyard.

The cloaked woman had come on a single horse and stood near the gate with it, another corporal watching her from a few feet away. She didn't carry any obvious weapons, only what looked like the front page of a newspaper, the single sheet rustling in a breeze.

A boulder of dread thunked down in Kaylina's gut.

"Jana Bloomlong," Vlerion stated without surprise as they approached.

"Lord Vlerion." Jana pushed her hood back, revealing lean features and thick gray hair clasped back from her temples. Jana looked sourly at Kaylina. "I should have known your clingy conniving female would be at your side."

"Is there a reason other women all have to call me names and put me down?" Kaylina asked, though she focused on the newspaper, more worried about Vlerion than defending herself. It appeared to be only the front page, as she'd thought, not an entire edition.

"They are envious of your beauty and the power the gods have granted you," Vlerion said.

"I think my father granted me that stuff."

The father she longed to meet. Speaking of envy, she felt a touch of it herself, knowing that her older sister had met Kaylina's father when she never had.

"The only thing I'm envious of is her ability to get honey made from altered plants," Jana grumbled. "*That's* the single difference in our mead. It has nothing to do with recipes or ability."

Kaylina didn't think that was true, but said, "There's honey in the preserve. The bees there defend their hives and have stung the taybarri, but maybe they'll like you more than them."

No chance. The taybarri were delightful. And Jana Bloomlong was the opposite of that.

"Maybe I *will* look for that honey. But not now. I came to speak with Lord Vlerion on another matter, tomorrow's edition of the newspaper. I was able to get an early copy." Jana smiled at Kaylina instead of Vlerion.

Kaylina grimaced, certain *she* was the reason Jana was here, trying to blackmail Vlerion or whatever she planned. She hadn't succeeded in having Stillguard Castle shut down or Kaylina executed. Was she now going to hurt Kaylina by hurting the man she cared about?

"Have your slowed mead sales forced you to take on a paper route?" Kaylina bared her teeth, not caring that she sounded snotty.

"My *sales* are fine. I have friends in the city, as well as in the royal castle, friends who keep me apprised on many matters."

Kaylina knew it was petty, but she hoped Jana learned that the head of the royal kitchen staff was shopping around for a new mead supplier.

Jana looked around the courtyard, making sure no rangers lurked close, then handed the newspaper page to Vlerion. The corporal was still watching her, but he wouldn't be able to read the words from there. Targon also remained in the area, keeping an eye on them, but he wasn't interfering. Not yet.

Vlerion squinted at Jana, then walked to a lamp mounted on a wall to read the article. Kaylina went with him, and he held the paper so she could see it.

She glimpsed her own name and sucked in a startled breath. It was down on the bottom corner, something about the grand opening of the Deep Sea Honeybee, the name Frayvar had given their eating house and put on the menu, despite everyone continuing to call it Stillguard Castle or—worse—the cursed castle.

As she tried to read that corner article—Vlerion had let it dangle as he focused on the larger story above—she realized it wasn't the one the corporal had mentioned. It wasn't the reason

Jana had come. Kaylina caught the words *mouthwateringly delicious* but made herself focus on the main article. As soon as she did, she slumped.

It started out with the first line all in caps: RANGER LORD VLERION CURSED BY DRUIDS TO BECOME A DEADLY BEAST. It didn't get better from there, going into great detail describing the creature he became and the great power he commanded to kill. Jana must have blabbed to a journalist, just as she had the queen.

Not only did the article identify Vlerion as a cursed killer beast, but it said he'd murdered Spymaster Sabor and was a threat to anyone who crossed him.

Kaylina looked toward Jana, surprised the article blamed Vlerion for the spymaster's demise. She'd assumed Jana had witnessed what really happened.

"Oh, did you want credit for Sabor's death?" Jana asked, as if she knew the exact line that Kaylina was on. Jana sneered. "You're getting credit for enough. I couldn't get Lord Havak to take that other article out. Enjoy the free publicity." Her gaze shifted to Vlerion. "Meanwhile, I hope you, Lord Ranger, enjoy having the populace of the entire city hunting you down. And your fellow rangers should go after you too when they find out." She waved to indicate the headquarters building, then lowered her voice, almost to a growl. "While you're fleeing for your life, maybe you'll have second thoughts about who you get into bed with." She squinted at Kaylina.

Kaylina tensed, tempted to spring over and throttle the woman.

This wasn't some back-alley newspaper printed up by rogue operators. Across the top read *Kingdom Crier*, the same newspaper that Kaylina had once read regularly for the Queen's Corner. Distributed throughout Zaldor, it was the most read paper in the kingdom, if not in the world.

"This hasn't been published yet." Vlerion pointed to the next day's date at the top.

"It will be distributed in the morning," Jana said, "unless..."

"What do you want?" Vlerion asked.

She smiled. No doubt, she'd been waiting for the satisfaction of having him ask. "I want you and your rangers to destroy the cursed castle that's been allowed to fester like an open sore in our city for far too long. And I want *her*—" Jana pointed at Kaylina's nose, "—out of business. At least, send her back to where she came from to distribute her druids-tainted drink there."

Vlerion lowered the paper and stared at Jana, his face flinty.

"If you do that," Jana said, "I'll talk Lord Havak into removing the article and printing something else. He only has that story because of me, and I told him I retained the right to have it removed if I wished. That's our deal. But if I don't return to him, he'll send it out, as is. To everyone in the kingdom. By dawn, it'll be in people's hands. Unless you agree to my terms and round up your rangers with all the explosives they'll need." Her pointing finger shifted in the direction of Stillguard Castle.

Kaylina, after seeing the sentinel shoot deadly purple beams out to kill Kar'ruk invaders, doubted Jana's plan would work even if Vlerion agreed to it. Which he wouldn't. Kaylina didn't know when she had come to know him so well, and to know his heart, but she did.

"Print your paper," Vlerion said coolly. "I will not be blackmailed. Not by you or anyone else."

Targon walked over, and Kaylina jumped. She'd forgotten they weren't alone.

He took the page from Vlerion to read it.

"This is the only chance I'm giving you." Jana looked at Targon as well as Vlerion. Did she think his captain would convince him that being blackmailed was a good idea?

Targon only grunted and handed the paper back to Vlerion,

who remained flint-faced and said nothing more. His muscles were tight though. Some part of him had to want to throttle the woman—*all* the people who were trying to manipulate him.

When her words fell on deaf ears, Jana finally looked at Kaylina, as if she might sway him.

Her gut knotted. If she wanted to, Kaylina very well *might* sway Vlerion. She hated the idea of giving up all that she and Frayvar had accomplished, and her heart protested the thought of giving up Vlerion. And that was what she would be doing if she left. His home was here, his career as a ranger, his duty to defend the kingdom and the crown—whether they deserved his loyalty or not.

But Kaylina teetered, wondering if it would be selfish to refuse to give up what she wanted for his sake. To make sure his secret remained safe and that the entire city wasn't targeting him.

Jana arched her eyebrows, waiting.

Vlerion noticed their held gazes and looked at Kaylina. Maybe he also saw the indecision in her eyes because he shook his head before speaking again to Jana.

"You will leave now, and be grateful the rangers are not arresting you. It is a crime to attempt to blackmail a kingdom subject, even more so an aristocrat."

Jana glowered at him and at Targon. "It's a crime to turn into a beast and slay innocent people. You'll be the one arrested when this comes out—or *executed*—and the rangers who knew about it will be suspect in the eyes of the law too."

"So be it," Vlerion said.

Targon didn't respond to the threat, though his eyes had grown wishful at Vlerion's mention of arresting Jana to deal with the problem. But, if her words were true, that wouldn't stop the distribution of the *Kingdom Crier*.

Jana stood in place, fuming for several long seconds. Kaylina realized she didn't care that much about Vlerion's secret. All she wanted was for her scheme to work so she could get rid of Kaylina and her mead, the threat to Jana's continued business success.

Kaylina glared at her. Too bad.

Jana opened her mouth to try who knew what else, but the ground shuddered.

"Another earthquake," someone called.

Targon and Vlerion remained calm, maybe not believing they had anything to worry about in the open courtyard. Kaylina braced herself, not trusting that the shaking wouldn't get worse.

Glass jars broke in the infirmary, and curses came from the barracks. The taybarri pawed and snorted in the stable. Wood snapped in one of the buildings, and the crash of furniture falling over reached them.

Jana didn't run—alas—but she did look warily around. "They always come in groups, don't they?"

Earthquakes? Kaylina had no idea what was normal.

"The last time a number of quakes struck the city," Vlerion said, "I was a little boy, and the Bushtop volcano erupted." Vlerion pointed toward the northeast where the Evardor Mountains loomed.

"Just what we need to add to the chaos," Targon said as the quaking grew less noticeable. "A volcano erupting. Bushtop took out one of the mountain villages with its flow, and it was years before all the ash here washed away."

When the quaking fully subsided, Jana looked at them again, as if she would resume her blackmail attempt.

But Targon made a shooing motion. "Go home, woman."

Jana hesitated, clearly reluctant to give in to defeat, then huffed dramatically and stalked out the gate with her horse.

Vlerion calmly ripped the newspaper. Kaylina thought he would shred it into dozens of pieces and toss it into a fire, but he was carefully tearing out the corner. The article about her and her mead, she realized. He handed it to her and *then* destroyed the rest of the page.

Touched by the simple gesture, the confirmation that he knew what was important to her, she stepped closer and leaned against him.

"Come with me to Stillguard tonight," she said, then, aware of Targon watching, added, "Please, my lord."

Targon snorted, no doubt aware that the tacked-on honorific was for his sake. "Nice that she says *please* and doesn't just use her powers to force you to comply."

Vlerion lifted his gaze toward the stars. Thinking about how annoying his captain's snark was? Or how irritating all these people trying to manipulate him were? Maybe both. But he slid his arm around Kaylina, silently promising that he wasn't frustrated with her.

She was glad, because she couldn't help but think about how this wouldn't be happening if her mead-making business had never begun. If she'd never come to Port Jirador.

"More seriously," Targon said, "you might want to leave the area for a while. When that gets printed..."

"*Now* you say I can leave ranger headquarters?" Vlerion's tone was more bitter than dry.

Targon lifted his head. "If you want to stay, we'll protect you from whatever comes of that, but it will be easier if whatever guards, bounty hunters, or assassins that people conjure up don't know where you are. If nothing else were going on, I would recommend you travel farther than the cursed castle a mile away, but..."

"I will not flee the city when you may need my sword." Vlerion looked at Targon. "I *will* go to Stillguard Castle, at least for tonight." He lifted his chin. "Kaylina needs assistance with washing dishes."

"By all the craters in the moon, you *are* controlling him, aren't you?" Targon asked Kaylina.

She lifted a hand and wiggled her fingers.

"Don't send your vile druid magic in this direction." Targon took the scraps of paper from Vlerion, said, "I'll burn these," then headed for the barracks building.

Vlerion nodded, though they both knew it wouldn't matter. Come morning, everyone in the city would be reading that article.

16

Temptation leads us down alleys full of muggers and thieves.
~ Dionadra, Essays on the Motivations of Men

When Kaylina led Vlerion into Stillguard Castle, their taybarri mounts choosing to bed down under a tree by the river, they found the dishes already washed, only a few lingering scents promising that another dinner service had passed while she'd been away. She lamented not being around to help and hoped her brother and the staff understood.

A single lamp burned, left out for her, though Frayvar couldn't have known if she would return that night. Glad for his thoughtfulness, she laid the short article about the Deep Sea Honeybee on a counter for him to see in the morning.

On the way over, she had convinced the taybarri to slow down as they passed under each streetlamp, giving her time to read it. Twice.

The journalist had praised the mead, hinted that the maker was druid-blessed, and urged others to visit and try it. There'd also been a line mentioning a young genius chef who made delicious meals. Frayvar would be ecstatic—and probably smug. In order to keep his ego in check, Kaylina would be sure to point out that *most* of the article had been about the mead.

"Not too much damage here," Vlerion said, though he waved at a waste bin that held a couple of broken glasses that must have fallen during the earthquake. "It's surprising, considering how old this castle is and how many years—*centuries*—there was no maintenance done. As far as I know, the Saybrooks never sent anyone over—never could find anyone willing to step foot in it—to do repairs or upkeep."

"Don't forget the live-in sentinel."

"You think the plant is the reason the roof never caved in during the centuries after the curse was laid and it was abandoned?"

"Certainly. And *we've* done a lot to tidy it up." Kaylina touched her chest and waved upstairs to indicate her brother, who was presumably asleep in his room. "Admittedly, we haven't repaired walls, roofs, or the floor."

"Maybe there *is* some magic keeping it together."

"If your mission in life is to grow vines out of the walls and strangle enemies, you need to make sure the mortar remains in sufficiently good shape."

Vlerion grunted. "I suppose that's true."

He stepped close, wrapping his arms around her, and rested his face against the top of her head.

She didn't know if he wanted to be close to her or felt the need for support. Maybe both? Even though he hadn't said anything to indicate he felt overwhelmed or beleaguered by everything that was happening, it all had to be emotionally taxing. Stalwart rangers probably weren't supposed to admit that they felt such things. This might be as close as he would get.

"I should show you to a room." More softly, Kaylina said, "I wish I could invite you to mine."

For a long moment, Vlerion didn't answer, merely holding her, but his silence was contemplative. "I brought along a potion Sergeant Zhani gave me."

Since Zhani had also given *her* potions, it took Kaylina a moment to remember he wasn't talking about the substance Sabor had thrown at him.

Vlerion released her, stepped back, and dug into a pouch at his waist. He withdrew and unwrapped two tiny vials with clear liquid inside.

"Those are supposed to... calm your libido?"

"Yes. Swallowing one should allow me to give you an enjoyable experience without the beast making an appearance."

Kaylina couldn't keep from making a face. She understood his reasoning for acquiring the concoctions, and she was touched that he wanted to give her pleasure, even when he couldn't take his own, but she didn't like the idea of sharing an experience with him that he wouldn't be able to enjoy himself. He would only be able to...

She rubbed the back of her neck and admitted she didn't *know* what he would be able to do. She'd only been with one other man besides Domas, the boyfriend she'd spent a couple of months with, the one who'd thought she was pretty and sexy but not normal.

Both men had been more experienced than she, but neither had spent a lot of time worrying about *her* pleasure before taking their own. She hadn't disliked sex with Domas, but she'd always had the vague sense that it should have been more satisfying. Her sister always made smug comments about how wonderful her nights with her husband were. Since she did *everything* better than Kaylina, it hadn't seemed that surprising that her bedroom experiences would be superior too, but Kaylina had wondered if she'd been missing something.

"That's not the usual expression of someone eager to get naked with me," Vlerion said dryly.

"I would *love* to get naked with you, but you know why I'm hesitant."

"Because you don't know about the heights of pleasure I can bring you to?" He managed a smile, amused despite everything going on.

Kaylina swallowed, wishing she could bring *him* to heights of pleasure. He needed a distraction from life far more than she. Not that his words—and that sexy smile—didn't intrigue, but...

"It's true that I don't know, but it's late. You must be tired. I'm tired. This isn't the time to experiment."

And yet... if he kissed her or even touched her, she wouldn't push him away. She would never push him away. Even when she *should*, she always longed to be close to him, to mold herself to his hard body, to bask in the thrum of warm energy that emanated from him, the power that cloaked him and enshrouded her when she was close.

"Perhaps not an ideal time, but..." Vlerion gazed toward a dark window, his strong profile half in light from the lamp, half in shadow. "You know what the morning could bring. I told Targon I would stay in the city, and I would like to, but the populace may rise up against me. I may be forced to flee." He grimaced at the lack of appeal. Had he ever fled from anything in his life?

She didn't know. "You can stay here. The plant will defend—"

"You. I believe that. Me..." Vlerion touched his chest. "I am certain it would prefer me to be dead. Nothing has changed. I'm still a threat to you. Although..." His gaze lowered to the vials.

He returned one to his pouch but opened the other. He poured himself a cup of water from the well bucket, then swigged the vial, making a face but following it with the water.

"You should have had mead with that." Kaylina leaned into the pantry and withdrew a handful of vanilla-honey cookies that she'd made a couple of days earlier. "Here. These will get rid of the taste."

"It wasn't that bad." Vlerion did accept a cookie and ate it. "This is much better."

"Naturally. It's been kissed with honey."

She watched him chew, the tendons in his strong neck shifting in the shadows, and a little thrum of excitement ran through her. Vlerion was here in the castle with her at night, and if the potion worked as promised, she could invite him to her room. Even if they couldn't do what they both wanted, she could lie in bed with him, embracing him as they gazed into each other's eyes, sharing warmth and company.

And maybe, while they were so linked, his hand would stray down her side, touching her where she'd only touched herself for many long months. Maybe, under the effects of the libido-dulling potion, he could give her what other men hadn't.

She bit her lip, shifting closer to him, wanting...

"I believe it will take some time to take effect," Vlerion said softly, lifting a hand to keep her back. His gaze lowered from her eyes to her mouth and then her chest.

A flush of heat swept through her, pooling at her core. All he had to do was check her out, and it turned her on.

He shifted his gaze toward the hearth. "Yes, it's not doing anything yet."

"How will we know when it's safe?"

He snorted softly and waved toward his crotch. Usually, she didn't stare at that particular area, but he *did* gesture to draw her eye.

"Oh," she said. "Yes, I see."

She wanted to feel smug that she could have that effect simply by being in the room with him but reminded herself that it was *dangerous* when he was aroused. He wasn't humming, not yet, but he was determinedly looking into the fire instead of at her.

"Maybe I should wait upstairs?" Kaylina asked uncertainly.

Naked and sprawled on her bed, she thought, ready for his touch, for him to do whatever he had in mind. But that might be dangerous too, if he was mistaken about when the potion took effect.

"Better for you to stay close so..." Vlerion looked at her again. "So I'll know."

His gaze was heady, intense with desire, and it pulled her like a magnet, but she gripped the cool edge of the counter to keep herself in place.

The call has been heard, the sentinel spoke into her mind, startling her.

Uhm, what?

He who heard wishes a response, wants to know if you've the power to send without the aid of the ashandar.

The what?

Maybe it was her imagination, but the sentinel seemed to sigh into her mind, impatient with her ignorance. *The artifact you used in the ruins.* It shared the memory of the sphere with her. *Come, and I will instruct you on how to use your power to call without it.*

I'm... kind of busy now. Can it wait until morning?

As soon as she shared the words, she realized she should prioritize the calling. If 'he who heard' was out there in the world somewhere—could that be her father?—then contacting him sooner would be better than later. Maybe he could come here and show her a few things. Maybe he could even use his power to help with all the problems floating around Kaylina. Would a full-blooded druid do something to assist humans? Maybe not, but even if all he did was show *her* a few things...

Like how to lift curses...

You will come, and I will instruct you on using your power.

Okay. On my way.

"The plant is requesting me," Kaylina said.

"Does it want more honey water?" Vlerion didn't sound surprised.

Maybe he thought it summoned her to serve it numerous times a day. No, not quite, thankfully.

"Not right now, but it said something may come of the call I sent out from the ruins, and it's going to help me reach… Well, it didn't say exactly. I don't want to make assumptions, but it might end up helping us."

Vlerion nodded and clasped her hand. "When you are done… I will come to you." He gazed intently into her eyes. "By then, it should be time."

Since her interactions with the sentinel—and other druidic items—had resulted in her being knocked unconscious before, she didn't want to assume they would be able to have their moment tonight, but she would hope for an opportunity. For whatever he was willing and able to give her.

"Okay." She smiled and rose on her tiptoes to kiss him on the cheek.

At least, she *meant* for it to be on the cheek. He might have moved, or maybe her own treacherous body shifted her aim, for their lips met. They touched with longing, aching, unquenched desire, regret, and need.

For some reason, she thought of him carefully tearing out her article and handing it to her before destroying the rest of the paper. Who would have thought the haughty ranger lord she'd met when she first arrived would turn out to be considerate? And devoted to her?

She kept herself from gripping his shoulders and pressing against him, but barely as her reservations about his plan vanished. She wanted whatever he would give—whatever he *could* give.

You will come, the sentinel spoke firmly into her mind, power accompanying the words. Compelling power that flowed into her, urging her to obey.

Maybe the sentinel communicated with Vlerion as well, because he leaned back, frowning slightly. His hands clasped her waist, and the interest burning in his eyes—the *lust*—promised the potion hadn't taken hold yet.

"You need to go," he said, his voice raspy.

"Yeah."

She waited for him to release her, raising her brows when his hands lingered, holding her. *Capturing* her.

He let go and stepped back, as if doing so were more difficult than riding into the dangers of battle. For him, maybe it was.

"I'll be back," she said.

"Yes." His lids drooped as he watched her leave.

The question of whether that potion, even once more time had passed, could truly affect him—the magic of the beast curse—came to Kaylina as she walked away.

17

You can't comply your way out of tyranny.

~ *Tenegarus Grittorik, lieutenant of the Righteous and Virtuous*

On the way up to see the sentinel, Kaylina stopped in her room. She opened a drawer in her bedside table and withdrew the packet Sergeant Zhani had given her, then extracted one vial.

When they'd spoken, Kaylina had been certain she would never use the elixir on Vlerion, not after learning it could have dangerous side effects, but Zhani's words *just in case* came to mind. She tucked the vial into her pocket before striding down the hallway toward the tower.

The sentinel's power wrapped around her and pulled her along, a tendril drawing her physically closer, demanding she obey its summons.

Irritation swept through Kaylina. Even though she accepted that sending out another call, or whatever the plant wanted her to do, could be beneficial, she resented it presuming to pull her about. Since it was even more of a huge eavesdropping spy than she, it had probably seen her with Vlerion and had wanted to interrupt them. To protect her, maybe, but also because it didn't approve of her being near one of the descendants of the original man the Daygarii had cursed.

"I'll spend time with whomever I wish," she said.

All along, the sentinel had been presumptuous, branding her without warning, forcing its communications on her, and killing others to protect her—or simply because it desired to. It cared nothing for humanity. It had admitted that. It was a Daygarii-created plant, through and through.

By the time Kaylina turned down the final narrow hallway, the irritation had turned to anger and more. Her hand warmed, that warmth flowing into her body and flushing her with a strange energy. A… magical energy?

As she approached the tower, vines dangling through the hole in the ceiling above the chair she'd left for climbing up, she noticed a faint green glow at the edges of her vision. Coming from the walls? The plant? No. *She* was emanating it.

That startled her, and some of her anger faded. With it, the glow also faded.

One of the vines rose up, the tip rotating toward her. It was like the head of a dog, interested in a rabbit it had spotted. But she refused to be the rabbit, or some obedient lackey. When the vine shifted toward her, probably wanting to touch her temple before she climbed up, she gripped it and kept it from advancing.

Energy buzzed up her arm. Her anger crept back into her, and she willed her power into the vine, silently ordering it to leave her alone. If she and the sentinel were to communicate, *she* would initiate it.

You are coming into your power. The sentinel sounded more amused than approving, though maybe there was some of both.

Yup. Can we get this over with quickly, please? I have a date.

You seek to mate with the cursed one.

Not exactly, unfortunately, but Kaylina had no intention of explaining their problem to a plant.

I invited him here so I could spend time with him before... Our world is about to get chaotic.

Compared to all that is in the universe, the machinations of men matter little.

Yeah, well, they're going to matter to us once tomorrow's newspaper is distributed.

A scornful scoff sounded in her mind, but the sentinel changed the topic. *To reach out to he who is now aware of you, who heard your call, you will draw upon the power within me.*

The vine twitched in her hand, trying to rise again to her temple. She continued to hold it away from her.

My father? Is that who you're talking about? I don't want to reach out to any random person with druid blood. Kaylina thought of the mountain men who'd shown up because of her call.

The sentinel answered by floating an image into her mind. The same handsome green-haired man with reddish bark-tinted skin that it had shown her before. Her father.

Or so she'd assumed. But had the sentinel ever confirmed that? She tried to remember.

I speak of he who planted the seed that created you, the sentinel said.

My father, she said.

Yes.

Glad for the confirmation, Kaylina nodded. The vine was still twitching, trying to initiate a stronger link.

She drew a bracing breath and lifted it to her head. Maybe it was silly, but she wanted control of the situation, of their communication. The sentinel couldn't assume she was here to serve it.

She touched the vine to her temple.

The sentinel is here to serve the Daygarii, it said, responding to what she hadn't spoken, *and those with enough of their blood to command a reasonable amount of their power.*

That's me?

We shall see.

Another vine lowered through the hole and snaked toward her.

How much touching do we need to do? Kaylina lifted her free hand—she still held the first vine in her other.

For this, multiple points of contact will facilitate. For the first time, you will draw upon my power. I will serve you, infusing you with enough to reach out without the aid of an ashandar.

Kaylina frowned but gripped the second vine. Others drifted down, touching her arm, snaking around her leg, and one curved around her waist.

Her heart pounded, and she admitted fear, despite the relationship she'd established with the sentinel. She'd seen these same vines kill people. None of them wrapped around her neck, but she would be trapped if the plant didn't let her go. She knew from experience that her knife wasn't enough to cut away the vines.

You have the power to force my limbs away if you wish, the sentinel said. *And soon you will have more power.*

With those words, invigorating energy swept into her body, making her skin flush and her scalp tingle.

Envision he whom you wish to communicate with, and call out to him, the sentinel instructed.

Kaylina did so, doing her best to form the face of a man she'd never met in her mind. Then, feeling a little silly, she tried to project the word, *Father,* toward him, wherever in the world he was. If he even *was* in this world.

His name is Arsanti t'el Avadorstar, the sentinel said.

Maybe I'll stick with calling him Father. Kaylina did file the name away, repeating it a few times so she could remember it. She imagined calling the name, as well as *Father*, out into the ether. No, across the North and South Dakmoor Seas, since one of the visions the plant had shared had been of him on a sailing ship.

Whether she effectively called to anyone or was able to send a message across a distance, Kaylina didn't know, but her skin continued to tingle with power, the sentinel's magic mingling with hers. So much energy coursed through her body that it was almost painful.

Yes, the sentinel said. *You are not as disappointing as I believed when I first drew you here.*

I'm so glad, Kaylina thought. *But we came of our own accord.*

Okay, they'd been tricked by that fake land agent, but...

The sentinel chuckled into her mind. *You came because I wished it. Not only to me in the castle but to this human metropolis near one of the remaining Daygarii preserves. It was your fate.*

I'm only here to make mead, she said, refusing to believe in fate. Even if such things existed for the heroes in stories, she wasn't such a person. She was just... Kaylina. Lover of honey. Maker of mead.

Anrokk, *daughter of Avadorstar, new protector of the future until the era of men passes and the Daygarii return.*

Kaylina swallowed. *Protector?*

She remembered Frayvar's translation of that plaque in the ruins, of how it had spoken of the Daygarii protecting the lands.

Curses don't last forever, the sentinel said. *You were birthed for a reason.*

I figured the reason was that my father was into my mother.

The sentinel chuckled again. *I imagine she did arouse him. Such is required for druids to procreate, as with many warm-blooded beings in this and other worlds.*

What am I supposed to protect?

An image of the preserve came to mind, as if she were seeing it from above, the trees dark green and dense as they spread from either side of the river and stretched into the foothills of the mountains. An area that had been left alone over the centuries, though it was surrounded on three sides by farm and grazing lands.

When you say curses don't last forever, do you speak of yourself? Or of Vlerion's curse?

I can survive longer, especially now that you have nourished me. The vines shifted along her skin, almost caressing her.

You're getting creepy again.

It is in your blood for plants and animals to be drawn to you. And men. It shared an image of Vlerion but also of Targon and several others who'd leered at her in recent memory. *You shall have to grow accustomed to it.*

Yeah... I probably won't.

Vlerion was the only one she wanted drawn to her.

Because you are drawn to him, to his beast. The sentinel showed her another memory, of the beast pulling himself out of the pool at the bathhouse, of powerful muscles under short damp auburn fur.

I'm drawn to Vlerion, Kaylina thought firmly, even as the sentinel showed her kissing the beast.

She'd been doing that to save herself, to get close enough for her power to work, to calm him, to get him to change back into Vlerion.

He's a good man, she added. *I love him.*

Tired of discussing this with a plant, Kaylina attempted to marshal her power again, sensing that they'd done what the sentinel wanted—what she wanted—and she didn't need to let its grasping vines continue to touch her.

Energy still coursed through her body, and she found it surprisingly easy to push them away. Maybe the sentinel let her. Either way, green light flared around her, and the air sizzled with shed energy. It felt good to use it, to have an outlet, and she let her head fall back, imagining using this magic to help Vlerion, to attack his enemies. There would be consequences, but would it matter? They were unimportant humans, an infestation on the land.

The thought alarmed her, and she opened her eyes and stepped back. Had it come from her? Or from the sentinel? Either way, she found it disturbing.

The vines hung limp now, not moving, and the sentinel was quiet in its pot. Maybe it had worn itself out by lending her energy. Had she succeeded in sending a message to her father? Would anything come of it? She didn't know.

The awareness that she wasn't alone came to Kaylina. She turned to find Vlerion in the shadows scant feet away, watching her through slitted eyes.

Her heart pounded with fear or anticipation or... she didn't know what. She felt like she'd been caught doing something wrong. Or maybe something forbidden.

But there was no condemnation in his gaze when he surveyed her from head to toe. "You are learning to use your power."

"Apparently." Kaylina tried to smile, but her mouth was dry, and she was oddly nervous. Why? This was Vlerion. Vlerion who'd promised to give her pleasure tonight... "Were you drawn by it?"

She meant it to be a joke, but he met her eyes with utter seriousness.

"I was." He stepped closer. "I always am."

He lifted a hand to her jaw, fingers light as they traced it. His touch sent a shiver through her, a longing for more. He brushed his fingers down the side of her throat, then followed the curve of her chest as he held her gaze.

Heat coiled between her legs, and she wanted to reach out, to touch *him*, but did she dare?

She couldn't tell from his face if that potion had kicked in. She didn't see the spark of danger in his blue eyes—yet—but they were intense. And he'd admitted being magically drawn. Could a mundane potion stop that?

Vlerion shifted closer, and she found herself backed against the wall. She trembled as he cupped her breast, thumb stroking her through the fabric of her shirt before drifting to her buttons.

"Vlerion," she whispered. "Are you… Can you tell if…"

Kaylina glanced to the side, toward the dangling vines. Even if he *was* okay, this wasn't the place for their interlude. It wasn't private.

"You've subdued it," he murmured, "with your power. Just as you can subdue me." For a moment, something sparked in his eyes. Indignation?

He couldn't have been too irked because he kept stroking her, shifting closer, inhaling her scent.

"I will thank you," he said softly, meeting her gaze again as his fingers unfastened her buttons and stroked her bare skin. "For all you've done for me, for all you want to do. For dealing with *that*." He tilted his head toward the sentinel as his fingers trailed lower, nails grazing the soft skin of her stomach. "To seek an answer for me."

Vlerion pushed her shirt open to look at her. Her nipples tightened under his appreciative gaze, his loving touch, but she couldn't help but worry that he hadn't answered her question.

If the beast roused, it wouldn't be safe here. The sentinel would come to life and attack. She was sure of it. And if it didn't? Her brother was in his room, a potential victim. And she… she could be a potential victim too. As his mother had warned, the curse could kill.

She needed to shift away, to push *him* away, at least until she was certain it was safe. But her body betrayed her, as it always did, and she turned into his touch, not away from it. She inhaled his masculine scent, appreciating it—and him—just as he did her. By all the altered orchards, she wanted this, wanted him to give her the experience she'd craved since meeting him.

As his explorations continued, fingers stroking lower, she trembled again. The heat in her core intensified, her body readying itself for him. He couldn't take her, not in the way of joining, but he used his fingers expertly, and she shifted and writhed as he stroked her, as he looked at her hungrily, as if he couldn't tear his gaze from her body.

He bent his face to her breasts, nuzzling them, and she couldn't keep from gripping his shoulders and arching toward him, wanting his mouth on her. A low growl rumbled in his chest as he complied, taking one nipple between his lips, sucking her gently.

She gasped, the arousal so intense that she jerked toward him before she could stop herself. She was vaguely aware of him unfastening her trousers as his tongue teased her, making her squirm and pant, breaths quickening.

"Vlerion," she whispered, lifting her hands to his head, digging her fingers into his short hair. She needed more.

"Your enthusiasm," he murmured, "is testing the potion."

Despite the words—the *warning*?—he didn't stop. She didn't *want* him to stop, but was he joking? His voice was husky, not calm or detached. Did she need to dig out that vial?

It was in the pocket in the trousers that were descending to the floor.

"Vlerion, should I…?" She didn't know what. Stop thrashing about? That would be hard as long as he was sliding his mouth so erotically over her nipple as his hand drifted lower, fingers stroking her core, sliding into her throbbing warmth. Dear moon gods, she almost came at his first touch there.

"No," Vlerion said against her skin, though he couldn't have known what she'd meant. She hadn't told him about the vial.

Nor did she want to use it. She didn't want him to stop. She needed this so badly and caught herself rocking toward him, her body begging for everything he could give.

She gripped his head harder, her breaths coming fast as he touched her intimately, more expertly than she'd ever touched herself. Somehow, he knew her and what gave her pleasure, intense pleasure. It was as if the magic that drew them together gave him knowledge of all that she longed for, physically and emotionally. From recognition in the newspaper to his tongue sliding down her stomach to replace his fingers.

Panting, with her thoughts scattered, she thought of pushing off his shirt, of touching him so that he would also enjoy this, but she remembered the danger in that. His lust. The beast.

Or would the potion succeed in tamping that down? If it did, would it mean her touch wouldn't affect him?

A twinge of disappointment ran through her, but the thought fled when his tongue slipped into her most intimate of spots. Throbbing desire and pleasure pulsed through her, and all she could think of was how incredible that felt.

She let out a garbled cry as Vlerion gripped her hips, pinning her against the wall as he lowered to his knees. He spread her legs, opening her to his touch. Maybe she should have felt vulnerable or shy, but eagerness made her give in to his movements, letting him look at her, letting him have all of her.

He growled. Maybe that should have alarmed her, hinting of the beast, but then he tasted her, stroking her with his tongue, and she couldn't think of anything but her own desire. He teased and titillated, bringing her closer and closer to the edge.

Such exquisite need rocketed through her that she arched away from the wall, begging aloud as she pushed toward him. His strokes turned into a gentle nip, then sucking that brought such relief and ecstasy that she cried out again, fingers digging in as she gripped him, waves and waves of satisfaction making her entire body shake.

As those waves washed over her, it took her a moment to realize that Vlerion had paused. He looked up at her as he gripped her, as she trembled in the aftermath of the climax, her breasts bare, her nearly naked body bathed in sweat.

He breathed heavily, pure lust burning in his blue eyes, and fear ricochetted through her as she realized the potion hadn't been enough. The beast was rising.

18

A BRIEF INDULGENCE, REGRET FOR A LIFETIME.
~ Assai, Priestess of Luvana

"Vlerion." Kaylina tried to pull her shirt closed as he stared at her, his eyes savage with naked lust, his muscles tense as he kept her pinned to the wall. "Thank you, but could you maybe hum a bit? You're looking a touch—"

With a growl, Vlerion rose to his feet, leaning in for a kiss, but he caught himself. He froze, closing his eyes, tension and great struggle twisting his face.

"Kaylina," he rasped, his hard muscles quivering, his body coiled, as if he would spring. No, as if the beast would erupt at any second. "Stop me. I don't want to hurt you, but I—" He threw his head back, the power radiating from him alarming. Dangerous.

Kaylina squirmed, trying to slip away. Her pants had fallen off —no, he'd taken them off—and she'd been too absorbed in her pleasure to notice. She couldn't reach her pocket. The vial.

Vlerion stepped back, releasing her, but she feared it was only because the change was taking him. She glanced to the side, to the vines she had worried about earlier.

They remained limp. The sentinel wouldn't help her.

As Vlerion staggered back, the rip of clothing announcing the change, she lunged for her pants and dug into the pocket. Fur sprouted from his skin as his muscles swelled, growing even larger and more powerful. His trousers split at the seams.

With shaking hands, she dug out the vial and started to uncork it, but Zhani's warning about side effects popped into her mind. The stuff could stop his heart.

But once he turned, he would take her as the beast, and she wouldn't be able to stop him, not this time. He hadn't engaged in battle first and wasn't exhausted. He was full of energy, of power. Of lust for her.

Kaylina uncorked the vial, but she couldn't bring herself to throw it. Even as his human teeth elongated and turned to fangs, and auburn fur sprouted, changing his face from that of her trusted Vlerion to a savage beast, she stepped forward and planted her hand against his chest.

She attempted to summon power, to send soothing magic into him, to turn him back. Was that possible? So soon after changing? She didn't know.

What if he had to find a release for his great power before the magic would fade? This time, there wasn't a blatant enemy to send him against. She couldn't sic the beast on another spymaster—or Jana Bloomlong.

His eyes met hers, no hint of Vlerion in their savage blue, and Kaylina forced herself to focus. If this was to work, it would take all of her concentration.

The brand on her hand warmed, and power flowed into Vlerion as a nimbus of green glowed around her again.

"Stand down, noble beast," Kaylina whispered, then hummed his song, wishing she had a better voice for music.

Paws gripped her shoulders, and the beast pushed her against the wall. Before, she'd wanted nothing more than for Vlerion to have her against that wall, but now, fear almost made her yank her hand back, to try to escape, to run. But she sensed that would break the magical link she had. Even if it wasn't turning him back, he showed some restraint. At the least, he hadn't yanked off his shredded pants to—

"Calm, please," she whispered, keeping her hand planted.

"My mate," he rasped, looking down.

Her shirt had fallen open again.

She shivered under the feral gaze, that lust-filled *hungry* gaze.

"I know you want this, my mate, but... I might not survive it. I know I promised we could be together before—" Kaylina still felt guilty that she'd lied to the beast about that, "—but the world is dangerous. Very dangerous. I need a protector, not... another danger."

His gaze rose to her face, and she thought he was listening, that she might be getting through to him—until a paw took her breast, claws grazing her skin.

"*My* mate."

"Vlerion," she said sternly, willing the magic in her blood to work, to give her the power to command him. She requested the sentinel to help too. As much as she hated needing its assistance, there were no other plants around that she could call upon.

The beast's mouth lowered toward her breast as his paw trailed down her skin, erotic but terrifying.

Her hand heated, her body thrumming with power. The beast growled, drawn, aroused.

She would have to throw the vial. As she lifted her hand, intending to spatter it against his chest, she sensed movement behind her. Commanded by her power, the limp vines reenergized, their tips lifting into the air.

The beast noticed and sprang back, landing in a crouch to face the threat. The vines flowed past her and toward him. He leaped back again, glancing over his shoulder. More vines sprouted from the mortar in the walls to either side of him.

"Don't hurt him," Kaylina ordered. "Just..."

What? Restrain him? Yes, that was what she needed until the beast magic wore off. He would hate it, but there wouldn't be side effects.

As the vines stretched for him, obeying her unspoken thoughts, the beast leaped back again. He wanted to run from the threat, she thought, but he gazed at her, disappointment mingling with his lust. He wanted *her* almost as much as his instincts demanded that he survive.

A vine whipped toward his arm. He caught it in the air, ripping it from the wall, and his powerful muscles surged as he tore it in half. He bit another off as it flicked near his head.

Snarling, he had to back farther as more vines reached for him. Too many for him to deal with. He shot her one last anguished look—as if he believed his mate had betrayed him—before turning and running.

Though she felt awful for having him attacked when he'd proven her protector again and again, that didn't keep her from ordering the plant to capture him. If she let him escape the castle, and, enraged that he hadn't been able to claim his mate, he attacked others, it would be her fault. What if he hurt Frayvar?

That thought propelled her to yank on her pants and run after the beast. All Frayvar would have to do was hear something, open his door, and lean out at the wrong time.

Kaylina ran down the hallway, buttoning her shirt as she went.

When she turned into the wider hallway, the beast was already gone, though broken vines dangled from several spots in the wall. At least Frayvar's bedroom door was closed. Later, she would be embarrassed that she'd probably made enough noise before

Vlerion had turned that her brother had heard. For now, that didn't matter.

A furious roar echoed from the floor below. The beast.

Kaylina ran down the stairs, glancing left and right at the bottom—afraid he crouched in the shadows and would spring at her. But more broken vines dangled from the walls, promising the sentinel was still protecting her. It had *tried* to capture him, as she'd asked.

Thank you, she told it before running outside.

Beyond the courtyard, it wouldn't be able to protect her, but she had to catch the beast before he went... where *would* he go? This time, she hadn't ordered him after anyone.

The queen had irritated *Vlerion* with her proposal, but Kaylina doubted the beast would care about that—or even remember. The queen hadn't threatened Kaylina. Even Jana, with her blackmail, had only wanted Kaylina to leave this part of the kingdom.

When she reached the back gate, it was closed. One of the taybarri came over. In the dark, she couldn't tell if it was Crenoch or Levitke, but a tail swished as a large furry head looked toward her—no, toward her pockets.

"Nothing good in there now. Did Vlerion come this way?"

The whuff sounded confused.

"Did he come outside at all? He... wouldn't have been himself."

No, Levitke spoke into her mind and looked toward Crenoch as he also ambled to the gate. *We heard a roar.*

"But you didn't see him?" Kaylina looked toward the front gate, thinking he might have run that way, but the taybarri would have noticed. "Okay, wait here, please."

Kaylina ran back into the castle, turning into the kitchen. The pantry door was open, and, yes, the movable flagstone that led to the root cellar and eventually the catacombs had been shoved aside. In the confined space, she noticed the beast's animal scent.

She ran and grabbed her sword and a lantern, planning to

follow him, but she paused. If the beast had gone into the catacombs instead of the city, there was less chance that he would encounter people—less chance that he would hurt anyone. If he *did* run into people, they'd likely be up to no good, right?

Grittor's face popped into her mind, and she grimaced. As she well knew, the Virts used the catacombs. But what were the odds that they were down there tonight?

"More likely, the beast will run around until the magic of the curse wears off," Kaylina reasoned. Tomorrow, he would wake as Vlerion and return.

She bit her lip, hoping she was right. Even though she shouldn't blame herself for this—*Vlerion* had been the one who'd wanted to reward her—she shouldn't have let him leave the castle. She should have tried harder to stop him. She should have thrown the vial.

Kaylina slumped against the pantry shelves. Yes, that was exactly what she should have done. If it had worked, he would have changed back into a man right there. Now...

Distant screams came from the catacombs.

"Shit."

Someone *was* down there. And the beast had found him. Or... them? More screams sounded.

Altered orchards, there might be bodies everywhere in the morning. Just as that awful article was printed, condemning Vlerion as the beast.

Kaylina swore again as she wrestled with indecision. If she went down there, she wouldn't have the sentinel to back her up. If the beast killed whatever victims he'd found, then turned on her, she might not be able to stop him again.

No, she still had the vial. She touched her pocket to reassure herself. And if she *didn't* go, there was a chance his magic would wear off while there were still threats, and that would leave him unconscious and vulnerable.

She set her jaw and descended into the catacombs. If the beast needed help, after she'd driven him away, she had to be there for him.

Kaylina walked quietly from the root cellar and into the catacombs, the passageways utterly dark aside from the wan light of her single lantern. The stone Kar'ruk statues looked no less ominous than the first time she'd come down here, and knowing they would hiss vapor at passersby didn't keep her from flinching when it caressed her cheeks.

She held her breath and hurried past the area. It crossed her mind that when the *real* Kar'ruk had invaded the city and been in the catacombs, they might have refilled the reservoirs of poison that the statues spat.

"Probably not," she whispered. If they had, the poison would have stopped the beast.

The screams ended before Kaylina reached their source. Cautious, she approached the underground lake where the fur shark had once attacked her.

A hint of yellow light shone on the water ahead, and her passageway ended at its rock ledge of a shore. The surface lay still, the faint trickle from the flow entering at one end not enough to disturb it.

Before leaning out of the passageway to look around, Kaylina paused and listened, straining her ears for the sounds of breathing, of anything. The trickle of water was all she heard.

She risked peering around, then froze, horror filling her at the sight of mangled bodies on the dock near the end of the lake. *Numerous* mangled bodies.

Men in green uniforms that she didn't recognize lay among blankets and packs, swords fallen from their hands, blood spattering the area. They looked like they'd been caught by surprise while camped for the night. All save a guard who was dead on the walkway close to Kaylina—he might have been awake and tried to defend the camp, but the beast had been too strong. Claws had slashed through the man's throat, leaving no doubt about who had been responsible.

She counted ten bodies before realizing that even more floated in the water near boats tied to the dock. And there were more near the start of the river that exited the lake, the dead lying half off the walkway that followed the wall.

Her gaze traveled back to the dock, and she counted the boats. Six of them, each large enough to accommodate a dozen men.

Had there been even more here? Men who'd managed to flee the beast while the others fought? Fought and died.

Kaylina shook her head in horror, hardly believing that what had started as an enjoyable night with Vlerion had turned into this.

But who were these people? The Virts didn't wear uniforms. And these weren't the colors of the Castle or Kingdom Guard.

Kaylina slumped against the stone wall. She couldn't bring herself to step over the dead body on the walkway to investigate. None of the men were moving, so she was fairly certain they were past help. She had to tell…

Who?

Vlerion was who she would usually go to.

Captain Targon was the logical choice, but she winced at the thought of explaining how the beast had come to be roused. Targon would guess the reason even if she didn't say, and he would be snarky and judgmental.

Maybe she would deserve it, but that didn't keep her from shying away from the notion. Maybe she could tell Sergeant Zhani. Zhani had enough rank that she could gather men, lead a team down here to investigate, and report to Targon.

Eventually, Targon would learn what happened, but Kaylina wouldn't have to be there for it.

"I wouldn't *have* to report it at all," she mused, wishing that didn't sound like cowardice.

It was tempting though. Days might pass before someone stumbled upon the bodies. The rangers patrolled down here from time to time, but she didn't think it was that frequent.

"No, I have to report it." As a ranger in training, it was her duty.

Besides, these people in their unfamiliar uniforms might represent a threat to Port Jirador or even all of Zaldor. What if this was part of an invasion force? The kingdom had enough trouble this week already.

"I hope you're okay, Vlerion," Kaylina said before heading back. "Wherever you are."

19

Nothing is so distasteful as giving a briefing to a superior after a failed mission.

~ Lord General Menok

Morning found Kaylina sitting at a table in the kitchen, her head hanging over a steaming cup of coffee, the vapors wreathing her face. She inhaled deeply, willing the liquid to give her energy. Oh, how she wished she were sharing a cup with Vlerion, smiling and joking as they enjoyed each other's company in the aftermath of their lovemaking.

But it hadn't quite been lovemaking. Oh, it had been amazing for her... up until the moment when the beast erupted. And it had turned into a disaster.

"Murder," she whispered, shivering.

She'd arrived at ranger headquarters before dawn and reported to a corporal on duty at the gate, asking him to let Targon know about the bodies when the captain woke up. Alarmed by the news, the corporal had gone straight to knock on the door. Kaylina had fled before the captain could come down to question her. It had been cowardly, and she knew it, but she hadn't wanted to endure Targon's snark. She had no doubt it would find her eventually, but, with luck, Vlerion would be at her side by then. He could share the enduring with her.

"Not the kind of sharing I'd hoped we would do after a night of intimacy," she murmured, then yawned.

Daylight had come, and gray clouds produced a soft drizzle outside. She'd tried to go to bed for a couple of hours after returning, but she'd been too wound up and had finally given up and made coffee. Frayvar, who'd apparently heard a few sounds during the night—he'd blushed and looked away after admitting that—had chalked it all up to sex.

He'd left early to grocery shop for the night's menu. With trepidation, she'd asked him to bring back a newspaper.

On the one hand, Kaylina didn't want to know if that story had printed. On the other hand, she *had* to know.

It worried her that Vlerion hadn't returned to Stillguard Castle. Even though he sometimes lost consciousness for an hour or two, especially after long and demanding battles as the beast, he should have woken up as himself by now. Unless... he hadn't been as successful at destroying the uniformed men in the catacombs as she'd believed. What if some of them had gotten the best of him? Or what if he'd come out of the catacombs and run into guards, and *they'd* taken him out?

Glum thoughts. Kaylina was relieved when the whuffs of numerous taybarri arriving reached her ears. But she doubted Vlerion was with them. Crenoch remained outside.

The ranger captain comes, Levitke spoke into her mind, something she was starting to be able to do whether Kaylina used her power or not. Either they were growing more in tune with each other, or the taybarri was maturing.

Is his expression calm or consternated?

Maybe *constipated* was the word Kaylina should have used, but she hadn't observed that the taybarri had the problems that humans sometimes had in that area. Probably thanks to all the grass and leaves they ate between meals of protein.

Levitke shared an image of Targon and two younger rangers riding along the river trail toward Stillguard Castle. Constipated probably *was* the right word for that expression.

You're getting more talented at communicating, Kaylina observed, wishing she could have a conversation with the taybarri instead of Targon. *Will you turn silver and become a mature elder soon?*

Amused whuffs sounded in her mind. The next image was of Crenoch rolling on his back with all four paws in the air, scratching an itch as he flapped his tail over the bank into the river.

I know he's *not maturing. I meant you.*

We are age the same.

Well, thank you for the warning about incoming... consternation. You're an excellent friend.

Yes. An image of honey drops accompanied the word.

I'll make some more as soon as I have a chance. Blackberries are coming into season. Maybe I can try them in the recipe.

From the kitchen, Kaylina couldn't see the tail swishing, but she believed it was occurring.

Better than pellets.

Oh, I know. Kaylina had never tried the protein pellets the rangers fed the taybarri, but, if she recalled correctly, they were made out of desiccated organ meat and who knew what else. Nothing appetizing.

Later, we ride into battle? The question didn't come with another image, but Levitke managed to convey boredom.

Kaylina had no desire to do that, but she said, *I have a feeling we will.*

Unfortunately.

More whuffs sounded beyond the gate, the new taybarri greeting Levitke and Crenoch.

Kaylina took a long bracing swig of coffee before standing up.

"Get out here, Korbian," came Targon's grumpy call.

With her sword belted on, Kaylina straightened her back and strode into the courtyard.

"Where's Vlerion?" Targon hadn't opened the gate, and he eyed the castle instead of her as she approached.

"I had assumed—*hoped*—he returned to headquarters after..." Kaylina glanced at the other rangers, a sergeant and a corporal mounted on their taybarri. "After."

"He did not. *I* assumed he came back here. Like a dog to its vomit."

"I can see you're going to be polite and genteel company today, my lord."

He gave her a scathing look and pointed inside. "If I walk in there, are vines going to jump on me?"

"Only if you threaten me." Or so she believed. She hadn't attempted to make a deal with the sentinel on Targon's behalf. She didn't care if *he* was able to visit her establishment or not.

"You'd better come out here then." Targon pointed at the river trail. "I'm in a threatening mood."

Kaylina wasn't entirely positive that was sarcasm rather than a more serious threat, but she wanted to know if he'd checked out the camp in the catacombs and knew who the uniformed men were. Who they *had* been.

"Yes, Levitke informed me of that."

Targon squinted at her.

Kaylina took a deep breath, opened the gate, and joined him outside.

"Wait here," Targon told his men and pointed for her to walk down the trail with him.

Ducks paddled in the river, not deterred by the rain. At the moment, it was little more than a mist that dampened Kaylina's cheeks. She might have considered the morning pleasant if the company had been better—if the night had turned out differently.

"What happened?" Targon stopped when they were out of earshot and leaned against a mature willow dangling branches over the river. "No, I know *what* happened. And since I've seen the lusty way you two ogle each other, I can guess *why* it happened, but what was the order of events that led Vlerion to that camp, and did he mean to attack those men, or were they in the wrong place at the wrong time?" Judging by Targon's grimace—that was almost a wince—those hadn't been criminals.

Kaylina wiped damp palms on her trousers. She'd been afraid of that.

"And by the way," Targon continued before she'd decided how to start her explanation, "next time you find something *that* significant in the middle of the night, tell me directly. Don't pass notes through my entire chain of command." He gave her an exasperated look. "As you, eavesdropper extraordinaire, should know, we have spies among the ranks. I know who some of them are but, I'm positive, not all. This story is going to spread like a venereal disease on a mixed-gender navy ship."

"I... I'm sorry." Kaylina hadn't thought of that, only that she hadn't wanted to deal with the captain's vitriol. She closed her eyes. Another mistake. "I apologize, my lord," she said sincerely.

For everything, she wanted to add. The lack of sleep and the stress of the last few hours—the last few *days*—caught up with her, and tears crept into her eyes. She scowled at the ground and blinked rapidly, not wanting Targon to see. He was the *last* man she wanted to cry in front of. Where was Vlerion? Again, she wished he were here for this.

"Just tell me what happened," Targon said. His tone wasn't gentle, but he'd softened it.

"Vlerion and I thought we had... a way to keep the beast from appearing if we... were together." Her cheeks flushed. She always hated discussing with Targon anything involving sex.

"And it didn't work," he stated.

"At first, it seemed to, but he got too, uhm." Still looking at the ground instead of Targon, Kaylina couldn't bring herself to say that her writhing nudity had apparently been so arousing that it had overridden the libido-dampening effects of the potion. It might have been true, but it would make her sound pompous and full of herself. She also didn't want Targon *imagining* her writhing nudity.

"Worked up. Then what? He mated with you and left, still as the beast?" Targon sounded confused.

"He didn't *mate* with me." Kaylina's cheeks heated even further. Her whole face was hot. "I mean, he wanted to, but I wouldn't let him. I was afraid that it wouldn't— Well, his mother warned me. And I don't want a *beast* lover anyway. I..." Dear craters of the moon, why was she going this far in depth with him?

"Yeah, I've seen Isla's scars. *All* of them."

All of them? Did that imply he'd seen her naked? Kaylina had a hard time imagining Isla wanting to be with Targon—and vice versa—but shook the thought away. It wasn't important.

"I wouldn't sleep with the beast either," Targon added. "Fortunately, he's never shown an interest in me in either incarnation."

"Lucky you," Kaylina muttered.

"I thought *you*, as someone who courts danger like a bee buzzing into every flower on the bush, might be intrigued and dumb enough to want him that way."

"No." She glanced up but only long enough to scowl at him. "Anyway, I summoned the plant to help me. I wanted it to hold him until he turned back into himself. But he was strong enough to break the vines, and he ran away. I was afraid he would hurt people and went after him. I don't know why he went into the catacombs, but I heard screams. By the time I got to that lake, those men were all dead. I didn't touch anything or explore farther down the river."

"*We* did." Targon waved to himself and his men, though they'd stayed behind and were watching as Crenoch and two other taybarri played in the river. "There were bodies all the way down that underground channel, and at least two washed up in the harbor. Claws and fangs killed everyone I looked at." Targon, who never seemed afraid of anything, shuddered. "He truly is a monster when he's in that form. I understand why Sabor was seduced by the idea of breeding beasts…" He paused to eye her, and Kaylina wished she hadn't shared that information when she and Vlerion had reported to him. "But he was a fool to believe he could tame that kind of power. I'm surprised *you* can."

"I had the sentinel's help."

"Nothing like plant tendrils getting involved in your sex life."

"It was nothing like *that*."

Targon waved away the comment. "Yeah, yeah, I get it. But that was a dumb move. For *both* of you. You *know* the consequences, what can happen when he changes. By now, you *must*."

"I do. I should have thrown the vial, but… I couldn't."

"What vial?"

Kaylina recalled that she hadn't mentioned Sabor's chemical attacks when she'd reported to Targon. She'd wanted to research them herself, at least the one that had forced Vlerion to change back. But maybe that had been a mistake. Maybe all the rangers who might encounter the beast should have the concoction.

No, not with the possible side effects Zhani had mentioned.

Targon cleared his throat and raised his eyebrows.

Kaylina was reluctant to explain, afraid he would demand some of the vials for himself, but since she'd accidentally mentioned it, she felt compelled and did so.

"Yes, Sabor was known to have an alchemist in his pocket."

Targon scratched his jaw. "Maybe he wasn't as foolish as I thought. If he believed he could handle the beast..."

"No, he *was* foolish."

Kaylina refused to feel bad for speaking disrespectfully about the dead. Sabor hadn't respected her when he'd lived.

"*He* didn't hesitate to throw the vial," Targon said. "I assume."

Kaylina glared up into his face, her earlier mortification forgotten. He was implying *she* was the foolish one.

"Sergeant Zhani said there could be side effects. That it might stop his heart."

"If it didn't before, it probably wouldn't have a second time."

Kaylina wanted to retort that he couldn't be sure, but... she hadn't considered that. It was probably true. Damn it, if she'd thrown it, that entire camp of men might not be dead.

Targon sighed and pushed away from the tree. "All right, don't tear up on me, Korbian. I get that you didn't want to hurt him. Better to be safe than sorry. Usually. But those men..." Targon pushed a hand through his graying hair, a haunted look in his eyes.

"Who were they? I didn't know."

"A mercenary company that usually works for the aristocrats in the Damark Province. Since it borders the mountains, and the nomadic desert tribes like to plague that pass, they employ mercenaries as well as rangers and the Kingdom Guard."

"I've... heard of Damark." Not a lot. Kaylina knew only that it was closer to her southern province than the capital. Her brother would know more.

"They grow a lot of spices down there, and the province is notorious for a chain of islands along the coast where gamblers can bet on whatever depravity they wish. It's a favorite destination of Prince Enrikon."

It took a moment for Kaylina to realize what Targon was

implying, that there was a link. "Were they the prince's mercenaries?"

"We don't know yet, but it's possible the kid isn't as dumb as we've been assuming. He may have hired forces under the assumption that he would need them, that his mommy and her co-conspirators wouldn't give up the power they've enjoyed these past years."

Meaning, Vlerion—the beast—might have killed men working for the prince, for the man who would, unless something drastic happened, become the next king of Zaldor.

Kaylina bent forward and gripped her knees, fresh fear for Vlerion clutching her heart.

"I have a meeting with Milnor later this morning where I hope to find out more," Targon said. "I wanted to get as much as I could from you so I wouldn't go in there blind. But it sounds like you don't know much either." At least he didn't say *as usual.*

"No. I... think it was chance that the beast ran into them. He was probably trying *not* to run into anyone while he was in that state."

"The state of being a horribly sexually frustrated beast looking for an outlet for release?"

That was probably correct, but Kaylina bristled at the implication that if she'd let the beast take her... No, all she would have had to do was use the vial.

"The beast is always dangerous," she said, "whether he's *frustrated* or not. It's the curse."

"Aren't you supposed to be finding a way to lift that curse?"

"*Yes.*" Kaylina couldn't keep the anguish from her voice.

Targon sighed, appearing frustrated himself. "You'd better stay here today. I don't know what's going to come of all this, but I'll send people out to look for—"

"My lord?" one of the rangers called and pointed up the river trail.

Vlerion was striding toward them, his face grim and a newspaper in his hand.

20

The pain of shame, greater than any wound.

~ *Winter Moon Priest Dazibaru*

Kaylina, relieved that Vlerion was not only alive but didn't appear wounded, wanted to rush forward and hug him. And, even though she shouldn't have been pleased about how the previous night had turned out, her body couldn't help but thrum at the memory of what she'd enjoyed *before* the explosions had started.

But, when their eyes met, Vlerion looked away. He wore an expression she'd never seen from him before. Shame.

Her anguish returned, and she wanted to shout that it wasn't his fault. But she was all too aware of Targon and the other rangers watching. She'd already confessed far more than she'd wanted to the ranger captain.

As Vlerion approached, he met her eyes again. His face was more masked now, and he nodded once to her.

The gesture felt so distant. She ached to pull him aside and talk to him alone.

But Vlerion stopped before reaching her and faced Targon while lifting the newspaper. Offering it to the captain?

"I've been investigating dead bodies in the catacombs and haven't had a chance to look at today's edition." Targon's tone implied he didn't *want* to look at it.

Why bother? Last night, the three of them had seen the version that had doubtless been printed.

"It's unexpected." Vlerion handed the newspaper to Targon, then took a deep breath and stepped around him to face Kaylina.

"She saw the graveyard of carnage you left in the catacombs. Don't distress her too much more today, Vlerion." Targon waved the newspaper and walked off.

Kaylina stared at his back, stunned by… Was that solicitude? From the man who always wanted her flogged?

Vlerion closed his eyes, not seeming to notice. Maybe he'd only heard that she'd seen the bodies.

"I… don't remember much." He opened his eyes but only so he could look past her head, staring toward the river without seeing it. "When I was… he. I think we thought we wouldn't run into anyone down there, but when we did… he was… not to be deterred. I remember snatches, rage, frustration." His voice lowered so much she barely heard him add, "Blood. Death. *Humans*. The worst it's ever been, that we've done. That *I've* done."

His eyes didn't moisten with tears the way hers had, but that shame returned to them. Anguish. Regret.

"It's not your fault, Vlerion." Kaylina gripped his forearm, wanting him to look at her, not *past* her. "It's the Daygarii who cursed your line, and then it's… me too. We both made bad choices last night. Let wishfulness lead us to… that."

"Yes." He sounded numb. Dead.

She hoped he didn't blame her. If she'd given in to the beast, he wouldn't have needed to flee and wouldn't have stumbled onto those men. He wouldn't have killed.

Unless he'd killed her. But she didn't know if that would have happened. His mother had survived. Maybe she would have too. Maybe it wouldn't have even been that bad.

Vlerion looked down at her.

"I'm sorry," she said, though she didn't know if he wanted an apology. She felt guilty, like she owed him one.

"*You* have nothing to apologize for."

"Are you sure?" Kaylina attempted a smile. "It seems right."

He laid a hand on hers. "I shouldn't have made assumptions about that potion. I should have found a way to test it first before coming to you."

"Like… on another woman? I wouldn't have been delighted by that choice."

"No. I don't know." Vlerion rubbed his face, and she noticed bruises darkening his stubbled jaw and a fresh gash on his scalp. The mercenaries must have landed a few blows before succumbing to the beast. "I know you've been frustrated—as have I—and I wanted to give you a reason to stay. To wait. Until…"

"I *will* stay. I know it's taking a long time to figure out this curse, but I'm learning more about what I might be able to do—and about my heritage—every day. Whether I want to or not." She tried her smile again, hoping to lighten his mood.

"You are. I have faith." He didn't return the smile. "In the meantime, however, it may be best if I leave."

Kaylina swallowed and glanced at Targon, wondering if the captain might be behind that choice, but he'd walked away and was reading the newspaper.

"Leave… me?" she asked. "Or…?"

"The city." Vlerion looked toward the newspaper and then around them, but there weren't many people walking the river trail this morning. Elsewhere, steam whistles blew, men shouted, and horse hooves clattered on the cobblestones, promising kingdom subjects were going about their day, but it was still behind the castle. "But you, perforce, as well. As long as I'm here..."

Kaylina shook her head. "You don't have to go. We'll stay away from risky situations." She waved toward the castle—toward her *bedroom*, though it had been the hallway near the tower where they'd had their interlude. "We won't let you turn again. When I'm not, er, *distracted*, you know I've been able to help soothe you. I can stay nearby if you want, in case anyone irritating walks up and vexes you. More irritating and vexing than me, I mean." She thought of the queen, though Jana Bloomlong filled that slot for her.

"It is not only that, although... last night was living out one of my nightmares, unfortunately. For that crime alone, I should be put to death." Vlerion lifted his gaze skyward, the soft drizzle dampening his cheeks.

By the moon gods, he wasn't thinking of his end was he? Admitting everything to the authorities and putting himself forward to be executed? Or... arranging for his death on his own?

"You can't..." Blame yourself, Kaylina wanted to say, but they were both to blame, weren't they? He'd made a poor choice, and she'd gone right along with it, even though she'd been concerned.

Her hand strayed to her pocket. After Targon's comment about the elixir not hurting Vlerion before, she doubly regretted that she hadn't thrown it at him, hadn't done her best to stop the beast.

Vlerion lowered his gaze to her hand—her pocket. "I remember you reaching for... What's in there?"

Kaylina hesitated. What if Vlerion grew angry that she'd asked Zhani for the elixir that Sabor, a detested enemy, had used on him? She believed Vlerion would understand—after all, he'd also been making requests from the Zhani pharmacy to stave off the beast—but couldn't put aside her trepidation as she delved into her pocket to show him the vial.

His eyebrows rose. There wasn't a label or anything to identify it.

Kaylina licked her lips. "It's some of the stuff Sabor threw at you in the alley. Not the acid but what broke the spell of the beast."

"And made me crumple helpless at his feet." Vlerion's tone was flat, his face hard to read.

"Yeah. I asked Zhani to figure out what it was so I could... Well, I thought, in case my power wasn't enough, it might be good to be able to make the beast turn back."

"That *would* have been good last night."

"Yes."

"But you were not able to reach it. He—*I*—stopped you?"

"I started to go for it, but I wasn't sure... Well, Zhani said there could be side effects. Like heart damage." Like it could have *killed* you, she thought but didn't say aloud. That seemed melodramatic after Targon pointing out that it hadn't the first time.

"I see."

"I didn't want to risk hurting you. I know the beast is dangerous, but I care about you."

Vlerion gazed into her eyes, his face softening, going gentle as it did for her but didn't for anyone else that she'd seen. Not even his old childhood friend, Lady Ghara.

"Because you love me," he said.

It was presumptuous of him to assume that, but it half-sounded like a question, so maybe he wasn't sure. Or maybe... was he in wonder?

"I do," she said.

"Even though I am a pompous aristocrat."

"Even though."

"Good," he said softly, holding her gaze.

Kaylina wished he would say that he also loved her, even though she was an irreverent, scheming, pain in the ass, but he glanced over his shoulder. Maybe because his captain wasn't far away, and the other rangers glanced over now and then, he didn't voice anything else.

Too bad. Kaylina knew he appreciated her and cared about her, but she would have liked him to say that he loved her. She believed it to be true, but one never knew for certain until one heard the words.

No, she decided as he continued to gaze at her with those gentle eyes, eyes that knew she had risked her life because she hadn't wanted to chance hurting him. Maybe she didn't need to hear the words. Maybe his love was there on his face.

Vlerion grasped her hand, drawing her from her musing. She thought he would take the vial from her. Instead, he curled her fingers around it, securing it in her grip. He leaned close to whisper in her ear.

"The next time you have reason to need it, do not hesitate. Throw it at me."

"Vlerion." She wanted to protest, even if he was right.

He brushed his lips along her cheek, kissing her briefly before leaning back and releasing her hand. He clasped his wrist behind his back, as if to remind himself that they dared not let their touches linger. That knowledge never stopped making her long for him.

"I do not intend to let the beast out again, so you should not need it. The rangers and the crown—" His brow furrowed, an acknowledgment, perhaps, that he didn't quite know *who* "the crown" was at the moment. "They may need me, so I won't do anything drastic, unless my superiors decide that is the right thing. But I will leave the area for a time, so that I can't be used. I don't want to be a catalyst for a civil war between mother and son—or the Virts and their family. At this point, I don't know what's most likely."

"But..." Kaylina looked toward the newspaper, wondering for

the first time if something different from the front page they'd seen had ultimately been printed. Why did he believe...

"I'll tell Targon where to find me in case he needs me," Vlerion said, "but it may be best if you and your taybarri don't know how to reach me. For your own sake as well as mine."

"You think I'll be so bereft without your touch that I'll ride out in the middle of the night to find you?" she asked before realizing the more likely reason. "Or... are there assassins again? People who might find me and question me about your whereabouts?"

"I don't know yet if there will be assassins, but I deem that feasible."

"I'd deem it *likely*," Targon said, catching who knew how much of their conversation. Newspaper raised, he walked closer to them. "After this, the prince *and* the queen may be after you."

"Yes," Vlerion said. "And since I rejected the queen's... proposal, she'll consider me more of a threat."

Targon grunted. "Maybe you should have accepted it. For the sake of peace in the kingdom. Besides, she's older than you. She'd croak eventually, and then you could find yourself a more amenable less-scheming soul to marry." He looked at Kaylina but didn't suggest she might fill that role.

She wanted to bristle at this future that didn't include her at all, but Targon had lowered the paper, and she saw an opportunity to slip it out of his hands so she could see for herself what it contained.

"And you'd be king," Targon added, not stopping her from taking it.

"A job I do not desire."

"It's in your blood, Vlerion. If the kingdom needs you, you must serve."

"I wasn't educated or prepared to take on such a duty." Vlerion looked toward the mountains, a reminder that he'd been trained to be a ranger, to ride alone or with a partner for days on end, battling deadly animals and enemies. More than once, he'd admitted he was more at home out there, far from crowds, far from people who might vex him to the point of changing. And hadn't the last months proved it was safer for all if he was out there? Since he'd met Kaylina, he'd changed—changed and *killed* —far more often than he had before.

"You'd still be a better choice than Petalira's bratty kid," Targon said. "If those mercenaries are any indication, Enrikon doesn't intend to give up his chance at power without a fight. But he'd be a nightmare for Zaldor. He'd give even less lenience to the Virts, and he's not shown respect toward the long-established aristocratic families that control the farms and ranches that feed the kingdom. They're bristling about the idea of him in charge too."

Kaylina looked at the front page of the paper but struggled to focus with them speaking beside her.

"As long as I am cursed, it is not a role I could accept. That is why my ancestor abdicated. One cannot protect and provide for the people by day and worry about turning into a monster that kills them by night. I suspect a political job would be more likely to make a man lose his cool and turn than..." He glanced at but didn't point at Kaylina.

"Vlerion." Targon gripped his arm and drew him away from her.

She wanted to hear what they said next but made herself stay put and read the paper. Not even the heading was the same as the one she'd read the night before, but the article did discuss Vlerion and it did reveal him as the beast.

A beast, it said, who protected people. She gawked in surprise as she read the words.

It claimed that when the ranger lord, Vlerion, saw threats to the kingdom, he changed and had the power of twenty men. He'd slain assassins, insurrectionists, Kar'ruk invaders, and diabolical traitors, such as Spymaster Sabor, who'd not only plotted to seize control and rule the kingdom himself but had been responsible for the hangings of factory workers whose only crimes had been complaining about onerous working conditions. After witnessing the vile acts of the spymaster, Lord Vlerion had taken the powerful beast form to slay the man. He'd had nothing to do, the newspaper assured the reader, with the death of King Gavatorin, who'd passed of natural causes. As a ranger and aristocrat, he'd always supported the king, never craving power for himself, even though he, as the only living male of the Havartaft line, was himself the rightful king.

After that, the article turned into a history lesson, speaking of King Balzarak, Vlerion's ancestor, and how prosperous Zaldor had been in the days when he'd ruled. For six centuries, since before the gold boom and the moving of the capital, the Havartafts had reigned, never expanding the borders too far, always focusing on doing good for the current subjects, rather than starting wars and annexing lands and absorbing peoples that would later be difficult to manage. The only mistake a Havartaft ruler had ever made had been trying to save the starving subjects around the capital by sending the rangers into the preserve to hunt, and they'd been cursed ever since.

"I don't understand," Kaylina murmured, though the article had, as far as she knew, gotten more details right about the curse than most iterations of Vlerion's story she'd seen and heard. He couldn't change to fight wrongs, unfortunately, and it was chance if he'd killed threats to the kingdom. He hadn't even been the one to slay Sabor, though she would happily let him keep the credit for that, especially if it turned into something that could help him.

But why would it? Who'd been responsible for this article, and toward what end had it been printed?

"How to read?" came Frayvar's voice from the side. He'd ambled out the gate and caught her mumbling to the paper. "I thought you'd mastered that, though Silana did mention that it took you until you were *six* to get the hang of it."

"We aren't all geniuses who can learn at three."

"Grandma said I was only two when I started reading recipe cards with her in the kitchen."

"That's why you're her favorite. What do you think of this?" Kaylina handed the newspaper to him, though he hadn't seen the earlier version and wouldn't know that it had changed.

While he read, she puzzled over who could have changed it—and why. The Virts?

She thought of Grittor, but how could he have influenced the newspaper printer? This wasn't the underground press that his people had started. Besides, just because he'd asked if the Virts owed her and Vlerion a favor didn't mean he would immediately become a supporter of the beast.

"Huh." Frayvar didn't sound surprised by any of it.

Only then did she remember that she'd never told her brother about Vlerion's curse. She'd promised Vlerion early on that she wouldn't and had struggled to keep that secret.

"That's not really what makes him lose it, is it?" Frayvar looked toward where Targon and Vlerion spoke under a willow.

"No, but— Wait, did you *know* about his curse? And what it does?"

"Of course."

"But I've been keeping that a secret from you."

Frayvar rolled his eyes. "I'm not a dimwit, Kay. Didn't we just establish that?"

"You didn't read a *recipe card* to learn about the curse." She reined in her sarcasm and wondered if he *had* read about it somewhere.

"Nope. I figured it out a while ago. You're a wonderful schemer, but you're not that great at lying." Frayvar handed the newspaper back. "It sounds like someone wants him to be the next king and is trying to get him the support of the common man. Even the aristocrats. Everyone who reads this newspaper, anyway. That article is trying to establish him as a folk hero."

"He's... a hero, I think, but not without..." Kaylina bit her lip, still hesitant to talk about the beast with her brother. Even if Frayvar had figured some things out, and he'd just read that article, Vlerion might not appreciate her babbling on the subject. Still, Frayvar *was* smart, and he was always a good person to brainstorm with. "He has some flaws," she said quietly. "The curse *gives* him those flaws. Once he turns, he can't control what he does. He barely even remembers it. He's killed... Sometimes, he gets people that deserve it, but I think he's killed some that didn't."

She *thought*? She winced at the dishonesty.

If those men in the catacombs were—had been—kingdom subjects, hired by the prince, the prince who was technically the rightful heir of the throne, they hadn't been doing anything wrong down there. Presumably, Enrikon had told them to lie low until he got a feel for the situation and whether or not he would need them.

"I did wonder about that," Frayvar said, "since you've been borderline obsessed with lifting his curse. Yes, I knew about that, even though you were trying to be vague. I assumed the beast thing might be... inconvenient."

"That's an understatement."

Kaylina caught movement, Targon returning. He was alone.

She turned, looking up and down the riverfront. Crenoch remained with Levitke and the other taybarri, and the two rangers who'd come with the captain were still there, but Vlerion had disappeared.

"Did you send him away?" Kaylina blurted, even though Vlerion had been speaking of leaving. It was hard to accept that he'd left of his own free will without saying goodbye. How long did he plan to be gone?

A lump swelled in her throat as she worried that he might not come back at all. What if he believed that leaving was best for the kingdom?

"Did you send him away, *my lord*," Targon said.

Kaylina looked at him in exasperation. How could he care about stupid honorifics right now?

More gently, Targon said, "If Prince Enrikon becomes king, policies might get tighter, rules more stringent, and lapses of enforcement less frequent."

"You mean Port Jirador will get even more *anal*?" Emotions made it hard for her to calm down and force reverence from her lips.

Targon's eyes narrowed. "The whole kingdom might become more stringent. You had better practice sheathing your tongue more often, especially when you're around aristocrats or anyone your superior."

"All you are is a superior—"

Frayvar gripped her arm and cleared his throat loudly to drown out the word *ass*.

Judging by the further narrowing of Targon's eyes, Frayvar might not have been entirely successful.

"Thank you for the advice, my lord Captain," Frayvar said. "We want to continue our business as law-abiding kingdom subjects, so we will certainly do our best to comply." He shot Kaylina a warning look.

She ground her teeth, detesting having her younger brother correct her, even if he was right. She managed to keep her mouth shut though. More than anything else, she was frustrated and upset about everything revolving around Vlerion.

"Also, my lord," Frayvar said, "would you and your men like something to eat or drink before returning to your headquarters?"

The two lower-ranking rangers looked wistfully toward the

gate. All the taybarri did too. More than Levitke and Crenoch whuffed with enthusiasm at the thought of breakfast.

"No," Targon said firmly, pulling himself onto his mount. "We have work to do."

He considered Kaylina. She braced herself, expecting him to command her to report to headquarters for training that she was not in the mood for.

"You stay here, Korbian. Out of trouble, out of sight, and, hopefully, out of the mind of anyone important." Targon waved vaguely toward the royal castle. "In a few days, I'll let you know if you'll be permitted to continue training with the rangers."

She blinked, at a loss for words. Seconds before, she'd resented the idea of being ordered to come train, but it sounded like he was considering kicking her out. Or… if the prince became ruler, was he a known misogynist who would forbid women from being in the rangers? If so, would Sergeant Zhani also be kicked out?

"Levitke." Targon clucked toward the taybarri, as if she were a simple animal. "Come with us. Korbian won't need you for a while, and other rangers probably will. I expect trouble to break out." He looked toward the city streets and the bridge crossing the river. "Any time now."

As the rangers rode away, Levitke hesitated and looked back at Kaylina.

She wanted to ask the taybarri to stay, enticing her with honey drops, though she doubted bribes would be needed. Levitke was a loyal friend and had helped her numerous times now.

Another lump formed in Kaylina's throat at the thought of losing Levitke as well as Vlerion.

"It's okay," she made herself say. "He's right. I need to stay here and work on the business. Frayvar's had to do everything by himself lately."

"That's the truth," he muttered as Levitke whuffed softly—in acknowledgment?—and padded off after the other taybarri.

"Though Sevarli has been really helpful. We might need to promote her."

"Why don't you ask her on a date?" Kaylina asked, though her brother's love life was far from the top of her mind at the moment. "I think she'd be delighted."

"A what?" Frayvar looked blankly at her.

"Are you *sure* you're a genius?"

"Grandma always said so."

Kaylina rolled her eyes.

As she started through the gate, the sentinel spoke into her mind. *I have received an update from he who planted his seed in your mother's garden.*

Kaylina halted. *My father?*

Yes.

21

The forest remembers.

~ *The Sentinel*

Kaylina headed up the stairs, fighting down yawns while bracing herself for snarky comments from the sentinel about what had happened during her *last* visit to its tower. Even though those vines had hung limp for most of the time she and Vlerion had been together, she knew it had seen everything.

She hadn't heard from it since they'd failed to stop the beast and she'd gone into the catacombs after him. It might be disappointed in her and would let her know.

She clenched her jaw, not slowing her stride. If the sentinel had news about her father, she wanted to hear it, no matter what censure came with it.

All sign of the broken vines had disappeared, magically drawn back into the walls again. At the hole in the ceiling, a couple hung down, as they often did. An empty pot lay on its side near the chair she used to climb up.

"Is that your way of saying you'd like more honey-water fertilizer and thank you very much, Kaylina, for taking time out of your increasingly busy and chaotic life to make it?"

The tip of a vine flicked a few times. It didn't make any noise, but it reminded her of when the taybarri batted their tongues against their lips irreverently. Apparently, the rangers didn't mind irreverence from their mounts.

Kaylina picked the pot up. "Since you asked nicely, I'll be most pleased to fill that for you after you give me the news about my father."

She half-expected the sentinel to demand she bring the fertilizer first, but, after a slight hesitation, it lifted the tip of a vine toward her face.

This time, she didn't play power games with it. After being up all night, she was too tired. Instead, she sat in the chair, placed the pot next to it, and yawned, halfway hoping the sentinel *would* knock her out. She needed some sleep.

"Go ahead."

The cool green tip pressed against her temple.

A vision filled her mind, the same man the sentinel had shown her before, leaning against the rail of a ship. This time, there were gray streaks in his green hair and creases in his forehead and at the corners of his eyes. It shouldn't have been surprising that he'd grown older, but Kaylina hadn't known how many years the druids lived. From the stories of the Daygarii, she'd sometimes gotten the impression that they were immortal.

In an earlier vision, he'd also leaned against a railing on the deck of a ship, gazing out to sea. Before, she'd seen him near the cliffs of her islands back home. This time, the fjords were visible, the spot where the North Drakmoor Sea transitioned into the Strait of Torn Towers. They were the same fjords she'd sailed past on the last couple of days of her journey to Port Jirador.

Is that where he is now? Kaylina couldn't help but feel hopeful.

Maybe her father could solve her problem. *Vlerion's* problem. Though Vlerion had a number of problems now, not only the beast curse. But if they could remove that constant threat...

She reminded herself that she didn't know if her father would help her in any way. He might arrive, think her a disappointing mess of a mostly human girl, and sneer and walk away.

He shared that he was sailing into the area, the sentinel spoke into her mind.

He can communicate with you?

From this distance, yes.

Could he... communicate with me? If he wanted?

You are not the sentinel.

Thank all the altered orchards.

Is that supposed to be an answer? Kaylina asked.

The sentinel waits. The sentinel watches. The sentinel listens throughout time.

And the sentinel was apparently in the mood to talk about itself in the third person.

"Definitely not an answer. Will my father come here? Is he on his way to see me? Does he want to try my mead?"

It was silly, but a part of her believed that he might be more impressed with her if he enjoyed her creations. From what her sister had said, he'd enjoyed the mead at the Spitting Gull, and hers was as good as what her family made. Silana, and even Kaylina's nemesis, Jana Bloomlong, had said so.

Not commenting on the mead question, the sentinel showed her the preserve, a meadow near the river, not too far from one of its entrances. Kaylina remembered running through that area at night when she and her brother had been fleeing the Kar'ruk. She even glimpsed the log that they'd darted across before falling—*diving*—into the river.

"That might not be my first choice of meeting places," she said, but it wasn't as far as the ruins. Since her taybarri had gone back with the rangers, closer would be better.

Not *her* taybarri, Kaylina corrected with sadness. If she didn't return to her ranger training, Levitke would be assigned to another.

Arsanti t'el Avadorstar will not enter the human den of overpopulation and depravity. The sentinel showed an image of Port Jirador to make sure she didn't misunderstand.

We call it the capital.

Distaste rolled off the plant. Kaylina didn't try to correct its feelings. Since the sentinel had lived here and kept an eye on the city for centuries, it probably had seen a lot of depravity, and it had doubtless witnessed the population in the area grow.

Should you wish to speak with Arsanti, you will wait for him in that meadow as the sun sets.

I will. Though nervous about meeting her father, Kaylina nodded firmly. *Thank you for relaying that message.*

I serve the Daygarii.

Kaylina decided not to ask if that included her. Previously, the sentinel had admitted being drawn to her druid blood, but she doubted it thought it was *serving* her. It probably referred to her father. No doubt, she should be appreciative that it wanted to defend her and hadn't killed her, like it had so many other visitors to Stillguard Castle over the years.

The vine lifted from her temple. She rose and started down the hall, but another question occurred to her, and she halted.

"Do you know where Vlerion went? If he left the city?" Kaylina remembered the plant showing her a vine that it could grow through the roof of the tower and use to magically see miles in every direction.

You are not now linked enough that you can feel where he went? The sentinel sounded... dry. And then it showed her encounter with Vlerion, her writhing against the wall as he lowered to his knees to give her the reward he'd promised.

Her cheeks flared with heat. It *had* been a reward. She should have wished it hadn't happened, since it had led to disaster, but that was hard. What she really wished was that he were here with her and they could have another night together—one in which they fully enjoyed each other's company without the beast arising.

"We should have gone to the bedroom," she muttered, though she doubted that would have mattered. The plant could probably spy through walls without trouble.

You remained so you could call upon me if needed.

They'd *remained* because she'd been too into the experience to think about going anywhere else.

Unfortunately, weary after our earlier joining, I lacked the power to halt the cursed one.

"I know. Me too. I would have had to throw the vial."

She *should* have thrown the vial, and yet... She recalled Vlerion's gaze when he'd realized she could have and hadn't... the love in his eyes.

Your power is not insignificant, and you are able to keep him from harming you, but you hesitate when it is possible that you might hurt him.

"Because I care about him."

Had you fewer feelings affecting you, your power would be greater. You would be closer to your Daygarii ancestors.

"I like my feelings." Kaylina yawned, wobbling and bumping the wall. She needed rest, but... "If I wanted to find he whom I'm *linked* to, how would I do that?"

Simply reach out with your power to sense his location. Because of the curse, he has magic about him and should be easier to detect than a normal insignificant human.

"So glad he's a *significant* human," she muttered.

The sentinel didn't reply. Kaylina, having no idea how to *reach out*, rested a hand against the cool stone wall for support and imagined Vlerion's face in her mind. She had called out before to Levitke, letting the taybarri know when she'd needed help, and, a couple of times, it had seemed to work. But she didn't want to call to Vlerion. She only wanted to know where he was going and if he was safe.

But, as she attempted to draw upon her power, weariness seeped into her body, making her limbs heavy. She yawned again, her lack of sleep making itself known. She only had time to think that she should head to her bedroom to rest before her body gave in to the fatigue and she slumped against the wall and collapsed.

22

He who least wants to unleash scorpions on his enemies should be given a jar of them.

~ Sandsteader proverb

Kaylina dreamed as she slept. Or was it a vision?

In it, Vlerion stood atop a watchtower in the mountains. It wasn't the same as the one Kaylina had visited—where she'd been kidnapped by Kar'ruk—but it was a similar stone building, giving a view of the surrounding mountains and trails through them. Instead of guarding a pass, this one jutted up atop a cliff, overlooking snow-crusted ledges and a great drop-off. Vlerion had climbed all the way to the crenelated roof to look out.

Or... *was* he looking out?

Wind tugged at his clothes, and he gazed toward the long descent below the tower. Moon gods' revenge, he wasn't contemplating jumping, was he? To end his life so he couldn't be a pawn for those who sought the power of the crown? Or was this more about the men he'd killed? That seemed more likely. He wouldn't shy away from a challenge, even a political one, but he'd implied earlier that the beast—that *he*—should be put to death because he'd killed others.

Fear shot through Kaylina as he stepped closer to the edge, looking thoughtfully down.

No! she cried, hoping he could somehow hear her through the dream and across the miles. *I love you, Vlerion.*

He knew that already, she reminded herself. And he was still up there, contemplating his own death.

The kingdom needs you, she added, thinking that might affect him more. *You swore an oath to protect it. Once we get the curse lifted, that'll be easier than ever. And I'm closer to achieving that than ever. My father is coming. I'm heading off to meet him, and I'll learn all that he can teach me. I'll ask him specifically about lifting your curse. Don't let a dark mood take away your future.* She might have scoffed at the idea that she of all people, she who'd had dark moods her whole life, could advise someone against giving in to one. *Don't let it take away* our *future. I love you, remember?*

Vlerion looked away from the edge and toward her, but he didn't step back. He merely gazed solemnly in her direction, his blue eyes troubled.

And then the vision faded, replaced by blackness, and then light.

Kaylina jolted awake to someone jostling her shoulder.

"Uhm, Kay?" Frayvar stood over her—she was sprawled on her back on the floor. "Are you sleeping or have you been horribly maimed by that plant? Er, did you put the empty pot on your chest or did it? Do you need me to get Doc Penderbrock? I heard fighting sounds in the alley earlier, so it may not be safe to leave the castle."

"I'm all right," she mumbled, pushing away the fog in her mind.

And the memory of that dream. *Had* it been a dream?

She swallowed, mouth dry. She worried it hadn't been, especially since she'd fallen asleep trying to use her power to find Vlerion. But she couldn't believe he would consider suicide, not when he'd said he believed she would figure out how to end the curse. Admittedly, that couldn't bring back the lives of those he'd killed, but if he could help others going forward, couldn't he find a way to make amends?

She didn't know. She wasn't in his place.

Maybe she should have been more negatively affected by killing Sabor, but, given the circumstances, she didn't believe she'd been in the wrong. He'd been a power-hungry asshole with delusions of self-importance. And he'd wanted to imprison her for her womb.

She shook her head. It was different, and she knew that. For Vlerion, those had been men—soldiers—who hadn't done anything wrong, not as far as they knew. Working for Prince Enrikon wasn't a crime. Even if he was an asshole too.

"My head hurts." Kaylina sighed.

"You might have hit it when you fell."

"That must be it," she murmured.

"*Did* you fall?" Frayvar gazed down at her with concern. "You're on the floor in the middle of the hall."

"I know. From what I remember, I kind of... collapsed."

His lips pursed together the same way Grandma's did when someone suggested a clearly inferior alteration to the Spitting Gull's menu.

"What time is it?" When Kaylina sat up, something heavy rolled off her stomach and clunked to the floor next to her. The empty pot. "Subtle, sentinel." She glared up at the hole but picked up the pot as she rose slowly to her feet.

Her headache intensified, pounding behind her eyes. She didn't know how long she had slept, but it hadn't been a *peaceful* sleep.

"A little after noon. I don't know how long you've been up here. I went to pick up groceries for tonight's service, but there were riots at three of the markets, so I had to flee before getting enough butter and flour. Tonight's diners may be disappointed."

"If there are riots, we may not get business tonight."

"People need mead and delicious racks of lamb even during trying times."

Kaylina headed down the hallway with him, the pot in her grip. "I'll hope you're right. Tonight, I can help—"

She halted, remembering why the sentinel had originally called her to the tower.

"My father," she blurted.

Frayvar paused at the top of the stairs. "You can help your father?"

"I, no. I mean, he's coming. I'm to meet him in the preserve at sunset."

"He… sent a message?" Frayvar's brows rose with skepticism.

"Yeah. Through, uhm, the plant."

Frayvar gazed back the way they'd come. "An interesting postal delivery system."

"More effective than the real one since Stillguard Castle still doesn't have a mailbox." Somehow, she couldn't imagine a druid posting a letter, even if the place *did* have a box.

"We should probably remedy that. People from out of town wanting to place orders for mead are currently having to send messengers to us." Frayvar brightened. "It's encouraging that they want our beverages enough that they're willing to do so."

"Kaylina?" came a woman's call from the courtyard. Was that Sergeant Zhani? "Are you in the castle?"

"Yes. I'll be right down!"

Dread swept into Kaylina as she worried what kind of news Zhani might have come to deliver this time. What if her vision of Vlerion…

She swallowed. What if what she'd seen him contemplating had happened?

Sergeant Zhani stood in the courtyard, not presuming to enter the castle again, and her taybarri waited outside the gate. A pang of longing went through Kaylina when she didn't see Levitke. It had only been a few hours, but she couldn't help but think Targon's parting meant Kaylina wouldn't be invited to continue training—or to continue riding taybarri.

"Is Vlerion okay?" Kaylina asked before Zhani could say anything.

"I… Do you know where he is?"

"No. Do you?"

"No."

Kaylina waved for her to speak about whatever had brought her. Not news of Vlerion's death, at least.

"People *are* looking for him," Zhani said. "Spymaster Milnor came into headquarters, cursing his name and demanding to see Captain Targon. Sadly, you weren't there training, so you couldn't make an excuse about having to use the latrine and run up to spy on their meeting."

"That *is* sad. I do love eavesdropping."

"Indeed." Zhani hesitated. "Will you return to training? I saw Targon order Levitke to stay in the stable and wondered… if you were okay."

Had there been a falling out? That was the question in her eyes.

"I'm not sure. Targon said for me to stay here for a couple of days." Or indefinitely. Kaylina frowned. "Until we see how things play out with the coronation of the prince. Or whoever."

Zhani blinked. "Vlerion isn't planning a coup or to put himself forward, is he? I rode past his rally and heard protestors arguing against the prince, but I didn't really think…"

"There's a rally? For Vlerion?"

"Did you see the newspaper article this morning?"

"Oh, yes."

"He already had supporters throwing his name around—I'm not from here, you know, but I understand his ancestors ruled before the current line. Now, the numbers of those supporters have grown. A lot. And they're being quite vocal today." Zhani lowered her voice. "There's talk that there might be civil war. There was already a standoff between the queen's forces and a bunch of men the prince brought along, but now that Vlerion might be in the running, things have gotten even dicier. I didn't think Vlerion had any interest in ruling, but a lot of people believe he'll be better for their agenda, whether it's the aristocrats or the commoners. I don't know what to think. Before you showed up, he was... maybe not a loner, exactly, since he commanded men, but he had the perfect mentality for a ranger, very content being off on his own or with a small group for weeks at a time in the mountains. I can't imagine him sitting on a throne, patiently listening to long queues of people with proposals and grievances."

"Maybe he could sit on the back of a taybarri instead of a throne," Kaylina said, though Vlerion had told her himself that he didn't want that job. If he did, he would have been attending those rallies and gathering men, not hiding out in the mountains.

Or... atop a tower perched on a cliff overlooking a deadly drop?

She glanced at the sun, wishing she had time to go look for him, but she couldn't miss her father's visit, not when he might offer a solution to the curse. If she could go to Vlerion with the answer to his main problem, he would be relieved, and he might forgive himself for the mercenaries' deaths.

"So he could ride away if the queues got too long and the people too onerous?" Zhani asked.

"Yes. Do you think that would help?"

Zhani shook her head. "No. He'd hate it."

"Yeah."

"Although... there is a Sandsteader proverb. He who least wants to unleash scorpions on his enemies should be given a jar of them."

"Is that like the kingdom saying, he who least wants power should be given as much as he can handle?"

"Yes. But we like to incorporate desert insects and reptiles in our platitudes." Zhani winked. "Makes them more memorable. Spend your life turning over rocks in search of gold, and you'll die to a rattlesnake's bite."

"You have a lot of venomous things over there, don't you?"

"It can be a deadly and forbidding place."

"Should you look wistful and homesick when you say things like that?"

"Probably not." Zhani smiled, but it faded as she contemplated Kaylina. "There's a reason I came besides discussing Vlerion's suitability as a kingdom monarch."

"Oh?"

"I heard—well, nobody told me, but when I heard about the mercenaries who were killed in the catacombs, I thought... maybe the elixir failed."

"Actually, I failed to throw it at Vlerion."

"Throw?" Zhani asked. "He needed to ingest it."

"Oh, *that* elixir. I was thinking of the one Sabor used that you got for me."

"I guess I should have considered that *it* failed too. For the events in the catacombs to have taken place."

"The, uh, libido thing seemed to work at first, but it wasn't quite enough. He got too into... things." Kaylina blushed.

"The magic that draws you two together may be too much. I've heard that blend works very well, so I was comfortable recommending it. At the time, I didn't quite understand the ramifications of what would happen if he became aroused."

"Yeah."

"Now, I regret offering it. I apologize to you and to Vlerion."

"It's not your fault. There's nothing to apologize for. We... made a mistake."

A taybarri whuffed, and they turned to find Jankarr riding up to the gate. Or maybe he'd been there the whole time and out of view beyond the courtyard wall. Zhani lifted a hand, as if acknowledging that he was waiting.

"Better to get this over with quickly," Jankarr said, then looked at Kaylina. "Have there been any disturbances in your catacombs? Other than what happened last night at that lake?"

"Not that I'm aware of."

"No noises of armies going through?"

"If they passed by, they didn't come up for mead."

"Captain Targon is assigning us to look for more mercenaries." Zhani pointed at herself and Jankarr. "He wants to know how many troops the prince has down there."

"Because you might have to fight them?" Kaylina realized she didn't know which side the rangers would take if mother and son ended up battling each other for the right to rule. For that matter, would they stand with Vlerion if he ended up making a claim? Or if, more likely, people tried to make a claim on his behalf?

"The captain didn't give a reason, but he wants as much intelligence as he can gather. As *we* can gather." When Jankarr met Zhani's gaze, he seemed surprisingly bitter.

Her expression more wry, Zhani told Kaylina, "We're both suspect right now, so we're being kept out of headquarters."

"Suspect?" Kaylina asked.

"Someone noticed when Spymaster Sabor was talking to me about you, and now Targon thinks I might be feeding information to Milnor. I'm not, but I do chat with Jankarr from time to time, and he's..." Zhani held an open palm toward him.

"Sabor *blackmailed* me into giving him information." Jankarr scowled. "He'd been doing it for over a year, threatening to have dire things happen to my family back home if I didn't snitch on my comrades."

"Yes, that's how he recruited spies." Zhani shook her head. "I never agreed."

"Unfortunately, I did," Jankarr said. "I had no choice. I understand why the captain was pissed when he found out, but I wish he would give me another chance. I haven't talked to Milnor at all. He may not even know I used to report to Sabor."

Kaylina had already learned about Jankarr being a spy, but she was surprised he was admitting it openly. Maybe he knew it had become widely known among the rangers by now.

"I know Targon's being careful, since this is an uncertain time, but it's insulting to be suspect when you've proven your loyalty to the rangers numerous times over the years." Zhani touched her chest and didn't look at Jankarr.

He winced and avoided Kaylina's eyes.

"I can imagine." Kaylina looked toward the sky again. "I need to head out of town. You're welcome to go into the catacombs through the root cellar here if you want." Only after she spoke did she remember that the sentinel, despite allowing Vlerion to visit, hadn't mentioned the rest of the rangers were welcome.

"Is it safe?" Jankarr asked.

"Maybe not, but the pantry is right there." Kaylina pointed to the wall between the kitchen window and the back door. "If you pass through quickly, vines might not sprout out to strangle you."

"*Might* not," Zhani said. "Encouraging."

"It *is* a cursed castle. I like to be realistic when telling people what to expect. We're still serving diners outside in the courtyard."

Jankarr snorted. "There's a vine-free catacombs entrance at the corner of Aspen and Seventh."

"No mead on the shelves on the way down though," Zhani said.

A boom sounded a few blocks away, and someone screamed. Kaylina tensed.

"We'd better check on that on the way to the catacombs," Zhani said.

Jankarr nodded. "I'm ready."

Kaylina watched them ride away, disappointed that she couldn't ask Zhani to accompany her to the preserve. "Maybe it's just as well."

The preserve also wasn't a safe place for rangers. Kaylina would have to go meet her father alone.

Why was that idea terrifying? Because she hoped he would help but dreaded that he wouldn't? That he wouldn't like her at all?

She tried to tell herself that it was encouraging that he'd come. At the least, he had to be curious about her.

"I do like being a curiosity," she murmured.

Kaylina told Frayvar where she was going and asked him to make some honey-water fertilizer for the plant. She didn't want to delay. That done, she grabbed her sword and gathered food, water, a bottle of mead, and a number of honey-based treats she'd made to accompany the tastings. Gifts for her father, if he would accept them.

When she stepped out the back gate, debating if she could rent a horse for the journey, a familiar sniffing noise came from one side. Levitke padded down the trail toward her, the taybarri's nostrils twitching, her dark eyes fastening on the treat-filled pack.

"Levitke," Kaylina blurted, running forward and wrapping her arms around her stout neck. "I thought you were locked up and forbidden from coming back here."

Her tail swished, and she whuffed.

"I don't suppose you'd like to take me to meet my druid father in the preserve?"

Levitke whuffed an affirmative.

"You're a good friend."

Levitke sniffed the pack.

"A good friend with transparent desires."

That earned another agreeable whuff. Kaylina took out a couple of cookies, offered them, then climbed onto the taybarri's back.

Another explosion sounded, this one closer to the harbor. On a nearby street, horse hooves sounded as riders—guards, probably—pounded in that direction.

"We'd better go before you're missed or the gates are locked and people aren't allowed to leave the city." Kaylina patted Levitke's furred neck.

The next whuff had a concerned note to it. Kaylina hoped that didn't mean the gate already *was* locked.

23

Do not claw a wound in your side to scratch at a flea.

~ Elder Taybarri Ravarn

The city gates weren't closed and locked, but more guards than usual manned them. Fortunately, they only questioned people coming into Port Jirador, not those riding out. Kaylina and Levitke passed through without having to explain themselves. A relief, but the taybarri glanced back a few times as they rode onto the highway, and that made Kaylina uneasy.

"Are you expecting rangers to chase you down and drag you back?" She rested her hand on the taybarri's furry shoulder, willing her power to let her understand.

No, Levitke spoke into her mind. *Men follow.*

"Rangers?"

No. Levitke picked up speed.

When Kaylina glanced back, she spotted two cloaked riders on horses. Despite a warm bright sun, they had their hoods pulled up, gripping them to keep their faces hidden when a breeze rustled through. The riders headed east on the highway—the same direction as Kaylina.

That wouldn't have been that unusual, but Levitke's warning that they were following Kaylina made her uneasy. Maybe they had been since she'd left Stillguard Castle. Followers would have been less noticeable in the busy city.

"Are they after you or me?"

Taybarri not special.

"You're *very* special."

Not to most men.

"Well, I'm not special to most men either."

Levitke's glance back conveyed skepticism.

Since everyone from the Virts to Spymaster Sabor to the rangers had wanted Kaylina since she'd arrived in the north, she supposed she couldn't support her statement.

"I didn't *used* to be special," she corrected.

Levitke gave the same glance backward, then picked up the pace even more. The horses following them had also increased their speed.

"You're faster than they are, right?" Kaylina couldn't guess why anyone would be chasing her—were these more kidnappers sent to use her as bait to lure Vlerion into a trap?—but she didn't want to be caught. She couldn't miss this meeting with her father.

Levitke roared and flashed, the world blurring briefly.

The taybarri magic only carried them twenty yards farther up the highway, but Levitke kept running, powerful muscles stretching her gait longer. Her tail streamed out behind her instead of swishing side to side as it did at slower paces.

Gradually, the riders fell behind but not *far* behind. The openness of the cleared farm and rangelands to either side of the highway, and the wide Stillguard River flowing toward the city and harbor, made it easy to see for miles. Levitke and Kaylina weren't out of sight when the taybarri carried her off the highway and onto a trail into the preserve, and Kaylina worried the men would follow. If they were trackers, they might not have any trouble pursuing them through the forested land.

Doubt rode with her as they passed trees, ferns, and bushes, and she wondered if she should have stopped, turned, and confronted the two riders.

But she didn't hear horses crashing through the foliage behind them, even when the trail narrowed, and Levitke stopped glancing back. Instead, the taybarri gazed left and right along the route ahead, a wariness to her head movements and nostril twitches.

It grew darker as they rode farther into the preserve, the dense canopy overhead creating deep shadows. Clouds must have gone over the sun as well. They still had a couple of hours until nightfall—until the meeting time—but it felt like twilight.

Levitke issued an uneasy whuff. Kaylina, now more practiced at sensing magical plants, noticed more than she ever had before. Maybe that was what made the taybarri uneasy. Kaylina assumed the altered vegetation had always been there, but maybe it had come out of dormancy. In the past, she'd witnessed the plants in the druid ruins shifting from a somnolent to an alert state. Could the call she'd sent out have caused this?

Or maybe her father was nearby, with his pure magical druid blood, and the plants were responding to him?

Since the undergrowth covered trails quickly in the preserve, and few visited the forest to keep it cut back, Levitke had to push through a lot of vegetation. She hopped over rotten logs and stumps and mossy boulders to keep the river to their right. Even so, they lost sight of it numerous times. Levitke did manage to keep the sound of flowing water within earshot.

The screech of a raptor came from the branches, startling Kaylina. Insects hummed, and a smaller bird sprang from a nearby bush, rattling foliage as it flapped its wings to fly away.

Men still follow, Levitke said.

"Maybe I should have rented a boat instead."

Kaylina recalled the strong current that had carried her and Frayvar downstream for miles before they'd been able to get out. She decided an attempt to row up the Stillguard would have ended with her carried in the opposite direction, floating out to the harbor.

Levitke leaped over a toadstool-dotted stump wider than a house, and a log came into view, stretching across the river.

"That's the spot where Frayvar and I went in. We're close."

A furry animal darted across the log, shadows making it hard to identify. It came to their side of the river and disappeared into the undergrowth. To the left, a vine dangling from a branch twitched.

Kaylina reminded herself that the plants and animals ought to like her for her blood, or at least leave her be, but the preserve felt ominous this afternoon. She couldn't help but wonder if something had changed.

"Maybe it's irked that we're being followed," she murmured.

As far as she knew, Daygarii magic didn't attack normal people who entered the preserve, not unless they hunted. Only rangers, men following the same career as those who'd poached here centuries before, were attacked whether they did anything or not. She doubted the people following her were rangers.

"You don't know who they are, do you?" Kaylina wondered if the taybarri might have caught their scent.

Enemies.

"I figured they weren't zealous fans after me for my mead recipes."

Levitke took them under the moss-blanketed branches of an ancient oak, where more vines dangled, the tips twitching. A snake curled up on a boulder hissed at them.

"I'm not looking for gold," she told it, thinking of Zhani's Sandsteader quotes.

The snake gazed at her and then back the way they'd come. Kaylina hoped it was irritated with their followers and not her.

"Levitke, that little clearing there. I think that's the spot."

The taybarri padded into an area that emanated magic, the source a ring of blue-capped mushrooms in the center. Kaylina didn't recognize the species or know if they were poisonous, but something about them kept other vegetation from growing within several yards of them. Even the branches were thinner overhead, and she glimpsed patches of the cloudy sky.

After Kaylina slid to the ground, careful not to land on any mushrooms, Levitke faced the way they'd come.

"Our pursuers aren't far behind, huh?" Kaylina spread her arms, willing her power to let her know if anyone with magical blood was nearby. Since she'd sensed the mountain men who'd come to the ruins, she figured a full-blooded druid would be even more noticeable, but the mushrooms were the only prominent things she noticed. To a lesser extent, she detected some of the vines and altered plants growing here and there. "Do we need to set a trap?"

Levitke crouched, her tail rigid, as she prepared to spring at enemies. Maybe she *was* the trap.

There was a chapter in the ranger handbook about using rope to make snares to catch enemies, but Kaylina hadn't practiced the various knots described for the purpose. Vlerion and Targon would probably consider that a failing.

Thinking of Vlerion made her hope she hadn't made a mistake in coming here instead of riding up into the mountains to look for that tower. But she didn't trust her visions enough to be certain they showed the future. The sentinel's instructions that she should meet her father here had seemed more concrete.

After she met with him, Kaylina would find Vlerion.

"I'll hide and be ready with my sling," she whispered, creeping past the mushrooms to stand behind a stout tree. A few vines dangled near her shoulder, and she tried to convey to them that she might need their help.

From the direction she'd come, a branch snapped, audible over the rushing river. Kaylina loaded a lead round into her sling.

Silence fell, save for the flow of water. The animals and insects she'd heard earlier had stopped making noise.

Something lofted out of the gloom—a dark ball-shaped item that she wouldn't have spotted if it hadn't struck branches on the way.

"Look out," she whispered to Levitke, afraid it was an explosive.

The object landed, bouncing twice before rolling to a stop against a tall mushroom. It hissed, a vapor rushing out, misting the meadow.

"Get out of there, Levitke," Kaylina whispered, backing up as tainted air reached her nose.

A poison? Or a sedative? She didn't know but held her breath and willed Levitke to leave the clearing without inhaling.

As Kaylina backed farther away, trying to hurry without tripping over roots and logs, Levitke charged in the direction of whoever had thrown it. Kaylina would have cursed if she hadn't been holding her breath. The air stung her eyes, whatever that stuff was spreading as it continued to spew out.

She turned and pushed into brush to the side of the meadow, angling away from the vapor while hoping to circle toward the men who'd thrown the device. In the dense foliage, she'd lost sight of Levitke. Already, her lungs demanded she breathe, but her eyes burned, promising the stuff was inimical.

She crept farther, trying not to make noise that would announce her location. Let her attackers believe she was writhing on the ground in the mushroom ring.

Ahead, branches snapped, leaves rustled violently. Levitke roared.

In fury? Pain? A battle cry?

Kaylina couldn't tell. Sweat dampened her palm around her sling as she tried to reach the skirmish with the element of surprise.

A blunderbuss boomed, close enough that it battered her eardrums. Fear for Levitke made her abandon stealth. She shoved aside branches as she hurried to help. A root tripped her, and she barely kept her balance and her sling loaded.

Through the leaves, the blue fur of the taybarri came into view. Levitke sprang about and flashed, fighting in a clearing of trampled vegetation her movements had made.

She snapped at a man with a sword and shield, the hint of a gray uniform visible under his cloak. A guard from the royal castle?

His hood had fallen back, but Kaylina didn't recognize him. Blood streamed down the side of his face as he leaped about with impressive agility, evading the taybarri snaps and being tangled in the brush.

A second man—the gunman—stood on a log, his hood remaining up, hiding his face. He lifted the blunderbuss and aimed at Levitke.

The branches and bushes didn't offer Kaylina enough space to use her sling. Afraid for her taybarri friend, she sprang onto a mossy boulder, roots half growing over it. From the elevated position, she hurled a round at the gunman. It struck his hand an instant before he fired. Her shot shifted his aim, and the pellets flew over Levitke's head.

She snarled, flashed, and appeared behind the swordsman. He must have expected the maneuver because he whirled in time to deflect her snapping jaws, his blade meeting her fangs with screeches.

Kaylina had to breathe, her lungs demanding that she gulp air. Fortunately, it didn't seem as tainted here. She still caught a pungent whiff of something foul but hoped she was far enough downwind that it wouldn't hurt her.

The gunman turned toward Kaylina, not appearing alarmed by her appearance. She slid another round into her sling, hoping she could reload faster than he.

But the man dropped the firearm and withdrew a throwing knife. Kaylina ducked down behind the boulder as he threw. The blade flew over her head and thunked into a tree trunk.

To her side, a vine twitched, its tip pointing at her. No, *behind* her. Was that a warning?

Attack! Kaylina yelled silently to it—to any vines in the area.

The brand on her hand warmed, and she sensed power flowing from it. Then, instincts promising it was a good idea, she scrambled over the boulder to the other side. Maybe getting closer to the gunman wasn't wise, but she stayed low, keeping her head below the bushes.

She came down, afraid to turn and put the gunman at her back, but a gasp from the spot where she'd been demanded a look.

Four vines had descended from the trees, and they gripped a man clenching a dagger in his hand, hefting him from the ground. There was a *third* person? She'd only seen two. This guy must have already been waiting somewhere along the way, ready to join the others and pounce. It had almost worked. He'd been an instant from catching her, probably intending to press that blade to her throat, a move she'd suffered far, *far* too often.

Keep him there, please, she thought, willing more power into the words.

The vines hefted him higher from the ground, and another snaked in, wrapping around his wrist.

"Spymaster," the man blurted. "She's got—"

Another vine whipped in and flattened across his mouth, like the brutish hand of a kidnapper.

Spymaster?

Branches rustled behind her. Kaylina whirled back, reaching for her sword, certain her sling wouldn't be enough.

The gunman was creeping toward her, but a huge blue blur arrowed in, slamming into him. Levitke knocked him five feet as she took him to the ground, smashing foliage. The blunderbuss tumbled free from the man's grip, hit a tree, and went off, pellets flying wildly.

An owl high above screeched and flapped away.

Kaylina looked toward the previous fight to make sure the swordsman wasn't poised to attack. But Levitke had defeated him. He had collapsed halfway in a bush, his throat torn out.

"Get off me," the man under Levitke yelled, his voice familiar. "You craters-cursed—"

Levitke shifted, using her bulk to smother his mouth, cutting him off even more effectively than the vine had silenced the other man.

Kaylina crept forward. The gloom was deep, but enough daylight remained for her to make out the face of the man—what wasn't smashed under a taybarri rear end. Levitke had chosen to *sit* on her foe to keep him still and quiet.

"You're a good girl, my friend," Kaylina whispered, not positive there weren't more enemies about.

Levitke whuffed and shifted her weight slightly, eliciting a groan from the pinned man. His hood had finally fallen back, and Kaylina recognized him.

"Spymaster Milnor," she said, surprised he'd come personally to do his dirty work. Had he intended to kill her? Or hoped she would lead them to Vlerion? That latter seemed more likely. "If you're looking for Lord Vlerion, he's not with me."

Milnor glared at her but couldn't speak.

Kaylina was tempted to leave it that way, but Levitke couldn't sit on him forever.

"Will you move off his mouth but not the rest of him?" Maybe she could convince some more nearby vines to help. Milnor would look good strung up from a tree with a tendril gagging him.

Levitke shifted her rump to the spymaster's chest but not without growling a warning at him.

"Where is he?" Milnor demanded, then spat, fur probably coating his tongue. "I know you know."

"I actually don't know."

The haunting memory of her dream—or her vision?—came to mind, of Vlerion on top of that tower, the wind tugging at his clothes, the promise of death gazing up at him.

She shook it away, refusing to believe he'd taken his life. Even if she knew for certain he'd been on that watchtower, she wouldn't have admitted it to Milnor.

"Why do you want him?" she asked.

"Why do you *think*? He's a threat to the proper succession. The rangers are refusing to obey the prince, the *rightful* heir. There shouldn't be a question about his coronation. But *Vlerion*, the traitorous bastard—" Milnor broke off with a gagging noise.

If taybarri fur had clogged his airway, Kaylina had no sympathy. "Vlerion is as far from a traitor as possible. He's been loyal to the crown all along. Even when the king and queen did nothing to deserve his loyalty. And you can..."

She trailed off because the spymaster was still gagging. Or... was he trying to breathe?

His legs kicked as he tried to thrash free of Levitke. She looked down at his face, then lunged away from him, whirling and baring her fangs.

Milnor grabbed for something wrapped around his neck. In the gloom, Kaylina hadn't seen it, but it had to be another vine.

Why? She hadn't used her power again to order the foliage to attack him.

For a moment, she stared as Milnor rolled over and thrashed about, trying to pull it from his neck, trying to breathe. She was tempted to let this play out, but Vlerion was still in trouble for the *last* spymaster who'd died at her feet. And there was a witness again—the man dangling from the branch, watching with wide eyes.

Sword raised, Kaylina stepped forward. Attempting to summon her power, she uttered the word she'd once spoken, somehow knowing it without ever having heard it.

"Sywretha!"

The end of the vine partially lifted from the spymaster without loosening its grip on his neck. It *hissed*, cold reptilian eyes turning toward her, and a tongue flicked out.

Kaylina cursed and backed away. "You're not a vine."

No, that was a glacier viper, a white-and-gray venomous snake she only knew from the ranger handbook. They weren't supposed to live at this low of an elevation.

No wonder Levitke had been worried.

The deadly snake hissed at Kaylina, showing its fangs as its long body tightened around the spymaster, fully cutting off his air.

Don't kill him, please, Kaylina thought toward it, willing her power to convince it to return to its den.

But her power met resistance, as if it had encountered a wall of energy. Or... a wall of someone *else's* power?

Before she could process the thought—and what it might mean—a snap sounded. Milnor's neck breaking. His flopping legs stilled in death.

The snake released him and slithered into the undergrowth. Levitke backed further to avoid its path, and she growled low in her throat, body tense.

A chill went through Kaylina, and she turned slowly toward the remaining man.

Eyes wide, he still dangled from the vines, and a fearful moan escaped his gagged mouth. Abruptly, he went rigid, and another snap rang out. Kaylina gaped in horror. There wasn't anything around his neck, no snake, no vine, nothing.

But his eyes rolled back in his head, and he went limp, as dead as the spymaster and the swordsman.

Though Kaylina stood still, her heart pounded, vibrating her whole body. She and Levitke weren't alone in the preserve, and she didn't know if an ally or an enemy had arrived.

24

SAFER TO NEGOTIATE WITH EVIL THAN SNUB YOUR NOSE AT IT.
~ Kar'ruk proverb

"Hello?" Kaylina called softly into the silence that had fallen upon the preserve.

Her palms were damp where she gripped her sword and sling, but she didn't lower the weapons to wipe them. If her father had arrived and been responsible for killing two men… she worried that meeting him was not as good of an idea as she'd envisioned.

A questioning whuff came from the brush behind her. Kaylina was glad for Levitke's presence but worried for her. She didn't think the Daygarii had considered the taybarri enemies, but they were associated with rangers, so she wasn't certain. If her father could snap a man's neck from a distance without touching him, without ordering a plant or animal or reptile to touch him, might he be able to do the same to a taybarri?

To her?

"I brought some mead and cookies if you'd like to… chat."

Kaylina looked toward the clearing with the mushrooms but couldn't help but glance at the dangling man's body, the vines still hanging him above the ground.

I am here, came a soft telepathic call in a language she'd never heard but somehow understood. Because of her blood? Was it possible to be born knowing a language?

After taking a bracing breath, Kaylina headed toward the clearing. She had to pass the fallen swordsman along the way. His death didn't distress her as much as the others. Because physical taybarri jaws had done it, not magic. Not Daygarii *power*. Which, even though she'd been using it, Kaylina still found creepy.

Inhuman.

That was the word that stuck in her mind as she approached the clearing.

No take weapons, Levitke suggested, trailing behind. *He has great power.*

Kaylina didn't know when she'd started feeling safer with a sword in her hands, but she did. Nonetheless, she followed the suggestion to sheathe the blade. This was her father. Hopefully, not an enemy. She also tucked away her sling, then wiped sweat from her brow before stepping into the clearing.

He stood in the center of the mushroom ring, as if he'd materialized there by magic. But he'd been sailing on a ship earlier, if the sentinel's vision could be believed. He couldn't poof into existence in different places. Probably.

The mushrooms started glowing a soft blue that matched their caps. The strange light pushed the shadows back enough to clearly show her father's face. Arsanti t'el Avadorstar. That was the name the sentinel had given.

His green hair was graying, as in the most recent vision, and age lines creased his face. His aura was more weary than scary and forbidding. Had it been a long journey to reach this place? His eyes gleamed as they reflected the mushroom light. Or maybe they even glowed faintly?

Kaylina wasn't sure, but, despite having two arms, two legs, and a torso similar to that of a man, there was an alienness to him, something that reaffirmed her earlier thought: inhuman. Not only did his skin have the reddish-brown tint of bark, but it looked rough, like bark. As if all of him were callused. His mouth was wider than typical for a human, his nostrils more flared, and his ears large. Even with the differences, his face had an elegance about it, his features pronounced, and Kaylina could see why her mother would have found him intriguing. Attractive.

As she studied him, he studied her, looking her up and down, regarding her curiously.

"Hi," she said when the silence stretched, a few insects chittering again, now that the battle was past. "I brought mead."

It was an inane thing to say, but if he'd liked her mother's drinks...

I have enjoyed that beverage in the past. And yours is also made from the bees who visit the plants we left.

How he could know that, she could only guess. "Yes."

She slowly removed her pack, withdrawing the bottle as well as some of her cookies. Had she been thinking things through, she would have brought goblets, but she hadn't known how long she would have to survive in the preserve and had stuffed in food rather than utensils.

I have wondered whether any offspring came from my minglings with human women and, if so, whether any developed the power of my kind and would be drawn to call upon me.

Kaylina opened the bottle and crept closer to hand it to him. "Were there a lot of minglings? With different women?"

Did she have more brothers and sisters than she knew about?

There were some. When I grew lonely for companionship. For many years, I have been the last of the Daygarii in this world, left to guard that which we left until such time as our kind wish to return. His eyes grew distant. Wistful? *That is...* if *they return. I believe... that will not happen before I pass.*

"Why did they leave?" Kaylina placed the bottle and two cookies in his hands, though he wasn't paying attention to her offerings.

The human population grew uncomfortably large and destroyed great forests and jungles in order to farm and build. My people felt crowded out, our habitats increasingly encroached upon. We are not so fecund a species ourselves and were surprised at the rapidity with which their kind gave birth and matured and spread. And spread. For many years, we debated whether to destroy humanity or to go to one of the worlds where no such beings exist.

"Destroy humanity," Kaylina mouthed.

He'd said it so casually. Would it have been a simple feat to accomplish?

She glanced back toward the dead men.

I, and others, voted to leave humans be for now, to only use our magic to protect some areas from their axes and plows.

"Like this preserve," Kaylina said.

Yes. There are other such places around the world. I have waited, as I said, to see if any of the seeds I attempted to plant would germinate and what the result would be. Arsanti gazed steadily at her.

"I guess that's me." Kaylina pointed to herself. "I have no idea if there are others. Uhm, we do have a term called *anrokk* though. I guess that came from your people. Is anyone with that animal affinity half druid?"

Not half. That is rare. His lips stretched in something between a grimace and a smile. *Not since the era of experimentation were there half-bloods. Not until* my *experimentation. Before then, it had been centuries since the Daygarii mated with humans. Those you call* anrokk, *and that is our word, are indeed distant descendants of our kind, but far more human than Daygarii blood flows through their veins today. You are different, the mating recent.*

"A little over twenty years ago, I gather."

Yes. That may be correct. Arsanti noticed the mead bottle in his hand and lifted it to his nose. *Your mother was on those islands, working in that eating house.*

"That's her."

She was beautiful and emotional.

"Sounds right."

She was not... the ideal choice for my experiment.

"Uh, okay." Kaylina didn't know what to say. She'd gathered from her sister's words that Arsanti had been a traveler and hadn't stayed that long, so she hadn't assumed he and her mother had been in love and devoted to each other, but Kaylina wasn't tickled to find out she'd been part of an experiment.

Her *mother would have been the logical choice, since she had an aptitude for many things. She first found the Daygarii honey near your island, made the drink from it, and she well understood nature and respected it.*

Kaylina blinked. "You were... hot for my *grandmother*?"

"She was unfortunately nearing the end of her reproductive years at that time."

"I'd imagine so." Kaylina subtracted twenty-two years from Grandma's age and decided she wouldn't have been terribly old then, and may well have been appealing, but she would have been nearing fifty.

The germination of the seed would have been less likely.

"Yeah, my *grandpa* might have objected to you germinating things in her too."

Arsanti gave her a confused look, as if he wouldn't have worried about whatever woman he chose being married. All he said was, *Since your mother was her direct descendant, I deemed it acceptable.*

"What were you trying to accomplish? With your, uh, minglings? I get that you wanted half-human offspring, but why?"

As I said, I'm the last of the Daygarii on this world and have been for a long time. It was... not exactly a punishment, like exile or banishment, but the collective suggested that since my vote had broken a tie and decided an important matter, I could stay here and protect our interests.

"What matter?"

Whether to let humanity survive or not.

"And you voted yes." Kaylina didn't glance at the dead men again but couldn't help but wonder what the druids who'd voted *no* had been like.

I did. But now, with age, I grow weary. One day, I'll not be able to protect that which my people left. Since they said they would one day return, I feel obligated to ensure the preserves remain untouched, the species that dwell in them safe.

"Are you the one that created the curses?" Kaylina remembered Vlerion and put aside her curiosity about her origins. She needed to ask her father how to lift Vlerion's curse.

No, but I helped plant the sentinel in the human city. He tilted his chin in what was probably the direction of Port Jirador.

"Three hundred years ago?"

Yes. I wasn't the only one remaining then. Some of the others who voted yes also stayed in this world for a time. He paused. *When there were others, I did not feel so isolated.* So lonely, his eyes seemed to say.

Kaylina opened her mouth to ask for more details about the curse—especially about *Vlerion's* curse—but he continued on.

I sought to leave offspring so that they could take my place. I believed they would have some power—our texts spoke of the experiments in the past—

"Didn't any of your people fall in love with the humans they, er, *seeded*?" Kaylina couldn't help but interrupt, affronted on behalf of her mother and any other women the druids had used for experimentation.

Arsanti gazed blankly at her. *Love? For... another species?*

He looked toward Levitke, who'd stood silently throughout this, watching from the edge of the clearing.

"Yeah, an intelligent species with feelings and hopes and dreams." Kaylina thought of how Silana had said their mother had fallen hard for her druid lover and had not been the same after he left. But for him... It sounded like she'd been one of many, and not even a first choice. Poor Mom.

I... cannot know what the Daygarii in the past felt, those who lived before my time. Arsanti set down the mead and cookies, then made a rope—or maybe *vine*—tugging gesture with his hand that might have been the druid equivalent of a shrug.

Kaylina wanted to lecture him on how people shouldn't be used in experiments but reminded herself of her most pressing need. She didn't want to offend him and drive him away if he had the knowledge to help Vlerion.

"Look, whatever the reason. I appreciate you coming here."

I was curious if my power would convey and you would have the intelligence to grasp it.

"*Something* conveyed." Kaylina turned the brand on her hand toward him. "The plant—sentinel—has been showing me how to use it. Sort of."

Interesting.

"Yes, I am. But I have a friend who's cursed to turn into a beast."

"The descendent of the Havartaft king who drew the ire of my people." Arsanti sounded stern. Talk about holding a grudge.

"Apparently. But *he* didn't have anything to do with that." Kaylina was tempted to argue that it hadn't even been a crime, but Arsanti's expression remained stern. He wouldn't want to hear that. "He's generations removed from the one who did. I know the druids put the curse on him, and I want to use my power to lift it. I'm trying to figure out how. Can you help me?"

She didn't ask if *he* had the power to lift it or would, having a vague feeling that he would prefer if she asked to learn rather than wanting to have things done for her. Of course, if she got the gist that groveling at his feet would prompt him to help Vlerion, she would put her pride aside and do so.

I knew she who placed the curse.

Was that promising? Kaylina raised her eyebrows hopefully.

"She foresaw a time when I and the other guardians would be gone from this world. She wanted to ensure this preserve, in particular, had a protector."

"Well, he—the beast—doesn't do that. He loses his mind and kills people."

Arsanti paused. Was that a surprise to him?

He kills those who threaten the preserve, he said.

"Uh, no. Among others, he kills those who threaten me." Kaylina considered bringing up the mercenaries.

Of course. Arsanti extended his hand toward her. *You have my blood, Daygarii blood. He would be drawn to you and seek to protect you.*

"I don't want him to be compelled to protect me because of my blood or magic or anything else except—" Kaylina kept herself from saying *love*, not wanting to explain her feelings to this man she'd just met. This strange non-human man. "Logical reasons," she finished, then added, "I also don't want him to turn into that monster, that killer, whether he wishes it or not."

She doubted Vlerion would *ever* wish it. Though maybe that wasn't true. He'd intentionally roused the beast, with the superior senses that came with that, to hunt the sage assassin who'd threatened her. He might not admit it, but there were times that power was handy.

The preserve must be protected, Arsanti said, as if it were a reasonable response to her statement.

"I told you he doesn't do that. Is that what he's *supposed* to do?"

I am certain of it, yes.

"Then the curse is broken. Can you lift it?"

I cannot.

Kaylina ground her teeth in frustration. "You can't or you *won't*?"

He gazed at her without responding.

"Did you try the cookies? They might put you in the mood to help your strange mixed-blood daughter." She attempted to smile but feared she was giving him her badger-baring-her-teeth-to-protect-her-young look.

Arsanti regarded the bottle and cookies at his feet, then picked up both. Maybe he would swig the mead, get drunk, and be more helpful then.

"Vlerion doesn't protect the preserve when he turns into the beast," Kaylina said again as Arsanti sipped from the bottle.

She didn't think that was sinking in for him. If the curse had never worked the way the female druid had intended, that made Vlerion's affliction even more distressing.

"Nobody does," she continued. "Well, maybe the cursed castle and the sentinel somewhat protect the area. People kind of remember why there's a link between that power and the preserve. But the Havartafts have kept their curse a secret, or tried to. At least until recently."

Until journalists had started printing stories about it…

"Nobody knows the beast is supposed to have anything to do with the preserve."

This is delicious. Arsanti held up the bottle.

Kaylina wanted to throttle him. Too bad humming songs from childhood didn't calm her the way it did Vlerion.

She took a deep breath and made herself say, "I'm glad you think so. The cookies have that honey in them too."

He nibbled thoughtfully on one of them and sipped again from the bottle. *The preserve must be protected. In addition to being the home for plants and animals and insects we wish to survive humanity's bruising touch, it houses our ancient ruins, the scattering above and the many below. Our libraries. Our memories. When the Daygarii return to this world, after the passing of man, they will wish for those items.*

"I get it. I'm not arguing against protecting this place. It's very pretty and only slightly creepy with all the twitching vines that can get pissed and kill people."

They protect the Daygarii as well. They protect you.

"I know. I figured that out and appreciate it." Mostly. Kaylina resisted looking at the dead men again. "But since Vlerion doesn't feel any urges to protect this place as the beast, I'm suggesting the curse wasn't done right. Or was a mistake altogether. Can't you revoke it?"

It is not indignation and anger over humans hunting here or destroying these plants that rouses the beast?

"No."

Finally, he was getting it.

Arsanti took another bite from a cookie. *It* is *possible something went awry and it's not being as effective as intended.*

"*Yes.*"

He frowned thoughtfully toward the mountains.

Was Vlerion in that direction? Kaylina had no idea, but she hoped her father wasn't thinking that he had to adjust the curse to make sure the beast killed every logger looking contemplatively toward the preserve. Dear moon gods, what if she inadvertently made things worse for Vlerion?

"Can't I protect the preserve?" she blurted. "Wasn't that the point of your experiment?"

His gaze returned to her. *Indeed. I didn't know if you would have the power, but I believe you have potential and will grow into it.*

"Yeah. When I'm not making mead, I can ride out here and keep an eye on things. There's no need for Vlerion to be cursed."

You would become a guardian and give yourself to protecting the preserve until such time as the Daygarii return?

Kaylina almost repeated a passionate *yes* but had the foresight to squint and ask, "What do you mean exactly by *becoming a guardian*? I was thinking it could be a part-time gig while I work at the eating house."

Should you give yourself to protecting the preserve, the curse on the Havartaft line might not be necessary, especially since it is not functioning as desired. It is not a simple matter, however, to alter a curse another has placed. I can confer with the ghosts of memory.

Kaylina had no idea what those were, but she liked the direction his thoughts were going now. Did that mean he knew how to lift the curse, despite his earlier obtuseness? That would be wonderful, but what did *give herself* to protecting the preserve mean? Arsanti was being vague about that, and she worried she wouldn't like what it entailed.

"Would I have to live here? And not get to run my business?"

Not get to be with Vlerion, she thought but didn't say. Of course, the preserve wasn't so far away that he couldn't visit her, but...

You would need to become as the sentinel, a watcher and protector of this place, of what lingers of the Daygarii.

"I wouldn't have to be turned into a tree or something, would I?"

A sentinel can have many forms.

"Many *plant*- or *tree*-like forms?"

They are of nature, yes.

"I'm not signing up for that. Besides, you've already *got* a sentinel." Kaylina waved in the direction of the city.

It is not ambulatory and cannot leave its pot, so it's not able to guard the preserve.

"It's pretty good at extending its influence beyond its pot," she muttered, memories of killer vines coming to mind. "Maybe I could get a wagon to load it in and a taybarri to pull it out here." She pointed at Levitke. "Then it could guard the preserve more easily."

This area is vast.

"Oh, I know. Finding Kar'ruk hiding in it isn't easy."

A guardian capable of walking, one with Daygarii blood, would be the ideal defender of these lands.

Great, a walking tree. Just what she'd always dreamed of being.

Should my offspring volunteer to become a guardian, and lead others with Daygarii blood to help protect the preserve, the curse may no longer be necessary.

"So, I just need to give up my life and my dreams for Vlerion to be free?"

Her earlier hope sank like a boulder in her stomach. She would give a lot to make it so he didn't turn into the beast, but could she give up herself? She had a feeling that whatever she became wouldn't be something compatible with a human being, with Vlerion, so she wouldn't even get to be with him. Maybe once in a while, he would come out and sit against the trunk of her tree.

"Gods." Kaylina bent over and gripped her knees. This *couldn't* be the only solution.

Before I make that promise, I need to research and see if it is possible to lift that curse. Amending it, I could possibly do, but since another Daygarii, one more powerful than I, placed it... He made the vine tugging gesture with his hands again before popping the rest of his cookie into his mouth.

"Well, let me know when you figure it out, okay? I need to think about things."

A *lot* of things.

You also need rest. You have been hunted.

"Tell me about it." Kaylina couldn't bring herself to thank him for helping. For *murdering* people. Especially not when she and Levitke had been doing okay on their own.

Rest while I research. Arsanti lifted a hand, revealing a leaf-shaped brand not unlike hers glowing green in his palm.

She stared at it, mesmerized. Had a plant—a sentinel—once marked *him* to help him learn to use his power?

The green glow extended to her, wrapped around her, and her eyelids and muscles grew heavy. In the middle of the clearing, she collapsed and fell asleep.

25

Never take for granted the value of a loyal comrade.
~ Ranger Captain Bonovar

Kaylina woke to early-morning light creeping through the canopy, a chill seeping up through the ground, and cool damp air blanketing her. She should have been cold, but warmth radiated from something pressed against her side.

She reached over and patted a large furry body. Levitke, the taybarri stretched out beside her, yawned.

"Thanks for keeping me warm," Kaylina murmured, deciding she'd slept through the entire night. When was the last time *that* had happened? "I think that was magically induced sleep."

Levitke whuffed in agreement.

"You're a good companion."

Levitke rose, shook herself like a dog, then wandered a few steps to pee on a fern.

"And not shy or modest," Kaylina added.

Her body was stiff when she rolled onto her side, but she

pushed herself into a sitting position to look around. She sensed the same altered mushrooms and other plants as the day before, but her father had disappeared. Off to research Vlerion's curse?

Hope and dread mingled within her. She wanted to fix him so he could be a normal person—the talented and noble ranger he was when the beast didn't encroach—and she'd thought she would give anything to achieve that, but could she sacrifice her humanity? Give up her dreams and everything she was?

"I don't know if I can do that, Levitke," Kaylina whispered as the taybarri wandered back over. "I wouldn't even get to be with him after his curse was removed, not if I turned into a tree or plant, some weird druid... *sentinel*."

Levitke nosed at the pack, and Kaylina dug out dried jerky for them to share, including a few cookies.

She didn't see the bottle of mead she'd given her father, so he must have taken it with him. Maybe it would give him a happy buzz, and he would see that he should wave his hand, lift Vlerion's curse, and leave her to protect the preserve as a human. *That* she would be willing to do. She could return to her ranger training and learn to be good at fighting so she could ride out on patrol and protect it with her sword, her taybarri, and her druid magic. Then she could return home and make love to Vlerion at night.

Kaylina groaned with longing for the notion, but thinking of him reminded her of the vision the sentinel had given her the day before. She jolted to her feet. She'd intended to check on him after meeting her father, not spend the night sleeping in the forest.

"We need to find Vlerion."

Levitke swished her tail and dipped her shoulder, an invitation for Kaylina to mount.

Before doing so, she looked around again for Arsanti. Would he expect her to wait here?

She dug in her pack for pen and paper and left him a note

saying that she would return. When she looked around for a place to leave it, two vines descended from a branch, startling her.

They tapped their tips together. It took her a moment to catch on and lift the paper. They captured it and held it so that Arsanti wouldn't miss seeing it hanging from the tree at the edge of the clearing.

"Thank you," she told them.

Kaylina swung onto Levitke's back, and they headed toward the boundary of the preserve, birds chirping happily. Rain started, and Kaylina couldn't share their cheer. At least the canopy kept most of it from pattering down on her head.

When they reached the edge of the preserve, Levitke halted abruptly. She looked toward four riders on the highway, their route taking them toward the mountains.

The men wore loose white-and-tan clothing that Kaylina had seen before. The sage assassins had favored that garb. Like them, these men carried swords sheathed across their backs or at their hips. She was too far away to see if they had sagebrush tattoos on their arms, but she wouldn't have been surprised if they'd been sent to hunt someone, regardless. They *looked* like a pack of bounty hunters.

She swallowed. Could they be after Vlerion?

Their horses trotted through puddles as they headed toward the watchtowers and the pass. In her vision, Vlerion had also been in that direction.

"It could be a coincidence," Kaylina whispered. "Lots of people go that way, right? Maybe they're leaving the city because of the trouble there."

Levitke's muscles were tight as she watched the men. They were past Kaylina and Levitke now, their backs toward them, and, in a couple of minutes, they would be out of sight, but the taybarri remained tense.

"Do you think they're assassins or bounty hunters, Levitke?"

A soft whuff.

"And that they're after someone?"

Another whuff of agreement.

"Vlerion?"

Levitke didn't know that. Like Kaylina, she probably had only suspicions.

"We'll head back and tell Targon."

She was tempted to trail the men, but, between the wide highway and well-trimmed grass and brush alongside, there was no way the assassins would fail to notice followers.

As soon as the men crested a hill and disappeared over it, Kaylina nudged Levitke's flanks, waving for her to head to town. The rain had stopped, but dark clouds promised it might return and come down harder.

Levitke startled her by running for the highway and turning not toward Port Jirador but toward the mountains. She chased after the assassins, her pace much greater than that of the men's horses.

Kaylina gripped the taybarri's fur tightly to keep from falling off. "What are you *doing*?"

The sage assassins had been amazing fighters, gifted by the altered plants they consumed, and even one had been too much for her to handle. She didn't know if these people had similar power, but there were too many for a single ranger trainee and a taybarri to take on, regardless.

Levitke didn't slow down. She charged for the hilltop.

A man shouted in his native desert tongue: *Something, something, Vlerion.*

Though surprised, Kaylina drew and loaded her sling as Levitke ran up the hill toward the crest. Swords clashed somewhere on the other side, steel clanging in the damp morning air.

"Bounty hunters," someone barked in Zaldorian. It was a familiar male voice, but not Vlerion's.

"Jankarr?" Kaylina asked in wonder.

Levitke crested the hill, and the battle came into view. Two black-clad rangers on taybarri wielded swords as their mounts leaped and bit at the four horsemen. The bounty hunters also wielded their swords, stabbing and slashing as they attempted to surround the rangers.

"It is Vlerion and Jankarr," Kaylina said.

What were they doing out here?

As Levitke bounded toward the fray, Kaylina picked out a target. She could ask questions later.

Though she hadn't had as much practice as she needed for firing from the back of a moving taybarri, she managed to clip one of the bounty hunters on the shoulder.

Vlerion looked in her direction, surprise widening his blue eyes, but her arrival didn't keep him from parrying a swing toward his head. He deflected the blade as his mount—he'd been reunited with Crenoch—lunged in, snapping at their attacker's horse. Right after, Vlerion launched his own series of slashes and thrusts.

Attacked from high and low, the bounty hunter struggled to keep his mount steady. It squealed and backed away as Crenoch bit and snapped.

Jankarr faced off against another white-clad assailant, his taybarri leaping about so the other enemies couldn't get behind them. The bounty hunters were quick and agile, but they rode normal horses, and horses were no match for taybarri.

A man on the edge of the skirmish drew a throwing knife. Kaylina fired another round, striking him in the side of the head. He reeled, catching his saddle horn to keep from tumbling off.

Levitke charged at his mount, slamming into the horse with her greater weight. The man's grip on the saddle horn couldn't keep him from flying off. He twisted in the air, managing to land on his feet, but Jankarr appeared behind him and lunged in, his face grim as he swung his sword.

The bounty hunter heard him and ducked to evade the attack, but it was a feint. Jankarr shifted the swing to slam the sword down onto the man's head.

Kaylina loaded another round into her sling, but she and Levitke were close enough now that they would be vulnerable to sword attacks. Dare she draw her blade against such skilled foes?

She was tempted to ask Levitke to back away, but her taybarri roared and went after a bounty hunter who'd lost his mount. He stood his ground, fearless at the huge taybarri rushing him, and lifted his blade to slash toward Levitke's snout.

Kaylina fired her round at his forehead. He jerked his sword up, forced to deflect the projectile instead of attacking the taybarri. The lead round clanged off his blade, but Levitke had reached him.

The man sprang to the side, avoiding her snapping jaws, but didn't see that Vlerion, still riding Crenoch, was waiting for him. Face utterly calm, Vlerion ran the man through with his sword.

One of the attackers shouted something, then wheeled his horse and rode away at top speed. He was the only bounty hunter still mounted, the only one, Kaylina realized as she looked around, still alive. The other three lay dead, their horses fleeing back toward the city, hooves pounding the highway.

"Kaylina," Jankarr blurted as she studied Vlerion, relieved, now that the battle was over, to find him alive. She'd been haunted by that vision. "What are you doing here?" Jankarr added.

"My taybarri thought Vlerion needed to be rescued." Or so Kaylina assumed. Levitke had known *something* was up. Maybe she'd caught the scents of her fellow taybarri.

Jankarr wiped his blade before sheathing it. "But I'm already rescuing him."

"Is that so," Vlerion said dryly. Dryly and calmly. With no signs of injury, he didn't look like the battle had bothered him in the least.

The situation reminded her of when she'd entered Spymaster Milnor's office to *rescue* Vlerion, only to find him sitting calmly at the desk. His face wasn't as grim as the day before, but there wasn't any humor in his eyes when their gazes met. He did, however, nudge Crenoch to ride to Levitke's side so he could lean over and hug her.

When Crenoch sidled up parallel to Levitke, the taybarri also leaned over. Not for a hug or anything affectionate but so he could sniff her snout a couple of times. After that, he turned a look—an *accusing* look?—up at Kaylina. He whuffed.

"Is he smelling cookies on your breath, Levitke?" After returning the hug and checking to make sure Vlerion truly wasn't injured, Kaylina delved into her pack.

Levitke lifted her head and swished her tail. Jankarr's taybarri, Zavron, also came over, ears perked at the rustling in the pack.

Jankarr and Vlerion watched with bemusement as Kaylina handed the last of her cookies to the taybarri, making sure to give Levitke one too. If not for her, Kaylina would have ridden the other way. The two rangers likely would have been fine without her intervention, but she liked to think she'd helped. And she was relieved beyond measure to have found Vlerion alive.

"Is it odd that she's giving our *mounts* cookies?" Jankarr asked. "And not us?"

"No," Vlerion said. "It's her druid blood. It compels her to do such things."

"And that's... not odd?"

"It is not. If you wish her to reward you with cookies, you must perform as well as the taybarri."

"I *did* come to rescue you," Jankarr said. "And warn you about the bounty and bounty hunters. What greater a performance could there be?"

"I already knew about the bounty hunters. This is the *third* group I've encountered since leaving the city yesterday." Though it wasn't visible in the distance, Vlerion glared sourly in the direction of Port Jirador—or maybe that glare was for the royal castle. Who'd put out the bounty? The queen? Because he'd turned down her proposal? Or was the prince responsible? Upset because some people wanted a King Vlerion and not a King Enrikon?

"I had no idea you were educating yourself on their existence so thoroughly," Jankarr said.

"Not by choice."

"It was at least noble and heroic of me to bring you your taybarri. You'll admit that, won't you? You'd be bereft in battle without Crenoch."

Now, Crenoch lifted his head and swished his tail.

"That was thoughtful of you," Vlerion said.

Jankarr nodded and gave Kaylina the same expectant look that Crenoch had.

"Uhm." She poked into her pack, hoping she had goodies left. "How did you get out here, Jankarr? I thought you were searching for more mercenaries in the catacombs."

When she caught Vlerion's grimace, she regretted mentioning them.

"I was, and I found them," Jankarr said. "Stealthily. I was able to overhear them talking about their plans."

"Apparently," Vlerion said, "the prince brought them along, as Targon guessed, in case he needs to fight the Castle and Kingdom Guard to take the throne."

Jankarr nodded. "I only found one platoon, but there are hundreds, if not thousands of men, stationed about the catacombs, waiting to fight if and when they're needed. Enrikon had them sneak in ahead of his arrival, figuring people wouldn't yet be on high alert and looking for trouble. The group I heard talking was discussing whether they would be sent after Lord Vlerion, now that people are arguing that he has a greater right to the throne than Enrikon." Jankarr looked at Vlerion. "Have you seen the chart showing your lineage in Taybarri Square?"

"I have not."

"It's just as well. A surly guard or maybe a Virt drew a giant, uhm—" Jankarr glanced at Kaylina, "—a phallic symbol next to your name. I think it was meant to be derogatory, but someone else came along and circled it with a heart, pointed the tip to your name, and added equally giant, uhm— Well, I think the whole picture is meant to indicate your suitability, heritage-wise and virility-wise, for the position of king."

"This is the intelligence you rode all the way out here to give me?" Vlerion asked.

"Well, you already knew about the bounty hunters, you said. I told you I'm trying to redeem myself."

"That's not necessary, not for me. Targon's the one irked about your double-agent status. You were his favorite commoner-rising-among-the-ranger-ranks story, you know."

Jankarr's humor vanished. "I didn't even think he liked me."

"I didn't say he liked you." Vlerion's voice was deadpan—or maybe he was tired—but he thumped Jankarr on the shoulder.

Jankarr's responding smile was wan. "You'll at least be pleased to know it didn't sound like the prince has anything to do with your bounty hunters. The queen, feeling jilted or threatened or both, has put a reward out for your head. She's the one who wants your death. Although..." Jankarr scratched his jaw. "Going by what the mercenaries said, the prince would be pleased to see you die too."

"Wonderful."

"The mercenaries don't want to fight you and eagerly await news of your demise."

"Remind me why I was pleased when you rode into my camp," Vlerion said.

"Because I brought your taybarri."

"That's right. Who would mooch from Kaylina if Crenoch weren't here?"

Crenoch turned his head to bat his tongue against his teeth toward his rider.

There weren't any cookies left in her pack, so Kaylina drew out a couple of pieces of jerky that she'd snatched from the pantry the day before. She handed one to each man.

"This doesn't look as good as a cookie." Jankarr accepted it but only after looking at Vlerion's hand to see if he was getting something better. "I'm possibly envious of my own taybarri."

Zavron let out a whuff that sounded smug.

"There's chili spice and honey in the jerky glaze," Kaylina said. "My brother made it. It's good."

Jankarr brightened. "I've heard he's a genius."

"He tells me that a lot." Kaylina decided not to be offended that Jankarr thought her odd and her brother a genius. Such was life.

Vlerion took a bite of his jerky while looking at Kaylina. "I am pleased to see you, but aren't you supposed to be in Stillguard Castle?"

"Oh." Jankarr snapped his fingers. "I forgot to share that intel with you. She's looking for her druid father. Did you find him?"

"Yes." Kaylina wished she could give Vlerion good news about his curse, but... she didn't yet know if Arsanti could do anything. Or if she could bring herself to pay the price he would demand if he could.

Vlerion and Jankarr raised expectant eyebrows.

Not sure how to explain the encounter, she groped for a way to start.

"If it helps, Jankarr promises he's done delivering the latest gossip to the spymasters." Vlerion's tone was light, but Jankarr winced.

"I believe that," Kaylina said, and she did. She also knew Spymaster Milnor... wouldn't be a problem anymore.

She needed to tell them about that too, but her gut knotted at the idea. She wished she could get away without admitting she'd witnessed Milnor's death. She would tell Vlerion in private, she decided, and let him inform Captain Targon and whoever else needed to know. At least, this time, she'd only been defending herself. Not that the authorities would deem that an acceptable reason for a commoner to kill a royal spymaster.

"I need to talk to Vlerion alone about it, please," Kaylina said. "It touches on a private matter between us."

"A matter of beastly importance?" Jankarr asked.

Vlerion gave him a sour look.

"Yes." Kaylina didn't see any point in denying that, not when the paper had shared almost everything.

"I'm glad I only recently found out about that," Jankarr said.

"Because you would have been conflicted about sharing my secret with Spymaster Sabor?" Vlerion asked. "Or because you would have been scared to ride alone into the mountains with me?"

"Definitely the latter. Sabor, I assume, already knew."

"He did. *Kaylina* isn't afraid to ride off alone with me."

"No, but she's odd. As we established." Jankarr gave her a friendly nod, a twinkle in his eyes making her inclined to accept the ribbing as a part of being a ranger rather than anything insulting.

In truth, having Jankarr teasing her again relieved her. He'd been so distant after she'd used her power to save him in the preserve.

"We specifically did *not* establish that," Vlerion said.

"I established it. You objected."

"As an aristocrat and your superior officer, my objection overrides anything you establish." Vlerion pointed up the highway toward the top of the hill. "Go keep watch while we talk. Let me know if a fourth group of bounty hunters shows up." After a pause, he added, "Please."

Jankarr's eyebrows flew up, and he looked at Kaylina.

"I taught him about how commoners like it when aristocrats say things like *please* and *thank you* to them," she said.

"Interesting. How did you impart such a *difficult*-to-master lesson on a noble?" Jankarr asked.

Kaylina raised her sling.

"Ah, of course. If I had breasts, I might try a similar method on Vlerion, but I think the outcome would be different for me."

"I can't believe you think *she's* the odd one," Vlerion murmured.

Jankarr waved in what could have been agreement or parting and guided his taybarri to the high point to keep watch.

Vlerion slid off Crenoch and walked away from the highway—and the bounty hunters' bodies. Though Kaylina wouldn't have minded the taybarri listening to their conversation, she also dismounted and followed him through grass that had grown tall as the summer progressed. It swished against their thighs, and they stopped under a pine, water from the rain still dripping from its needles.

"There's something I'd like to discuss with you, as well," Vlerion said quietly, "but tell me about your night first, if you wish."

A part of her wanted him to go first, to tell her about *his* night—and whether he'd stood atop a watchtower and contemplated jumping. But did it matter if he had? He was here, alive, and facing bounty hunters. If he'd wanted to die, he could have let one of them win. She frowned at the thought of riding over that crest in time to see him fall to an enemy's blade, and was glad he hadn't.

"It went that well?" Vlerion smiled slightly, though his eyes held worry as he watched her.

"It was... eventful. And I didn't learn quite what I hoped to learn." She hesitated, wondering how much she should tell. "I asked about your curse."

For an instant, hope sparked in his eyes, but he must have guessed from her tone and expression that she hadn't learned how to lift it.

"My father doesn't know if he can alter it in any way, but he's going to look into it. Apparently, instead of attacking friends and foes alike, the beast is supposed to be moved to specifically attack those who threaten the preserve. My father said that if someone else volunteers to... dedicate their life to guarding the preserve, your curse might not need to continue."

"Someone else?"

Kaylina touched her chest. "Me."

26

Bogged down in the minutiae of living, we fail to see others designing our future.

~ "Sorrows of Men," by the bard Nogorathi

"You'd have to turn yourself into a *plant*?" Vlerion asked as Kaylina finished summing up her conversation with her father.

"I'm not sure exactly. It might be more of a tree. A walking tree maybe. He mentioned ambulation being important."

Vlerion stared at her, his jaw slack. He'd folded his cloak across a damp boulder for them to sit on, and they perched shoulder-to-shoulder as they spoke. Now and then, Jankarr looked at them from the top of the crest, but he didn't signal any danger approaching.

"From what I gathered," Kaylina added, not sure if Vlerion was appalled, too stunned to speak, or some of both, "something like that is what he had in mind when he planted his seed in my mother."

"His seed?"

"Got her pregnant. That was intentional. A *mingling*. He did it with other women too. He wanted to pass along his druid blood and hoped a half-human Daygarii would develop enough power to watch over the preserves—there are more than this one, I guess—until such time as their people return." Kaylina didn't mention the implication that humanity was expected to be extinct by then. It seemed grim. "I am the result of an experiment."

She tried to keep her tone light but probably sounded bitter. Logically, it shouldn't have mattered—it wasn't as though the man she'd *thought* was her father had been a great guy who'd loved her mother either—but the truth stung. Feelings did not obey logic.

"That is something I understand completely," Vlerion said wryly, waving at himself.

She opened her mouth to deny that he'd been an *experiment*, but he probably felt similarly. As they'd discussed before, he wasn't a normal human either. And his mother's marriage to his father had been arranged, nothing born out of love.

Vlerion wrapped an arm around her shoulders. "So, you were destined to be a tree, and I a beast. That's why we're drawn to each other."

"Are those entities usually linked? I've read a lot of tales and don't remember one called 'The Beast and the Tree'."

"We're linked because..." He gazed gently at her. "Because."

"Yeah." Kaylina leaned against him, not having the words to articulate it better than he, but she did feel inextricably bound to him. By magic. Maybe even by fate. If the sentinel and the magic in her blood had played a role in her coming north, to the city next to the preserve, maybe she and Vlerion had been destined to be together.

"I trust it goes without saying that you can't accept his... proposition, if that's what you'd call it," Vlerion said. "It doesn't sound like he even knows if he can lift my curse."

"He's looking into it."

"Even if he can..." Vlerion looked gravely into her eyes. "You've a future as a brilliant mead maker and irreverent but honorable ranger. You can't give that up, certainly not for something I was born with."

"Something it's not your fault you were born with. Something you shouldn't have to endure."

"It is what it is. And everyone knows about it now. The first bounty hunter spoke before he attacked, saying he'd never hunted a beast. Like it was a sport, and he hoped I'd change so he could mount my head on his wall when he killed me."

"Did you kill him?" Kaylina assumed, since Vlerion wasn't looking over his shoulder, he'd thus far dealt with the bounty hunters who'd come after him.

"Yes. I didn't give him the satisfaction of changing into the beast to do so, though I was tempted, if only to show him how great his folly had been in coming after me."

"*Were* you... tempted? Almost roused?" She knew he was much more likely to grow furious enough to turn into the beast on someone else's behalf—usually on *her* behalf—than on his own.

"No. I didn't even hum. I hope he was disappointed as my sword pierced his heart."

"A lot of people are dying this week," she said, thinking of the spymaster. She hadn't shared that yet but needed to.

Vlerion closed his eyes, his face bleak. "I'm aware."

She cursed herself, belatedly realizing her words would make him think of the mercenaries again. If Jankarr had spoken the truth and they were rooting for Vlerion's death, she didn't feel as bad about the loss of some of them as she had the day before. Though she supposed it was because they knew the beast had killed their comrades that they wanted the queen's hunters to slay him.

"Did you go to one of the watchtowers yesterday?" Kaylina caught herself asking, even though she'd decided earlier not to bring it up. But she had to know. Had that vision been true? Had he almost jumped? And if so, what had stopped him?

Vlerion opened his eyes and looked at her again. Was that wariness in their blue depths?

"Yesterday, when Targon drew me aside, he asked me to check the watchtowers while I was on my way out of town, yes. He wanted to make sure nothing had happened to the rangers manning them. He said, with the way things had been going of late, he wouldn't put it past the Kar'ruk or other enemies to take advantage of the chaos from the king's death."

"Ah."

That was a lot more information than she'd asked for, and she sensed he'd used it to avoid answering the question she wanted to know. Maybe he sensed that she already knew. From the beginning, he'd not doubted that she had power. Even before she'd fully believed it, he'd known.

"Everything was... okay up there?" Kaylina wouldn't ask, she decided again. Not if he'd had suicidal thoughts. If he wanted to admit that, she would listen, but she wouldn't pry.

"The rangers were at their posts." Vlerion looked toward the grass and the highway—away from her. "The trek to check on them gave me time to think."

"Hopefully about how much better your life will be once your curse is lifted." She smiled and patted his thigh.

He squinted at her. "Something that will not happen because I forbid you from letting yourself become a tree."

"Don't worry. I'm not interested in that. I *do* want to fulfill my destiny as a brilliant mead maker and an irreverent but honorable ranger." She held the smile, since he was still squinting at her. Doubting her? Afraid she *would* make that sacrifice for him? "If my father comes back and says he's able to remove the curse, I'll bargain with him, or I'll come up with some scheme that will appeal to him, to what he wants. At the least, I'll promise to keep an eye on the preserve as my normal human—mostly human—self, as long as he lifts the curse."

Vlerion politely did not point out that being *half* human didn't make her *mostly* human. But she looked human, damn it. And she loved him the way a human woman would.

"I believe you *will* scheme," he said after scrutinizing her a while longer.

"Yes. I'm good at it."

Whether it would work on a Daygarii druid... that was another question. But she wouldn't give up easily.

"So I've observed."

Vlerion rested his hand on hers, and she grew aware of the heat of his thigh through his trousers. Maybe they shouldn't have been this close, but with Jankarr nearby, she wasn't tempted to climb into his lap and kiss him. Not *that* tempted, at least. Vlerion looked like he could use a kiss.

Up on the hill, Jankarr and his mount stirred, taking a few steps and looking in the direction of the city. It was too far for them to see, but trouble might be on the way. Crenoch and Levitke joined them on the hill and looked off to the west.

"What did you want to talk about?" Kaylina guessed they wouldn't have much more quiet time together—if one could call the aftermath of battling bounty hunters *quiet time*.

"Choices to be made."

"That involve me?"

"They shouldn't, though you would be, at least tangentially, affected." Vlerion regarded her. "As I said, I had time to think while riding. Under Targon's advisement, I fully intended to lie low, as he put it. But that felt to me like... hiding."

"When there are bounty hunters looking for you, hiding is an excellent idea." Kaylina didn't point out that he didn't appear to be doing a good job of it.

"I prefer confronting conflict, not shying away from it."

"By leaping in and roaring while swinging your sword?"

"Usually, only Crenoch roars. Unless..." Vlerion tilted his palm toward the sky.

Yeah, she'd heard the beast roar often.

"But hiding isn't in my nature, and I don't think my hiding is what the kingdom needs." Vlerion looked toward the west, as the others were doing, though from their position, they couldn't see down the highway. "Even if I were killed, I believe the prince and the queen might start a civil war, each vying for the crown. Petalira may not have a blood claim, but she's made it clear that she doesn't want to give up the power she's enjoyed, and I know she has allies who've also come to enjoy their power in these past years."

"There's at least one less ally." Kaylina used the opening to tell him about Milnor.

Vlerion didn't look surprised. "He may have acted independently of the queen. Or she may have asked him to handle me, and he, like his predecessor, decided to go through you."

"Yeah. I'm not sure why you think I'd only be *tangentially* involved in your life."

"A naive statement, perhaps."

"How are you going to confront the conflict that keeps finding you?" Kaylina thought it would be smarter for him to hide—to get entirely out of the province, maybe taking his mother with him—until matters were resolved, but she wasn't surprised that he wouldn't do it.

"By offering a third option for the people to rally behind." He sounded grim but determined.

"You're going to put yourself forward as a candidate for the throne?"

"Yes. I don't know if the rangers will stand with me or not. They've no loyalty to Queen Petalira, except maybe Targon, but the prince is another matter. There are some who aren't old enough to remember what a brat he was as a teenager—and, by all accounts, still is—and he's been out of the capital for almost a decade. There are others who won't want to fight the succession, what's in Gavatorin's will. But I have a case. I'll have to make it quickly and talk to a number of the Kingdom Guard captains. They'll be less likely to stand with me than the rangers, but if my comrades back me, some of them might. And I believe the Virts will fight for any change of regime that could benefit them."

Kaylina nodded. "I agree with that."

"Once it's known that I'm back in the city, I'll have a lot more than a few bounty hunters trying to kill me. Since I threaten *both* of their plans, Petalira and her son may work together to take me out."

"Are you *sure* you don't want to hide instead?"

He laughed shortly. "No."

But his eyes said he was sure.

"Well, I can talk the sentinel into offering its protection. If the rangers won't help you, Stillguard Castle will. And *I* will."

Kaylina wouldn't have been surprised if he scoffed and said there wasn't anything she could do; despite her burgeoning druid powers, she doubted that thought was wrong. She didn't have enough magic to sway an entire city.

But Vlerion nodded and met her eyes. "I know you will."

He meant it. His faith that she could do something filled her with emotion.

"I love you," she blurted impulsively.

She'd meant to say it aloud for a while, but it came out unexpectedly, and she blushed, as if she'd misspoken. But he was about to throw himself into danger—*more* danger. It was the right time.

Besides, he'd already presumed that she did; he'd even stated it, and she'd agreed. This wasn't that much different. Yet speaking the words somehow felt more vulnerable.

Vlerion nodded at her again, and placed his hand on hers again. "I love you too."

"Oh." She swallowed. "Good."

He drew her into a hug, which she returned, warmth for him spreading throughout her body.

"This isn't dangerous, is it?" She doubted he'd taken any elixirs this morning.

"Not with Jankarr on the hill."

"I didn't know his presence was that inhibiting. We should have invited him to Stillguard Castle the other night."

"I don't care for *company* when I am with a woman," Vlerion said. "Having that plant there was bad enough."

"I barely noticed it." She was positive the vines had been limp, though she admitted she'd been too busy enjoying herself to watch.

"Good." He sounded smug.

She smacked his chest but couldn't bring herself to draw back. "How can I help with your... quest for the crown?"

"It's not that, not exactly. As I told you, I don't want that job, nor do I believe myself qualified."

She leaned back to look at his face. "But you're going to try to oust the queen and the prince, right? You just said..."

"I worry for the kingdom if the prince takes the crown. Even if things remained as they have been... the Virts will be the first to tell you that hasn't been ideal. It's fine for the aristocrats maybe but not for the commoners, and there are a lot more of them than us."

"We're a prolific sort, we commoners."

"Indeed. We were creeping toward war even before Gavatorin passed."

"So, are you planning to... get rid of Petalira and her son?" Kaylina couldn't muster a real objection to the idea, but she doubted Vlerion had assassinations in mind. Even if the queen deserved it after trying to have *him* killed.

"Round them up and force them into exile. There's a historical precedent for that when it comes to coups. You can ask Frayvar about it."

"You're assuming I'm not well-read on such matters, huh?" She wasn't but put on an indignant face.

"Were they covered in your pirate sex adventures?"

"Those were seafaring romantic adventure novels, thank you."

"That covered historical events?"

"Sometimes. Would it really be a coup if your great-great-great grandfather was king? Coup implies an unlawful taking of power, doesn't it?"

"Yes. Future historians can decide."

"Okay, let's assume you succeed. You don't want to be king yourself. What, then?"

"I don't want to think too far head, since the odds of this working are slim. You'll note my current lack of an army." Vlerion nodded toward the hilltop, where Jankarr and the three taybarri were still looking to the west. "But if it works, I'll step into the king's shoes, then call all the heads of aristocratic families in the various provinces to attend a meeting, and I'll find an equal number of representatives of commoners, and we'll discuss what kind of government would be best for Zaldor going forward."

"Like… you'd dissolve the monarchy?" The idea daunted Kaylina. It was hard to imagine so many centuries of history, of the Zaldor Kingdom gone, just like that.

"I'll take advice from people wiser than me on whether to do that. It would be a monumental undertaking, and there are many who wouldn't desire that kind of change—indeed, who would fight it fang and claw." Vlerion shrugged. "It may simply be that they will desire to keep the current system and will find someone else with a blood-tie to the throne to rule in my stead. I suspect the aristocrats will want that."

"Which is why you're inviting commoners to the meeting? And giving them an equal vote?"

"Yes. Remember, this is a hypothetical meeting that probably won't ever come to fruition. I'll more likely die before dawn tomorrow."

"Don't do that. If you die, I'll be devastated, especially after you just spoke of your love for me. I'll let my weirdo father turn me into a tree."

"Perhaps I could be buried under your roots."

"A future king should be more optimistic."

What sounded like a soft bird whistle came from the hilltop. From Jankarr. When they looked at him, he pointed in the direction of the city, his expression grave.

"I feared we couldn't linger long," Vlerion said, rising.

Kaylina had no idea what Jankarr had seen but stood and handed Vlerion his cloak. They tramped through the grass to the highway and up to join the others. Levitke whuffed. In agitation? Crenoch and Zavron paced about.

As Kaylina had noted before, they couldn't see the city from the hilltop, but they did see black smoke rising from its direction, wafting up to join the clouds.

"Port Jirador is burning again," Jankarr said.

27

There won't be any bad guys. That's the problem with civil war. You're fighting your own people.

~ Lord Vlerion of Havartaft

Kaylina rode down the highway with Vlerion and Jankarr, drizzle dampening their skin and the taybarri's fur. Wind whipped at their faces. Their mounts set a fast pace, and her pack thumped against her back with each lope of Levitke's powerful legs.

The rain wasn't keeping the city from burning, and urgency filled them all. Nobody complained about the pace. There wasn't as much smoke as when the Kar'ruk had invaded, but Kaylina didn't know if that was because fewer buildings were on fire or the rain was tamping it down.

"You wouldn't think the queen or the prince would want to burn the city they're trying to take control of," she muttered.

Vlerion glanced at her, but they were cresting another hill, and the walls came into view ahead, the smoke hazing the air and making it hard to see the harbor and the royal castle on its plateau. Jankarr withdrew a spyglass and held it to his eye.

"Are the gates open?" Vlerion asked.

"No," Jankarr said. "There are a bunch of guards turning people away."

"They may let us pass," Vlerion said.

Kaylina remembered the castle guards who had opened the portcullis for him to leave.

"Wait. Those aren't guards. Or at least not *only* guards. I see green uniforms. More of those mercenaries." Jankarr lowered the spyglass and looked at Vlerion. "They're not going to let you in."

"No," he agreed.

Jankarr looked at Kaylina. "I don't know if they'll let *us* in either. It depends on what's been happening today."

Distant booms rang out from the city.

"Sounds like there's fighting around the base of the plateau," Vlerion said. Another boom floated to them. "And more. There's smoke coming from— Is that ranger headquarters?" He pointed.

Jankarr lifted the spyglass again.

Worried for her brother, Kaylina wanted to ask him about Stillguard Castle too.

"There are too many buildings in the way to say for sure," Jankarr said, "but it's the right direction. I don't think we should assume the mercenaries and rangers are on the same side. When I left, there was some debate about whether we would back the prince before he was officially coronated. And you could tell people were hoping he *wouldn't* be officially coronated."

"Could we slip in through the catacombs? Is that entrance we once used still being guarded?" Kaylina pointed off the highway, toward the farmlands where she'd once escaped through a shed with an access point.

"If it is, it won't be as heavily guarded as the gates. Let's try it." Vlerion directed Crenoch to run off the highway and into the fields, the grass nipped low by the cows and sheep from the nearby estate.

"Can you tell if there are fires burning around Stillguard Castle, Jankarr?" Kaylina asked. *In* the castle, she thought, but she believed the sentinel would come to its defense. Of course, vines, even magical vines, couldn't put out fires.

Jankarr peered through the spyglass again. "It's hard to tell from here, but I don't think there's smoke coming from that part of the city."

"Thank you. I'm relieved."

"Yes. We can stop by for mead after vanquishing whatever bad guys are menacing Port Jirador." Though Jankarr's face remained concerned, he managed a wink for her.

"There won't be any *bad guys*," Vlerion said. "That's the problem with civil war. You're fighting your own people."

"There are some who would argue the prince is bad," Jankarr said. "He's at least snotty and unappealing."

"A loathsome crime punishable by death."

"*I* thought so."

Vlerion glanced at him. "Have you even met him?"

"Yeah, I had to guard his yacht four summers ago when he was in town for a meeting. He called my taybarri fat and said the rangers had gone downhill since they started letting commoners in."

Crenoch whuffed three times and glanced at Jankarr's taybarri. Zavron bared his teeth and batted his tongue in return. Kaylina wasn't sure how much the young taybarri communicated with each other through those whuffs but suspected Crenoch had agreed that Zavron was on the chunky side.

More booms drifted across the countryside as they rode, their mounts' breathing growing heavier. Kaylina rested her hand on Levitke's shoulder, willing some of her power into the taybarri. Her hand tingled faintly. If the magic worked as desired, she didn't know, but Levitke's head came up, and her tail swished a bit.

Thanks for riding hard for us, Kaylina thought to her.

Taybarri in danger, Levitke responded.

All her friends back in ranger headquarters, yes.

The shed came into view ahead, the same squat stone building that Kaylina remembered. Seeing it also brought to mind the low doorway and the ladder leading down to the catacombs. There wouldn't be room to take the taybarri that way. Levitke and the others would be distressed not to be able to help, especially if they believed their kin in danger.

Vlerion dismounted when the taybarri stopped. "Crenoch, you three will have to find another way into the city. We're going to—"

Two Kingdom guards in chain mail stepped out of the shed, swords in their hands.

"Nobody's allowed into the catacombs," one said, looking warily toward the group, especially the taybarri.

Vlerion and Jankarr drew their own swords. The guards' faces blanched as they either recognized who they would have to deal with, or simply knew rangers in general were well trained.

Kaylina slid off Levitke's back and drew her sling, still preferring that weapon to the sword.

"Do you want to fight us?" Vlerion asked calmly.

"No, my lord."

"Do you want us to take your weapons and tie you up, so your superiors believe you tried your best to stop us?"

"Yes," the other man said.

"*No.*" The first guard scowled at him.

"No?"

"That would be dishonest and dishonorable."

His buddy shook his head and gave Vlerion a plaintive look, but the other guard kept scowling at him. He sighed and said, "No, my lord."

"All right." Vlerion nodded at Jankarr, and they sprang for the guards.

Kaylina loaded her sling, intending to help, but, as always, Vlerion moved with preternatural speed and struck with the power of a bear. He disarmed and downed the first man as easily as if the guard hadn't been trying to fight back, then turned and took the second from behind. Jankarr held his sword on the guards as Vlerion tied them up.

"Those bonds won't keep that long," Jankarr said.

"Our taybarri will watch these men," Vlerion said.

Levitke blew out air and looked toward the city. Kaylina doubted she would stick around for guard duty. Would the mercenaries at the gates let taybarri pass if they didn't have riders? She didn't know. In general, people seemed to believe them simple animals instead of the intelligent beings they were.

Crenoch swished his tail and issued a questioning grunt.

"No, you can't eat them," Vlerion said.

Kaylina highly doubted *that* was what Crenoch had asked, but the guards' faces grew even paler.

Vlerion left them tied and sitting against the shed, then waved for Kaylina and Jankarr to follow him inside.

"Let's hope the presence of mercenaries at the gate means there aren't any left in the catacombs," Jankarr said as they descended a ladder into darkness.

"That would be ideal." Vlerion didn't say that he would rather not have to kill more men, but Kaylina knew it was true. As he'd already implied, he didn't think the people they encountered would be bad guys. They were all kingdom subjects. "There used to be a lantern down here."

Kaylina heard him patting along the wall.

"If the guards want to keep people out," Jankarr said, "they've probably taken away any lights."

"Did you bring a lantern?"

"Originally, when I went down into the catacombs, yes, but I lost my pack in a skirmish. If Sergeant Zhani hadn't been with me, I would have lost my head."

"She's good and calm in a fight. Did she go back to headquarters?"

"To report what we heard to Targon, yes."

"I didn't pack before Targon shooed me out of the city," Vlerion said. "Kaylina, did you bring a lantern?"

"Sorry. Only cookies." Kaylina had cinderrock matches, since she'd been thinking she might need to start a campfire in the preserve, but she hadn't intended to traipse through dark tunnels. "Hold on. I have an idea."

Numerous times now, the brand on her hand had glowed green. Usually, it happened when she was interacting with the sentinel or using magic for something else, but maybe she could entice it to do so on its own. She gazed at it in the dark, willing her power to create illumination.

It was easier than she expected, the brand tingling and her hand warming. Strong green light flared from the leaf-shaped mark on her skin, bathing their faces and the walls around them, including a crumbling archway and tunnel leading toward the city.

Jankarr gaped at her. "Well, isn't that... *handy*?"

Kaylina had a feeling the word *odd* or *weird* had been on his tongue, but he smiled, seeming pleased by his punny replacement.

"Yes," Vlerion said firmly and rested a hand on her lower back so they could walk together and lead the way.

Feeling like a human lantern, Kaylina tilted her hand toward the passageway ahead.

Mostly dirt, their tunnel wasn't as well built as the centuries-old catacombs, and they had to step over numerous fallen stones and mounds of dirt. There were more than she remembered from her first journey, and she recalled the earthquakes. They might have shaken stones free. She eyed the arched ceiling as they walked, hoping a quake wouldn't occur while they were underground.

When they passed into the catacombs proper, without running into anyone save the Kar'ruk statues hissing at them from alcoves, Kaylina started to hope they would be able to reach ranger headquarters without encountering any trouble greater than the two guards.

A few distant booms came from above, the ground trembling faintly, but not with the alarming vigor of the earthquakes. Now and then, when they passed near sewer channels, with grates open to the air above, they would hear blunderbusses firing and swords clanging. It sounded chaotic, and Kaylina imagined citizens hiding in their homes, watching with wide eyes as they wondered what was happening. Again, she worried for her brother. Just because Stillguard Castle hadn't been on fire earlier didn't mean he couldn't be in danger.

"Are we heading for the Steam and Strigil?" Kaylina wished they dared veer off to check on Frayvar, but Vlerion would need to unite with the rest of the rangers and check in.

"It's the closest access point to ranger headquarters," he said.

"It's not a favorite place of mine."

"You prefer the nursery across from your nemesis's inn?" Vlerion asked.

"No, I don't like that area either."

"I'm surprised a woman would object to a steam house full of naked men," Jankarr said from behind them. "Lots of fit, athletic rangers and guards go there after training."

"You think she should seek them out for a date?" Vlerion asked.

"If I were a woman, *I* would. Unless she prefers powerful, wealthy aristocrats. Those are less likely to lurk in the public baths. They're also often older and flabbier."

"I had no idea you'd done such a thorough assessment of the clientele."

"I've been there often. It *is* one of my favorite places. There's a pretty girl who comes down and scrubs your back, wipes you with a cool towel, and brings wine. They *should* serve chilled mead. I'll suggest it the next time I'm there."

"I'll look forward to an order from the bathhouse," Kaylina murmured, not commenting on the rest.

Her main objection to the place was that assassins had tried to kill her on her last visit. Further, the beast had shown up and ripped their heads off. The memory of a headless man floating in one of the baths came to mind whenever she thought of the bathhouse.

Voices came from a tunnel at an intersection they were nearing, and they fell silent. Ahead, rubble littered the ground, and Kaylina eyed the walls and arched ceiling, spotting a few missing stones. Again, she thought of earthquakes and what might happen if they were down here when one occurred. Those stones had probably fallen during one of the last quakes.

When Vlerion paused at the corner to peer into the darkness toward the voices, Kaylina suspected that was the way to the Strigil. Maybe he would opt for another route.

"Put your hand out, please," he said softly.

Kaylina wanted to joke that it wasn't a candle that could be snuffed in an instant, but the voices sounded again, closer, and she didn't risk speaking. When she willed the magic to stop flowing, the glow actually did stop quickly.

"Handy," Jankarr whispered again.

"Ssh." Vlerion drew his sword.

Kaylina opted for her sling but rested a hand on his back so she would feel if he moved.

A hint of light came from the direction of the voices and soon grew brighter. It looked like numerous people with lanterns were heading their way. A snuffling noise floated to them. A taybarri? Kaylina wished they would encounter rangers, but it sounded more like a dog. One brought along to track people?

"Should we retreat?" Jankarr whispered.

"Rocko's got his scent," came a young voice, the words clear.

His? Were they hunting someone in particular?

Vlerion stiffened against Kaylina's hand, somehow knowing even before the next words.

"Lord Vlerion's?" another man asked. "He's down here?"

"He *has* to be. Rocko smelled his boot. The lady who sold it to us said it was his."

If the men hadn't been drawing closer, Kaylina would have joked that Vlerion shouldn't have been so careless about leaving his boots behind all those times he'd changed into the beast. All she did was squeeze his shoulder. She didn't know if it was reassuring or a question about whether they would fight.

"Hurry. We'll get a reward if we bring in his head. The prince said so."

Vlerion shifted and whispered, "Scoot back into that tunnel. I'll deal with this."

"You'll deal with it with me at your side," Jankarr said, stepping past Kaylina.

She let him, happy to back up so she could use her sling from a distance instead of leaping into a sword fight.

The dog bayed with excitement, its barks thunderous as they rang off the stone walls in the confined tunnels. Another hound joined in. How many people were down here looking for Vlerion?

The footsteps quickened, men shifting from walking to running as they followed the dogs.

"Don't forget to throw that potion if you need to," someone said.

Dread swept into Kaylina. These people knew they might face the beast, and they'd come prepared.

28

A HOUND ON THE TRAIL OF A RABBIT, DETOURED ONLY BY THE chattering of a squirrel.

~ Ranger Founder Saruk

Two dogs came racing out of the dark tunnel ahead of the men, ears flopping as they bayed and ran toward Vlerion, Jankarr, and, behind them, Kaylina. She hated the idea of harming animals and willed her power to turn them away.

Go back to your men. Only death waits for you here.

But their hunting instincts drove them toward the prey their handlers had commanded they find. Vlerion.

He crouched with his sword, waiting calmly. Again, Kaylina willed the dogs to run away. No, to find better prey. She tried to put the image of a rabbit in their minds, one waiting farther down the tunnel. Such a tasty rabbit!

The brand warmed her skin. A sign that her magic was working, she hoped.

"Come on," she whispered.

Baying even *more* eagerly, the hounds veered to run past the group. They breezed by close enough that Vlerion could have struck them, but he merely kept his blade ready and tracked them with his gaze.

The dogs ran through the intersection and continued on into the catacombs.

"Guess they sensed you could turn into a deadly beast and wanted nothing to do with you," Jankarr said.

"Indeed," Vlerion murmured, but he gave Kaylina a long look over his shoulder.

She smiled, happy that he knew she'd helped. She might never be as skilled a sword fighter as they, but she could do something.

"There they are!" A man in a green uniform came into view, carrying a lantern in one hand and a sword in the other.

Six more uniformed troops accompanied him. The prince's mercenaries.

If they thought anything of the dogs running past their prey, they didn't show it.

"A bonus to the man who kills him," an older mercenary in the back said. He carried a blunderbuss, his lantern hooked over the firearm.

"These guys aren't as smart as the dogs." Sword raised, Jankarr stepped up, crouching to the right side of the tunnel.

"Indeed," Vlerion repeated, taking the left.

Their stances meant they didn't intend to let anyone get past to Kaylina. She appreciated that, but it also meant they blocked her view, and she couldn't use her sling without risking hitting them. There weren't any more dogs or other animals, only the men, greed in their eyes, the thoughts of earning a reward propelling them into a foolish battle.

Vlerion hummed as he lunged in to greet the mercenaries who charged at them. Jankarr sprang forward at his side, keeping enough distance so they didn't risk hitting each other.

Metal clanged as swords met. In the confines of the tunnel, the rangers opted for stabs more than slashes, but it grew clear that they had plenty of experience fighting that way. Their swift parries and ripostes kept the mercenaries at bay, though those men weren't inexperienced themselves. They also had practice fighting together in close quarters, and they deflected most of the rangers' attacks, even making room for their allies behind them to lunge through gaps and try to strike Vlerion and Jankarr.

Though her allies were outnumbered, Kaylina believed they would eventually be victorious against the mercenaries, especially since the tunnel limited how many could come at them. She did, however, worry about the mention of potions. Which one had something that could knock out the beast—or maybe knock out both men, whether Vlerion shifted or not?

While searching for someone delving into a pocket, she spotted the older mercenary raising his blunderbuss. Like Kaylina, he had to wait for a clear shot, lest he hit his own men, but his height made it more likely he would find an opening.

She glanced around for something to stand on, needing height herself to target him. Rubble near the walls caught her eye. She had to run back several paces to reach a pile large enough to climb. The blunderbuss fired as she scrambled up, and she swore, glancing back.

As he fought, Vlerion must have been keeping an eye on the gunman. He crouched low, and the spattering of lead pellets clattered off the wall near his head.

One of the mercenaries swore and staggered away from the fight, grabbing the back of his shoulder. The idiot gunman had caught one of his own troops.

Another mercenary surged forward and took his place, lunging toward Vlerion while he crouched low. But Vlerion deflected the series of attacks and resumed his natural stance, even disarming one of the mercenaries and stabbing him in the abdomen.

The man cried out and staggered back. Another swordsman in green took his place.

From the top of the rock pile, Kaylina aimed her sling at the mercenary leader in the rear, the man reloading his blunderbuss.

Jankarr glanced at Vlerion as they fought. Because he hoped Vlerion would turn into the beast? Jankarr, dealing with a difficult opponent, kept being forced to step back.

Kaylina almost fired, but Vlerion jumped over a leg sweep, and she paused, afraid of hitting him. Even from the rubble perch, she struggled to get a clear shot over their heads.

Vlerion deflected a combination of slashes and stabs, then kicked his attacker's sword arm aside. The man fumbled his weapon and stepped back. Vlerion used the pause to dart closer to Jankarr's battle and slash at his foe's head. The mercenary glimpsed the blade coming and ducked, but that gave Jankarr an opportunity to rush in and stab him in the chest.

In the back, the leader raised his blunderbuss. For a couple of seconds, Jankarr and Vlerion were both to one side of the tunnel. That gave Kaylina a clear shot, and she took it.

Her round slammed into the leader's forehead. He jerked to the side, the blunderbuss firing wide again, shots striking the wall and ceiling. One clattered not far from Kaylina's side, and she ducked as shards of stone broke off.

Attempting to remain calm, she reloaded as the skirmish continued.

"Use the potion," a man fighting Vlerion yelled. He glanced back at his leader, his eyes wide and desperate, as Vlerion pushed him with an unrelenting series of attacks.

The mercenary wasn't quick enough to deflect one, and Vlerion's sword cut deeply into his cheek.

"Sergeant!" the man blurted, a plea.

"He's not the beast." The leader reloaded as he glared at Kaylina. "It won't do anything."

"It might help," someone shouted. "Try it. On both of them. We're outmatched!"

As if to lend evidence to the statement, a mercenary screamed as he went down to Vlerion's deadly blade.

The leader snarled, but he leaned his blunderbuss against the wall and delved into a belt pouch. Kaylina took careful aim above the heads of her allies, rising on tiptoes and lifting her sling to make sure her round didn't hit them.

The man pulled out a vial of familiar blue liquid.

Kaylina rushed her shot, afraid to let him throw it, afraid the side effects that hadn't stopped Vlerion's heart when he'd been the beast might do so when he was a mere man. Or what if it hurt Jankarr?

Her round sped past Vlerion's head, less than an inch from his ear, but it hit her target, thudding into the leader's chest. Unfortunately, it only pissed him off.

"Bitch," he snarled and hurled the vial.

It sped toward *Kaylina* instead of Vlerion.

Cursing, she leaped off the rubble, or tried. A rock shifted under her heel, and she flailed, barely keeping from falling on her ass.

Vlerion, without a break in his fight, reached up and snatched the vial out of the air. Kaylina almost laughed in relief—and admiration for his athleticism. Had he even looked at the vial as he caught it?

Without hesitating, Vlerion finished off the mercenary in front of him. As Jankarr defeated his own opponent, the leader, the last man standing, grabbed his blunderbuss and spun to run.

Vlerion lowered his sword and looked like he might let the man escape—he had to be tired of killing kingdom subjects—but Jankarr drew a throwing knife and hurled it. It sank deeply into the back of the leader's neck, and he pitched to the ground, the firearm clattering from his grip.

More voices sounded in the distance, someone yelling, "Sergeant Taymorak?"

Was that the older mercenary? It didn't matter. They were all down, dead or dying.

Vlerion and Jankarr calmly cleaned the blood off their swords as they watched the tunnel, ready if more men charged into view, though Jankarr also wiped blood out of his eyes. He'd taken a gash to his forehead, and several cuts in his sleeves pointed to other minor wounds.

"Sergeant Taymorak?" came the call again. "Do you want us to come help or keep guarding the exit?"

More voices followed, but their uncertain questions were too quiet to make out. The men were around at least one bend more than a hundred yards distant. In the maze of tunnels, it was hard to tell.

"The rest of the platoon could be up there." Vlerion backed away from the bodies, waving for Jankarr and Kaylina to do the same. "Unless we want to fight even more men, we'll have to find another access point."

"Will any others be unguarded?" Kaylina asked.

"I don't know."

"I never thought I'd say this—" Jankarr used his sleeve to wipe sweat from his brow, "—but I wouldn't mind seeing the beast pop out and help with these guys."

"If the beast *pops out*, he would be as likely to kill you as our adversaries," Vlerion said.

"That's dreadful. The newspaper didn't mention that."

"The *newspaper* is propaganda put out by someone who wants a regime change."

"But Korbian has seen the beast, hasn't she? And she lived to tell about it." Jankarr looked at her.

Kaylina still hesitated to speak of it, since she'd kept Vlerion's secret for so long, but, with the way things were going, it seemed likely Jankarr might witness a change. He should know at least some of what to expect so he would be prepared.

"He only changes if he's inundated by strong emotions," she said when Vlerion didn't answer.

He was gazing down the tunnel, probably contemplating if they could get by the men ahead. And contemplating if they would get in trouble for killing the mercenaries. Since those men were after him, it seemed fair, but what if Prince Enrikon and his forces came out on top? What if he ended up the king and commander of the rangers? He would drive Vlerion out if not put him to death, with the latter seeming far more likely.

"Men trying to kill him doesn't elicit *strong emotions*?" Jankarr whispered.

"He's used to that." Kaylina didn't explain the humming.

"Go." Vlerion gestured them back down the tunnel they'd come through. "We'll find another access point."

Jankarr went with him but whispered, "Vlerion, if the mercenaries believe you're down here, they'll have them all guarded."

Once full darkness ensconced them again, Kaylina willed the light to emanate from her hand. It obeyed almost cheerfully, as if her blood was happy to have her call upon her powers. Something told her she would call upon them a lot more before the day was through.

"Let's go to Stillguard Castle," she suggested.

Another hound bayed behind them. Great.

"*Everyone* knows about that access point," Jankarr said. "It'll be guarded too."

Kaylina winced, fearing that was true. The Virts had been using the passageway before she'd ever come to Port Jirador.

Vlerion looked at her as they walked, picking up the pace

when the hound bayed again. "Will the plant guard what's *below* the castle?"

"I don't know. I don't think it ever attacked the Virts when they were using the root-cellar entrance."

It was possible they'd learned to go swiftly up the ladder and out the back door before any vines appeared.

"I might be able to convince it to do so, even if it doesn't usually," she added.

Jankarr gave her a weird look.

"Are you going to call me handy again?" she asked.

"If vines pop out of the walls to strangle our enemies, I might."

"If that happens, you'd better offer to stock her pantry and wash her dishes," Vlerion said.

"The plant's power has grown since I started feeding it the honey-water fertilizer." Kaylina waved away the other comments. "I bet it could send vines out underneath its foundation."

"Do you feed Vlerion honey-water fertilizer too?" Jankarr asked.

"No. He won't even drink my mead."

"Vlerion, that's rude."

"You talk a lot for a man bleeding from four wounds."

"It's at least *six* wounds, and I'm using my tongue to keep my mind off the pain." Jankarr dabbed at the cut on his forehead.

They reached an intersection, and Vlerion pointed down the tunnel that led toward Stillguard Castle. "We'll check it. It's closer to ranger headquarters than most of the other access points, so it's a good choice. If we can get through."

"If we can, and there's a lull in the fighting tonight," Jankarr said, "one of us might be able to sneak away and report to Targon."

"Yes." Vlerion nodded to him. "Good of you to volunteer for that."

"By then, my wounds will be festering, and I'll need the doc to look at them." Jankarr considered Kaylina as they jogged down the new tunnel. "Will you bathe me before I go?"

"With honey fertilizer?"

"Or warm sudsy water and a gentle sponge." He winked at her.

Well, at least he wasn't avoiding her eyes anymore.

Vlerion glared at Jankarr. "Are you no longer finding her *odd*?"

"Oh, she's terribly exotic, but the pain, remember." Jankarr touched the back of his hand to his forehead and pantomimed fainting. "I'm distracting myself."

"Why couldn't Sergeant Zhani have come to warn me about bounty hunters?" Vlerion grumbled.

"She's feeling guilty about providing an elixir that didn't fully work," Kaylina said.

"It's not her fault I was too…" Vlerion waved vaguely, glancing at her curves but quickly turning his focus back to the route ahead.

"Virile?" Kaylina suggested.

"Horny."

"That too."

Jankarr looked back and forth between them. He didn't seem to have figured out that Vlerion's lust was more likely to rouse the beast than having people try to kill him. Kaylina wouldn't be the one to explain it to him.

When they entered the first chamber near the root cellar, a voice came from that direction. It didn't belong to Frayvar or anyone else Kaylina had heard before, and she squelched the glow of her brand.

Vlerion and Jankarr stopped, Vlerion sighing faintly.

Kaylina also wished it could have been easy. She knew Vlerion never minded fighting, but he didn't want to kill more people. She pulled out her sling while hoping the mercenaries, or whoever stood guard, hadn't ventured up into the castle and done anything to Frayvar or the staff.

"I'm bored," someone said. "Vlerion isn't going to show up here. He's probably not even in the kingdom anymore. Why can't we go up into the inn and get a drink?"

"It's a cursed castle," someone with a gruff voice said, "not an *inn*."

"They've got drinks, don't they?"

"The mead is *delicious*," another man said.

It wasn't the time for Kaylina to feel proud or pleased by a random stranger's accolade, but she promptly decided she didn't want that man killed.

"The girl who makes it is delicious. You think she's up there? We could alleviate our boredom on her."

The men guffawed—there had to be at least six of them—and made comments about how exactly they might all do that.

Kaylina rescinded her desire for any of them to be spared.

A soft growl came from her side. Vlerion.

She found his arm and rested her hand on it, his muscles tense beneath her grip. An irritated part of her wanted to sic him on the mercenaries, but there'd been enough killing.

"I'll handle this," she breathed.

Vlerion planted his other hand on hers, as if to capture her. That was fine. She hadn't intended to spring into the middle of the mercenaries and challenge them to a sword fight.

Are you awake? Kaylina called silently up to the sentinel.

A sense of sarcasm wafted back to her along with a view from the tower of men fighting in the streets around the castle, fires burning in nearby buildings, and explosives going off all over the city.

It is a little noisy tonight, she agreed. *Are you aware of a group of men between me and the root-cellar ladder?*

Since I am potted instead of planted in the ground, my senses are less effective at discerning what is occurring below the castle, but I can tell you are there. The fertilizer you instructed your inferior half-

sibling to make was not as refreshing as yours, else I would have more power.

Apparently, not everyone thought Frayvar was a genius.

Kaylina didn't know if it would work when they weren't touching, but she attempted to send some of her power up to the tower, enough to enhance the sentinel's reach.

Ahhhh, it breathed into her mind. *Excellent. I sense eight men.*

Good. Can you lock them up behind vines? Without killing them? They're not done fantasizing about sexual acts, so it would be impolite to slay them.

Humans have a strange notion of courtesy.

Yes, we're a quirky species.

You are not one of them, not fully, else I would not desire to soak up your power and serve you.

Kaylina kept herself from saying what a shame that would be. She needed the sentinel's assistance.

"Are you doing something now?" Vlerion murmured, his arm still tense under her hand. "Using your power?"

"I'm chatting with the sentinel about using *its* power."

"I feel you doing something," he murmured, easing closer so that his shoulder brushed hers. Drawn to her power?

"Lending it support."

"Did you hear something?" one of the men barked.

Kaylina winced. She had thought they'd been speaking quietly enough that the mercenaries wouldn't hear.

Vlerion released her, stepping in front of her and drawing his sword. Jankarr also brushed past her, and they strode toward the root cellar.

"There!" someone yelled.

Reluctantly, Kaylina drew her sling and followed the men. Vlerion and Jankarr stepped into the influence of the lanterns the men had lit in the chamber outside the root cellar. Surprisingly, nobody sprang out at them.

Wary, they glanced at each other and eased forward. Coming behind them, Kaylina couldn't see much. When Vlerion halted, standing up straight, she got an inkling that an attack wasn't on the way. After a long look from side to side, Jankarr gazed back at her with his mouth dangling open.

"You still want her to give you a bath?" Vlerion asked him, twitching his fingers to invite Kaylina to join them.

"Maybe not. She's a little too... uhm." Jankarr looked apologetically at her without finishing.

"Handy?" she suggested.

"Yeah."

Vines had captured all eight men, not only securing them to the stone walls, their feet dangling inches above the ground, but also smothering their mouths so they couldn't yell for reinforcements. Or comment on how delicious Kaylina was.

Looking proud, Vlerion clasped her shoulder and guided her toward the ladder. The mercenaries stared at her instead of Vlerion or Jankarr as they passed, several of their gazes locking onto her hand. Her brand had started glowing again. A side effect of lending the sentinel power?

She was glad the men were gagged. They would have harsher words for her weirdness than *handy*.

In the root cellar, Vlerion went first up the ladder. The flagstone trapdoor was askew, and voices floated down.

Fortunately, Kaylina recognized these voices.

"One of them is coming," Frayvar blurted.

"Are you ready?" Sevarli asked.

"I'll crush their heads in," Frayvar said with surprising vehemence.

He was the least aggressive person Kaylina knew.

"It's us," she called up to forestall head-crushing.

Frayvar had to be poised with his cast-iron frying pan again.

"Thank all the warring gods for peace," Frayvar said with such relief that Kaylina worried they'd had a fraught time since she'd left.

Vlerion and Kaylina stepped out of the pantry and into the kitchen, Jankarr coming behind. He shoved the door shut and dragged a crate full of sacks of flour over the flagstone.

Frayvar stood near the hearth and was, indeed, holding the big pan. His shirt was rucked and hanging out, and a bruise darkened his cheek. Behind him, Sevarli stood with two huge butcher knives in her hands. Her shirt was ripped at the shoulder seam, and two of her buttons were missing.

"You kids having a good time up here?" Jankarr asked.

"*Hardly*," Sevarli said. "Those goons groped me when they came through. Did you kill them?" Her voice was savage, her eyes promising she hoped the answer was yes.

"I hit one in the head," Frayvar said, "but two others jumped on me and punched me. I thought I was dead, but vines shot out of the wall, and their commander ordered them to hurry up and get down there in case Lord Vlerion came that way. They're trying to *kill* you, my lord."

"I know." Vlerion waved at the pan. "Good work defending your castle."

"The vines scared them more than me with my pan," Frayvar admitted.

"You clubbed one good though," Sevarli said. "I appreciate that as much as appropriately timed vine growth."

Frayvar smiled at her.

"What now?" Kaylina asked Vlerion while firmly shutting the pantry door.

"Probably nothing until one of us can sneak away to talk to Captain Targon." This time, Vlerion didn't look to Jankarr. Maybe he'd decided he would have to risk that errand himself.

Since so many people were hunting him, Kaylina would have preferred Vlerion to stay in the castle with her. They could hide out and let Petalira and her son fight things out for themselves.

Except that it hardly mattered which one won. They both wanted Vlerion dead.

Kaylina gripped his arm and leaned her forehead against his shoulder, exhaustion seeping into her. "When did my life get so difficult?"

"The day you met me," he murmured, stroking the back of her head. "Do you regret it?"

"Yeah."

He snorted softly. "But you still love me."

She slumped against him, too tired to tease him for being pompous and overly self-assured. "Yeah."

29

There is no way to placate a bitter rival.

~ Chef Sayler Amentour III

Despite her weariness, Kaylina joined Vlerion when he climbed into a tower that looked over the courtyard wall and out to the city. It was the front tower opposite the one belonging to the sentinel. Oddly, he hadn't chosen the plant's room for his viewpoint.

She stood at his side as he gazed out the window, past the trees at the corner of the property. The branches allowed only a partial view but hid the window from anyone who might be spying on Stillguard Castle from the streets.

Vlerion's sword hand flexed as explosions continued to go off and men fought in the streets. He had to be as tired as she, but his jaw kept tightening, and she knew he wanted to be out there, fighting with his men, not hiding in the castle. That was especially true when they spotted rangers riding taybarri over one of the bridges.

At the moment, there was no fighting in the streets and alleys adjacent to the castle, but a couple of bodies promised there had been. Kaylina wondered if the sentinel had sent out any of its purple beams to slay people. She didn't ask.

Vlerion tensed when a cloaked figure appeared at the front gate and gripped the iron bars.

"Whoever wins, they'll come for you," Jana Bloomlong called up, looking toward the sentinel's tower, its purple glow seeping out the window.

"Does she mean me or you?" Kaylina asked quietly, though she doubted Jana knew Vlerion was there. She couldn't even be certain Kaylina was there, could she?

"They'll kill you, girl, for being a druid freak. And you'll deserve it."

"Guess that answers my question," Kaylina murmured.

"You bribed the Virts, didn't you? They went in and convinced the printer to change what *should* have gone out in the newspaper." Jana's words were slurred. Was she drunk? "They tried to turn that Vlerion into a cursed folk hero. He's a criminal. Just like you are! Did you sleep with Grittor? He's the one who was behind things, who has friends on the newspaper—friends everywhere. Is there anyone you won't sleep with for favors, you slut?"

"That favor was for Vlerion," Kaylina murmured but not loudly enough for Jana to hear. Let the woman rant to herself and not be certain if anyone heard her.

With her diatribe delivered, Jana slumped against the bars, then slid down them. Something clinked against the cobblestones. A bottle of alcohol?

Vlerion rested a hand on Kaylina's shoulder. "She's no threat to you, not right now."

"I know. I wasn't thinking of braining her with my sling."

Not much, anyway.

"By tomorrow morning, I suspect there will be others for you to brain."

"You know how to get a girl excited."

"I do know that." Vlerion gazed at her.

She flushed, remembering *how* excited she'd been when he'd pressed her against the wall, not that far from where they were now. If only that elixir had worked to keep him from turning into the beast. They could have… No, she reminded herself. They couldn't have joined fully. That had been the whole point of the elixir, to keep him from being aroused.

She leaned against him, wondering if they would get a chance to be together. If she had to agree to turn herself into a tree to have his curse lifted…

Vlerion wrapped his arm around her shoulders, but the moment didn't last nearly long enough.

"You may get an opportunity to use your sling *before* tomorrow," he said, looking out the window.

Though she didn't want to, Kaylina turned her head to follow his gaze. Jana Bloomlong had disappeared, and hundreds of uniformed men were heading up the main street that led past Stillguard Castle. The main street that led *to* it.

Kaylina leaned out the window to peer around the curve of the tower. Across the roof of the keep, she could make out more troops on the river trail behind the castle. As they approached, the clink of armor and arms drifted to her, the whispers of voices.

"How many people are coming?" she asked.

"An army," Vlerion said grimly. "I may have missed my opportunity to report to Targon and ask for his help."

Some of the approaching men wore green uniforms—the mercenaries—but others were dressed in the gray of the Kingdom Guard. They'd combined forces.

As the troops drew closer to the castle, Kaylina spotted representatives of the Castle Guard as well. A feeling of foreboding crept into her at the implications. Either the prince had managed to convince the Castle and Kingdom Guard that he was the rightful heir and they had better do his bidding, or the queen had agreed to work with him, sending the troops that had formerly helped protect her and her husband to join her son's men.

Earlier in the day, they'd been battling each other. What had changed?

Kaylina looked at Vlerion's profile and answered her own question. Before he had fought the mercenaries in the catacombs, his enemies had only *suspected* that he was in the city. But now they knew. Had that knowledge compelled them to declare a truce and work to defeat him? To *kill* him?

His face was as grim as ever. He had to be thinking something similar. Maybe he already knew for certain that was what had happened.

"We can defend Stillguard Castle if we need to." Kaylina tried to sound reassuring. That was, after all, why she'd wanted Vlerion to come here. If they had to make a stand, this was the best spot.

"You, me, Jankarr, the serving girl, and your brother with his frying pan? Against an army?"

"Don't forget about the sentinel." Kaylina wondered if she ought to run down and make it a fresh batch of fertilizer. It had been snippy about Frayvar's version.

"Ah, of course. You, me, Jankarr, a girl, your brother, and a plant."

"It's a bad-ass plant." Kaylina didn't think she needed to point out that it had nearly killed his boss. And it *had* killed others.

"I won't deny that. I'm tempted to ask you if it can shoot some purple beams, but..." Vlerion spread a hand toward the approaching army.

"Those are kingdom subjects?" Kaylina guessed his objection.

"Yes. I remain conflicted. I don't want to spend the rest of my life in hiding, but I was slow to reach my decision, and now I've lost what could have been the advantage of surprise."

"You don't think you could walk out there, tell them they're following the wrong guy, that *you're* the rightful king, and they should turn on their superiors?"

Vlerion snorted. "The mercenaries from another province would certainly not do so. And the Guard... likely not, not without some catalyst. If the rangers were among them, that would help, but I can't be certain of where they stand." He leaned out the window to study both streams of approaching men. Some, especially toward the back, were mounted on horses, but Kaylina didn't see any taybarri. "No, I do not see any rangers now."

"Hopefully, because they aren't interested in trying to kill you, not because anything happened to the majority of them." Kaylina remembered Vlerion and Jankarr's earlier concern about fires around ranger headquarters. What if the prince, knowing Vlerion's colleagues might protect him, had ordered them taken out first?

"They would not be easily defeated." Did Vlerion sound like he was trying to convince himself of that?

In open battle, the rangers were unparalleled fighters, but deception could take down even great warriors. Jankarr might not have been the only spy among the ranks. What if another had helped facilitate a defeat from within?

Vlerion thumped a fist on the stone windowsill. "I need to find Targon and talk to him."

"Late in the night, you might be able to sneak by the army, maybe swim up the river without them noticing." Kaylina pointed toward the cloudy sky; it was growing darker with the approach of twilight. "You could also go back through the catacombs and find another access point. They can't all be guarded. Everyone's out *there*." Kaylina flung her hand toward the growing army, feeling it wasn't much of an exaggeration.

More and more men were filing onto the main routes to the castle, and some were coming from the opposite direction now too, from the city gates. Despite the options she'd mentioned, Kaylina couldn't help but feel trapped.

That feeling increased as the army reached the courtyard walls, men on foot and men on horseback surrounding Stillguard Castle. And were those siege engines on the way, being pulled by teams of oxen?

Vlerion had looked at her as she'd suggested ways he could escape but didn't move from her side. He wouldn't leave, she realized, even if he believed he could slip past the army. Because she was here. He had to worry they would capture—or kill—her to get to him. Or, by now, maybe they hated her too and would happily kill her independent of him.

It took a ridiculously small amount of the total army to surround Stillguard Castle, troops ten deep in the street and alleys and along the trail out back. They'd blocked access to the river. The only way out would be through the catacombs, and Kaylina suspected men were marching toward her root cellar too. That access point was too well known and this army too large for the leader—whoever was commanding it—not to have that covered.

With luck, the troops would be afraid to advance through the root cellar entrance with their allies dangling from vines down there.

Kaylina was about to ask the sentinel if it still had the men ensnared when someone on a white stallion rode through the army, the troops parting to let him pass. She couldn't tell who it was since he didn't wear a uniform, instead clanking in full plate armor with a helmet and visor covering his face. A blue cloak without ornamentation spilled down his back to his horse's flanks. His mount was *also* armored.

"Maybe you should ask the plant to send out its purple beam," Vlerion murmured.

Did he already know who that was?

Six more armored men on horses came behind the figure, each

carrying a firearm and wearing a sword at the waist. Bodyguards? When the cloaked man stopped in front of the castle gate, the six troops fanned out protectively to either side of him, glaring defiantly up at the glowing purple tower.

They were mercenaries, not the Castle Guard. Men who'd been paid well to be loyal and protect the prince?

That was who this had to be. Kaylina was surprised Enrikon hadn't sent a minion to lead the army, but maybe he felt suitably protected.

"Can the beast's claws tear into plate armor like that?" Kaylina asked.

"Yes, but the *beast* is also vulnerable to hundreds of men with swords and firearms."

"You're intimidated by that little army? Goodness."

Vlerion slanted her a sidelong look.

"You'd better run off and find Targon and the rangers and bring back help." She smiled and patted him on the back.

"I'm not leaving you here alone when there's a *large* army surrounding your castle."

Kaylina wanted to say that she and the sentinel could protect the castle, but she doubted that was true. Even as the prince sat astride his mount, teams wheeling cannons came through. They pointed one at the front gate and three others at the sentinel's tower.

"We may all need to flee," she admitted.

Vlerion started to respond, but the prince rode a few steps forward to speak.

"Lord Vlerion of Havartaft," he called, his voice echoing strangely since he hadn't lifted the visor.

"Guess someone told him you went this way in the catacombs," Kaylina said.

"I am giving you the opportunity to surrender and walk through that gate to meet your fate. If you do not, I will unleash the full might of my army on that castle and raze it to the ground. No mercy will be shown to anyone within its walls."

Kaylina bristled. Even if she would stand at Vlerion's side in a fight, Frayvar and Sevarli were innocent civilians. And what about Jankarr? He hadn't disobeyed any orders, as far as she knew, and didn't deserve to be *razed* along with the castle.

"And if I *do* surrender?" Vlerion called, startling her.

Any hope she'd had that he might hide—or flee—disappeared. Not that she'd expected that.

The armored figure twitched, the visor turning to look toward their dark tower. He had been addressing the front of the castle, or maybe the plant's glowing window. As if Vlerion would make his last stand from there. *Kaylina* might, but she was a weirdo with druid blood.

"The castle will be left alone, and your... common-born mead maker and her kin may live." Enrikon said *common-born* with the same sneer one might use when speaking of a leech attached to one's leg.

"Someone's been filling him in since he arrived," Kaylina murmured.

"So it seems."

"What happens to Vlerion if he walks out there?" Kaylina called.

He looked at her, as if he hadn't expected her to speak, but he didn't try to cut her off.

A long pause followed before the prince spoke in an incredulous tone. "Is that the *mead maker*?"

"What, I'm not allowed to ask questions?" she muttered.

"You didn't curtsy and put *Your Highness* at the end," Vlerion said. "Though it may be *Your Majesty* by now, I suppose. Usually, there's a ceremony, but this regime change isn't going as smoothly as typical."

"If she wants to live," Enrikon called, "she had better learn her place. Mute and on her knees when royalty is nearby."

"My *knees*?" Kaylina went from bristling to seething as she squinted at the sentinel's tower, wondering if the prince was close enough to the walls for it to attack. And if its purple beam could penetrate that thick armor. If the beast's claws could...

"You didn't realize that my pomposity is barely existent compared to that of some nobles," Vlerion said.

"I did not, no."

Vlerion rested a hand on her arm and looked at the prince. She thought he might make comments about her known irreverence and Targon's suggestions of flogging, but he didn't. Maybe this wasn't someone he would banter with. If so, she approved.

"I would also like to know what happens if I walk out there," Vlerion called.

He didn't add *Your Highness.* Maybe nobles didn't have to be as obsequious.

"You will be executed for the crime of killing kingdom troops." The prince pointed, and a hulking man in chain mail stepped forward, carrying an axe meant for beheading.

Kaylina rocked back. The prince wanted to execute Vlerion right *there*? While she watched? While the entire city did?

"I'll remind you that the castle and your audacious mead maker will be spared. That is the deal I offer. You've my word that your death will be her life."

"I need time to consider your gracious offer." Vlerion spoke in the calm, detached tone he so often used when addressing others —especially those who vexed him.

Too bad. Kaylina thought vitriolic sarcasm would have been more appropriate.

"You may have one hour," Enrikon called, then lowered his voice to address the men who'd placed the cannons. He didn't speak so quietly that Kaylina couldn't hear him. "Give him something to think about during that hour." He waved toward the tower.

Watch out, Kaylina warned the sentinel.

Of course, came the dry response. *Did you think I was napping while the castle walls were surrounded?*

I don't know your sleep schedule. Brace yourself. They'll have explosives as well as those cannonballs, I'm sure.

The sentinel didn't answer.

Kaylina debated whether to ask if it could shoot a beam at the prince. If she commanded it, and the plant succeeded in killing him, it would be murder, and she would be to blame. But she had no intention of letting Vlerion commit suicide. For that matter, she also didn't want to have her castle razed.

While she debated, the first cannon fired. Kaylina gripped the windowsill and leaned forward.

As the cannonball sailed over the courtyard wall and directly at the sentinel's tower, a purple beam shot out. She'd been envisioning it hitting the prince, but it struck the projectile. It exploded in a white and purple spray of light, and pieces of metal pelted down in the courtyard and the street, pinging off people's armor.

Three more cannonballs blasted toward the tower. Three more cannonballs blew up before reaching it.

Kaylina looked at the prince, hoping he would be scared and ride off, possibly while wetting himself. But he merely sat on his mount inside his armor, gazing through his visor at the display.

"Bring the explosives," he called over his shoulder. "If Lord Vlerion doesn't come out within one hour, we will blow up the castle and the entire block around it if necessary."

The prince turned to ride away, the men again parting to make room for him. He pointed at the axeman—at the *executioner*—to stay where he was. To wait for Vlerion.

Shoot him, Kaylina caught herself commanding the sentinel.

Repercussions be damned. The world would be better without that asshole.

The glow of the tower brightened, purple light bathing the courtyard and walls.

"Look out!" one of the troops yelled. A Kingdom guard. Someone who'd been there when the Kar'ruk invaded.

The prince jerked about and dove—no, he *fell*—from his horse, alarmed as a beam shot from the tower window. It grazed his shoulder as he tumbled and crashed to the ground. Right away, Kaylina knew it hadn't been a fatal blow.

The sentinel fired again. But Enrikon was on hands and knees and crawling away, his armored men blocking the tower's line of sight. When the beams struck, they hit soldiers, not the prince.

"Stop!" Kaylina cried, then issued the order silently through her link to the sentinel. *Stop, please. Not the men, just the prince.*

But Enrikon kept scrambling away, using his men for cover. The sentinel fired several more times but couldn't reach him. A soldier screamed as a beam cut through his throat, killing him.

Stop! Kaylina ordered, this time summoning the power of her blood, willing the sentinel to obey. The cursed plant was all too happy to kill *any* humans. Her hand warmed, her whole body tingling as power flowed toward the tower. *Stop.*

The beams ceased, and the glow lessened.

"Do we fire back?" one of the men at the cannons called.

The prince didn't answer. Kaylina didn't know where he'd gone. He was probably still on his hands and knees.

"Hold," someone else said. Their military commander, most likely. "Give Vlerion his hour." Whoever he was, the man sounded grim. Almost sympathetic toward Vlerion.

When she was sure the beams wouldn't start up again, Kaylina bent over and gripped her knees for support. She stared at the wooden floorboards but only saw the beam cutting into that soldier's throat, killing him. She closed her eyes, but the image remained, seared into her retinas, as if she'd looked directly at the sun. She'd killed that man, as surely as if she'd drawn a blade across his throat herself.

Vlerion rested a hand on her shoulder. "Are you all right?"

"I may throw up on your boots."

"Don't, please. I need to address that army."

"You can't go out there."

"I'm not going out the gate. I'll speak to them from the wall."

Kaylina straightened, though her stomach lurched with queasiness. "They can *shoot* you on the wall."

"After that display, they'll think twice about firing anything in the direction of the castle."

"At least wear some heavier armor." She waved to the leather torso-piece he wore, all the rangers ever wore. That wouldn't stop a cannonball.

"I don't have any."

"Blighted moon craters, Vlerion. You're a wealthy aristocrat. *Why* don't you have full plate armor like that pompous idiot out there?" Kaylina thrust her hand toward the window, as frustrated with the prince for accidentally avoiding death as with herself for ordering it.

"The taybarri won't abide metal on their backs."

"What? Since when?"

"Since always. It's in *The Ranger's Guide to Honor, Duty, and Tenets.*"

She looked blankly at him.

"Didn't you finish it?" Vlerion managed a smile, though she surely couldn't. He even had a teasing tone when he said, "You've been in training for weeks."

She knew he was trying to lighten her mood, but she didn't want it lightened, damn it. Everything was so frustrating. "I don't know how to explain this to you or the author, but it's not riveting to read. The chapter on medicinal uses for roots and fungi is more torturous than cleaning pots and pans."

"Our founder, Lord Saruk, wrote it. He was full of knowledge and had an earnest desire to pass it along to others, but he didn't have a practiced pen."

"Or ever meet an editor. *Vlerion*." Kaylina didn't know what she wanted from him. Maybe only to share her frustration.

He stepped forward and hugged her. For a moment, they stood there, taking support from each other as twilight crept over the city and the soldiers lit lanterns. It wasn't a long enough moment, not for Kaylina.

"I will go out and speak with the army." Vlerion released her and stepped back. "With luck, the prince is busy receiving medical attention for his grievous wound, and I'll be able to talk without interruption, at least from him, for a few minutes."

"I hope it *is* a grievous wound." But she knew it wasn't. Unfortunately.

"Captain Lethermon will listen, I believe. The rest... We'll see. As I said, the mercenaries will have no allegiance to me."

"Is that the guy who called hold?"

"Yes." Vlerion stepped toward the stairs but paused to look back. "Whatever happens to me, I forbid you from letting your sentinel or your father turn you into a druid-human-plant rooted in the preserve."

"You'll have a hard time forbidding anything if you're dead." Kaylina didn't want him to contemplate his passing. She wanted him to have a reason to fight to live.

"That's why I'm forbidding it now. Preemptively. You have a future, as a ranger if you want it, but most certainly as a mead maker, as whatever else you wish to be. You're too young to sacrifice yourself to be a nanny for the preserve."

"Surely, I'd be more of a bodyguard than a nanny. With the power of the Daygarii."

"You'll be swatting axe wielders with vines and hissing at them. I forbid it all, Kaylina."

"You're still kind of pompous, Vlerion."

"Yes, I am. Pompous and forbidding."

"The only way to ensure I don't become a tree is for you to live and stay at my side."

"If I live," he said quietly, "you might be even more likely to make that sacrifice."

Kaylina wished she'd never told him about her meeting with her father, about what Arsanti had proposed. Why was she always compelled to honesty with him?

30

Feed and water nature today, and reap a reward tomorrow.
~ *Daygarii saying*

Vlerion headed downstairs to don his gear and—if he followed Kaylina's suggestion—grab a huge pan to use as a shield when he walked out of the keep to address the army. Meanwhile, Kaylina went to the tower with the sentinel. After watching its beams kill men, even after she'd commanded it to stop, she didn't want to stand beside it, but she might need its help again. If the army launched cannonballs at Vlerion, she would ask the sentinel to fire more beams, and she didn't know if she would bother stopping it a second time.

Nervous, she watched the courtyard below for Vlerion to walk out. The front ranks of the army—and several cannons—were visible through the wrought-iron gate. Surprisingly, nobody had tried to batter it down yet. The stone walls around the courtyard remained sturdy, despite the centuries of neglect, but Kaylina knew from past experience that the rusty, creaky gate could barely restrain a half-hearted taybarri offensive. A battering ram would easily take it out.

Distraction, a soft voice sounded in Kaylina's mind.

Levitke?

Make distraction. The taybarri had to be nearby to communicate, and Kaylina thought she was behind the castle, but platoons of soldiers were back there. Would Levitke have been able to get that close?

An image of her and several other taybarri and rangers came to Kaylina. They were swimming in the dark river, approaching and attempting to avoid notice as night deepened. Along the way, they'd had to sneak past three barges loaded with soldiers.

You need a distraction so you can get through the men and into the castle? Kaylina guessed.

Yes. Bring message.

You're bringing one? For Vlerion?

Yes.

Is it one that he needs to hear before he addresses this huge army and tells them... whatever he's going to tell them? It crossed Kaylina's mind that Vlerion speaking forcefully—she couldn't imagine him speaking cajolingly—from the courtyard wall might work as a distraction, drawing all eyes toward him.

But Levitke responded, *Yes.* She also shared an image of Captain Targon looking surly—as usual.

Kaylina didn't know if that meant Targon was with the rangers in the river or if he'd sent the message. Either way, Vlerion had wanted to speak with him.

I'll see what I can arrange, Kaylina replied.

The sentinel started pulsing powerful purple light, emanating it farther from the tower than usual. Uneasy murmurs came from the soldiers in the street, proving they'd noticed it. Noticed it and were staring at it, she hoped.

"Are you eavesdropping on my telepathic conversations?" she asked it. "Can you do that?"

A feeling of smugness emanated from the pot behind her.

"I'll take that as a *yes*." Kaylina leaned out the window to check if Vlerion had come out to the courtyard yet. She didn't see him. "Will you stop him if he shows up down there? I'm going to run to the kitchen and try to figure out a distraction for my friends."

If the troops on the river trail were looking toward the front of the castle, they would notice the pulsing light, but it wouldn't be as obvious from back there.

An image popped into her head of vines stretching across the front door to keep Vlerion from exiting.

"I guess that'll work." Kaylina slid through the hole in the floor. "But don't gag him like the guys in the root cellar," she called back.

As she ran down the hall toward the stairs, she groped for a way to distract the soldiers on the river trail. They were the ones the rangers and taybarri would need to get past. She imagined herself and Frayvar running into the courtyard banging spoons against pans.

"Sounds like a good way to get shot," she whispered.

She was two steps from the bottom when an explosive detonated somewhere nearby, white light visible through the windows. Only then did she realize that she hadn't heard any explosions for a while. Probably because the people who'd previously been fighting each other had joined forces to come here. Everyone was after Vlerion now.

Shouts came from the troops behind the castle. Had they seen the rangers in the river? Who had lit the explosive?

When she paused in the kitchen to look around for something capable of making a distraction, she spotted her brother in the pantry, pushing a… was that the huge storage hutch from the dining hall? He was shoving it into the pantry. The crate that had been on the trapdoor earlier was tipped sideways under a shelf.

"Everything okay?" Kaylina asked.

"Did you know there are *soldiers* in the root cellar?" Frayvar asked in a squeaky voice.

"Yeah, but they're bound by vines. Or they *were*."

Maybe the sentinel hadn't been able to keep the men restrained while it was launching magical beams at enemies out front.

"One stuck his head up through the trapdoor not thirty seconds ago," Frayvar whispered, putting his shoulder against the heavy wooden hutch to shove it deeper. "He didn't look *bound*. I hit him with a broom, and he ducked back down long enough for me to push the flagstone back in place."

"What happened to Jankarr?" She put her shoulder against the hutch to help her brother push.

"He went outside a minute ago."

With a final shove, the hutch fully covered the trapdoor. If the mercenaries *had* been released, that would hopefully keep them from pushing up into the castle.

Kaylina rose on tiptoes to look out a window. Sword in hand, Jankarr stood at the back gate. He had it open partway and was waving to someone outside.

Her first thought was one of betrayal, that he was letting the army in. But, when he pulled the gate open wider, rangers on taybarri rode through. Water dripped from their fur and plastered the men's hair to their heads. A firearm boomed right outside the wall. The last rider—Targon—cursed and flattened himself to his taybarri as it ran through the gate.

"Rangers!" someone outside belatedly shouted.

It sounded like the soldiers had been drawn off by that explosive, but they ran back into view now, their weapons drawn.

Jankarr slammed the gate shut and locked it, then dove to the side when a soldier raised a blunderbuss.

"Look out," he warned the others.

The taybarri split and ran to either side of the gate, stopping along the wall where the thick stone protected them. Outside, the soldier with the blunderbuss poked the firearm between the bars and leaned close, seeking to target someone.

A vine erupted from the mortar by the gate, the tip flicking toward his face. He shrieked, dropped the blunderbuss, and sprang back.

If two of his comrades hadn't grabbed him by the arms and pulled him away, the vine might have wrapped around his neck. Instead, it snapped in the air like a whip as more vines grew out of the mortar between the stones. They wove between the bars, creating a latticework that the men wouldn't be able to attack through.

"Guess the sentinel isn't completely out of steam," Kaylina said.

The soldier's blunderbuss had fallen through the gate, and Jankarr picked it up.

"Now, if you could disarm the rest of the army, that would be great." Jankarr spoke toward the vines while staying well back from them.

"It's not powerful enough to affect that many or reach far beyond the castle walls," Kaylina called through the window. "At least, I assume so from what I've seen it do."

"What good is it then?" one of the rangers grumbled.

She grabbed a few cookies from the pantry—she had to smash her chest against the corner of the hutch to reach them, but since someone was thumping at the trapdoor from below, she didn't dare move it. Then she stepped out the back door to greet the rangers.

"It's been doing its part," Kaylina said as Levitke ran up to her, dripping water onto the cobblestones. "The sentinel shot Enrikon, but the prince dove-fell off his horse and avoided a lethal blow."

"It tried to *kill* the prince?" Targon asked. "Our potential next monarch?"

"I only suggested disarming," Jankarr murmured.

"The prince has given Vlerion an ultimatum," Kaylina said. "He's either to walk outside and hand himself over to an executioner with an axe the size of a plow blade, or the army will raze the castle."

"It would be a shame to lose that." Targon looked dourly at the keep.

"With me and my brother and Sevarli in it," Kaylina added, wondering if Targon would say that still wouldn't be much of a loss.

Levitke's nostrils flexed as she noticed the cookies. Kaylina gave her one, then walked to the other taybarri, distributing most of the rest to them.

"I guess it *would* be a shame to lose my *anrokk*," Targon said somewhat grudgingly.

Once the taybarri had received treats, Kaylina handed the last one to Jankarr.

"I warrant a cookie this time instead of a dried strip of meat?" He looked touched as he accepted it.

"That was a delicious piece of glazed sirloin, and you know it," Kaylina said.

"It was pretty good, but it wasn't a dessert. Rangers, like taybarri, adore sweet things, you know." Jankarr waggled his eyebrows in her direction.

"How come *he* gets cookies when *we* swam through the icy river, risking discovery by an entire army, and got *shot* at on the way into your castle?" Targon asked.

The three other men who'd accompanied him nodded.

"I perform like a taybarri for her." Jankarr winked and chomped into his cookie.

"I'm surprised Vlerion allows that," Targon said. "Where is he? After all that effort, he'd better be here. I need to talk to him."

"He is. He—" Kaylina turned, then remembered she'd asked the sentinel to stop Vlerion. Since she didn't hear him orating from atop the wall, she assumed it had succeeded but hoped it hadn't used drastic means. Just because the plant was allowing him inside the castle now didn't mean it liked him. "I'll get him for you."

Kaylina jogged back inside, through the kitchen and great hall, and into the vestibule. Vlerion stood two feet from the great double doors but was rooted in place. No, *vined* in place. One had sprouted from the wall and wrapped around the wrist of his sword arm.

"Sorry," Kaylina blurted. "Your allies were coming, and I wasn't sure where you were, so I requested the plant ask you to wait."

"Ask," Vlerion murmured, eyeing the vine grasping his wrist like a shackle. "It frames questions in an interesting manner."

"It does, yes, I've noticed." Kaylina made a shooing motion at the vine while projecting her thoughts toward the sentinel's tower. *Let him go, please.*

"I've been attempting to have a conversation with it to see why it's holding me, but it doesn't speak with me the way I assume it speaks with you."

The vine released Vlerion and disappeared back into the wall.

"You mean it doesn't insert smug and presumptuous emotions into your mind while talking about how inferior humans are?" Kaylina took Vlerion's hand and pointed toward the kitchen.

"If that's what it does to you, I may be relieved it doesn't speak with me."

"You should be." She led him into the kitchen. "Targon is here.

I thought you might like to talk with him before addressing the army."

"*Captain* Targon would like to speak with his subordinate, yes." Targon leaned against a counter, pushing a hand through his short wet hair to flick water out.

Jankarr and the other rangers had also come inside. Sevarli had disappeared, but Frayvar was in the kitchen, mixing dough to make who knew what. He baked when he was nervous.

"He seems crabby," Vlerion said.

"I didn't give him a cookie."

"He didn't perform suitably?" Vlerion asked.

"Not like a taybarri." Jankarr smirked.

"If we could delay the jabberwocky," Targon said, "there's a humongous army outside that wants to kill you."

"I did notice them." Vlerion tilted his head toward the dining hall. "Do you want to speak in private? Or does it matter?" He nodded toward the other rangers.

Targon speared Jankarr with a dark look. Jankarr sighed but didn't look confused about his captain's suspicion.

Kaylina didn't weigh in, but she wanted to hear Targon's update—if he knew anything that could help with the situation, in particular.

Thumps came from the floor of the pantry.

"What is that?" Targon snapped.

He *was* crabby. Kaylina went to check for more cookies.

"Mercenaries in the root cellar are trying to break in." Frayvar said.

Targon glowered in exasperation at the pantry, then pointed to his men. "Deal with that. We don't need an invasion force coming up from below."

"Yes, my lord." The rangers tugged the hutch out of the pantry, and Jankarr lifted the flagstone, showing his sword before his face.

"Shit," someone barked from below. "Rangers."

"Follow me, men," Jankarr called cheerfully and jumped down.

Arms folded over his chest, Targon didn't leave the counter he was leaning his hip against. Apparently, he trusted his men to handle the mercenaries.

Once they were out of sight, Targon looked pointedly at Frayvar and Kaylina.

"Oh, I'll finish the bread later." Frayvar hurried out of the kitchen. "Sevarli, are the intruders still leaving the gate alone?" he called to wherever their server was keeping an eye on things from.

"Vines grew across the front one," came her distant voice.

"Oh, good."

With him out of the kitchen, Targon turned his I-want-privacy-to-speak-with-Vlerion look on Kaylina.

"I'm not as good at taking hints as my brother," Kaylina said.

"I knew the day I met you two that he was the smart one."

"Because he didn't hurl a sling round at a ranger?" she guessed.

"That was one reason."

"Talk, Targon," Vlerion said. "She'll eavesdrop if you send her away."

Targon scoffed but didn't deny it. "Fine. I came to tell you that we've got trouble, but you probably figured it out."

"When the trouble started firing cannons at the castle and pointed out my executioner, yes."

"Here's the gist of what I got. I was called into a meeting in the royal castle with the queen this afternoon when the prince stormed in, demanding to talk to his mother. Petalira had been asking me to swear my loyalty and that of all my men to her. She was vexed that Enrikon unexpectedly brought legions of mercenaries with him and had used them to capture the harbor and a couple other key points in the city. She gave me a whole list of reasons why her son wasn't mature enough to be granted command of the entire kingdom. This was happening at the same time as she found out that none of her bounty hunters had been successful yet—she was *pissed* when you turned down her marriage proposal, Vlerion—and that Spymaster Milnor was missing."

Targon paused to eye Kaylina. She couldn't imagine how he'd learned about Milnor's death, since Vlerion hadn't reported in to Targon since she'd told him, but his squint suggested he somehow knew. Or at least *suspected* she'd been involved in that. He didn't ask, however. Instead, he returned to briefing Vlerion, as if he were the lower-ranking officer reporting to his superior.

"Enrikon has had men looking for you too. Since the newspaper printed. No, before that. Since the beast took out some of his mercenaries in the catacombs. He also offered up a fat reward to whichever one bagged you." Targon made a throat-cutting motion.

"We heard about that," Vlerion said.

A few clangs and shouts drifted up from below—the rangers dealing with the mercenaries, presumably.

"What's been going on here with our people?" Vlerion asked. "When Jankarr, Kaylina, and I were riding back into the city, we saw smoke around headquarters. Was it attacked?"

"Yes, that happened after I left the castle. I wasn't dumb enough to outright reject Petalira's demand that I promise the rangers will serve her, but I didn't want to give an oath and then be foresworn. I told her I'd serve whomever the senior lords deemed to be the rightful leader and was coronated. From the curses she sent after me, she took it as a rejection. I don't know for *certain* that she sent the armored men in plain clothes who showed up, lobbing explosives into our compound, but I believe so. They were doing some poor acting to try to make us believe they were Virts, but they were too well trained with weapons to be factory workers. Besides, I recognized a few faces from the Kingdom Guard. Not local boys. They were from neighboring towns. She must have ordered them brought in when she learned her son had arrived with an army. The rangers defeated them and got their explosives away from them but not before the miscreants lit fires and blew a hole in Penderbrock's infirmary. He's extremely vexed about that, since he just got a new organization system put in and half his medicines were destroyed."

Vlerion looked toward the keep wall, as if he could see what the army was doing outside. This discussion was taking up a lot of his hour. Kaylina was tempted to check a window to see if the prince had returned.

"Anyway," Targon said, also glancing toward the walls, "before I left the royal castle, Enrikon suggested to his mother that they set their differences aside for the time being, combine their armies, and take you out. They're worried that there's a growing sentiment among the commoners and some aristocrats that *you're* the man who should rule Zaldor next."

Kaylina expected Targon to scoff again—his entire demeanor and delivery had a surly, exasperated bent to it. Instead, he gazed at Vlerion when he finished and raised his eyebrows.

"Are you asking me to?" Vlerion spoke quietly and arched his own eyebrows.

"No. That would be sedition. Unless you were to slay Petalira and Enrikon and take the crown for yourself. Then I'd simply be obeying my new monarch and commander." Since Targon still looked surly, it was hard to tell if he hoped that would happen.

"I was thinking of exiling them, not killing them," Vlerion said.

For the first time, Targon shifted away from the counter, straightening as something sparked in his eyes. Was that hope?

"Then you're contemplating it? You always said you had no interest, and I agree that your brother would have been more suited for it, but, by all the altered orchards, you'd be a better pick than Enrikon. And Petalira, even if she had a blood right to the throne, which she doesn't, spends far too much time *scheming*."

Targon scowled at Kaylina, whom he'd also accused of being a schemer.

Her brother called her that all the time, and it wasn't *un*true, but she glared back at him. She didn't appreciate being compared to Petalira, friend of Jana Bloomlong—an even *schemier* schemer —who wanted to see Kaylina dead. No doubt, she'd cheered when the army had arrived.

"The Virts won't accept Petalira," Vlerion said. "It would be more of the same going forward, which they've proven numerous times this year they object to."

"I would hope you wouldn't give in to all their demands either," Targon said. "You need the aristocrats' support if you're going to do this, and the Virts are their underpaid exploited employees, needed to run their farms and factories."

"At least you admit their working conditions are abysmal," Kaylina said.

Targon chopped his hand through the air. "You could figure out what bones you need to throw them to keep them content later."

"Yes," Vlerion murmured and looked to Kaylina, holding her gaze.

Targon, she realized, wouldn't know what Vlerion had truly been contemplating. Taking control of the monarchy only to turn it over to someone else. As far as she knew, he'd only shared his thoughts with her, trusting her with them. She appreciated that, though it was far more daunting being the confidante of possible future *king* Vlerion than ranger lord Vlerion.

"That can be *after* Petalira and Enrikon are... exiled." Targon added.

Did that pause mean he preferred they be killed?

Since he'd slept with the queen, Kaylina found the captain's willingness to entertain that idea appalling. Though maybe it was *because* he'd slept with her, and seen firsthand her scheming, that he believed she needed to be killed and not exiled.

"Petalira is watching this from a tower along the royal castle wall," Targon said. "We could see her from one of the bridges. She must have shooed out the archers so she and her bodyguards would have a good view. She doesn't want to miss seeing Stillguard Castle annihilated and you killed."

"If I'm killed, it's not *supposed* to be annihilated," Vlerion said.

"Uh-huh. How much do you trust Enrikon to follow through with his promise?"

"I trust him not to want to be shot again by that plant."

"You think it's going to rise to your defense?" Targon asked skeptically. "It *can't* care who takes the throne."

"Kaylina does," Vlerion said quietly.

Targon opened his mouth, his eyes implying he had snark in mind, but he paused and considered her.

"Yes," he finally said. "I believe she does. Does she control it or vice versa? I thought that thing was an unknown, but if it shot the prince… Korbian, did you *ask* it to do that?"

Er, how much trouble would she get in if she admitted that? She didn't feel any guilt about the sentinel hitting the prince, but that guard it had killed…

"When he said he was going to have Vlerion killed… yes. I was frustrated. But it kept attacking after I asked it to stop, and it hit some men." Kaylina swallowed. "It killed a man. At least one. So, yes, it's an unknown. It will sort of help me sometimes, but it doesn't obey me explicitly. It… likes killing humans, I think."

"Well, it's Daygarii, so of course it does." Targon didn't sound that upset about the death, maybe because his men were now under the castle, killing more troops.

"It's powerful and has a mind of its own," Kaylina said so there wouldn't be high expectations. "I can often talk it into helping, but I can't guarantee the results."

"I need to address the army before my hour is up," Vlerion said. "I was about to do that when you arrived, Targon."

"What are you going to say?"

"I'm going to argue that I'm a better candidate to rule than Enrikon and ask them to come over to my side."

"A part of me hoped you'd say that, and that I was coming here to swear my sword—and that of all the rangers—to you, but the pessimistic part of me thinks they're going to shoot at you the second you walk into view. You should have made your bid *before* the army amassed at the castle gates. None of them are going to cross the line to the other side while all the others remain. They would be risking being stoned or outright killed as traitors."

"I know, but they *amassed* with surprising swiftness."

"I should have tried to talk you into this yesterday instead of sending you to check the watchtowers," Targon said. "Honestly, I didn't think you would entertain it. Not only because you lack interest but because of the curse."

Vlerion tilted his head toward Kaylina. "She spoke to her druid father about lifting that."

"Is that possible?"

"We'll see. I'm forbidding Kaylina from letting him turn her into a tree." Vlerion managed a faint smile for her.

"Uh, okay." Targon appeared more bewildered than amused.

"If I survive the rest, I'll talk to her father myself and bargain with him, see what can be done." Vlerion took a deep breath and faced Targon, his face graver than she'd ever seen it. "The rangers will support me in my bid?"

He was asking Targon to sign his men up for a mission that might be suicidal. If none of the guards turned... If none of the mercenaries turned... There were thousands if not tens of thousands of men in the city and the surrounding areas. And how many rangers were stationed in Port Jirador? A few hundred at most.

Though he had to have considered all of that, Targon nodded without hesitation. "Yes. They're standing ready at headquarters and awaiting my order."

"Thank you."

Targon stepped forward and handed him a sealed scroll. "That came for you while we were putting out the fires at headquarters. You've a few Virts willing to swear to support your bid too, though they're not fighters, so I would reserve them for *schemier* operations."

"If they can influence the newspapers, that's enough."

"We'll see." Targon pointed in the direction of the front gate. "If that army doesn't like what you have to say, you won't survive long enough for the printing of the next edition."

Grunts and scuffs and more than one curse came from the root cellar. Targon turned, his hand going to the hilt of his sword. Jankarr's head appeared, but blood ran from a fresh cut on his jaw, and he hurried to scramble through the trapdoor, rolling to get out of the way quickly. The other three rangers also came up, one injured and being helped by his comrades. They pulled him free, and Jankarr surged to his feet.

"Problem?" Targon asked.

Jankarr and another man rushed to push the flagstone into place, then shoved the hutch back over it.

"No problem." Jankarr's cheer didn't match the blood on his face as he slumped against the hutch.

"We drove the mercenaries back," one of the other rangers said, "and killed a couple of them, but a whole platoon showed up with explosives. They called us traitors and chased us back here."

"We weren't *chased*," Jankarr said. "We tactfully retreated."

"You weren't real tactful when that arrow hit you in the ass."

"It only grazed my hip." Jankarr clasped a hand to a gash in his clothing—and in his flesh.

"You screeched like a dying pig."

"It was my parents who gave me that hip. I'm partial to it."

Targon sighed. "That was a lot of words to say we're all trapped in here."

"Yes, Captain."

All sets of ranger eyes—even Targon's—turned toward Vlerion. They'd made their choice in coming here. Now, he was their only hope to escape the night alive.

Kaylina wished she could say that she and the sentinel could turn the tides, but if the plant had been forced to withdraw the vines in the root cellar to deal with the attacks out front, there was a limit to what it could do with its power. A hard limit.

Frayvar and Sevarli jogged into the kitchen.

"Teams with battering rams have arrived," Frayvar said, "and some of the troops are throwing potions at the vines blocking the gate. Or maybe those are acids."

"They've also got a bunch of men with rope and grappling hooks," Sevarli added.

Targon looked at Vlerion. "You're up. I hope you've been practicing your speech."

Vlerion didn't feign confidence. His expression was bleak, but he nodded to Targon, then hugged Kaylina and headed for the front door. As he walked out of the kitchen, he gave her a long look back over his shoulder, the kind that meant he had regrets, and he didn't know if he would see her again.

31

The harder life is, the more easily people will vote for change.
~ *Dionadra, Essays on the Motivations of Men*

One ranger remained in the kitchen with Frayvar and Sevarli with orders to shoot the mercenaries if they blew open the trapdoor and tried to enter. One remained by the back gate in the courtyard, also with orders to shoot anyone who got through the vines or climbed over the wall. Another was stationed in a rear tower to back him up.

Jankarr went with Vlerion to the front courtyard, grimacing after Targon told him to redeem himself by doing *the right thing* if Vlerion was threatened. Kaylina feared that meant Targon expected Jankarr to leap in front of an arrow to save their future king if necessary.

She climbed up to join the sentinel so she could watch Vlerion address the army—and coerce her botanical ally into helping any way it could. She held her sling in case she needed to fire through the tower window, but the meager weapon was laughable against armored men. Unless they succeeded in getting through or over the wall and into the courtyard, they wouldn't be close enough for her to shoot effectively.

Of course, as she eyed all the cannons and siege engines that had been rolled in, she deemed that likely. The courtyard walls weren't *that* high or thick. After all, Stillguard Castle had been an inn for generations before it had been cursed. Centered in the core of the city, it had probably been hundreds of years since it had repelled an enemy invasion, if it ever had.

It was somewhat mollifying that the men setting up the equipment and stuck in the front lines kept glancing nervously toward the sentinel's tower. By night, its glow was all the more noticeable.

"We need to keep him alive while he addresses the army." Kaylina glanced at the plant. "If we survive the night, I'll bring the biggest pot of honey water you've ever seen up here."

The sentinel shared an emotion of amusement that she was bribing it. At least it was still willing to communicate with her.

Vlerion stood in the courtyard below. Bracing himself? No, waiting. Crenoch trotted up to join him, and he spoke quietly to the taybarri.

Crenoch swished his tail, lifted his head, and whuffed firmly. Vlerion surprised Kaylina by wrapping his arms around the taybarri's neck and burying his face in Crenoch's fur.

Emotion swelled in her throat at yet another sign that Vlerion thought he was going to die. She wanted to call down that she and the sentinel would have his back—no, tonight it was his *front* that would be vulnerable—but she hesitated to yell anything the soldiers near the wall might overhear. Vlerion probably wanted his appearance to be a surprise.

After a moment, he swung up onto Crenoch's back. Was that what he'd been asking? If his mount would risk his life by going up to the wall with him?

Vlerion *would* look more impressive, more like the ranger hero he was, on a taybarri's back.

As they rode toward narrow stone steps leading to the top of the wall—it would be a tight fit for Crenoch—Jankarr jogged after them. Vlerion lifted a hand to stop him and shook his head. Jankarr said something—a protest?—and pointed to the other front tower. From her position, Kaylina couldn't see through its window, but she knew Targon had gone up there with a bow.

Vlerion shook his head again, spoke firmly, and pointed to Jankarr, then up to Kaylina. Asking him to protect her?

No, she had the sentinel. She didn't want Jankarr to sacrifice himself for anyone but agreed with Targon that he should go up there with Vlerion to help in case snipers started firing.

"You go with him, Jankarr," came Targon's harsh whisper from the other tower.

But Vlerion held his hand up again, and Jankarr's shoulders slumped. With Crenoch balancing carefully on the steps, he rode up to the wall near the gate.

"Damn it, Jankarr," Targon snarled. "This isn't the time for you to disobey your commanding officer."

"I'm not disobeying you, my lord. I'm obeying him." Jankarr pointed solemnly to Vlerion's back.

Kaylina expected Targon to scoff, but he didn't. Maybe he accepted that if they somehow made this work, Vlerion would one day be their king.

Jankarr did remain at the base of the stairs, ready to charge up if something happened and Vlerion needed help.

Kaylina watched Vlerion as he rode into view of all the soldiers out front. Enough lanterns and braziers burned in the street that people spotted him quickly. The men in the alleys could probably see him as well. It grew quiet in the streets, the voices stopping, the preparations for storming the castle pausing.

"At least they're not shooting him on sight," she whispered.

"People of Zaldor, my countrymen and colleagues, I am Vlerion of Havartaft, ranger, defender of the borders, and warrior who's always fought on behalf of the kingdom. As you may know, my ancestor, Balzarak, once ruled the kingdom, as his ancestors did before him, going back to the Era of Expansion, of the first gold discoveries in the Evardor Mountains. That was a time of great prosperity for commoners and aristocrats alike." Vlerion's words rang out strongly and loudly, but the army stretched for blocks, if not miles, and it wouldn't carry to them all.

"Is there any druid magic that can help amplify his voice?" Kaylina asked the sentinel as Vlerion continued, letting anyone who wasn't aware know who he was.

She couldn't imagine how druid magic could achieve voice amplification but envisioned a trumpet flower.

A wispy tendril of magic flowed from the sentinel and touched her brand, making it tingle. Then a larger tendril of their combined power, probably visible only to them, stretched over the courtyard and toward Vlerion, attaching to his back. If he felt anything, he didn't show it, only continuing to speak, but the power made his voice louder, allowing it to carry over the rooftops for many blocks in all directions.

"Thank you," Kaylina whispered.

An arrow fired, not from the army but from the adjacent tower. No, the *roof* of the adjacent tower. Targon had climbed out the window and stood up there, his bow in hand. His arrow soared over the courtyard wall, over ranks of men, and to a rooftop two buildings farther up the street. It struck someone who'd been hiding in the shadows of a brick chimney, and a bow fell from the man's fingers before he dropped. Targon's arrow protruded from his throat.

Vlerion continued speaking, but he lifted his hand without looking back, acknowledging Targon's protection. Kaylina didn't know if the archer had been about to fire or merely put there to do so at an inopportune time, but she was glad Targon had keen eyes and had caught him.

A question emanated from the sentinel as it showed her a hypothetical Vlerion with green light glowing from him, making him look like he'd been blessed by a god. Or by one of the Daygarii.

"Let's not go that far. Suggesting he's magical or aligned with the druids in some way might creep people out."

An indignant feeling came from the sentinel.

"Sorry. It could also make him an easier target for snipers. Uhm, speaking of that, can you tell if any more are out there, aiming at him? Or where the prince went?"

She hoped Enrikon was cowardly hiding somewhere, afraid to be struck again.

A vision washed over her eyes. As it had once before, the sentinel showed her what the vine poking through the roof of its tower could stretch up to see.

It didn't focus on any nearby snipers and instead swept out over the streets all around the castle, each filled with rows and rows of soldiers. It paused to focus on a flat rooftop six blocks away.

Beside a large brick chimney, the prince stood with his six bodyguards around him and pointed angrily toward Vlerion. Assuming he could *see* Vlerion from that distance. He'd retreated well out of range of the sentinel's beams. Too bad he didn't look incapacitated from the earlier blow.

"Unfortunately," Kaylina murmured. "What building is that?"

Without the sentinel's help, she couldn't have seen that far, and she had no idea.

The view shifted, showing her a sign out front. Sluice and Pick Industries.

While she debated what to do with that information, the view shifted again, sharpening as it focused on something farther away.

"As you've possibly heard," Vlerion continued speaking, "the shameful secret that I've attempted to keep to myself my whole life has been exposed."

Kaylina frowned at his words. It wasn't *shameful.* And nothing about the curse was his fault. But maybe he meant to set himself up as sympathetic to these strangers? Or explain why he hadn't let it be known before?

"My ancestor, King Balzarak, during a time of famine, ordered rangers into the preserve to hunt. All he wanted was to feed our people, but the Daygarii we'd believed long gone from the area appeared, and they cursed him for sending the rangers to poach in their protected forest. With their foul magic, they cast a spell on him, making it so he turned into a powerful beast."

Surprisingly, that revelation resulted in a few cheers from the crowd. Kaylina reminded herself of the revisionist newspaper article saying the beast *protected* the kingdom instead of attacking anyone in his path.

The cheers were squelched, sergeants and captains telling their soldiers to shut up. Kaylina was surprised they weren't yelling over Vlerion, trying to shut *him* up. Though, with the magic amplifying his voice, that would have been difficult. But surely any second, the army would start its siege.

A touch of vertigo struck her as the sentinel's vision reached the plateau by the harbor, swept up the rock, and focused on the front of the royal castle. It was quiet up there, only a few guards on duty on the walls.

"Because they're all *here*," Kaylina grumbled, "sent to make sure Vlerion dies tonight."

The sentinel focused on a tower on a front wall, one with a balcony that overlooked the city and the harbor. As Targon had described, the queen was up there, with guards to either side of her. There were also several older men and women in rich greens, blues, and golds. Aristocrats? Advisors? Kaylina didn't recognize any of them. At first, she didn't recognize Petalira either because she had a fancy gilded spyglass to her face. It pointed straight at Stillguard Castle. At Vlerion.

Petalira lowered it and snapped something to a man in gray and black next to one of the guards. Chin to his chest and timid-looking, he nodded and rushed into the tower.

"I'll wager she's sending a message to her son, telling him to keep Vlerion from talking. Or to shoot him."

The sentinel didn't opine on that. Reading someone's thoughts from more than a mile away was probably beyond its abilities. It showed a few more seconds of the queen on the balcony, ranting and gesturing to those around her, people who nodded firmly. One patted her on the arm.

Then the sentinel drew back, focusing on the prince's building again. Enrikon was also ordering people around, two military commanders. He pointed emphatically toward Stillguard Castle.

"I think you're going to need to wrap up your speech soon, Vlerion," Kaylina murmured, wishing she could do something.

But the prince was too far away for the sentinel to attack. All of their true enemies were. Down below, the mercenaries and guards were simple men and women doing their duty, following orders, as their oaths compelled. That they were listening to Vlerion at all might be considered treasonous by their superiors.

A boom rang out, and Vlerion dropped low on Crenoch's back as a cannonball shot overhead. A purple beam slashed out from the tower, scant inches from Kaylina's ear. It intercepted the cannonball before it reached the castle.

When it hit, shrapnel flew, some clinking off the wall near Vlerion, some hitting soldiers. An arrow sailed from Targon's tower. As with the other, it avoided armor by striking its target in the neck: the cannon operator. The man pitched backward, disappearing from view behind the smoking weapon.

Kaylina hadn't realized Targon was such a good shot but couldn't be surprised, and she was grateful to him.

"A little late that time," Vlerion called up to his tower.

"I wanted to see what the plant could do," Targon called back.

They both sounded utterly calm, as if that hadn't been an assassination attempt.

"It doesn't like me very much. I'd rather not count on it for my defense." Vlerion nodded to Kaylina.

Thinking she'd been responsible for the beam lashing out? She shook her head, but he'd already looked away, down to Jankarr, who was coming up the steps toward him.

Vlerion saw and lifted his hand again.

"I'll carry on," he called.

Jankarr looked like he would protest, but, as orders came from the army for more men to load cannons, an earthquake rumbled through the city. Kaylina gripped the edge of the window for support as Vlerion watched for more trouble from below.

A curse came from the other tower. Targon.

Kaylina peeked out to check on him. He hadn't fallen, but that roof had a steep slope. His bow was lowered, and he gripped a lightning rod for support. Stones tumbled from the courtyard walls, old mortar giving way. The floorboards creaked under Kaylina's feet, and she hoped the castle could withstand these quakes.

Out in the streets, the troops looked around but didn't break formation, not until a stone corbel on the corner of a roof snapped and fell, crushing someone. Men shouted, and some started to run, but it was too crowded for them to go far.

"Stay where you are," a commander barked. "Man those cannons!"

The tremors grew less pronounced, and the troops recovered

their equanimity. Kaylina supposed it was wrong to hope a great chasm would open in the street and swallow the entire army. She had no idea if such things ever happened outside of the adventure novels she read.

"Jankarr," Kaylina called softly, spotting him standing in the gatehouse archway, probably hoping it would shelter him.

He jogged over to the tower and looked up at her.

"The prince is on the rooftop of the Sluice and Pick Industries building. Will you tell..." Kaylina groped for a name. Who would he tell? Targon was trapped here with them. How could they get a message to the rest of the rangers? "Someone," she finished lamely.

Jankarr looked in the direction of the Sluice and Pick, though he couldn't see it through the wall and intervening buildings. He nodded firmly at her. "Yes."

Risking falling ceiling stones, he ran into the castle. Kaylina didn't know who he would tell, but maybe he was checking to see if the way through the catacombs had opened up. Maybe he could reach someone who could put the intelligence the sentinel had given her to use.

"As you can see," Vlerion called, sitting straight on Crenoch's back as the tremors finished. "It's possible the gods are not pleased with the current regime. I will not speak ill of the dead, but those who watch over us may know that neither Gavatorin Senior nor Junior created as fair and prosperous a kingdom as existed in the past. Perhaps that is why the gods have been causing the quakes. I don't know. I'm a simple soldier, like you, sworn to protect the borders."

Kaylina almost snorted at the idea that the *gods* had anything to do with the earthquakes, but the people who'd been scrambling about, readying cannons for more attacks, paused again to listen to Vlerion.

"I know what life is like when the gods aren't pleased with

you," Vlerion added. "Though in my case it's the Daygarii who weren't happy with my family. That is why my predecessor stepped down all those years ago, and it is why the Havartafts have not attempted to reclaim the throne. But these are trying times, with uprisings within and threats from without." Vlerion waved in the direction of the northern Evardor Mountains, to the frozen lands beyond, where the Kar'ruk made their homes, and many eyes tracked his movements. The Kar'ruk invasion was recent enough to be in people's minds. "It is time for a Havartaft to return to the throne. Should you switch your allegiance from he who lacks experience with war to a soldier, to *me*, I'll use the curse to my advantage. With the help of one who was born with Daygarii power, the beast will rise to protect the city—the entire kingdom—whenever it is threatened." Vlerion risked turning his back on the crowd to look toward Kaylina in the tower.

Those watching him also shifted their gazes to her. Kaylina wanted to shrink down below the windowsill. She couldn't imagine people would be delighted by anyone with Daygarii power. As Jankarr had for weeks, they would think her a freak, an oddity. Not normal.

"The mead maker!" someone called with enthusiasm.

Well, maybe that guy wouldn't mind her.

Someone else yelled at him to shut up.

"She has the power to control the beast when the curse arises," Vlerion continued. "But she has also sworn to obey me, the rightful King of Zaldor." He looked back at Kaylina, offering a slight smile.

"Obey, right," she muttered. When some of the eyes turned toward her tower again, Kaylina lifted her arms and curtsied toward Vlerion. If this would help him, she would pretend to agree, but she whispered, "I'd better get another reward for that when the curse is lifted."

"I promise the beast's protection for you all," Vlerion said, turning back to the army, "but you must join me. I'll not allow the prince or the queen to have me assassinated, as they've tried to do *many* times already. And you know in your hearts that you want something better for the future of the kingdom. You want to be led by someone who has slept on the cold ground as often as in a soft bed, someone who's been injured more than fifty times in the line of duty, someone you can depend on to put the interests of the kingdom—of *you*—ahead of his own."

"Shut that treasonous bastard up," a yell boomed from a distant rooftop. From the rooftop of the Sluice and Pick Industries. The prince must have found a megaphone or another way to amplify his voice. "Commander Dashul, follow the orders I gave you before I left. Storm the castle, and kill that usurper!"

Still on the courtyard wall, Vlerion gripped his sword hilt. But he couldn't do anything to the prince from there. Neither could Kaylina or the sentinel, not with Enrikon so many blocks away.

Unfortunately, that commander heard the order and obeyed.

"Batter down the gates!" he yelled to his men. "Climb the walls, and kill anyone who resists arrest."

A few of the soldiers hesitated, looking to Vlerion for different orders, but the majority leaped to obey their commander. They were trained to do so without questioning right or wrong.

The troops with ropes and grappling hooks surged toward the courtyard wall while those manning the cannons lit fuses. A group with a battering ram approached the front gate.

Vlerion drew his sword, clearly intending to defend the wall rather than run. As Kaylina had acknowledged earlier, with the back gate and the catacombs entrance guarded, there was nowhere to run anyway.

"Help him defend the castle, please," Kaylina told the sentinel, "while I think of... something."

What, she didn't know. She, Vlerion, and Targon could hardly keep out an army. The men with ropes were spreading out to find undefended spots along the wall.

The sentinel shared an image of Vlerion glowing again, as if to say, *You should have let me limn him with magic.*

"You may be right."

But, as the battering ram struck the gate, Kaylina doubted it would have been enough.

32

NOT ALL TESTS ARE DESIGNED BY OTHERS.

~ Lord Professor Varhesson, Port Jirador University

Two of the taybarri who'd arrived with Targon's group rushed to the front gate, roaring through it at the men wielding a battering ram. They paused when they saw the rippling lips and fangs, but more troops crowded them from behind, weapons raised as they urged their comrades to continue. Perhaps reassured by their numbers, the soldiers kept battering, and the rusty hinges creaked, already close to giving.

On the rooftop of the nearby tower, a *crack* sounded, Targon firing a black-powder weapon into the air. A short blunderbuss, Kaylina thought at first, but it launched something akin to fireworks, and white and blue flashed in the night sky above the castle.

The shot fired, Targon dropped the weapon—or the signaling device?—and picked up his bow. He didn't aim at the troops with the battering ram or those climbing the courtyard wall. Instead, he picked targets in the crowd. Officers. Mercenary officers, mostly, but he fired at a captain of the Kingdom Guard as well.

The thought of trying to snipe people—especially fellow kingdom subjects—from a distance chilled Kaylina, but the logical part of her admitted it was wise. Targon didn't have enough arrows to make a dent in the army, but if he could take out key officers—the one answering to the prince, in particular—it might make a difference. At least *some* members of the army had been listening to Vlerion and hadn't looked like they wanted to attack.

"We need to help," Kaylina told the sentinel, her words almost drowned out by the bangs at the gate.

And had she heard a bang at the rear gate too? Yes, an answering taybarri roar sounded behind the keep. Was that Levitke?

Crenoch roared from the wall as he and Vlerion rushed to hack the ropes of men attempting to come over near a corner. Dozens of grappling hooks clinked as they found purchase on the stone.

"Can you destroy those with your beam?" Kaylina asked the sentinel, willing it to take some of the power in her blood if it needed more energy.

Instead of beams, vines grew along the top of the wall, then lowered over the other side, toward the men climbing. Someone screamed, and Kaylina imagined one killing a man. She shuddered at the thought of lending her power to that, but what choice did they have?

Vlerion leaped off Crenoch's back so they could face in different directions, working independently to keep men from reaching the top of the wall. Targon fired another arrow into the army. The battering ram crashed through the front gate and, with a great screech of metal, tore it off the hinges.

Before the men could run into the courtyard, the taybarri charged them. Further, two beams shot from the sentinel, one buzzing loudly as it passed near Kaylina's ear. They sped over the heads of the taybarri to strike soldiers in the faces, searing into their brains.

Stomach churning, Kaylina looked away. The sentinel had to strike at places the men weren't armored, but the goriness made her want to throw up. She was supposed to make mead, not war. She wasn't meant for this.

Two more beams lanced out. Once they finished their deadly work, Kaylina made herself lean out with her sling. It was a paltry weapon against an army, but she spotted a man who made it to the top of the wall before Vlerion reached him or a vine took him down. He charged at Vlerion. Crenoch had run down the wall in the other direction, snapping at the hands of another man trying to pull himself over.

Vlerion spun, his blade a blur as he defended against a barrage of sword strikes. It didn't take him long to turn parries into an attack of his own, slipping past the soldier's defenses and sinking his blade into a vital target. He shoved the man off the wall, then ran to meet two more who were pulling themselves over the top.

His faint humming reached Kaylina's ears. It struck her as more ominous than ever.

She fired her sling at the man farthest from Vlerion, hitting the soldier in the forehead as he tried to pull himself onto the wall. He lost his grip on the stone and fell back out of sight.

Vlerion reached the other climber, his sword raised, but the man let go, preferring the fall to dealing with him.

Power, the sentinel whispered into Kaylina's mind, and a vine curled around her ankle.

Startled, she almost jerked away, but she'd offered whatever assistance she could give and nodded. With the vine like a conduit, the sentinel drew energy from her. It needed her power to make more vines, to try to keep men out.

The taybarri were defending the front gate, blocking soldiers from getting through that way. Unfortunately, the troops ordered to climb the wall had countless ropes and grappling hooks.

As Kaylina's power flowed from her and into the sentinel, it sent out more beams and grew more vines. But her energy drained quickly, her muscles growing weary. She sank to her knees by the window.

War horns blew in the distance. Announcing more men joining the army? Was every soldier in the city—in the province—here to storm the castle?

Kaylina lost sight of Vlerion as he ran down the wall to attack more climbers who'd bypassed the vines to reach the top. Bleakness crept into her, and she leaned her forehead against the cool stone by the window. She only had so much power to give, and there were so many enemies. What happened when the sentinel ran out of energy too?

"Is there any chance my father is around and could help?" she asked. "Sentinel, can you call to him?"

It shared a sense of exasperation. Right, it was already doing everything it could.

An explosion came from inside the castle—from the kitchen. Kaylina jerked her head up.

"Kay!" Frayvar yelled from downstairs.

Fear for her brother slammed into her. It had to be the mercenaries from the catacombs. Or maybe some men had gotten past the taybarri and ranger at the back gate. Either way, she needed to help him.

Muscles weak, Kaylina had to draw her sword and use it like a cane to push herself to her feet.

"Keep fighting, please," she told the sentinel. "I'll be back to help."

She hoped.

When she slid through the hole and landed, her legs gave way, and she fell off the chair she'd been using as a stool. She pitched to the floor, cursing, and willed her body to find more energy.

"Need some help, Kay!" Frayvar yelled.

Another explosion almost drowned him out. That had definitely come from the kitchen—or the pantry leading down to the catacombs.

Teeth gritted, Kaylina pushed herself to her feet. Using the wall for support, she half-ran and half-shambled down the hall toward the stairs.

Explosions erupted outside the castle, and she feared the cannons were targeting the walls—if not Vlerion directly.

Stay alive, she cried silently to him, though she didn't think he could hear her.

When she reached the bottom of the stairs and turned into the kitchen, one of the rangers was dropping to his knees, four soldiers with axes and swords surging out of the pantry—out of what had *been* the pantry. The trapdoor had been blown open, the hutch knocked back, and shelves ripped free. Broken jars and dented tins were scattered all over the floor.

Frayvar ran forward with his frying pan and clubbed a man about to run the ranger through. Sevarli hurled a clay pitcher at the chest of another.

Kaylina reached for her sling, but one of the intruders spotted her and rushed in her direction with his sword. He raised it, aiming for her head.

Glad she still held her own sword, Kaylina swept it up in time to block. Canopy parry, Zhani would have called it, to be followed by a tree-cavity thrust. Kaylina did exactly that, stabbing her sword into his torso. Unfortunately, chain mail deflected it, and the man whipped his blade down to attack her again.

She skittered back out of the kitchen, fear giving her limbs new energy, but she barely managed to deflect another blow, this one at her chest. She knocked the man's sword into the banister at the bottom of the stairs.

"There are more coming up from below!" Sevarli yelled.

"I see them." The ranger had regained his feet, but he was fighting too many, with his back to a counter, limiting his room to maneuver.

"One got into the dining hall," Frayvar warned.

Kaylina wanted to glance over her shoulder in that direction to make sure nobody was about to leap out at her, but her foe pressed her, stabbing again toward her chest.

Frustration flooded her veins, and she drew on the dregs of her power as she deflected the attack, imagining druidic magic amplifying her sword and her movements.

Her hand glowed green, and the intruder glanced toward it, the light distracting him. She swept her blade toward his throat. He wasn't so distracted that he couldn't parry, but her sword also flashed green. The light stunned him, and he staggered back. She swung again, but his eyes must have been too blinded to see it. Her blade cut into his neck, and she pushed him back.

As he pitched to the floor, someone grabbed her from behind, a strong wrist clamping down on her sword arm.

"Let go," she snarled, kicking backward.

She clipped her attacker's leg, but it wasn't enough to loosen his grip. He pulled her back farther, and a second man appeared, pushing her against the stone wall in the dining hall.

Kaylina twisted her wrist, trying to pull her sword arm free, but she didn't have enough strength to overcome two men. They were the green-uniformed mercenaries from the catacombs—or maybe they'd come over the wall to get inside. With enemies everywhere, who could tell?

One pressed a dagger to her throat and snarled, "Make that tower stop attacking our people, you cursed druid bitch."

"We know you control it," the other said as the sounds of

fighting continued from the kitchen. He glanced at her brand, a faint glow still coming from it.

Weariness stacked inside of Kaylina like lead weights, and she didn't think she could summon more power. She'd given too much to the sentinel.

Frayvar, Sevarli, and the ranger were too busy with their own battle to help her. Kaylina longed to call for Vlerion, but he had to be overwhelmed, dealing with all the attackers outside.

A man's scream came from the top of the wall near the back gate. Kaylina had no idea if Vlerion, Targon, or the vines had been responsible, but her captors leaned in close, as if *she* had been. With fury in their eyes, they tightened their grips.

That dagger bit in, drawing a drop of her blood. Fear made her muscles tremble as much as weariness. For the first time, she believed she might not survive the night. They *all* might die here.

"Make that cursed thing stop, you freak," the knife man snarled, speaking slowly. "Or I'll kill you right here."

"Okay," she whispered, feeling a drop of her warm blood trickle down her neck. "But I need to concentrate to communicate with the sentinel. The plant. Give me a minute, and don't—"

He jerked the knife from her throat but only to stab it into her arm. Kaylina couldn't keep from screaming as fiery pain erupted from her biceps.

"No minutes." The man swept the blade back to her throat. "It's killing our people. Make it stop, *now*!"

Kaylina closed her eyes, trying not to cry out again, trying to keep tears of pain—and fear—from leaking through her lashes.

A roar sounded in the courtyard, and she didn't know whether to be hopeful or more afraid. That hadn't been a taybarri. The beast had arisen.

33

If you want to die, threaten an animal's mate.

~ Ranger Sergeant Mlokar

The mercenaries pinning Kaylina against the wall didn't understand the ramifications of the new roar, didn't know the difference between the taybarri and the beast.

"If we kill her, the attacks might stop," one said.

"I don't know. Didn't Fozrik say this place has been cursed for centuries? She's just a girl."

"Yeah, but she's linked to it. Look at her hand. She's a *freak*." The knife bit deeper.

Kaylina tried to summon a few shreds of magical power, enough to stretch from her hand to his, to bite into his palm and fingers, like stinging nettle, so that he would—

"Shit." The man swore and jerked his hand back, fumbling his knife. "What was that?"

The beast appeared in the doorway to the dining hall, another great roar reverberating from the stone walls. With his clothes in shreds and his boots and sword missing, he threw his arms wide, muscles flexing under his auburn fur.

Blue eyes savage, the beast snarled, "My mate!"

Cursing vehemently, the men released Kaylina and leaped back. They jerked their swords defensively toward the beast. His powerful muscles rippled under his short fur as he surged into the dining hall.

The mercenaries reacted quickly but not quickly enough. When the beast charged them, he evaded their sword slashes, ducking or dancing away, then leaping in behind the attacks. He knocked both blades to the floor, the weapons clattering against stone. When the beast sprang upon Kaylina's attackers, his claws tore through armor and into flesh. His jaws sank even deeper.

The men's screams assailed her ears, making her wince, but with her arm throbbing with pain and blood saturating her sleeve, she couldn't feel sympathy for them.

A severed hand flopped down at her feet, and her stomach churned again. This battle was too much for her—too much for *anyone*—to have to endure. Muscles weak and drained of energy, she slumped against the wall for support.

The beast finished the mercenaries and spun toward her, his gaze raking her up and down.

"Thank you, but there are more enemies," she hurried to say, afraid his mating instincts would make him forget that.

Kaylina had to convey that there weren't only more enemies but a *lot* more enemies. Since Vlerion was no longer defending the wall, the troops would have an easier time getting over.

The beast snarled. An acknowledgment? Instead of leaping on her, he sprang toward the doorway.

A clang came from the kitchen, where a battle still raged, more mercenaries trying to overcome the ranger guarding the pantry entrance. When the beast roared, the ranger spun toward him, his eyes as wide with fear as those of the mercenaries he faced.

"Outside." Kaylina ignored the pain in her arm and put a hand on the beast's muscled back.

Even though the kitchen held numerous enemies, she worried he would mistake friends for foes, attacking anyone who came within reach of his deadly claws.

The mercenaries looked at his powerful form, at the blood dripping from his fangs, and they turned and fled down the ladder and back into the catacombs.

The beast crouched, as if to spring at the ranger.

"*Outside*," Kaylina said more firmly, willing her flagging power to influence him.

She also tried to share an image of all the mercenaries and soldiers storming over the wall, but doubt swept into her. Her ability to control the beast was never as great as others believed.

And he snarled, as if he resented it, until she added an image of the men out there pinning her against a wall. She emphasized that they were from the same side as the guys who'd just done that to her.

The beast spun toward her. His eyes were wild and savage, with no hint of humanity in them, but she glimpsed understanding in them. He lifted a claw to her face and touched her cheek before racing outside.

Kaylina wanted to slump against the wall again, but dozens of men had made it into the courtyard, and both gates had been battered down. As powerful as the beast was, he couldn't beat all of them alone.

"We need to help him," Kaylina told the ranger. "That's Vlerion."

The man looked toward the trapdoor in the destroyed pantry, the way clear now that the mercenaries had fled, and hesitated for a long second. But then he nodded to Kaylina, lifted his sword, and walked out ahead of her.

"I hope we survive for your bravery to be rewarded," she told him as they entered the chaos.

Vines were visible along the top of the wall, grabbing people and keeping them away, but there were far fewer now. The sentinel's power was waning as much as hers.

"You're the brave one for standing face to face with *that*." The ranger pointed his sword at the beast, who was already tearing into men who'd leaped down from the wall. Despite his wariness, the man rushed to engage with others who were trying to attack the beast from behind.

Wincing as her wound stung, Kaylina loaded her sling. At least the man had stabbed her in the left arm instead of the right.

Shouts and roars came from outside the rear gate. Kaylina fired at a mercenary when he was glancing back and caught him above the ear. She spotted another ranger riding a taybarri through the courtyard, slashing at enemies, and wondered where Targon had gone. Did he have any idea how to survive this? By now, he had to have run out of arrows.

As if summoned by her thoughts, Targon ran around the back corner of the castle and into view. Blood ran from gashes on his head and hands, but he was still fighting, using his sword now that his quiver hung empty. He charged up to two men as they leaped down from the wall.

More roars came from beyond the courtyard walls—were there taybarri out there now too?

"In here, Sergeant!" Targon yelled through the broken gate as he battled the two men.

Kaylina was confused until Sergeant Zhani and several other rangers rode into the courtyard. Their mounts bit mercenaries as they slashed with their swords, taking people down from their elevated positions.

Relief swept into Kaylina. These had to be rangers from headquarters that Targon had summoned when he'd fired those flares. They'd managed to fight their way through the army to come help. And more taybarri roars in the streets promised some were out there fighting.

The beast also roared, furious about something. He hefted one of his opponents over his head with his strong arms and threw the man—the body—in front of Zhani's taybarri. Growling, he faced the newly arrived rangers, and fear overrode Kaylina's relief. If the beast was unable to tell friend from foe and killed their own allies...

Again, he roared at one of the taybarri. It bolted toward the far side of the courtyard, carrying away its startled rider.

"Control him," Targon barked at Kaylina as more rangers—more *taybarri*—hesitated to run into the courtyard. They were fearless against the soldiers, but the beast was another matter.

Even though he was utterly terrifying, Kaylina put away her sling and ran toward him. She had to guide him, to ensure he was the protector of people—at least those sworn to their side—that Vlerion had promised he could be with her help.

When he saw her, he threw his arms wide, flung his head back, and roared. Hopefully, more with frustration with all these men swarming around him than with her.

"Only attack those who attack you, my mate." Kaylina stepped close and touched his furred chest, though she couldn't help but eye those flexing paws—the sharp claws slashing through the air.

She envisioned the mercenaries in green uniforms and attempted to share the image with him. In this state, he might be closer to an animal than a man, and more able to receive her silent communications.

When the beast spun away, roaring again, she feared she didn't have the energy—the *power*—left to influence him. But he avoided a ranger and sprang toward two mercenaries with blunderbusses jumping down from the wall. They were raising their weapons and had meant to shoot him in the back. But when he ran toward them, pure snarling, deadly power, they hesitated. His muscled legs carrying him swiftly, the beast reached them before they could recover. He bowled into both, sending their weapons flying.

Levitke lunged in front of Kaylina, startling her. Jaws snapped, and the taybarri caught an arrow that had been flying toward her, launched from an unknown archer's bow. Levitke broke it in two and spat it out.

"Thank you," Kaylina rasped, feeling foolish for standing in the middle of the chaotic courtyard. Maybe she could direct the beast from a doorway. "Extra cookies for you later."

Kaylina hoped there would be a later.

Levitke roared, then rushed toward steps leading up to the wall where the archer crouched. He saw the taybarri coming and jumped off on the other side.

"Control him without exposing yourself." Targon ran in from the side—he must have seen the close call—and pushed Kaylina against the keep wall, no gentleness in his touch. "Stay out of the way so you don't get trampled or killed."

Before she could issue a retort that would *not* have been reverent, he whirled away to engage more attackers that were trying to get at the beast's back. The troops understood that he was Lord Vlerion, that he was who they'd all been ordered to kill.

Kaylina kept her link with the beast, feeling attached to him by her magic, and guided him whenever he turned toward a ranger without any recognition in his fierce eyes. Several times, she whispered a, *No*, in his mind, sharing with him the green-uniformed men again, and he whirled away, attacking the mercenaries.

Sweat beaded on her brow, as if she were fighting herself. The effort of using her magic drained her as much as sparring in the arena with Sergeant Zhani.

Bodies soon lay all over the courtyard. More than one ranger had been wounded, and the awareness that they were still outnumbered overwhelmed her again.

More and more guards and mercenaries flowed through the broken gates, and a cannon fired out front. Commanders shouted to their men to keep up the fight, to wear them down.

Kaylina worried it would work, especially when the beams stopped lancing out to halt the climbers. And the vines disappeared from the top of the wall. She sent a silent question to the sentinel.

A weak sense of fatigue came from it, immense fatigue. It had done all it could.

A cannonball slammed into the wall, causing a section to crumble and exposing the keep. The next attack might tear down the castle itself. Then it would be razed, as Prince Enrikon had threatened. Prince Enrikon, who was hiding blocks away instead of leading his men in his battle and risking his life alongside theirs.

Disdain and anger simmered within Kaylina, but she couldn't summon any more power. She could barely stay on her feet and leaned heavily against the wall for support. At least her link with the beast didn't take a lot of energy. She could see a green tendril of magic tethering her to him, and she could continue guiding him.

But for how long? A taybarri cried out, and a ranger went down. A soft rain started falling, as clangs and booms echoed all around her, and she couldn't help but see their demise in it. She wondered if the catacombs access point was open, if they could flee that way.

She opened her mouth to call to Targon, to suggest they try, but she paused, sensing someone nearby, someone with power. Someone familiar.

Kaylina looked toward the nearest tower, one at the back corner of the keep that faced the rear gate and the river. As Targon had stood on another rooftop before, the new arrival perched there now. Her father, green-and-gray hair damp about his shoulders, gazed down at the battle.

How had he sneaked in and gotten up there? Kaylina had no idea, but when their eyes met, she silently asked if he could help. No, if he *would* help. He had the power. But did he care what befell Vlerion? Or even her?

He was gazing thoughtfully at the beast, and then his gaze followed the tendril linking him to her.

You have battled well together, Arsanti spoke calmly into her mind.

Yes, but there are too many. Won't you help your daughter? Your experiment? Kaylina couldn't help but sneer at that last word.

His eyebrows twitched. *The preserve must be protected.*

Yeah, and if we die here tonight, we can't do it.

We?

She pointed at the beast. *We're a team. We're* mates.

Yes. I do see that. Arsanti spread his arms, and power flowed from him.

It didn't attack the assailants but instead wrapped around the castle and entered the sentinel's tower through its window. His power infused the plant, as hers had done earlier, but he was a full-blooded Daygarii and had much more to share.

Kaylina sensed the sentinel perk up, refreshed as druid magic filled its limbs and leaves, granting it fresh energy. Within seconds, purple beams lanced out again, striking soldiers and mercenaries in the courtyard. One arced over the wall to blow up a cannon. Vines again grew from the wall, snatching climbers and blocking the gate and the gap from the earlier strike.

A tattered cheer went up from the rangers as they realized the sentinel wasn't attacking them and was instead evening the odds. Arsanti gazed down at Kaylina, then pointed at her, and a surge of power infused her, the same as he'd given to the sentinel.

It was like a jolt from the strongest cup of coffee, sending refreshing energy through her. Sensing the beast starting to grow weary, she attempted to siphon some into him. He could put it to use far more than she.

A snort of amusement sounded in her mind. Her father.

Allow me, he said.

Power flowed from him and into the beast, who roared with appreciation for the rejuvenating vigor. He sprang to take down three more opponents.

"We can't get out!" a mercenary near the gate yelled, the vines blocking the way. "We're outnumbered!"

"No retreat!" someone outside bellowed.

A beam lanced from the sentinel's tower and struck in the area that the order had come from. A man screamed in pain. Kaylina hoped the sentinel had taken out the officer in charge. If those in command died or were too wounded to give orders, the army might back off.

A boom sounded, and a cannonball soared straight for the tower. The sentinel blew it up with another beam, but tremendous irritation emanated from it. Then the ground shook.

Another earthquake.

For the first time, Kaylina was paying attention to the sentinel when it happened and realized the epicenter was at its tower. In its *pot.* It had to be responsible. Had it been all along? For every earthquake that had shaken the city?

Kaylina didn't know, but this one rocked the ground more than any of the others had. Pieces of the wall crumbled, giving a view of the army outside and the buildings around. As stone fell—a nearby house collapsed completely—with chunks landing on people, the army looked around in fear. For the first time, men broke ranks and fled for safety.

Kaylina expected to hear the prince with his megaphone again, ordering everyone to stay until someone got Vlerion. But no bellows came from that direction. It was unlikely, but she hoped Enrikon's building collapsed, and rubble crushed him.

A tremendous cracking of rock came from the direction of the harbor. Thunderous snap after snap, it kept going, as cacophonous as a landslide. Distant screams also came from that direction. Kaylina didn't understand what was happening until the sentinel shared an image with her, along with a sense of smugness.

The edge of the plateau on which the royal castle perched was crumbling, sloughing down into the harbor.

Kaylina gripped the wall for support as the vision played out in her mind. If not for all the noise coming from that direction, she might have thought it an image of a hypothetical future, but the screams and tremendous snapping of rock promised she was witnessing the present.

Mouth dry, Kaylina struggled to swallow. The entire plateau didn't go down, and only the front section of the royal castle and courtyard crumbled into the harbor, but it was still devastating. Nobody caught in the fall could have survived.

With a jolt, Kaylina realized the queen, if she'd remained in that tower, watching Stillguard Castle, would have been caught. The queen and the advisors who'd stood with her.

"By the wrath of all the gods combined," Kaylina whispered, looking toward the tower.

That smugness came to her again, the sentinel proud that it had put her father's power to such effective use.

Kaylina rubbed her face with trembling hands, far more sick than smug at all the carnage, but, as she had noted often, the sentinel felt nothing but disdain for humans. And since they'd been attacking it, she didn't even know if she could blame it for its response.

As the last tremors from the earthquake subsided, Kaylina looked up toward the tower where her father had perched, but he was gone. A hawk flew nearby, and she briefly thought it might be

Arsanti, but she'd never heard of magic that suggested the druids were able to turn into birds or animals.

"Doesn't mean it's not possible," she whispered.

It would explain how he'd gotten onto the tower to help. Or had he simply come to watch her and see if she had developed enough power to guard his preserve?

"Protect him!" Targon barked.

Kaylina spun, fear for Vlerion igniting anew. He'd collapsed and was turning back into a man.

She didn't know if someone had thrown a potion, or he'd run out of energy on his own, especially after Arsanti had left. The power that had been flowing into the beast had left along with him.

Sling in hand, as if *that* would be enough to help, Kaylina ran toward Vlerion. Fortunately, several rangers and taybarri were running toward him too and formed a ring around him. He wasn't moving. His shredded clothes were loose on his body, and blood seeped from numerous wounds, but his chest rose and fell with breathing. The curse magic had simply worn off.

Kaylina and the rangers stood ready, but, in the aftermath of the great earthquake, silence crept over the city. The enemies in the courtyard who weren't already dead or too injured to continue slunk to a gap in the wall that wasn't blocked by vines. They slipped through, a few sending long looks toward Vlerion before leaving. Kaylina had no idea what they were thinking. That he'd done what he said he would do? That he was a monster and a threat to all? That a beast couldn't rule the kingdom? Who knew?

Through the gaps, Kaylina couldn't see much of the surrounding area, but what she *could* see was soon empty of people. Once the enemies from the courtyard dispersed, nothing stirred out there. Rubble remained, and a cannon half blown to pieces lay on its side, but stillness settled around the castle.

At her feet, Vlerion stirred. Kaylina dropped to her knees beside him and touched his chest.

Never before had she seen him wake so quickly after the curse wore off, but maybe the power her father had infused him with had helped. Whatever the reason, she wouldn't complain. When his blue eyes opened, the savagery of the beast gone and a hint of pain in them, she turned her touch into a hug, though she was careful not to brush any of his injuries.

Less careful, he returned the hug, pulling her down and crushing her against his chest.

"We did it," she whispered, referring to how the beast had let her guide him, more than anything else.

Targon, blood dripping from his sword as he stood nearby, snorted. "That *earthquake* did it." After a pause, he added, "Unless you're going to tell me that you made that happen."

"Not me." Kaylina looked toward the sentinel's tower.

"The *plant* did it? Did it do all of them?"

"I think it might have."

Vlerion, arms still around her, turned his head to look in that direction.

"Do you tell it to?" he asked quietly.

Since she'd admitted she'd asked it to shoot the prince, she couldn't blame him for thinking that a possibility. But she'd seen something they couldn't yet be aware of—the destruction of the front of that plateau and the royal castle, and she didn't want to be held accountable for that.

"No," she said. "Someone fired a cannon right at its tower, and that pissed it off."

Targon grunted. "It would have been nice if it had gotten that pissed off *before*." He scowled around the courtyard. "I've lost men here, and the guards and the mercenaries... hundreds must have died."

Kaylina opened her mouth, intending to explain that her

father had arrived and given the sentinel power, but if nobody had seen him, did she want to share that? He wouldn't want credit for helping human beings. She had no doubt he'd only acted to help *her*, to make sure his experiment lived and could do the duty he'd created her for. Besides, would the rangers even believe that someone had appeared and disappeared here, somehow getting past all the combatants?

"Sometimes, you have to get shot at a few times before you get really disgruntled," was what Kaylina finally said.

"I get disgruntled as *soon* as someone attacks me." Targon must have decided Vlerion was safe, for he stepped away and called, "Sergeant Zhani, Corporal Zintner, find all our injured. Jingus, ride back and, if the streets are safe enough, get the doctor."

"Yes, my lord," came their replies.

Vlerion sighed, looking like he also expected to be assigned a duty. A hand to his gashed ribs, he grimaced as he pushed himself into a sitting position. Kaylina leaned back so he could do so, but she also touched his chest.

"You're too injured to do anything else tonight," she told him.

"I am not."

"Look, your head is bleeding. What if someone cracked you in that spot with a sling round? You'd pass out again."

"There's only one person here with a sling," Vlerion said.

"Yeah, and I'll use it on you if you try to get up."

Targon looked back at them. "Sometimes, she vexes me like a thorn under my nail, and sometimes I like her."

Vlerion nodded. "I've experienced similar feelings."

Kaylina squinted at him. "I may use my sling on you even if you *don't* get up."

"She's quite the shrew, isn't she?" Targon said. "At least she's got nice tits."

Just when she started to think he wasn't a total asshole...

"Are you sure it's *me* you'd like to pelt with your sling?" Vlerion gave Targon a dark look but appeared too weary for growling or truly forbidding glares.

Kaylina started to answer that she had fantasies involving deadlier weapons for Targon, but a ranger leaned into the courtyard and yelled, "Captain, you've *got* to see this."

He pointed in the direction of the harbor and the royal castle—what remained of it. Kaylina had little doubt about what *this* was.

"Bring a spyglass if you've got one, my lord," the ranger added.

"Jankarr's got my spyglass," Targon grumbled as he headed for the gate. "Someone find him."

Kaylina wondered where Jankarr had gone—apparently not to report on the prince's whereabouts to Targon. She reached out to the sentinel.

Do you know where the ranger Jankarr went? she asked it, sharing an image of him.

A sense of indifference came from the sentinel. What did it care for a random human?

Kaylina formed an image of a huge pot of honey-water fertilizer in her mind. The kitchen and pantry were in bad shape, but she could hopefully find intact jars of honey to fulfill the promise. The bribe.

A vision of the Sluice and Pick building came to mind again. She thought the sentinel was confused about who she wanted an update on, but it would be good to know if the prince was still there, so she didn't ask it to stop. As it had before, the vision closed in on the rooftop of the building. The prince and two of his bodyguards lay amid puddles of blood.

That shocked her until she saw a man in ranger blacks. Jankarr. But he also lay on the rooftop, blood leaking from wounds. Damn, those looked like *fatal* wounds, but his eyes were open, and he looked at a man pointing a sword at him and speaking. It was one of the prince's bodyguards, and there were two men in Kingdom Guard uniforms too. They all had swords out and were pointing back and forth from Jankarr to the prince. With his throat slit, Enrikon had to be dead. But Jankarr...

"We have to go," Kaylina blurted, surging to her feet.

"What?" Vlerion blinked. "You threatened me if I got up."

"I know, but we might already be too late." She whistled for Levitke and Crenoch, then repeated, "We have to go. Trust me."

Vlerion pushed himself to his feet, his face grim. "I do."

34

We don't always get the future that we want, but surviving to get a future and a chance to do good for others is more than many are given.

~ Grandma Korbian

Drizzle fell from a sky that hid the stars and the moon, only streetlamps brightening the night. Vlerion held his sword and looked around for threats as he and Kaylina rode toward Sluice and Pick Industries. Several rangers on taybarri came close behind them, bows drawn as they peered into alleys and at rooftops.

Numerous guards remained in pairs and small gatherings, but nobody raised a weapon toward their group. The mercenaries had disappeared, save for those who'd died with scorch holes through their armor, selectively struck by the sentinel's beams.

Kaylina hoped the rangers thought to check inside Stillguard Castle to make sure Frayvar and Sevarli were okay—and that the mercenaries who'd come in through the catacombs entrance were all gone. Worried by the sentinel's vision, she hadn't gone inside to look before taking off with Vlerion.

Fortunately, with no attacks along the way, it didn't take them long to reach the three-story brick building. It hadn't been damaged too badly by the earthquake. One of the two guards she'd seen in the vision stood on the rooftop near the edge, his sword still in hand. He looked down at their approach, his eyes locking on Vlerion, and he sheathed the blade and held his hands up. The worried expression on his face seemed to say, *I didn't do it.*

Kaylina's gut twisted as the taybarri stopped and she slid off Levitke. The fear that they were too late returned.

"Jankarr's up there," she told Vlerion. "And, I think, the prince."

Vlerion nodded curtly, dismounted, and ran toward the front door. Since the ride had been short, she hadn't explained much of what she'd seen. She also hadn't wanted to worry him about something that might not be true—or at least that hadn't happened yet. The sentinel's visions weren't always entirely accurate.

But she had a feeling this one had been, and she had to make herself hurry to keep up with Vlerion as he charged through the first floor and up a set of stairs in the back. Afraid of what they would find on the rooftop, she was tempted to walk slowly, or not go up at all. But Vlerion might need help. *Jankarr* might need help. If only she knew how to use her powers to heal, but she suspected druid magic would more readily repair damage to plants than humans.

When the stairs led them to a landing, the door already open to the rooftop, Vlerion paused to look before surging out. He was still armed and wary—rightfully so.

Prince Enrikon lay on the flat rooftop, as dead as she'd seen in the vision. The same two guards and a sole remaining bodyguard were there, having moved little. Maybe they'd been arguing right until Vlerion rode up.

All three men eyed him warily. None lifted their weapons.

After determining that they weren't a threat, Vlerion ran across the rooftop to the only other person alive up there. Or *was* he alive?

Jankarr was lying on his back and didn't move, not even his head. Tears threatened Kaylina's eyes as she worried he'd already passed. There was so much blood under him that she didn't see how he could be alive.

But when Vlerion came into his view, Jankarr's glassy eyes blinked a few times, and he even managed a smile.

She hurried over in time to hear him whisper, "I'd hoped... you would come."

Vlerion wiped moisture from his own eyes before kneeling and gently clasping his comrade's hand. "What have you done, Jankarr?"

Vlerion looked over at the prince's body and the dead bodyguards.

Jankarr didn't try to look. He already knew what had happened.

After Kaylina had told him where Enrikon was, Jankarr had managed to get over here to kill him. He was the only one up there who could have done it. It occurred to her that Enrikon's bodyguard, or maybe one of his dead comrades, must have cut Jankarr down. But they'd been too late to save the prince. And the Kingdom guards? Had they been helping defend Enrikon or had they run up and tried to help Jankarr because they wanted Vlerion and the rangers to come out on top?

She didn't know, and she doubted Vlerion, focused on Jankarr, would ask. She was tempted to try to find a doctor, but the experienced men all looked like they knew what she didn't want to believe, that Jankarr's wounds were fatal, that nothing could save him.

"What needed to be done," Jankarr rasped, then coughed weakly, blood leaking from the corner of his mouth.

Movement behind Kaylina made her jump. But it was only Targon. He stepped out onto the roof and looked around, his gaze lingering on the prince's body before shifting to Vlerion and Jankarr.

"If you... had done it..." Jankarr continued. "It would have been... a coup. Murder. But now... you're the... logical successor."

"Damn it, Jankarr." Vlerion's voice was hoarse, and he wiped his eyes again.

Jankarr smiled, but another round of coughs made it short-lived. His eyes closed, and Kaylina thought he was gone, but when Targon walked up, they opened again.

"Captain?" Jankarr whispered.

Targon nodded. "You redeemed yourself, Jankarr." Even his voice was thick with emotion. "Not bad for a commoner."

With those words, Jankarr looked like he'd finally found peace with himself. His gaze slid back to Vlerion. "Rule well, brother."

Vlerion squeezed his hand. "You'll be remembered."

Kaylina saw as well as sensed the life fade from Jankarr's eyes. She turned away, struggling to control her own emotions.

Vlerion rose, gripped Targon's shoulder, then walked to her. He pulled her into his arms and rested his face against her hair, the support as much for himself as for her, she believed.

Weary and numb, she leaned into him and returned the hug.

"You can't go through with your plan now, you know," she murmured.

"My plan?"

"After that speech you made and after all the sacrifices..." Kaylina pointed to Jankarr's body and thought of all the others on both sides who'd died that day. "Your offer to rule can't be pretend. You can't step down. Targon swore the rangers to you. Jankarr died for you. You have to be king."

Vlerion was silent for a long moment as he digested that. He wanted to reject the notion—she could tell—but could he?

"My grandma would say, we don't always get the future that we want." Kaylina could have laughed at how different this year had turned out for her than she'd dreamed. "But surviving to get *a* future and a chance to do good for others is more than many are given." As she recalled, she'd stuck her tongue out when Grandma had offered that advice to her.

Vlerion, being more mature, did not. "I think you're right."

Too bad he looked nothing but reluctant and bleak about that admission.

Kaylina tried to think of words to give him hope for the future, or at least to distract him. "Of course I'm right," was what came out. "That's why it was ludicrous for you to claim that I would obey you."

"Yes, it was."

As she held him and gazed past his shoulder, the same hawk as before soared across the skyline. It flew from the harbor and toward their rooftop, alighting on the chimney.

Sensing its power, Kaylina stepped back. She used a sleeve to dry her eyes, not sure her druid father would understand feeling sorrow for the passing of a human. Probably not.

"Vlerion." Targon stood at the edge of the rooftop, facing the direction of the harbor, though taller buildings in the way obscured the view of the destruction to the royal castle. Even so, he'd probably heard the report from his men.

Vlerion released Kaylina and joined him. Their backs were to the chimney when the hawk shifted into Arsanti and jumped down to the roof.

Earlier, she'd been thinking how she hadn't believed the Daygarii could change into birds or animals. As she witnessed it, she realized the thought had been silly. They'd cursed Vlerion to change into a beast. Of *course* they had that power.

The bodyguard swore and ran to the stairs, apparently more alarmed by the appearance of a Daygarii than anything else that had happened that day. The guards lifted their swords but stayed back.

As Arsanti walked toward Kaylina, Vlerion started to reach for his own blade, but he seemed to realize who had come and stopped himself. She nodded that it was okay, though she didn't know for certain that it was.

Let us talk, my offspring. As before, Arsanti spoke into her mind instead of aloud.

"Okay." Kaylina walked to a private corner of the rooftop with him.

"Who is that?" Targon gripped the hilt of his own sword.

"I think that's Kaylina's father," Vlerion said.

Targon scrutinized Arsanti. "Huh. You're lucky she turned out so pretty."

Kaylina, who'd noted before that her father was handsome, if in an exotic and alien way, shook her head.

They are an odd race, Arsanti said.

Funny, they've thought me *odd.*

At least Domas's condemnation about how she wasn't normal no longer rang in her mind whenever she considered her differences.

Because you are more like us— Arsanti touched his chest, *—than like them.*

Kaylina didn't agree, but he looked pleased, so she didn't contradict him. She didn't have the energy left to contradict anyone.

Thanks for coming to help today, she said.

He clasped his hands together in front of his chest. It could have meant *you're welcome* or been a gesture of agreement. *I am pleased that you've come into your powers.*

Somewhat. I feel like I have a lot to learn.

Yes, the preserve can teach you, even as you guard it.

"Uhm," she said aloud, feeling Vlerion would want to be a part of this conversation. "About that... I'm willing to protect the preserve, but..."

From across the rooftop, Vlerion frowned and walked toward them.

"He doesn't want me to let myself be turned into a tree," Kaylina finished. "He wants... me."

"Yes," Vlerion said firmly, squinting at Arsanti. Ready to argue, to defend her. As always.

I see that now. Arsanti continued telepathically, but the words reached both of them.

"Honestly," Kaylina said, "I'd rather find a way to avoid turning into a tree too. But... will you lift Vlerion's curse? Did you find out if you could?"

Maybe she shouldn't have asked that aloud with Vlerion there. If the answer was no, that it couldn't be done...

I have researched how to alter it, but I cannot altogether remove that which was placed by another.

Even though he'd warned her that might be the case, Kaylina couldn't keep from slumping with disappointment.

"There has to be a way. I promised him I'd lift the curse. I promised his *mother*," she added, as if that made the vow even more important.

"You say you can alter it?" Vlerion tilted his head, sounding more hopeful than Kaylina.

What alterations could possibly make his curse acceptable? She struggled to see anything short of removing it as a failure.

In some small ways, that may be possible. Arsanti eyed him. *If I assist you in this, you must vow to help my daughter protect the preserve.*

"I would have *always* been willing to do that," Vlerion said with exasperation.

The rain picked up, and wind gusted across the rooftop. Targon looked like he wanted to arrange for Jankarr's body—and those of the other rangers who'd died—to be taken back to headquarters. Nobody lingered by the body of the prince, those once loyal to him either dead or gone.

Appearing unconcerned by Vlerion's exasperation, Arsanti calmly said, *Rangers once poached there.*

"Because they were *starving.*"

And your ancestor ordered them to.

"Because they were starving," Vlerion repeated.

Kaylina shifted her weight, worried this meeting wasn't going well.

As the new king, you will serve your people so effectively that they will know how to grow and maintain a surplus of food so such actions are not necessary, Arsanti said sternly.

Vlerion looked like he wanted to argue but admitted, "The domestication of livestock for food has grown far more popular in these northern provinces, so most people have meat available year round. We also have vessels capable of taking out fishermen even in the stormy winter seas."

So any poaching would be without necessity and could be treated as a criminal charge. Arsanti watched Vlerion closely as they spoke. Could her father read his mind and tell if Vlerion was telling the truth?

"It could be, yes. Thanks to the curse on Stillguard Castle, people haven't dared hunt in the preserve anyway."

Excellent. The sentinel will remain in that keep to watch over Daygarii interests.

"Oh, good," Kaylina muttered. "I'd be bereft without it demanding I feed it honey fertilizer every other day."

What alteration to your curse do you seek? I saw that my daughter could control you as the beast, and that you fought well together.

Arsanti nodded at Kaylina, looking pleased again. By the success of his experiment, no doubt.

Vlerion's voice turned harsh with exasperation—or maybe *frustration*—when he responded. "I don't want to turn into the beast every time I experience *lust*." He glanced back at Targon, maybe regretting that he'd spoken loudly, but it wasn't as if Targon didn't know about their problem. "I want to be able to control when I turn and not go crazy and be a threat to everyone when it happens."

Arsanti stroked two fingers down his jaw a few times as he considered that. *From what I have researched, it was never intended that you turn into a beast due to lust. And, if anger, only because the preserve was endangered. As to turning savage and threatening all those around you...* He waved a hand vaguely. *Would people fear the beast if he were not so dangerous?*

"Yes," Vlerion said firmly.

Arsanti looked skeptical. *My daughter will have the power to steer you toward the targets you desire, as she did today. And you would also be able to use the power of the beast to defend your kingdom. Do you not desire that?*

Vlerion blew out a long breath, then nodded. Yes, he'd promised to do that in his speech. He might even *want* to be able to turn into the beast to more effectively defend the people of Zaldor. Assuming he could keep from harming innocents. He looked toward Kaylina.

You two would have to remain linked, Arsanti said, *but that is desired, regardless, is it not?*

"Yes," Vlerion said again, as firmly.

Kaylina hesitated. "I do want to be linked with him—I love him—but I also want him to be able to control his own destiny, not worry about what will happen if I'm not around. And would his descendants also still be cursed?"

For the first time, it occurred to her that if she and Vlerion married and one day had children, *her* descendants would be cursed.

That is what she who placed the curse intended, that a beast would always exist and arise to protect the preserve until such time that the Daygarii return to this world.

Kaylina looked bleakly at Vlerion. This didn't feel like much of a victory.

Surprisingly, he smiled. "Someone told me we don't always get the future that we want."

"I told you that twenty minutes ago."

His smile widened. "Indeed." His expression grew more somber as he faced Arsanti again. "All I ask, if it's possible, is that the beast not arise from feelings of passion. Lust. I don't want to risk hurting your daughter. The rest... We can control the rest."

Kaylina was tempted to object, but Vlerion *had* learned to control the beast—until she'd arrived. Maybe what he requested *was* all he needed.

Yes, Arsanti replied. *I understand the modification to the curse that you desire. But applying the magic required to make changes is not without risk to the recipient.*

Concern crept into Kaylina. After all they'd endured, after Vlerion had promised the people that he would rule the kingdom, what if something went wrong, and he died? Was it worth it to risk that? For an *alteration*?

Vlerion gazed steadily at Arsanti. "I understand. As long as there is not a risk to Kaylina, I accept that there may be one to me."

My daughter need not be present.

"Oh, I'm not leaving him alone." Kaylina kept herself from saying *to endure crazy druid magic* but stepped forward and clasped Vlerion's hand as she faced her father.

I see. Arsanti looked up into the rain and toward ominous

clouds that had descended over the Evardor Mountains, shrouding their peaks. *The moon is right, the weather agreeable.*

What did he consider *un*agreeable weather?

This may be done now, Arsanti added, turning back to them. *If you are ready, I will call upon the power of nature to accentuate that which I possess.*

Nerves fluttered, Kaylina's concern deepening as she wiped rain out of her eyes.

"Do it," Vlerion said.

Arsanti lifted both arms toward the night sky, and power crackled in the air around him. Green light limned his body as he tilted his head back, his eyes closed. Lightning branched across the sky overhead, and he stretched his fingertips toward it.

Was he calling to it? That was more like the power of the *gods* than nature, wasn't it?

More lightning flashed. The next branch streaked toward the rooftop.

Kaylina wanted to spring away and take cover, but she sensed the magic in this and that her father was calling the storm. She tightened her grip on Vlerion's hand as he stood stoic and unflinching beside her.

A gust of wind struck her in the chest like a battering ram. She stumbled back, losing her grip on Vlerion's hand. The gale knocked her to the rooftop, her shoulder hitting hard. She grunted in pain, the blow jarring her injury as she rolled several yards. Somewhere behind her, Targon cursed, also knocked back.

When she stopped, rising to hands and knees to look back toward Vlerion, Kaylina found he hadn't moved. If anything, he appeared frozen in place by her father's magic, his gaze locked on Arsanti.

Again, lightning flashed in the sky. Two branches streaked down, one striking Arsanti and one Vlerion.

Kaylina screamed, terrified for him. His body stiffened as white light flared all around them, the brilliance swallowing them.

Arm lifted, she had to squint her eyes shut and look away. Only her other senses—her Daygarii blood—told her that great magic flowed down from the sky, the lightning a conduit that stretched from the clouds and linked the two men.

Then Vlerion screamed, utter pain wrenching the cry from his body.

Kaylina surged to her feet, but the world went dark before she'd taken two steps. At first, she thought something had happened to her, that she was being knocked unconscious—*again*—but the lightning was what had disappeared, leaving the rooftop shrouded in darkness. After the intense brightness, she struggled to see anything.

"Vlerion?"

His scream hadn't lasted long. She peered toward where he'd been, blinking her eyes and willing them to adjust.

"What was all *that*?" came Targon's voice from the far side of the roof.

Kaylina shook her head, arms outstretched as she carefully walked forward. She didn't sense her father's magic anymore, nothing about him at all. Had he left? Had he *died*? What if he'd called down more power than he could handle?

As she edged closer, her eyesight returned, and she picked out Vlerion. He was crumpled on his side and not moving.

"Vlerion!" Kaylina blurted and stumbled toward him. She dropped to her knees and touched his shoulder. A buzz of magic made her fingertips tingle. "What did you do, Arsanti?" she demanded, looking around.

He'd spoken of risks, but...

"He's gone." Targon walked up beside her and pointed toward the night sky. A hawk was flying away, heading out to sea.

If he survives, Arsanti spoke into Kaylina's mind, *his curse will be within his power to control.*

If he *survives*? She couldn't bring herself to thank her father, not until she knew...

Not until she knew.

"Vlerion?" she whispered, her throat tight.

He didn't stir under her touch.

"He'd better be alive," Targon said.

Kaylina touched Vlerion's throat, his skin damp from the rain, and found his pulse. Did it seem faint? She wasn't sure, but she could feel it. His heart beat steadily, not erratically.

"That's something at least." She shook his shoulder gently.

Again, he didn't stir.

"I'll get Penderbrock," Targon said.

"Okay."

Kaylina doubted a human doctor would be able to do much for someone afflicted by druid magic, but she was glad Targon had volunteered. She was too weary to handle anything else that night, maybe even summoning the energy to stand up and get down from the rooftop.

"Vlerion." She slumped down beside him and rested her cheek on his chest. "You shouldn't be so quick to trust druids."

"Not a tree," he rasped so faintly that she questioned if she'd heard the words.

"What?" She lifted her head.

His eyes remained closed.

His hand shifted enough to touch her cheek. "You are not a tree."

Ah, he was content as long as he'd kept Arsanti from turning her into a guardian?

"You're astute." Kaylina wrapped her fingers around his hand, encouraged that he was conscious. "You're going to make a good king."

Vlerion groaned softly. Whether it was because of the pain from the ritual or the future that fate had granted him, she didn't know. With the words spoken, he lapsed into unconsciousness again.

35

The yearning to be together is rooted in the desire to leave behind loneliness.

~ Publican Dalrik

After Doc Penderbrock cleaned and wrapped the knife cut in her arm, Kaylina bathed and put on a night dress, then dozed in the chair in her room. A lamp burned low on a table, and Vlerion slept under a blanket on her bed. She opted for that word—*slept*—instead of admitting he was unconscious and hadn't stirred since he'd spoken on that rooftop.

When Targon had returned with rangers to collect Jankarr's body, he and his men had also carried Vlerion down from the building. It hadn't been hard for Kaylina to talk them into taking him to her castle rather than their headquarters, probably because it was closer. It also sounded like the headquarters compound would need as much rebuilding as Stillguard.

With her help, Penderbrock had stripped Vlerion of his armor and torn clothes to treat wounds left by the prince's army. There had been surprisingly few, given how eventful the battle had been. Penderbrock, puzzled that Vlerion was unconscious, had checked his head several times for lumps until Kaylina had admitted he'd been touched by druid magic. She was reluctant to explain her father to others—the world already thought she was an oddity—nor did she think Vlerion would want her detailing everything about the curse. If that ritual hadn't worked... would he want people to know?

During one of the times she dozed off, the romantic adventure novel in her lap clunked to the wood floor. The soft noise made Vlerion stir, and she sat up, hoping he would waken.

Dawn hadn't yet arrived, and she wouldn't have been surprised if he slept through the day, but she couldn't help but long for reassurance that he would survive. And that Arsanti's magic had worked.

Vlerion's eyes opened, and he sat up, the blanket that had covered him slipping to his waist. Chest bare, save for a couple of bandages, he blinked a few times as he looked around. His eyes were surprisingly alert.

With her own eyes more sleepy than alert, Kaylina smiled at him as she picked up her book to set next to the lamp.

"How are you feeling?" She looked at his bandages, though her gaze strayed to his bare chest, the handful of bruises not doing anything to mar his appeal.

She remembered him fighting, first as a man and then as a beast. In both incarnations, he'd been amazing, his strength, stamina, and agility allowing him to deliver far greater blows to his enemies than he'd received himself.

Not sure she should be ogling the chest of a wounded man, she looked into his eyes.

"Good." Vlerion sounded surprised.

He lifted his arms and flexed his muscles experimentally. Then he pushed the blanket to the side so he could stand. Stark naked, he swung his arms and rotated his hips, all of which made it even harder not to ogle him.

"I'm fuzzy on what your father did to me, but I actually feel... amazing." Vlerion looked curiously at her, as if she might know.

"Well, you were struck by lightning."

His eyebrows rose. "It must have been invigorating."

"It knocked me halfway across that rooftop." Technically, a gust of wind had done that, but Kaylina doubted he cared about precision. "Do you remember... anything?"

Do you remember if my father succeeded in altering the curse? was what she wanted to ask, but would Vlerion be able to tell yet? Arsanti had *said* he'd been successful, but who could trust a father who'd turned into a bird and flown away without saying goodbye?

Vlerion stopped swinging his arms and lowered them to his sides. "I... remember Jankarr's death."

"Ah." That hadn't been what she'd wanted to remind him of. She rose from her chair, stepped close, and wrapped her arms around him.

She could *feel* the vigor he'd spoken of, almost like a magical power that emanated from him. The power of the beast?

He didn't seem close to a change—if anything, he appeared more calm and relaxed than usual—but she knew without a doubt that he was still magical. That which had always drawn her continued to draw her, and she had to resist the urge to let her hands roam, to let her hug of commiseration turn into an erotic exploration of his body.

"I also remember some of the battle," Vlerion added, gazing toward the wall as he sorted through his memories, unaware of her rising desire. "But that's also fuzzy, after... you know..."

After he'd turned into the beast. Yes, she knew.

"I'm sorry for all that you lost," she whispered.

"Thank you." Vlerion returned her hug, holding her close. "Given everything, I feel surprisingly serene. The aftermath of druid magic, I suppose." He looked around the room and then down at her—or maybe at himself. "I also feel naked." He sounded a little puzzled.

"The lightning," she said, smiling.

"It ripped my clothes off?"

"Incinerated them."

"*Really*?" Vlerion touched his bare chest, as if wondering why *he* hadn't been incinerated.

"No. I think the lightning was mostly funneling power into my father. After we got you here, I helped Doc Penderbrock remove your clothes so he could treat you. They were ripped and bloody anyway, due to..."

"The beast."

"Yeah."

She mulled over a way to ask him if he could tell if the curse had changed.

Maybe he was also wondering that because he lifted a hand to stroke the back of her head, then cleared his throat with surprising diffidence. "Would you like to also get naked?"

Still in his arms, Kaylina leaned back so she could look into his eyes. They held wariness, curiosity, and was that trepidation? Maybe he wanted to test whether lust would still bestir the beast.

"Of course, you don't *have* to undress." Vlerion gazed down at the curves under her night dress.

As always, his interest lit flames that had already been smoldering within her. A thrum of excitement coursed through her at the thought of finally, *finally* being with him.

"If you simply stand here in my arms with your appealing parts pressed against mine a little longer, we'll find out." Vlerion smiled, but that trepidation lingered in his eyes.

"Should I... get one of the elixirs?" she felt compelled to ask, though she didn't want to dampen his libido—to dampen anything. She wanted it to be safe to join with him.

Was it?

"No more potions." Vlerion slid his hand from her head to trail down her side, brushing her through her night dress.

Her nerves lit with pleasure, the stimulation driving away her weariness. Oh, how she'd longed for him to touch her—to be *able* to touch her without repercussions.

"Okay," she whispered.

"I want to test... I want you." The hint of a growl in his voice sent a titillating rush through her. She wanted *him* too. But did that growl indicate the beast? Or only his interest as a man?

Kaylina peered into his eyes again, looking for that glint that entered them when he was on the verge of changing. Vlerion gazed back at her, his humanity intact.

He lifted a hand, as if to unlace her night dress, but he paused and raised his eyebrows. Silently asking if it was okay. If she trusted him not to turn.

"I want you too," she whispered aloud, giving her permission.

"Good." He reached for her laces as he lowered his mouth to kiss her, his lips hungrily taking hers.

His passion almost surprised her, making her think of a pent-up panther that had been locked in a cage and finally released, but his touch roused her swiftly. In the scant seconds it took him to slip off her night dress and pull her against his hot, hard body, she was pressing eagerly into him, kissing him back. She matched his passion as she wrapped her arms around his shoulders, molding herself to him.

Without breaking their kiss, Vlerion lifted her and laid her on the bed. She kept her grip on his shoulders, pulling him down with her so their bodies would stay together, deliciously close.

His hands slid over her bare skin, raising gooseflesh as he

stroked and cupped, eager to finally explore her. Equally eager, she ran her own hands along his muscled planes, relishing the heat of his body, the intriguing mix of smooth skin and raised scars. Her mighty warrior had survived many, *many* battles to be here with her tonight.

Vlerion's lips and tongue caressed her as his hands roamed, he as intrigued with her body as she with his. There was no hesitancy in his touch, no question of whether things would go awry this time. She found herself trusting that, trusting *him*. Maybe he could already tell the beast wouldn't arise.

She hoped so because she longed for this, for him. She couldn't imagine stopping again.

She slid her hands over his firm flesh, exploring him as she'd never dared before. She luxuriated in running her fingers over the hard bulges and indentions of his muscles, the taut tendons of his neck, the fierce masculinity of *him*. And his mouth—it tasted so good against hers, so tantalizing as his lips and tongue moved against hers.

Before long, she squirmed in his arms, her breaths quick, her hands flexing around his hard shoulders. His lips tasted magnificent as they kissed, and she inhaled his warm scent, reveling in his aura of power.

When his fingers trailed over her bare breast, teasing her sensitive flesh, she shifted toward him. The heat in her core intensified, his every touch stoking the fire within her. His hand slid lower, and she trembled with anticipation.

She remembered being in the hallway with him, her back against the wall, his mouth pleasuring her. She wanted that again but, this time, longed for him to find his own release, as well.

Hoping to convey that, she kissed him hard, willing her thoughts to wash over him. She wished him to know how badly she wanted this for both of them.

A hint of magic warmed her, adding to the flush of desire she already felt, and maybe she *did* manage to share her thoughts with him.

"Kaylina," Vlerion rasped, shifting over her, his hard length pressed against her. "You're impossible to resist."

"Don't resist," she whispered, her mouth against his. "Take me." She pressed up against him, so delighted, so *aroused,* that she could scarcely wait. "Hard."

"I don't want to rush with you," Vlerion said, but his breaths were quick too, his muscles coiled with barely restrained power.

"We can go slow later," she whispered, twisting and shifting under his continuing touches. "I want—"

He slipped his hand between her thighs, making her gasp. Yes, *that* was what she wanted. She spread her legs in invitation, craving more.

Vlerion growled his approval, or maybe his desire, and lowered his mouth from hers so his tongue could trace her damp skin, finding sensitive flesh that quivered under his touch. He licked and sucked his way along the curve of her breasts, taking her nipple in his mouth even as his fingers found her core.

Gasping again as sheer pleasure swept through her, she forgot her explorations of his body. She needed to grip his shoulders, to hang on to him as she trembled. He sucked gently, then teased her with an exquisite nip that ignited raw need in her. She couldn't keep from crying his name, urgency making her thrust toward him.

He smiled against her skin, then descended lower, his tongue trailing down her abdomen as he ignited her every nerve. Her muscles quivered, her need intensifying. She arched toward him, wanting what he'd given her before, wanting more this time.

As he had in the hallway, he descended lower, bringing his mouth to her core. He gripped her hips, capturing her, and breathed in her scent as he tasted her fully. His movements were almost frenetic this time, his body taut with his own need. There was no potion lessening his libido.

She caught herself looking to his eyes, afraid the beast might come, but when their hungry gazes met, Vlerion was present with her. Full of lust and even a little savage, perhaps, but he was still a man. A man who'd wanted her for as long as she'd wanted him. There was so much tension in his body that she expected him to give up this prelude and spring upon her at any moment, to satisfy his own great need.

Kaylina wanted that, but she wanted this too, for him to complete this exquisite preamble that would lead to their joining. This time, he could have her afterward; he wouldn't change into the beast. She groaned, wanting him so much. His every lick and touch made her fire blaze hotter, and she caught herself gasping for air—for him.

He sucked at her, nearly taking her over the edge, before shifting back to teasing strokes of his tongue.

"Vlerion!" she cried, panting now, her need making her impatient.

It crossed her mind that this was where things had gone wrong before, where the beast had risen. Maybe they should have stopped, but he delved hungrily into her, and she couldn't do anything but pant and writhe, unable to form words.

"Gods, Kaylina," he said, almost a snarl as he kissed and stroked, licking her so provocatively, making her whole body shake as he carried her closer and closer to her climax. "You make me so..."

"Crazy," she gasped, bucking into him.

He slid his tongue fully into her as he gripped her hips, probing, thrusting, and she lost the ability to form thoughts. She simply reacted, pushing toward him as her aching need built and built.

He was panting too, seeming as aroused as she by his intimate touches. She rubbed his scalp, longing to do more for him, but it was hard to think about anything but her own intense pleasure.

When he sucked in the most exquisite spot, she found her release, exploding like one of the cannonballs blasting toward the castle. She imagined the fireworks of a beam blowing it out of the air as she crashed over the edge, her ecstasy even more euphoric than the first time.

"Hard," Vlerion said, finishing his sentence. He surged up so they were face to face, his powerful body hard against hers.

"What?" she panted, thoughts scattered as waves of pleasure kept sweeping over her.

"You make me so *hard*," he growled, his eyes fiery with his own need.

She glanced down, eyes full of his straining length pressed against her, eager to sink into her. The desire in his gaze was so intense that she longed to quench it, to bring him a release that would make all the months of waiting worth it.

"I need you," he rasped, "to be ready again. To take me."

She wrapped her arms around his shoulders, pushing her body against his.

"I'm ready for you... all the time," she said, kissing him. It was too difficult to speak, to convey that she woke up dreaming of him, needing him, every morning, and she fantasized about him whenever they were together, embarrassingly ready for him more times a day than she could count.

He lowered his hand, stroking her again with his fingers. Checking to make sure she was indeed ready? Even that innocuous touch made her throb, more than prepared to accept him. She clenched around him and nodded her eagerness, kissing him again as she stroked him, willing him to feel the same amazing pleasure she had.

"I love you, Kaylina," he said, almost in wonder as he shifted his length to enter her.

So eager to have him enjoy himself that it hurt, she pressed toward him, willing him to drive into her. She wanted him to experience ecstasy such as he'd never known with another woman.

He slid into her, slowly at first, making sure she was okay, but his raw power coiled in him, and she knew he wanted more. He wanted her fast and hard. She nodded, willing him to take all the pleasure he could.

Like the panther she'd envisioned before, he sprang, plunging in deep, filling her like no one had before. The delicious friction took her from her earlier satisfaction to needing him all over again.

A groan of pure intense pleasure escaped him as he withdrew just enough to drive in again. They rocked together, panting each other's names, inarticulate growls and words matching their frenzied motions. She came again before he, his stamina on the battlefield extending to stamina in this arena, but she clung on, giving everything he needed even as satiation filled her. She wanted this for him so badly that she kept stroking him, kept kissing him, giving him everything he must have wanted since they first acknowledged their attraction.

Finally, he threw back his head, roaring like the beast as he exploded into her. Kaylina whispered words of love, her legs wrapped around his hips, capturing him even as he kept her pinned. Neither of them was leaving the other.

"Never," she whispered, kissing him on the neck as the tension finally left his body, and he emanated vast satisfaction.

"Hm?" He nuzzled her ear as his breathing returned to normal.

"I'm never leaving you," she whispered. "And you're never leaving me."

"So certain, are you?"

"Yeah."

"Because of your druid powers?"

Feeling a little naughty, she said, "My tits."

He laughed softly, his breath warm against her neck. "They are amazing."

"And only for you."

"I know." He sounded smug. "Your legs are still clamped around me."

"I like you between them."

His eyes gleamed. "Good."

Arms wrapped around Vlerion, legs tangled with his, Kaylina rested her face against his chest, their bodies damp in the aftermath of their lovemaking. Daylight shone through the window, the sun having risen—and then some—while they'd been busy enjoying each other's company. A thousand tasks awaited both of them, but Kaylina didn't want to get out of bed, didn't want this time to end.

"Maybe we won't be disturbed for a while," she murmured. "After all, you were struck by lightning. Nobody should expect you to take on kingly duties for a couple of days, right?"

"I'm sure Targon will show up soon, wanting my help." Vlerion tightened his arms around her, probably also wishing they could stay in bed together longer.

A knock sounded at the door.

Kaylina scowled. "If that's him, I'll shoot him with my sling."

She must have spoken loudly enough to be heard through the door because the words that wafted through sounded nervous. "Ms. Korbian? It's Sevarli. The castle is a huge mess, but Frayvar and I got the kitchen tidied up enough to make breakfast. A couple of rangers who said they have to be stationed here now to protect Lord Vlerion helped. Well, we *convinced* them to help. With bribes. Anyway, I brought up some bacon and biscuits if you're hungry."

"That sounds lovely," Kaylina called and was about to get up to go to the door, but Sevarli must have taken the words as an invitation to enter.

Vlerion swept a blanket over them as the girl walked in.

"Oh, my apologies." Sevarli looked away from them but continued inside to deliver a tray.

It held a basket of freshly baked biscuits, jam and butter, perfectly crisped bacon, and two cups of steaming coffee. The mixture of aromas tantalized Kaylina's nose and made her stomach growl.

"That smells *amazing*," she said. "If Frayvar doesn't ask you to marry him one day, *I* will."

Sevarli blinked.

"I might object to that," Vlerion murmured, watching Kaylina through his lashes.

Kaylina plucked up a piece of bacon and put it in his mouth. *His* stomach growled at the first taste.

"Maybe not," he amended.

She laughed and grabbed a piece for herself, hurrying to say, "Thank you," to Sevarli.

She was already backing toward the door. "You're welcome. I'll see to it you're not disturbed for a while," she promised as she shut it.

"You've hired quality staff." Vlerion's slice of bacon had already disappeared, and he was eyeing the rest of the plate.

"Oh, I know it."

They scooted into a sitting position to enjoy the meal, and Vlerion gazed contentedly at her as he sipped his coffee.

Kaylina slathered biscuits with jam and butter for both of them but paused as she handed one to him. "You realize... that because you're still cursed to turn into the beast, and I'm still an *anrokk*... Are you bothered that we'll never get a chance to know if we'd be attracted to each other the same way if not for the magic drawing us together?"

"No," Vlerion said without hesitation. "I've known for a while that the magic is what brought us together; it's not what keeps us together." He brushed her hand as he accepted the biscuit. "Are *you* bothered?"

"No," she said, also without hesitation. And she wasn't.

EPILOGUE

Scions of the past, giant trees of the present.
~ Daygarii saying

"That's the sweet, the semisweet, and the dry." Kaylina pointed to bottles set along the great table in the dining hall at Havartaft Estate, crystal goblets lined up by each to facilitate tasting. "For those who like to be more adventurous, I've brought my new juniper-pine mead, a blueberry-vanilla melomel, and a sweet and tart cinnamon-apple cyser."

"I've had quite enough adventure for this month—this *decade*," one of the guests, Lady Arrowcraft, said with tartness of her own, "but I would enjoy placidly tasting the apple one. Oh, and the blueberry. Perhaps *all* of them."

"Is there anything you don't do placidly, Hanlah?" Lord Banderdorn said.

"At my age, no. Though I understand from Lady Banderdorn that you are an expert on placid. Or was it *flaccid?*"

The two aristocrats shared edged smiles, not-so-politely

continuing the insults they'd been engaged in since Kaylina had arrived.

Isla Havartaft had invited a group of nobles to a tasting party and dinner, talking Kaylina into bringing mead and Frayvar and Sevarli into cooking. A great business opportunity, Isla had promised. The aristocrats, despite sniping at each other, had made enthusiastic comments about the mead, so maybe it would prove worth it. Even those who hadn't yet stolen sips had been pleasant with Kaylina.

Funny how much more often that happened now that Vlerion was king, and she was known to be his lady friend. Oh, he hadn't had his official coronation yet, since the city was recovering from the upheaval in the streets and the utter shock of having half the royal castle fall into the harbor. But Gavatorin's funeral had taken place a couple days earlier, with Enrikon's and Petalira's deaths being respected at the same time. The bodies of the queen and several other nobles had eventually been found in the harbor. Thankfully, at least in Kaylina's eyes, not many staff and guards had been in that section of the castle when the earthquake struck.

She was glad that few people had any idea that the sentinel and, in a roundabout way, *she* had ultimately been responsible for that. True, it had been her father who had fed power into the plant, allowing it to create such a great quake, but he'd only come to Port Jirador because of her.

"While I can appreciate the fruit meads," Isla said from the head of the table, "my favorite is the semisweet. It's delicious. Ah, Trudlia?" She flagged down one of the staff. "Bring those little slips, will you? In case any of our friends want to put in a bulk order after they've tasted Kaylina's delights."

"I *am* planning on hosting an end-of-summer birthday celebration for my mother," one of the ladies said, "and she loves anything sweet. Perhaps some of that cyser would go over well with her and the guests..." She picked up a goblet and raised hopeful eyebrows toward Kaylina.

Kaylina had intended to pour the drinks one at a time, speaking a little about each mead, but other hands came in, grabbing goblets and pointing at preferred bottles. While Kaylina doled out samples, some of the nobles clearing their throats and making it known that they wanted fuller goblets, Sergeant Zhani walked into the room.

As she often did of late, she'd accompanied Kaylina out to the estate. To train whenever they had an opportunity, Captain Targon had told Kaylina. Zhani hadn't said anything to contradict that, but Kaylina believed her trainer had also been assigned to be her bodyguard when she left Stillguard Castle.

After Vlerion's speech from the courtyard wall, a lot of people knew that Kaylina was special to him. Many of his enemies had fallen that day, but, as he'd pointed out, there would be more. Though he would prefer it otherwise, they might target her. It was a future that Kaylina accepted, as long as it meant she had him.

"These nobles are thirsty," she said when Zhani joined her. "I don't think I'll be able to break away for training this afternoon."

"I didn't expect that. I've been wandering around the estate, taking in the art and historical pieces." Zhani waved toward a waist-high vase near the door.

Kaylina wagered she'd been looking for assassins that might be *skulking* amid the art and historical pieces. Hopefully, she hadn't found any.

"Also, Frayvar kicked me out of the kitchen," Zhani added.

"He's seventeen. He's not allowed to kick anyone out, certainly not a sergeant."

A sergeant and a *princess*, Kaylina thought but didn't say. Vlerion had finally filled her in on that, on how Zhani had come to the kingdom to escape an arranged marriage, but it was a secret, and Kaylina hadn't told her brother. For that reason and others, she was glad that Zhani had survived the battle. Not all of the rangers had.

Jankarr's face floated through Kaylina's mind. He'd done Vlerion a service—he'd done the *kingdom* a service—but she would never forget that she'd had a role in his death. If she hadn't told him where Prince Enrikon had been...

"Technically, it was his assistant," Zhani said.

"Sevarli?"

"Yes. I suggested that a touch of finely chopped misako leaf in the dough would add flavor to Frayvar's biscuits. The herb is a culinary favorite where I'm from, and I've noticed that people here aren't that aware of it. But she was offended on his behalf, stating almost ferociously that the food is perfect, not bland. Mind you, I didn't *say* it was bland. But she ushered me out as if I'd called everything odious. I've had gentler treatment at the hands of the Kar'ruk." Zhani looked more amused than offended.

"Sevarli has a crush on Frayvar. She probably hoisted you out because of your beauty, not your quirky culinary sense."

"I did wonder about that, but that's not why I came over." Zhani lowered her voice. "I've been meaning to thank you for coming to Jankarr's funeral. He was a friend."

"Of course." Kaylina had never considered *not* going. She'd been relieved that the event had been well-attended by the rangers, with even Targon coming and speaking a few words. She'd worried that Jankarr's comrades wouldn't forgive him for working for Spymaster Sabor. As if he'd had a choice. "I didn't know him as well as I would have liked, but he seemed a good friend to Vlerion and others. It's unfortunate that he died the way he did."

"I think it is too, but, from what I heard, he got a chance to redeem himself, and he probably wouldn't have wanted to go any other way."

"Yes." Kaylina thought it was cruel that Targon had claimed

Jankarr *needed* to redeem himself, but she didn't say so. All the rangers had their handbook on tenets and honor and taybarri grooming memorized, and they lived and died by it. She didn't know if she would ever fully be one of them, but at least Targon didn't seem to expect that. She'd given him a bottle of mead at the funeral, and he'd accepted it without a snarky word.

"More of the dry, please, my lady." A noble who'd guzzled his first generous sample held out his empty goblet.

The honorific surprised Kaylina—she was certainly no lady—but she noticed Isla heading her way and didn't comment on it, simply pouring more mead for the man.

Zhani didn't bat an eye at the *my lady*. She also noticed Isla coming and stepped back. "I'll check the perimeter of the estate. This is a big event, and we don't want any shenanigans interrupting it."

"What kind of *shenanigans* would interrupt a mead tasting?" Kaylina asked.

And why did Zhani considered it a *big event*?

But Zhani was already heading for the door. Another woman had arrived, one in plain clothes with her dark-blonde hair drawn back in a tight braid. Targon's sister, Shylea.

Kaylina blinked as Zhani greeted Shylea without surprise. Had Isla invited her? The last Kaylina had heard, Vlerion had promoted Shylea to the position of spymaster. Was she here on business? Or to try the mead?

More guests lined up for refills, distracting Kaylina. Isla let her fill a couple more goblets, then drew her aside.

"Some of your guests might go home smashed," Kaylina told her. "The alcohol content in my meads is higher than you'd guess."

"Oh, I expect they'll be drunk by dinner." Isla looked toward the door, but Zhani and Shylea had disappeared, and it was empty. Only the delectable scents from the kitchen wafted in.

Frayvar had already sent out a couple rounds of appetizers, including spiced oysters that had made Lord Saybrook—the famous grandfather of Ghara Saybrook, who was, to Kaylina's relief, not there—pound him on the back and ask if he wanted a job as head chef at his estate. Frayvar had declined. After all, he had to oversee the rebuilding of the kitchen at Stillguard Castle in anticipation of normalcy returning to the city and clientele flocking to their eating house.

"May I speak with you privately for a moment?" Isla asked, though she'd already drawn Kaylina across the room.

"Yes, my lady," Kaylina said with a twinge of nerves.

A server bringing snacks and water made Isla pause before continuing. When Kaylina had accepted this invitation, she'd suspected Isla wanted to speak privately with her, especially when Vlerion had said he had to work and wouldn't be able to make it.

He'd had to work a *lot* in the last two weeks, and not at the ranger duties he enjoyed. When it came to running a kingdom, especially one that had seen great upheaval, there was much to straighten out, especially since he'd brought in Grittor as an advisor on matters regarding the Virts and the common man, and they were making changes.

Though she'd returned to her training with Sergeant Zhani, Kaylina had barely seen Vlerion during the days. He did, fortunately, make time to visit her at night in Stillguard Castle, which was quickly being repaired. Vlerion had offered work to anyone who wished fair pay fixing the damage from the siege. It was in better shape now than at any point in the time Kaylina and Frayvar had been there.

The hammering and banging from the construction crews almost drowned out the noise she and Vlerion made as they enjoyed each other's company in her room in the evenings. In her room, in some of the guest rooms, in the dining hall, and once in the partially repaired pantry while a dinner service went on outside. That had been an accident, but she smiled at the memory—at *all* the memories. It had been insufferable waiting all summer to be with Vlerion, but their times together now made the wait seem worth it.

"I wanted to see how you're doing," Isla said when the server departed, leaving tarts and cookies on a plate in her hands, "and how things are going between you and Vlerion." She considered Kaylina. "That's quite the smile. Are you imagining your business expanding as reports of your mead go far and wide?"

"I do imagine that often, but this smile was for, uhm, other things."

"My son."

Kaylina's cheeks warmed. "He *can* make me smile, yes."

And scream and cry out and beg... None of which Kaylina intended to discuss with his mother.

"Good. If I understand things correctly, he will still become the beast, but it's more... voluntary now? His, ah, *passions* won't make him change? Is that right?" Isla must have received some of the details from Vlerion, but maybe she wanted to hear Kaylina's version. Or just that everything was going well, and he—the beast—wasn't a threat to her anymore.

Kaylina appreciated that his mother cared. "That's right. We don't have to worry about the beast when we're..."

"In the bedchamber?"

"Yeah." Why were her cheeks so warm?

"Or the pantry?" Isla's eyes twinkled.

"He *told* you about that?" Kaylina couldn't imagine Vlerion confiding details of his sex life with his mother, but... she supposed she hadn't seen them together that often and didn't fully know what they discussed.

"He did not. Your brother told me about the *completely inappropriate*—in his words—thumps, bangs, and moans emanating from his pantry the other night and how they interfered with his concentration while he was making a persnickety remoulade."

"Oh." Kaylina dropped her face in her hand. "I thought we were being quiet. Relatively quiet."

"I understand your brother sanitized the entire space afterward." Isla sipped from her mead goblet. "Three times."

"That's a little overdramatic. He only sanitized it two times after the mercenary battle, and there was blood everywhere."

"I'm relieved the mead wasn't damaged."

"Me too. It was all bottled up in the cellar. Most of the battle took place above it or out in the catacombs. As to the rest, Vlerion and I are doing well. Thank you for asking." Kaylina bit her lip, studying Isla's collarbone for a moment, before adding, "I am sorry I wasn't able to lift the curse. Even my druid father couldn't do that. I know I promised you and Vlerion... Well, I believed I'd be able to do it."

Isla patted her on the shoulder. "You did your best, Kaylina. I'm relieved it's not as bad as it was. For both of you."

"We're very happy now. We've been happy, uhm, almost every night."

"Given how busy he's been these last couple of weeks, that's impressive."

"Yes." Kaylina blushed but couldn't keep from grinning. "He is."

"Of course. He's my son." Isla winked.

One of the staff appeared in the doorway and cleared his throat. "I am honored to announce the entrance of His Majesty, King Vlerion."

Kaylina touched her chest, delighted. He'd found the time to come out to the estate? She hadn't expected that.

Dressed in an emerald-green tunic and black trousers that fit him perfectly, showing off his broad shoulders, muscled form, and trim waist, Vlerion stepped into the doorway. The attire surprised

Kaylina since, thus far, he'd ignored suggestions from would-be advisors that he wear anything but his ranger uniform. She liked the look, however, finding him dapper and handsome, his hair recently trimmed, his jaw shaven.

"Nothing is official, Hastion," he said quietly to the servant as he scanned the room, his gaze settling on Kaylina. "You can still call me Vlerion, and you don't need to announce anything here, in the house where I grew up."

"Yes, Your Majesty." The man bowed deeply and would doubtless continue doing proper introductions instead of the casual—or nonexistent—ones that Vlerion preferred.

Vlerion sighed but also patted the man on the back before striding toward Kaylina, giving the mead-sipping aristocrats in the room the briefest of nods. He might not have done more than nod to his mother, either, but she spoke to him.

"It's good to see you, my son. Have you given thought about where you'll live yet, as king?" Isla glanced around the room, as if to suggest Havartaft Estate. When she'd shown up in town for Jankarr's funeral, she'd admitted, not for the first time, to being lonely out here with only the staff for company. "I can't imagine the plateau that the royal castle—the *remains* of the royal castle—rests on is structurally sound anymore."

"I don't think it is, Mother." Vlerion clasped Kaylina's hand. "I would feel obligated to live in a central location, however, one with quick access to ranger headquarters and other important points around the capital."

"He gets up before dawn to train every day before his meetings," Kaylina told Isla. "I think he believes he still might be called out to patrol the borders."

A quick wistful look in his eyes was the only indication Vlerion gave that he would *prefer* risking his life guarding the borders to meetings with self-important aristocrats, bureaucrats, and Virts, all eager to push their agendas.

"Perhaps he merely wants to keep himself fit for you, my dear." Isla smiled at Kaylina as she sipped her mead.

By now, Kaylina shouldn't have blushed when discussing such things, but she did anyway.

"I do appreciate fitness," she murmured.

Vlerion squeezed her hand. "Since Kaylina needs to fertilize that needy Daygarii plant every day, I'd thought to stay in Stillguard Castle with her. It's centrally located, being repaired, and the lingering curse will keep away the riffraff."

"I don't think it's appropriate for the king of all of Zaldor to reside in an eating house, son."

"An eating house and meadery," Kaylina said.

That earned her a tart look from Isla.

"It's modest enough that it may send the message I wish going forward," Vlerion said. "I don't feel future kings should reside above the people, looking down at everyone."

"Also, petitioners may be distracted by the mead and never make their way to your office upstairs," Kaylina suggested.

"*Yes*. I'd be delighted by that."

Isla snorted softly but didn't argue for Vlerion to live at Havartaft Estate.

"Perhaps he could visit out here on the weekends," Kaylina suggested. "He'll need breaks away from his work, and that lake with the dock is quite peaceful."

"It is indeed." Isla gave Kaylina a pleased look when Vlerion nodded in agreement.

"Perhaps *we* can visit on the weekends," he suggested to Kaylina, then dug into his pocket.

Isla noticed and backed away, giving them space. She also shushed a couple of the noisier nobles and pointed at Vlerion.

Kaylina waited curiously.

"I've already given you a sword," Vlerion said as he drew out a black velvet jewelry box. "But this is more customary in this part of Zaldor."

Kaylina was tempted to remind him that she'd only accepted the sword as a loaner, but she was too interested in what he would unveil and why he would do it in front of all these people. He'd always struck her as someone to favor private places for intimate moments. Only when he opened the box to reveal a beautiful gold ring with the Havartaft silver-and-black emblem on a flat circle did she realize this might have more significance than a simple bauble.

"Unlike the sword," he murmured, smiling, "this *is* a family heirloom. I hope you'll accept it."

Kaylina started to answer, but he took a deep breath, as if bracing himself for battle. No, for something that made him *nervous*. Battle never bothered him.

What he intended to do slowly dawned on Kaylina, and emotion welled within her, tears threatening to creep into her eyes.

Vlerion bowed low over the ring, holding it out toward her as he lifted his gaze to meet hers. He licked his lips—he *was* nervous. "Kaylina Korbian, master mead-maker, ranger trainee, possessor of blood as odd as my own—"

Isla rolled her eyes. Maybe she'd expected something more poetical.

"—and woman who melds perfectly with me," Vlerion continued, "woman I love... Will you marry me?"

Conscious of all the eyes now turned toward them, and the gravity of the moment, Kaylina tried to rein in her tendency toward snark and irreverence. But she couldn't help but whisper, "You're asking me? Not making it an order?"

"Based on my past experiences with giving you orders, I thought you might be inclined to reject me if I did that."

"Never that, but I'm glad you're learning." Kaylina gripped his hands and started to give him an answer, but she paused as a thought occurred to her. “Will I have to call you *Your Majesty* all the time?”

“Only in public.”

She might have curled a lip.

His eyes glinted with humor. “I’ll also have to call *you Your Majesty.*”

“Oh. That’s fair. Uhm.” Before that moment, it hadn’t dawned on Kaylina that he was asking her not only to wed but to be queen. The gravity finally knocked the irreverence out of her. She swallowed and caught *herself* taking a bracing deep breath before raising her voice to officially reply. “Yes. I will marry you.”

“Excellent.” Vlerion straightened and kissed her, murmuring against her lips, “I look forward to spending the rest of my life with you.”

Aware of polite claps amid somewhat drunken cheers from the nobles, Kaylina wrapped her arms around his shoulders to return the kiss. “I look forward to that too.”

When they parted, both inhibited by all the people watching, Vlerion slid the ring onto her finger and clasped her hand, nodding toward the table.

“Would you like to try some mead?” she asked before remembering that he didn’t drink alcohol.

But… could he now? They’d proven—night after night—that strong emotions no longer aroused the beast. Only the need to defend the kingdom or the preserve did.

Vlerion nodded, as if following her thoughts. “If you’ve something manly enough for me. The fruit ones are too girlie.”

“*Really*,” came an indignant comment from his mother, who hadn’t backed so far away that she hadn’t caught their every word. She was currently enjoying a goblet of the blueberry-vanilla.

Kaylina led him toward the table. “I have a juniper-pine mead that should suit you. I gathered the needles from extremely manly and virile trees in the mountains near a ranger watchtower. It's likely battles have taken place under their boughs. There might even have been dried Kar'ruk blood on the needles."

"*Perfect*," Vlerion said, his eyes gleaming with approval.

THE END

Thank you for reading The Curse and the Crown series! If you enjoyed the books and have time to leave a review, I would appreciate it. If you want to see more in this world, let me know!

- https://www.facebook.com/LindsayBuroker/
- https://www.instagram.com/lindsay_buroker/
- https://twitter.com/GoblinWriter
- https://bsky.app/profile/lindsayburoker.bsky.social

Made in the USA
Las Vegas, NV
29 November 2024